Romney Vane

William E. Gladstone

Statesman and patriot, four times prime minister of England

Romney Vane

William E. Gladstone
Statesman and patriot, four times prime minister of England

ISBN/EAN: 9783337308728

Printed in Europe, USA, Canada, Australia, Japan

Cover: Foto ©Raphael Reischuk / pixelio.de

More available books at **www.hansebooks.com**

WILLIAM E. GLADSTONE

Statesman and Patriot.

FOUR TIMES PRIME MINISTER OF ENGLAND.

———

*It is held
That valour is the chiefest virtue, and
Most dignifies the haver; if it be,
The man I speak of cannot in the world
Be singly counterpoised.*
—SHAKESPEARE.

———

BY

ROMNEY VANE.

———

Illustrated by Numerous Rare Engravings.

———

CHICAGO:
DONOHUE, HENNEBERRY & CO.
407-429 Dearborn St.

TRIBUTE TO

WILLIAM EWART GLADSTONE.

In the London "Times" May 23, 1898.

BY

LEWIS MORRISON.

Ay, thou hast gained the end
    Of long and glorious strife,
Consoled by love and friends,
    Thrice blessed life!
If all the immortal die,
    What gain hath life to give?
If all the immortal live,
    Death brings no sigh!

Oh, long life lit with praise
    For duty nobly done,
High aims, laborious days,
    And the crown won!
Why should we mourn and weep
    That thou dost toil no more?
At length God gives thee sleep,
    Thy labors o'er!

The crying of the weak
    Called not to thee in vain.
Thy swift tongue burned to speak
    Relief to pain.
The lightning of thy scorn
    No wrong might long defy.
Thy truth for lives forlorn—
    Thy piercing eye!

Good knight! No soil of wrong
    Thy spotless shield might stain ;
Thy keen sword served thee long,
    And not in vain.
Oh, high impetuous soul,
    That, mounting to the light,
Spurnedst the dull world's control
    To gain the right!

'Mid strife the century dies—
    Massacre, famine, war,
The noise of groans and sighs
    Is borne afar;
The monstrous cannon roar,
    The earth, the air, the torn,
'Mid thunderings evermore
    Time's dawns are born.

But thou no more art here,
    But watchest far away,
Calm in some peaceful sphere,
    The eternal day.
O, thou who long didst guide
    Our Britain's royal will,
Invisible at her side
    Aid thou her still!

O, aged life and blest,
Wearing thy duteous years,
Entered thou on thy rest;
We shed not tears!
Thou hast thy labors to thy country given.
Thy eloquent tongue, thy keen untiring brain,
Thy changeless love of man, thy trust in Heaven,
Thy crown of pain.

3

PREFATORY NOTE.

It is not at all remarkable that at least twenty authors are appealing to the reading public to consider their stories of the illustrious career of William Ewart Gladstone; the wonder is that there are not a hundred instead of a score. Such a story deserves to be told by a thousand lips and sketched by a thousand pens. At best, these biographies can only be fragmentary, and when in years to come Mr. John Morley shall have accomplished his task as Mr. Gladstone's literary trustee, and shall present the world with "The Life of Gladstone"—in one cares not how many volumes—even then, it is more than probable that a thousand points of interest will escape the vigilance of that careful and erudite biographer. If a man should sit down to tell the story of his own life, the half would not be told; how then can he tell completely the story of the life of another?

Notwithstanding the number of those who have entered this romantic field of biography, it has seemed good to me also to offer a Life of Gladstone, especially addressed to American readers. My memory stretches over the main periods of Mr. Gladstone's public career. In the morning of my years my enthusiastic admiration for the great statesman took on the form of homage which grew in depth and sincerity during ten stirring years through which I was permitted the privilege of following and working where Mr. Gladstone led. I regarded him then, and I regard him now as the ideal political leader. I believe no greater Englishman has lived for a thousand years. During the many years in which I have enjoyed the privileges of citizenship in these United States, I have watched Mr. Gladstone's career with intense delight, regretting most sincerely that he never found the opportunity of visiting his "kin beyond the sea." Had he ever set his firm foot upon our hospitable shores, he would have had a welcome that would have echoed from Cape Cod to the Golden Gate, and from the mountains to the sea. But, "the golden bowl is broken," and Mr. Gladstone sleeps the long, dreamless sleep in the great Abbey where kings and warriors and priests lie sleeping.

I am ambitious to lay my wreath on the great statesman's grave, and to tell to my American fellow-citizens, as best I may, the story of that great, full-orbed life that has become a deathless legacy to his country, and a glory to our age.

ROMNEY VANE.

CONTENTS.

CONTENTS.

EULOGIES OF THE GREAT STATESMAN.

Those who knew Mr. Gladstone most loved him best; in proof of which, witness these ungrudging testimonies of those who fought with him side by side or in opposition in the great political conflict in which he engaged.

Salisbury, Balfour, Devonshire, Harcourt, Roseberry, Dillon.

"He will leave behind him the memory of a great Christian statesman, whose character, motives and intentions could not fail to strike all the world. He will leave a deep, a most salutary influence on the political and social thought of the generation in which he lived, and he will be long remembered, not so much for the causes in which he was engaged, or the political projects he favored, but as a great example of which history hardly furnishes a parallel—of a great Christian man."—*Lord Salisbury.*

" He brought to our debates a genius which compelled attention, he raised in the public estimation the whole level of our proceedings, and they will be most ready to admit the infinite value of this service, who realize how much the public prosperity is involved in the maintenance of the worth of public life and how perilously difficult most democracies apparently feel it to be to avoid the opposite dangers into which so many of them have fallen."—*Right Hon. L. J. Balfour.*

" Deeply as we regret the difference of opinion which caused the separation between Mr. Gladstone and many of those who had been his most devoted adherents, we never doubted and we do not now doubt, that in that as in every other matter with which during his long public life he had to deal, he was actuated by no other consideration than that of a sense of public duty and by his conception of that which was in the highest interests of his country."—*The Duke of Devonshire.*

" His life has been a lesson which has not been, and will not be, forgotten. There is not a hamlet in this land where his virtues are not known and felt. They feel that his heart was ever with the weak, the miserable and the poor. They remember how much of his life was spent in labors to alleviate their lot. They know that to him they were always his flesh and blood. His sympathies were not confined by any narrow bounds. The ruling passions of his heart were freedom and peace—freedom not only for his own, but for every people, and peace with freedom—the glad tidings of great joy, the gospel of that religion to which he was devotedly attached. His voice went forth, wherever they might dwell, to all who were desolate and oppressed."—*Sir William V. Harcourt.*

"There was no man, I suspect, in the history of England—no man, at any rate, in recent centuries, who touched the intellectual life of the country at so many points and over so great a range of years. But that was in fact and reality not merely a part of his intellect, but of his character; for the first and most obvious feature of Mr. Gladstone's character was the universality and the humanity of his sympathy. I do not now mean, as we all know, that he sympathized with great causes and with oppressed nations and with what he believed to be the cause of liberty all over the world, but I do mean his sympathy with all classes of human beings from the highest to the lowest."—*Lord Roseberry.*

"Even when racked with pain and with the shadow of death darkening over him, his heart still yearned towards the people of Ireland, and his last public utterance was a message of sympathy for Ireland and of hope for her future. His was a great and deep nature. He loved the people with a wise and persevering love. His love of the people and his abiding fa'th in the efficacy of lib rty and of government based on the consent of the people, as an instrument of human progress, were not the outcome of youthful enthusiasm, but the deep-rooted growth of long years, and drew their vigor from an almost unparalleled experience of men and affairs. Mr. Gladstone was the greatest Englishmen of his time; he loved his own people as much as any Englishman who ever lived; but through communion with the hearts of his own people he acquired that greater, wider gift, the power of understanding and sympathising with other peoples."—*John Dillon, M. P., in behalf of Ireland.*

CHAPTER I.

> Time is eternity.
> Pregnant with all eternity can give,
> Pregnant with all that makes archangels smile.
> —*Edward Yong.*

We are fast coming to the close of the greatest century of all the years of time. Every decade of these later years has been richer in direct influence on the well-being of humanity than any century of the years of old. Science, art, literature, religion, social life have all made such marvelous strides that the world of 1898 seems altogether another kind of world from that of 1800. No period of the world's history has been as productive of great men and women in every department of life as this great cycle which is now hastening to a glorious close. On the bench and at the bar; in the pulpit and on the throne; in the laboratory of the scientist and in the boundless fields of exploration; in the dreamland of the poet and the cloister of the saint; by the furnace fires of the inventor and the campfires of the warrior; in the legislative halls of the nations and at the desks of seminaries, schools and colleges; in the marts of commerce and in the factories of toil—great men and women are to be found in crowds and throngs: greater men and women than the world has ever seen before. This is an age of the sons of Anak, the pygmies are dreams of the dead past, the age of the giants has come.

One of the greatest of all the names of this century is the name of William Ewart Gladstone. An American lady writing of him says:

There have been intellects more brilliant, leaders more dashing and magnetic, but there is no other man of the century who has combined in himself the qualities of statesman, orator, political financier, scholar, author, friend of humanity, and illustrator of the highest virtues of domestic and public life. There has been no other man who has better shown that highest form of moral courage, the standing firmly for what is believed to be right, though such a stand deprives him of office and public favor. There has been no other life of this, or perhaps of any century, so filled with splendid achievements and so consecrated to high purposes.

The years of Mr. Gladstone's life have run parallel with the years of the century, and in those years he has exerted a wonderful influence. They have been what they were very largely because he was what he was. The clay bears the impress of the potter's hand, and master minds are moulders of the centuries. It was Mr. Gladstone's hand· that let loose the half-imprisoned genius of freedom, and gave to England civil and religious liberty. It was Mr. Gladstone who dared to preach the grand political gospel, on which our great Republic is builded—that the toiler in the factory and the mill, and the prince in his palace and the nobleman on his wide domains, are equal. "Are they not," he said, in the midst of aristocratic sneers, referring to the working classes of England, "your own flesh and blood?" What his friend Lord Tennyson sung, Mr. Gladstone beat into the unwilling brains of the frivolous and prejudiced among the English aristocracy:

> Howe'er it be, it seems to me
> 'Tis only noble to be good;
> Kind hearts are more than coronets
> And simple faith than Norman blood.

It will be the purpose of the following pages to set in order the story of Mr. Gladstone's great public career. But Mr. Gladstone will have an abiding place in the heart of the world because of his kind and gentle spirit. Never did a heart beat with warmer human sympathies than the heart of him who was four times Prime Minister of England. Behind the statesman stood the man, quick to sympathize and quick to help. A thousand illustrations might be cited—let one or two suffice.

It is January the 7th, 1885. Prince Victor, Duke of Clarence, will reach his majority to-morrow. He is the prospective heir to the throne of England. Mr. Gladstone writes a letter of congratulation to the young prince; and in every line and between the lines the father's heart is beating tenderly for the royal lad who to-morrow will be a man. Let us read the letter. It is doubly interesting now, seeing that prince and statesman have both passed into the silent land:

HAWARDEN CASTLE, January 7, 1885.

SIR: As the oldest among the confidential servants of Her Majesty, I cannot allow the anniversary to pass without a notice which will to-morrow bring your Royal Highness to full age; and thus mark an important epoch in your life. The hopes and intentions of those whose lives lie, like mine, in the past, are of little moment; but they have seen much and what they have seen suggests much for the future. There lies before your Royal Highness in prospect the occupation, I trust at a distant date, of a throne, which, to me at least, appears the most illustrious in the world, from its history and associations, from its legal basis, from the weight of the cares it brings, from the royal love of the people, and from the unparalleled opportunities it gives, in so many ways and in so many regions. of doing good to the almost countless numbers whom the Almighty has placed beneath the sceptre of England.

I fervently desire and pray, and there cannot be a more animating prayer, that your Royal Highness may ever grow in the principles of conduct, and may be adorned with all the qualities which correspond with this great and noble vocation.

And, sir, if the sovereignty has been relieved by our modern institutions of some of its burdens. it still, I believe, remains true that there has been no period of the world's history at which successors to monarchy could more efficaciously contribute to the stability of a great historic system, dependent even more upon love than upon strength, by devotion to their duties, and by a bright example to the country. This result we have happily been permitted to see, and other generations will, I trust, witness it anew.

Heartily desiring that in the life of your Royal Highness every private and personal good may be joined with every public blessing, I have the honor to remain, sir,

Your Royal Highness's most dutiful and faithful servant,

W. E. GLADSTONE.

The kind fatherly heart that prompted this letter was the same heart that prompted him to visit again and again the bedside of a poor crossing-sweeper, and on bended knees to breathe words of prayer and lift the cross of hope before the eyes of the dying boy. The same heart that led him to plead with the sons of an old friend, plead with frequent and pityful entreaty, that for their dear father's sake they would quit the paths of folly and lead a noble life, and he did not plead in vain.

One of the elements of character that endeared Mr. Gladstone to all hearts was the grand catholicity of spirit that made him appreciative of all good work by whomsoever wrought. As an example, it is worthy of note that Mr. Spurgeon, the prince of English preachers, a Nonconformist of the Nonconformists, an avowed opponent of the Church as by law established, more than once received words of kindness and encouragement from this great churchman and statesman. He respected the sower who sowed good seed, and did good work in the world, by whatever name he was called. And it will interest the admirers of Mr. Gladstone and the friends of Mr. Spurgeon alike, to know that on the occasion of Mr. Spurgeon's last illness the great statesman wrote the following letter of condolence to Mrs. Spurgeon:

HAWARDEN, July 17, 1891.

MY DEAR MADAM: In my own home, darkened at the present time, I have read with studied interest daily accounts of Mr. Spurgeon's illness; and I cannot help conveying to you the earnest assurance of my sympathy with you and with him; and of my cordial admiration of his splendid powers, but still more of his devoted and unfailing character. May I humbly commend you and him in all contingencies to the infinite stores of the Divine love and mercy, and subscribe myself, my dear madam,

Faithfully yours,

W. E. GLADSTONE.

Mrs. Spurgeon immediately responded, and the dying preacher summoned his failing powers to write the following postscript which was probably one of the last efforts of the preacher's busy pen:

P. S.—Yours is a word of love such as those only write who have been into the King's country, and have seen much of His face.   My heart's love to you.—C. H. SPURGEON.

It is hardly necessary here to refer to Mr. Gladstone's profound religious character.   Later on we shall see him in the early mornings, walking to the hamlet church to share in the sacred communion.   The spirit that possessed him may be gathered from these beautiful stanzas from one of the devotional hymns he wrote:

> O lead my blindness by the hand,
>   Lead me to thy familiar feast;
> Not here and now to understand,
>   Yet even here and now to taste,
> How the eternal Word of Heaven
> On earth in broken bread is given.
>
> *   *   *   *
>
> O let the virtue all divine,
>   The gift of this true Sabbath morn,
> Stored in my spirit's inner shrine,
>   Be purely and be meekly borne,
> Be husbanded with thrifty care
> And sweetened and refreshed with prayer.

Archdean Farrar, who knew him well, speaks of him as "the highest type of Christian gentleman" he had ever known.

He has passed from these scenes of time, but his name and his fame and the wise words he has spoken will never die.

> What wreaths that cannot fade
> Upon thy bier are laid!
> Greece weeps her truest friend, and Italy
> Remembers thee in tears;
> Bulgaria, Armenia mourn for thee,
> Friend of their friendless years,
> One radiant Form appears,
> Smiling while she weeps—'tis Liberty!
> O chieftain true and rare!
> Sleep! We have not forgot,
> Within ten thousand hearts thy hopes shall move,
> Thy spirit slumbers not.

CHAPTER II.

"Life is the gift of God and is divine."—H. W. Longfellow.

William Ewart Gladstone first saw the light at his father's home, 62 Rodney street, Liverpool, on the 29th of December, 1809. He was the third son. It was the habit of Mr. John Gladstone to discuss all manner of questions with his children; nothing was taken for granted between him and his sons. A succession of arguments on great

GLADSTONE'S BIRTHPLACE.

topics and small topics alike—arguments conducted with the most good humor, but also with the most implacable logic—formed the staple of the family conversation. Such conditions were pre-eminently calculated to mould the thoughts and direct the course of an intelligent and receptive nature. There was the father's masterful will and keen perception, the sweetness and piety of the mother, wealth with all its substantial advantages and few of its mischiefs, a strong sense of the value of money, a rigid avoidance of extravagance and excess, everywhere strenuous purpose in life, constant employment and concentrated ambition.

"In William Ewart Gladstone we have the same restless energy, the same sympathy with struggling nationalities, the same business aptitude, the same appreciation of great men, the same far-sightedness, and also the same longevity. The great qualities of the father have been modified by surrounding circumstances, but the generic similarity is conspicuous. It was amid surroundings such as we have indicated that W. E. Gladstone began life. The father's active participation in parliamentary contests opened wide the door for the buzz of political questions at his house. It also created the conditions for the familiar association and intercourse with men of high quality and large caliber. It is easy to understand how the teaching and influence of a man of genius like George Canning should remain a permanent factor in the intellectual development of a young lad. It became then, as it has remained since, an important influence in the evolution of a great career."

Speaking of Mr. Gladstone's ancestors, who were entirely Scotch, being proprietors of a moderate property near the town of Biggar, in Lanarkshire, Mr. George W. E. Russell says: "The title of the estate from which they took their name was Gledstane, afterward modernized to Gladstone. This patrimony dates back some six hundred years, but during the last century or two the family history runs on different lines. The grandfather of William Ewart Gladstone was a corn merchant at Leith, and in the course of his business had a shipload of corn consigned to him. The vessel conveying the grain arrived in due course at Liverpool, and his eldest son, John, was dispatched to that town to carry out the sale. The skill and aptitude exhibited by the young Scotchman in carrying through the business attracted the attention of one of the leading corn merchants, on whose advice he settled there. He commenced his business career as a clerk in his friend and patron's house, and lived to become a principal partner in the firm, and one of the leading merchants of Liverpool. His career was successful throughout; he was at once a keen and active politician, a generous philanthropist, and a splendid man of business. He was always in earnest, and had built up his position in life by shrewd sense, great activity and unsullied honor. These great qualities, combined with a restless energy, naturally brought him to the front in all matters connected with the town of Liverpool. In politics he was to all intents and purposes a Liberal-Conservative of those days. In 1812 he presided over a meeting called for the purpose of inviting Canning to become a candidate for the borough. The contest which ensued laid the foundation of a life-long friendship between John Gladstone and George Canning. The influence of his great friend converted Mr. Gladstone to Conservative principles, and in 1819 he entered the House of Commons, representing in succession Lancaster, Woodstock and Berwick. Mr. John Gladstone was, by Sir Robert Peel, created a baronet in 1845, and died in 1851 at the ripe age of eighty-eight.

The England on which Mr. Gladstone opened his eyes had made very little material progress since the days of Queen Elizabeth. Travel and means of transportation were at the tedious rate common to the days of the Patriarch Job, when "the camel was for safety and the horse for speed." There were "*fast* stage coaches," as men then counted fastness. But the omnipotence of the monarch we call "Steam" was only "a dream of hair-brained fanatics." It was nevertheless a dream destined to become wonderfully true. There was no system of public government education; but the rate-payers were compelled to support paupers. Almost everything was taxed from the cradle to the grave. There were church taxes, window taxes, cart-wheel taxes, horse taxes, taxes on malt, taxes on hair-powder and taxes on silver plate. More than seventeen hundred articles were subject to taxation. There were taxes on the ribbon of the bride, and on the brass nails of the coffin. The man who indulged in horse riding in those days had to ride a taxed horse with a taxed bridle along a taxed road. It was a land of beautiful liberty and abounding taxation. And, as Sydney Smith said, the great hope of the Englishman was that when at last life's pilgrimage was ended he would "be gathered to his fathers, and enter a land of rest and peace where he would be taxed no more."

But England was nursing noble souls when this century was young. The temple of literature was thronged with such men as Scott and Byron, Wordsworth and Coleridge, Southey and Shelley and Keats, Campbell and Lamb; and by the sluggish tides of the Mersey a cradle was being rocked in which lay a smiling boy destined to be the glory of his country, the honor of his age.

It is not mere idle curiosity that longs to know all that can be told of the early days of illustrious men.

By a most happy accident we have fallen upon some very pleasant reminiscences of Mr. Gladstone's boyhood days by one of the very few surviving comrades of those far away years. Mr. Graham and Mr. Gladstone were boys together.

The great Commoner of England outlived most of his contemporaries. Those men who were privileged to listen to his first parliamentary utterances are now few and far between. The companions of his boyhood, even of his ripening manhood, have practically disappeared. How very few

are left who can say "I remember Gladstone as a lad"—
fewer still, "I remember Gladstone as a boy!"

But Dingwall, that far northern royal burgh, famous as
being the place which Mr. Gladstone's mother claimed as
being "her town," and over which, in matters municipal,
Mr. Robertson (Mr. Gladstone's grandfather) presided,
lays claim to possessing among its townsmen one who, as a
boy, romped with Mr. Gladstone, took part in his boyish
games, and discussed with him the problems of child's
imagination. If England has in Mr. Gladstone a "Grand
Old Man," Dingwall has a "Grand Old Man" in Mr. Graham. That venerable and worthy gentleman for a long
period of years acted as local poor inspector, and, though
past eighty, he is still possessed of powers, mental and
physical, that are the envy of many men not more than
half his age. Mr. Graham's likeness to Mr. Gladstone is
remarkable.

"Excuse me, sir," said a friend to him, "but how like
Mr. Gladstone you are!"

Mr. Graham, with an ever-ready laugh, retorted that, not
only was he like Mr. Gladstone, but he had the pleasure of
knowing him as a boy.

"I visited Mr. Graham the other evening," says a recent
writer, "and on glancing around the snug room in which we
sat together I noted no fewer than four portraits of Mr.
Gladstone laid open to view. One represented him at the
age of three score and ten; another when he had, as Mr.
Graham aptly put it, 'crossed the line,' (that is eighty
years); another represents him as taken quite recently along
with Mrs. Gladstone; and in a fourth he stands before a
Midlothian audience in his recent campaign, exhorting them,
in one of his most fervid perorations, 'not to put their
trust in squires, in parsons, nor in acres, but to listen to the
voice of the people's will, and stand by Ireland in her
attempt to realize her aspirations.'"

Filled even now with boyish life and vitality, and possessing a memory and imagination as fresh and keen as ever he has known them to be, Mr. Graham plunged into many interesting reminiscences of his early youth. His quick eye caught sight of the large portrait of Mr. Gladstone that lay beside us near the window.

A glimpse at the familiar face of the venerable statesman served to put his memory on the proper rails, and the old gentleman, rising from his seat and pointing at the portrait, said : "Isn't that like him? But, oh, he is changed since I knew him first! You need not look surprised, for I knew Mr. Gladstone seventy years since. We were playmates here in Dingwall together, and many a happy day have we spent in each other's company."

And, so saying, Mr. Graham shot his memory back over the long vista of seven decades and gave me his impressions of Mr. Gladstone as a boy. Mr. Graham was a special favorite with Mr. Gladstone's mother. During the summer vacation she used to bring her boys to Dingwall on a visit to their relatives and friends there, and on such occasions she invariably sent for "the little boy Graham" to keep the youngsters company.

"Willie was always my favorite," said he, "and, though he was a couple of years older than I was, we were close companions during those long and happy summer days. We would scamper along the country roads together, both of us nimbler in the feet than we now are, I warrant; we would explore the woods together, go in together for all forms of sport and frolic, and often even take our meals together."

"And, Mr. Graham," I asked, "was there anything about the boy that was remarkable—was the child, so to speak, father to the man?" Mr. Graham replied that, even to his child mind, there did always seem a charm about the boy Gladstone. His mind was as alert as his body, and he never lost a chance to extract information from things the most commonplace. "He was so inquisitive," remarked the old gentleman, laughingly, "he was never content with a simple answer to a question, but probed everything to the very bottom ere he appeared anything like satisfied." From what Mr. Graham said, it appears that Willie Gladstone delighted to tear all sorts of subjects to shreds, and then, microscopically, to examine each shred separately, as he plied questions with the view of eliciting answers.

"I remember," said Mr. Graham, "we were one day standing together watching the operation of potato planting, and we fell on discussing the proper distance that should be given between the plants. We argued the subject out to our own satisfaction, and when he had pumped all the information possible on the point from me, I was highly amused to see him take from his pocket a memorandum book, in which he took a note of all the information he had gained on the subject. This note book he called into requisition very often, jotting down scraps of information gained from day to day, and making memoranda of the most commonplace subjects."

"And what kind of a companion did young Gladstone make?" I asked.

"He was always lively," replied Mr. Graham, "always thirsting after instruction, and delighted in prying into the root of things. But he was not so eager for fun and trickery as I was, but would often be thoughtful. And nothing pleased him more than reading. He would go and buy a treatise or tract on some special subject, and pore over it, mastering its contents. He was a queer fellow that way," added the old gentleman, laughing.

Then came the rehearsal of an interesting incident of their Sunday-school experiences, in which young Graham, on one occasion at least, proved "too many" for young Gladstone. The task submitted to the scholars was the formidable one of repeating from beginning to end the 119th Psalm, and

Mr. Graham still distinctly remembers the keen interest taken in the feat by Mrs. Gladstone, whose memory he cherishes. It is no mean tribute to his powers of memory as a child that he was the only scholar who succeeded in performing the task successfully. "That was no little thing for a wee boy to do, was it?" laughed Mr. Graham. At least I can say that I did what even a Gladstone failed to do, and what I would certainly fail to do now, I fear."

Mr. Graham mentioned a circumstance in connection with Mr. Gladstone in those days which, however trivial it may have seemed at the time, was, in the light of subsequent history, prophetic. Just as Mr. Gladstone knows now how to take care of our national finance, and how to put our resources to the best advantage, he seemed, even as a boy, to be entrusted by his mother, to some extent, with the household purse. Said Mr. Graham, "Mrs. Gladstone used to say laughingly, 'Go to the Chancellor of the Exchequer [meaning her son William], and tell him to give me some money.'"

CHAPTER III.

> O. years, gone down into the past,
> What pleasant memories come to me.
>
> *—Phœbe Cary.*

> Strange to me are the forms I meet,
> When I visit the dear old town,
> But the native air is pure and sweet
> And the trees that o'ershadow each well-known street,
> As they balance up and down,
> Are singing the beautiful song:
> " A boy's will is the wind's will,
> And the thoughts of youth are long."
>
> *·—H. W. Longfellow.*

Mr. Gladstone was possessed of a most wonderful memory. It was perfectly phenomenal in its scope and retentiveness. It served the great statesman and scholar as a sacred treasure house, to which he has committed ten thousand facts in compact and orderly arrangement. It is said of Mr. Gladstone that "he never forgets." After he had reached his eighty-fourth year, he, at the wish of some friends, began recalling the memory of early days. He went back to the days of his boyhood and bid the dead past reappear. So pleasant and interesting are these reminiscences that we can not resist the temptation of presenting a few of them here, seeing that they refer to events and impressions of his very early years.

Mr. Gladstone called to mind the grand old coaching days, when the Tony Wellers of the time were men of very considerable importance. "The system was raised," he said, "to the highest degree of perfection, far exceeding that of anything of the kind to be met with on the Continent."

When a boy, going to school at Eton, between the years 1820 and 1830, he went from Liverpool to Eton by coach. The coach changed at Birmingham. He gives this graphic description of the scene, after the lapse of three score years and ten : "Our coach used to arrive at Birmingham about 3 or 4 o'clock in the morning, when we were turned out into the street till it might please a new coach with a new equipment to appear. There was no building in the town, great or small, public or private, at that period, upon which it was possible for a rational being to fix his eye with any degree of satisfaction." Mr. Gladstone lived to see this same Birmingham one of the most beautiful cities upon the face of the earth. He remembered Edinburgh in the days of Lord Moncrieff, of Dr. Gordon, of Dr. Thomson and Bishop Sandford.

He speaks in these early reminiscences pleasantly and gratefully of some weeks spent in Edinburgh and the neighborhood with that prince of Scottish preachers Dr. Chalmers, whose wonderful "Astronomical Discourses" marked him out as one of the greatest intellectual giants the pulpit of Scotland had seen since the days of the immortal John Knox.

Speaking at a great meeting in Dundee in 1890, Mr. Gladstone gave some interesting memoirs of the condition of commerce in his boyhood. This memory serves to indicate how strongly the love of the beautiful had possession of him in his early youth :

"It is hardly an exaggeration to say," Mr. Gladstone observed, "that at the time when I was a youth of ten or fifteen years of age there was hardly anything that was beautiful produced in this country. I remember at a period of my life, when I was about eighteen, I was taken over to see a silk factory in Macclesfield. At that time Mr. Huskisson, whose name ought always to be remembered with respect among all sound economists, and the government of Lord Liverpool had been making the first efforts, not to break down—that was reserved for their happier followers—but to lessen, to modify, or perhaps I should say, to mitigate, a little if possible, the protective system. Down to the period of Mr. Huskisson silk handkerchiefs from France were prohibited. They were largely smuggled, and no gentleman went over to Paris, without, if he could manage it, bringing back in his pockets, his purse, his portmanteau, his hat or his great-coat, handkerchiefs and gloves. But Mr. Huskisson carried a law in which, in lieu of this prohibition of these French articles, a duty of 30 per cent. was imposed on them, and it is in my recollection that there was a keener detestation of Mr. Huskisson, and a more violent passion roused against him in consequence of that mild, initial measure than ever was associated in the other camp, in the protectionist camp, within the career of Cobden and Bright. I was taken to this manufactory, and they produced the English silk handkerchief they were in the habit of making, and which they thought it cruel to be competed with by the silk handkerchiefs of France, although even before they were allowed to compete the French manufacturer had to pay the fine of 30 per cent. on the value. It was in that first visit to a manufactory at Macclesfield that—I will not say I became a free trader, for it was ten or fifteen years later when I entered into the full faith of that policy—but from what I saw then there dawned on my mind the first ray of light. What I thought when they showed me these handkerchiefs was: How detestable they really are, and what in the world can be the object of coaxing, nursing, coddling up manufacturers to produce goods such as those, which you ought to be ashamed of exhibiting."

It will interest many readers who are personally familiar with North Wales, who have seen the sun rise over Snowden's crest and Conway's castled towers, and who have spent many happy hours at those grand "watering places," Rhyl, Llandudno, Bangor and Canarvon, which we should designate "Summer Resorts," to hear Mr. Gladstone tell of traveling along the North Wales coast as far as Bangor and Carnarvon, when there was no such thing as a watering place, no such thing as a house to be hired for the purpose of those visits that are now paid by thousands of people to such multitudes of points all along the coast. It was supposed that if ever any body of gentlemen could be found sufficiently energetic to make a railway to Holyhead, that railway could not possibly pierce the country, and must be made along the coast, and, if carried along the coast, could not possibly be made to pay. So firm was that conviction that "I well recollect the day," Mr. Gladstone, added "when a large and important deputation of railway leaders went to London and waited upon Sir Robert Peel, who was then Prime Minister, in order to demonstrate to him that it was totally impossible for them to construct a paying line, and therefore to impress upon his mind the necessity of his agreeing to give them a considerable grant out of the consolidated fund. Sir Robert Peel was a very circumspect statesman, and not least so in those matters in which the public purse was concerned. He encouraged them to take a more sanguine view. Whether he persuaded them into a more sanguine tone of mind I do not know. This I know, the railway was made, and we now understand that this humble railway, this impossible railway, as it was then conceived, is at the present moment the most productive and remunerative part of the whole vast system of the North Western Railway Company."

Of the Liverpool of his boyhood, Mr. Gladstone said: "When my recollections of her were most familiar, she was a town of one hundred thousand persons, and the silver cloud of smoke which floated above her resembled that which might appear over any secondary borough or village of the country.   I refer to the period between 1810 and 1820, and it is especially to the latter part of period that my memory extends.   I used as a small boy to look southward along shore from my father's windows at Seaforth to the town. In those days the space between Liverpool and Seaforth was very differently occupied.   Four miles of the most beautiful sands that I ever knew offered to the aspirations of the youthful rider the most delightful method of finding access to Liverpool, and he had the other inducement to pursue that road, that there was no other decent avenue to the town.   Bootle I remember a wilderness of sand hills. I have seen wild roses growing upon the very ground which is now the center of the borough.   All that land is now partly covered with residences, and partly with places of business and industry.   In my time but one single house stood upon the space between Rimrose brook and the town of Liverpool.   I rather think it was associated with the name of Statham, if my memory serves me right, the name of the town clerk of Liverpool."

He told also on this occasion a pleasant and romantic story of Hannah More, which links Mr. Gladstone with a far distant past.

"I believe," he said, "I was four years old at the time, and I remember Hannah More presented me with one of her little books—not uninteresting for children—she told me she gave it to me because 'I had just come into the world and she was just going out.'"

CHAPTER IV.

SCHOOL DAYS AT ETON.

Ah, happy hills ! Ah, pleasing shade !
Ah, fields beloved in vain !
Where once my careless childhood strayed,
A stranger yet to pain !
I feel the gales that from ye blow,
A momentary bliss bestow,
As waving fresh their gladsome wing,
My weary soul they seem to soothe ;
And, redolent of joy and youth,
To breathe a second spring !
—Gray's Ode on Eton College.

The father of Mr. Gladstone was not slow to recognize
the brilliant mental powers of his gifted son, and wide
awake to the grand opportunities that lay in the path of
every earnest youth, he resolved to aid him in every possible way to fit himself for a career of usefulness and honor.
To this end the boy Gladstone was entered a scholar in the
famous Eton College in September, 1821, being then in his
thirteenth year.   The dew of early youth was on his brow,
and he was declared to be "the prettiest little boy that
ever went to Eton."   As a scholar he was by common consent acknowledged to be God-fearing and conscientious,
pure-minded and courageous, and humane.   He was never
seen to run, but was fond of sculling, and even then given
to that fast walking which he has practiced all his life.   At
school he distinguished himself by turning his glass upside
down and refusing to drink a coarse toast at an election dinner, and for having protested against the torture of certain
wretched animals which were then regarded as fair game on
Ash Wednesday.   Some of his schoolfellows, failing to

appreciate this early evidence of his chivalrous disposition, Mr. Gladstone offered to write his reply in good round hand upon their faces. In the school debating society he naturally took a high place. In one of his earliest recorded speeches, he declares that his "prejudices and his predilections have long been entitled on the side of toryism." So tory was he that, seeing a colt of the name of Hampden entered for the Derby between two horses named Zeal and Lunacy, he declared he was in his proper place, for Hampden in those days was to him only an illustrious rebel.

Celebrated as this school was all over England, it must be admitted that the pupils were in no great danger of being overworked. In 1845 the time devoted to study did not amount to eleven hours per week. An old Etonian thus speaks of the nature of the studies pursued :

"The books used in the fifth form—besides The Iliad, The Æneid, Horace, and, I think, some scraps of Ovid for repetition merely—consisted of three 'Selections' or 'Readers'—Poetæ Græci, which contained some picked passages from Homer's Odyssey, Callimachus, Theocritus, etc., together with Scriptores Græci and Scriptores Romani, which were similarly made up of tit-bits from the best Greek and Latin prose writers. A lad would go on grinding at the above scanty provender from the age it might be of twelve to that of twenty with little or no change. Plautus, Terence, Lucretius, Persius, Juvenal, Livy, Tacitus, Cicero, Demosthenes, the tragedians (except in the head master's division), Aristophanes, Pindar, Herodotus, Thucydides—in short, all but four of the great authors of Greece and Rome, and those four poets were entirely unknown to us, except it might be through the medium of certain fragments in the 'Selections' aforesaid, where I believe that the majority of them were wholly unrepresented. It seems almost incredible that a young man could go up to the University from the upper fifth form of the first classical school in England, ignorant almost of the very names of these authors. Yet such was the case sometimes. It was very much my own case."

When but eighteen years of age Mr. Gladstone, under the *nom de plume* of "Bartholemy Bauverie" contributed some remarkable articles to the *Eton Miscellany*. He wrote on "Eloquence," on "A Chorus of Euripides," and followed by a powerful article on "Ancient and Modern Genius Compared." After taking the part of the moderns as against the ancients—though he by no means depreciates the genius of the latter—the essayist, in concluding his paper, thus eloquently apostrophises Canning:

"It is for those who revered him in the plenitude of his meridian glory to mourn over him in the darkness of his premature extinction; to mourn over the hopes that are buried in his grave, and the evils that arise from his withdrawing from the scene of life. Surely if eloquence never excelled and seldom equaled—if an expanded mind and judgment whose vigor was paralleled only by its soundness, if brilliant wit, if a glowing imagination, if a warm heart, and an unbending firmness—could have strengthened the frail tenure and prolonged the momentary duration of human existence, that man had been immortal! But nature could endure no longer. Thus has Providence ordained that inasmuch as the intellect is more brilliant, it shall be more short lived; as its sphere is more expanded, more swiftly is it summoned away. Lest we should give to man the honor due to God—lest we should exalt the object of our admiration into a divinity for our worship—He who calls the weary and the mourner to eternal rest, hath been pleased to remove him from our eyes."

Then, after comparing the death of the object of his early hero-worship with the death of Pitt, he says, finally, "The decrees of inscrutable Wisdom are unknown to us; but if ever there was a man for whose sake it was meet to indulge the kindly though frail feelings of our nature, for whom the tear of sorrow was to us both prompted by affection and dictated by duty—that man was George Canning."

With the daring of youth he ventured into the realms of poetry. His next contribution was entitled "Richard Cœur de Lion," an effort in verse. This poem consists of some two hundred and fifty lines, and the following passage may be taken as a fair sample of the whole:

> Who foremost now the deadly spear to dart,
> And strike the jav'lin to the Moslem's heart?
> Who foremost now to climb the leaguer'd wall,
> The first to triumph, or the first to fall?
> Lo, where the Moslems rushing to the fight,
> Back bear thy squadrons in inglorious flight.
> With plumed helmet, and with glitt'ring lance,
> 'Tis Richard bids his steel-clad bands advance;
> 'Tis Richard stalks along the blood-dyed plain,
> And views unmoved the slaying and the slain;
> 'Tis Richard bathes his hands in Moslem blood,
> And tinges Jordan with the purple flood.
> Yet where the timbrels ring, the trumpets sound,
> And tramp of horsemen shakes the solid ground,
> Though 'mid the deadly charge and rush of fight,
> No thought be theirs of terror or of flight,—
> Ofttimes a sigh will rise, a tear will flow,
> And youthful bosoms melt in silent woe;
> For who of iron frame and harder heart
> Can bid the mem'ry of his home depart?
> Tread the dark desert and the thirsty sand,
> Nor give one thought to England's smiling land?
> To scenes of bliss, and days of other years—
> The Vale of Gladness and the Vale of Tears;
> That, pass'd and vanish'd from their loving sight,
> This 'neath their view, and wrapt in shades of night?

We are happy in being able to present from Mr. Gladstone's own pen a picture of the Eton of his boyhood. In a paper on Arthur Henry Hallam, contributed to the *Youth's Companion* for February, 1898, we gain glimpses of Eton and Eton life that are exceedingly interesting, as well as a record of one of Mr. Gladstone's earliest and most sacred friendships :

"Far back in the distance of my early life, and upon a surface not yet ruffled by contention, there lies the memory of a friendship surpassing every other that has ever been enjoyed by one greatly blessed both in the number and in the excellence of his friends.

"It is the simple truth that Arthur Henry Hallam was a spirit so exceptional that everything with which he was brought into relation during his shortened passage through this world came to be, through this contact, glorified by a touch of the ideal. Among his contemporaries at Eton, that queen of visible homes for the ideal schoolboy, he stood supreme among all his fellows; and the long life through which I have since wound my way, and which has brought me into contact with so many men of rich endowments, leaves him where he then stood, as to natural gifts, so far as my estimation is concerned.

"While intimacy was at this particular time the most delightful note of the friendship between Arthur Hallam and myself, I am bound to say that it had one other and more peculiar characteristic, which was its inequality. Indeed, it was so unequal as between his mental powers and mine, that I have questioned myself strictly whether I was warranted in supposing it to have been knit with such closeness as I have fondly supposed. Of this, however, I find several decisive marks. One was, that we used to correspond together during vacations, a practice not known to me by any other example. Eton friendships were fresh and free, but they found ample food for the whole year during the eight or eight and a half months of term time. Another proof, significant from its peculiarity, I find in a record more than once supplied by a very arid journal, which at that early period I had begun to keep. It bears witness that I sometimes "sculled Hallam up to the Shallows," a point about two miles up the stream of the Thames from Eton. Working small boats (whether skiff, "funny"—such was the name,—or wherry) single-handed was a common practice among Eton boys, and one which I followed rather assiduously; but to carry a passenger up stream was another matter, and stands as I think for a proof of setting extraordinary value upon his society. Another recollection, more considerabe, bears in the same direction. Except upon special occasions, the practice was that the boys breakfasted, or "messed," alone, each in his room. Now and then a case might be found, in which two, or even three, would club together their rolls and butter (the simple fare of those days, which knew nothing of habitual meat breakfast), but this only when they lived under the same roof. I had not the advantage of living in Mr. Hawtrey's house, and indeed it was severed from that of my "dame" by nearly the whole length of Eton, as it stood in what was termed Weston's yard, near those glorious and unrivaled "playing fields," (I speak of a date seventy years back. The stately elms were then in their full glory. I fear that the hand of time has not wholly spared them,) whereas my window looked out upon the church-yard, with the mass of school buildings interposed between our dwellings. Notwithstanding this impediment we used, for I forget how many terms, regularly to mess together, and the point of honor or convenience was not allowed to interfere, for the scene of operations shifted, week about, from his room to mine, and *vice versa.* It was a grief to me, in my posthumous visits to Eton, to be unable to identify his room, consecrated by the fondest memories, for it had been sacrificed to the necessary improvements of an ill-planned but most hospitable residence.

"It was probably well for him that he participated in no game or strong bodily exercise, as I imagine that it might have precipitated the effects of that hidden organic malformation which put an end to his life in 1833, when he was but twenty-two years old. But at these meals, and in walks, often to the monument of Gray, so appropriately placed near the 'churchyard' of the immortal 'Elegy,' were mainly carried on our conversations. It is evident from notices still remaining, that they partook pretty largely of an argumentative character. On Sunday, May 14, 1826, I find this record in my journal: 'Still arguments with Hallam, as usual on Sundays, about articles, creeds, etc.' It is difficult for me now to conceive how during these years he bore with me; since not only was I inferior to him in knowledge and dialectic ability, but my mind was 'cabined, cribbed, confined,' by an intolerance which I ascribe to my having been brought up in what were then termed Evangelical ideas—ideas, I must add, that in other respects were frequently productive of great and vital good.

"The common bond among all the boys of any considerable prominence at Eton was the association for debating all unforbidden subjects, which has already been named and which is known as 'The Society.' Such institutions are now very widely spread; but at the date when this one was founded, in the year 1811, it might claim the honors of a discovery, for it was in exclusive possession of the field. During its career of about four-score years it has supplied the British Empire with no less than four prime ministers. It fluctuated in efficiency as the touch of time and change passed over it; but during the period of Arthur Hallam's membership it was regenerated by the introduction of that rare and most often precious character, an enthusiast, by name James Milnes Gaskell.

"This youth had a political faculty, which probably suffered in the end from an absorbing and exclusive predominance in mind and life such as to check his general development of mental character, yet which in its precocious ripeness secured for him not the notice only, but what might also be called the close friendship of Mr. Canning, that commanding luminary of the twenties, doomed to die at Chiswick in 1827, in the very chamber in which Mr. Fox had breathed his last only twenty-one years before. Gaskell found our society, if not at the point, yet afflicted with a premonitory lethargy, almost of death; but he breathed life by his assiduity and energy into every artery and vein of the body, and gave to Arthur Hallam a worthy field for the training of his eloquence and the exhibition of his always temperate but yet vivid and enlightened ideas, stamped with traditional Whiggism, yet incapable of being permanently trammeled by any artificial restraints.

"I have mentioned that we were inhibited from debating any events not more than fifty years old, and I recollect the growling of our famous Doctor Keats when we fished out from the Indian administration of Warren Hastings a question lying very close upon the line. But Gaskell was equal to the occasion. He had a small but pleasant apartment in a private house, which his private tutor was privileged to occupy. In this room four or five of us would meet and debate without restraint the questions of modern politics. Here we reveled in the controversies between Pitt and Fox. I think we were mostly, if not all, friendly to Roman Catholic Emancipation, and to those initial measures of free trade which Huskisson, supported by Mr. Canning, devised with skill and supported with courage, in the face of bitterness of hatred from the 'harassed interests,' which I think underwent at least mitigation in the later stages of the controversy."

CHAPTER V.

STUDENT LIFE AT OXFORD.

> "Deeper, deeper, let us toil
>   In the mines of knowledge,
>   Learning's wealth and freedom's spoil,
>   Win from school and college.
>   Delve we there for brighter gems
>   Than the stars of diadems."
>
> —*Charles Mackay.*

> "1 have a debt of my heart's own to thee,
>   School of my soul! old lime and cloister shade,
>   Which I, strange suitor, should lament to see
>   Fully acquitted and exactly paid:
>   The first ripe taste of manhood's best delights,
>   Knowledge imbibed, while mind and heart agree,
>   In sweet belated talk on winter nights,
>   With friends whom growing time keeps dear to me,—
>   Such things I owe thee, and not only these."
>
> —*(R. M. Milnes) Lord Houghton.*

In the brief interim between the school days at Eton and
the college days at Oxford, Mr. Gladstone enjoyed the
privilege of the private teachings of Doctor Turner, who
afterward became Bishop of Calcutta. At this period his
habits of study became systematized and fixed. A born student, he now so arranged his time that a certain number of
hours each day were allotted to close exacting, study. In
these formative years of his life, from the age of eighteen
till he was twenty-one, wherever he was, whether with his
tutor, or at home, or at Liverpool, at the University, or spending a vacation in the country, it was his constant rule to
devote at least six or seven hours a day to good hard work.
From ten o'clock till two, and then for two or three hours

in the evening he was diligently engaged in study. This course was the fixed order of his young life. Nothing was allowed to interfere with this plan. These hours were sacred. Life was very real and very earnest. Mr. Gladstone pursued his studies with an ardor that fell little short of devotion

CHRIST CHURCH, OXFORD.

"He is such an ardent creature" said Lord Beaconsfield on one occasion with a touch of satire in the utterance. It is to the order and ceaseless ardor of these early days that Mr. Gladstone owed largely the accuracy and completeness of the wonderful scholarship of his riper years.

In the year 1829—the year in which Doctor Turner, his tutor, was appointed Bishop of Calcutta—Mr. Gladstone was entered as a student of Christ Church College, Oxford. This college has always been regarded as the most aristocratic of all the colleges of aristocratic Oxford. "An Oxford man" has always been looked upon and is looked upon still as a man of conservative sentiments and aristocratic prejudices. The training at Christ Church College had precisely this influence on the mind of Mr. Gladstone. Loyal to the old-time traditions of his country, and true to the deepest and most sacred convictions of freedom, he became saturated with those influences which gave Macauley the right to speak of him not many years later as "the rising hope of the Tory party."

In the month of December, 1878, nearly half a century after the Christ College days, in an address delivered at the opening of the Palmerston Club, Oxford, Mr. Gladstone, in referring to this matter, said :

"I trace in the education of Oxford, of my own time, one great defect. Perhaps it was my own fault; but I must admit that I did not learn, when at Oxford, that which I have learned since—viz., to set a due value on the imperishable and inestimable principles of human liberty. The temper which, I think, too much prevailed in academic circles was, that liberty was regarded with jealousy, and fear could not be wholly dispensed with. I think that the principle of the Conservative party is jealousy of liberty, and of the whole people, only qualified by fear ; but I think the policy of the Liberal party is trust in the people, only qualified by prudence. I can only assure you, gentlemen, that now I am in front of extended popular privileges, I have no fear of those enlargements of the constitution that seem to be approaching. On the contrary, I hail them with desire. I am not in the least degree conscious that I have less reverence for antiquity, for the beautiful and good and glorious charges that our ancestors have handed down to us as a patrimony to our race, than I had in other days when I held other political opinions. I have learned to set the true value upon human liberty, and in whatever I have changed, there; and there only, has been the explanation of the change."

Little did the young student of Oxford dream that a time would ever come when he would entertain such principles as these, or give utterance to such radical sentiments. It only needed that the young recluse of Oxford should be brought face to face with the people, that he should know their wants and their weakness, their hopes and their aspirations in order that the scope of his convictions should widen and his groundless prejudices should vanish.

Mr. Gladstone's influence at Oxford was of an eminently salutary character. One who knew him well in these days speaks thus of his University life: "Lord Lincoln's friendship for Gladstone was of the stanchest, and equally creditable to both. If Gladstone owed something to the Duke of Newcastle's patronage, Lord Lincoln owed a great deal more to his friend—as he ever generously confessed—for the lesson in good conduct which he derived from him. There was a very fast set at Christ Church, of which the Marquis of Waterford was the guiding spirit, and wealthy young noblemen were under strong temptations to join that set. Late supper parties, gambling and nocturnal expeditions to screw up the doors of dons or to break the furniture in hard-reading men's rooms, were among the least of the freaks in which the gay young 'tufts' indulged, and it required some moral courage even to condemn their follies by word too openly. A midnight bath in Mercury—that is, the fountain in the midst of Tom Quad—was often the penalty which outspoken critics were made to pay, for the 'tufts' administered a retributory justice of their own, much after the fashion of the Mohawks. But they never dared touch Gladstone, although he did not scruple to give them his mind about the worst of their pranks, and many well-disposed youngsters like Lord Lincoln instinctively rallied to the strong young fellow who did not know what fear was, and who, notwithstanding that he was so reasonable and steady, took such pleasure in healthy amusements and cheerful society. For it must not be supposed that Gladstone was ascetically inclined. He was one of the most hospitable men at Christ Church, which was saying a good deal."

Speaking of this period, and especially of the religious tendencies of the University, Mr. Gladstone says: "At the time I resided at Oxford, from 1828 to 1831, no sign of what was afterward known as the Tractarian Movement had yet appeared. A steady, clear, but dry, Anglican orthodoxy bore sway, and frowned this way or that at the first indication to diverge from the beaten path. Dr. Pusey was at the time revered for his piety and charity, no less than admired for his learning and talent, but suspected, I believe, of sympathy with the German theology, in which he was known to be profoundly versed. Dr. Newman was thought to have about him the flavor of what he has now told the world were the opinions he derived from the works of Dr. Thomas Scott. Mr. Keble, 'the sweet singer of Israel' and a true saint, if this generation has seen one, did not reside in Oxford. There was nothing at that time in the theology or in the religious life at the University to indicate what was so soon to come."

In his able sketch of Mr. Gladstone's career, Mr. Walter Jerrold says, in referring to the spiritual side of the life at Oxford during these four years: "We do not find any striking movement in progress; the Catholic Emancipation question had created some stir, and was yet a sore subject with many. The famous Tractarian Movement, with all its far-reaching effects, did not commence until a few years later. Gladstone, who was looked upon as the most religious member of his set, was always an earnest student of theology as well as a man of strong moral feeling. It is not, therefore, surprising to find that he was at this time very desirous of entering the church. He, however, never really

decided upon such a step, and finally commenced his political career in accordance with the wishes of his father.   It
is strange to reflect upon that the two most remarkable men
at Oxford during the early thirties, each wishing to take up
certain work, should not only take up with other work, but
doing it, should rise to the prominent positions of leaders
of men.   William Ewart Gladstone, wishing to enter the
church, became in course of time, Prime Minister of England, and the acknowledged political leader of the people ;
while his friend and contemporary, Henry Edward Manning, wishing for a life in the world of politics, was forced
by circumstances to seek some other path, entered the
English Church, became Archdeacon, seceded to the Church
of Rome, and died a Cardinal."

When Mr. Gladstone went to Oxford he met many of his
old Eton friends there.   Others had entered the University
of Cambridge, among whom were Arthur Henry Hallam,
George Selwyn and Richard Monckton Milnes, better known
in our day as Lord Houghton.   Tennyson was also at Cambridge enjoying that fellowship with Hallam that he has
made immortal in the pages of "In Memoriam."

An interesting episode transpired about this time, well
worthy of brief notice.   The debaters of the Oxford Union
were attracting great attention.   Speaking of this debating
Society, an Oxford man of that day says :   "We could
hardly name any institution in Oxford which has been more
useful in encouraging a taste for study and for general reading than this club.   It has not only supplied a school for
speaking for those who intended to pursue the professions
of the law and the church, or to embrace political life, but
furnished a theater for the display of miscellaneous knowledge, and brought together most of the distinguished young
men of the University."

The relative position of Shelley and Byron in the rank
of great poets of the age was at this time exciting consid-

erable interest in the public mind. Shelley had been expelled from Oxford, and in the judgment of many of his admirers had been very badly used by the University. A notable debate took place in Oxford on this question, in which, by special arrangement between Cambridge and Oxford, certain Cambridge men took part. Hallam, Milnes and Selwyn drove over from Cambridge to speak in the interests of Shelley. The debate was opened by Sir Francis Doyle on behalf of Shelley. Only one Oxford man was found to stand as Byron's advocate, and that was Henry Edward Manning, who became afterward the Cardinal Archbishop of Westminster. Manning was regarded as the most eloquent and persuasive member of the Oxford Debating Union. But his eloquent and impassioned plea for Byron was all in vain. At the end of the debate, by a vote of ninety to thirty-three, the palm of superiority was awarded to Shelley. Referring to this incident many years afterward Lord Houghton, one of the speakers from Cambridge, observed—at the inauguration of the new buildings of the Cambridge Union Society in 1866—"At that time we (the Cambridge undergraduates) were all very full of Mr. Shelley We had printed his 'Adonais' for the first time in England, and a friend of ours suggested that, as he had been expelled from Oxford, and been very badly treated in that University, it would be a grand thing for us to defend him there. With the permission of the Cambridge authorities they accordingly went to Oxford—at that time a long, dreary, post-chaise journey of ten hours—and were hospitably entertained by Mr. Manning of Balliol and Mr. Gladstone of Christ Church. Mr. Gladstone was at this time only a 'freshman,' and could not take any part in the debate, although he was present as a 'probationary member.'"

Very interesting information concerning this great debating society may be found in the reports of the late Librarian, Mr. E. B. Nicholson.

The Oxford Union came into existence in the spring of 1823, and fifty years later it celebrated its jubilee by a banquet, at which Lord Selborne took the chair. It is not a little remarkable that Mr. Gladstone's Ministry included no fewer than seven of the early presidents of the society, viz., the ex-Premier himself, Lord Selborne, Mr. Lowe, Mr. Cardwell, the Attorney-General, Mr. Goschen and Mr. Knatchbull-Hugessen. Although the Union owed its origin to a few Balliol men, three-fifths of the members of the United Debating Society came from Christ Church and Oriel. The Wilberforces attained great distinction in the society.

From 1829 to 1834 is described as the most active and most brilliant period in the history of the Union. In the course of these five years the presidency was held by (amongst other) Mr. Gladstone, Mr. Sidney Herbert, the Duke of Newcastle, Lord Selborne, the Archbishop of Canterbury and Mr. Lowe. Mr. Gladstone made his first speech on the 11th of February, 1830, and was the same night elected a member of the committee. The following year he succeeded Mr. Milnes Gaskell in the office of secretary. His minutes are neat; proper names are underlined and half printed. As secretary he opposed a motion for the removal of Jewish disabilities. He also moved that the Wellington Administration was undeserving of the country's confidence: Gaskell, Lyall, and Lord Lincoln supported; Sidney Herbert and the Marquis (now Duke) of Abercorn opposed him. The motion was carried by 57 to 56, and the natural exultation of the mover betrayed itself in such irregular entries as "tremendous cheers," "repeated cheering." The following week he was elected president.

It was also claimed that in this society the undergraduate might learn for the first time to think upon political subjects, and could improve his acquaintance with modern history—especially that of his own country. The sharp encounter of rival wits was useful in expanding the mind and in enlarging the scope of its impressions. Further, it was remarked that unless a student was so perverse as to set himself entirely against the prevailing tone of feeling which pervaded all classes in Oxford he would probably acquire from conviction, as well as prejudice, a spirit of devoted loyalty, of warm attachment to the liberties and ancient institutions of his country, a dislike and dread of rash innovation, and admiration approaching to reverence for the orthodox and apostolic English Church. All this "leads by an easy and natural step to serious meditation upon the vital matter of religion, and this contributes more than anything to strengthen the good resolutions and to settle the character of a high-minded young man. He becomes distinguished for polish of manners, steadiness of morals and strictness of reading." The opponents of Oxford culture affirmed, on the other hand, that its tendency was toward intolerance and bigotry, both in religion and politics.

In those stormy times it was impossible that the Reform Bill should escape notice. In the summer of 1831 the theme was taken up for debate in the Oxford Union. Mr. Gladstone made a bold and exhaustive speech on this occasion in determined and uncompromising opposition to the bill. The speech was delivered when the young orator was only in his twenty-second year. Charles (afterward Bishop) Wordsworth said it was better than any speech he had heard during the five days' debate in the House of Lords, which he had closely followed. Lord Lincoln, a fellow-student and friend of Gladstone, wrote to his father, the Duke of Newcastle, and said : "A man has risen in Israel." This vigorous onslaught on Lord John Russell's reform bill stamped the speaker as a finished orator, and within eighteen months of its delivery Mr. Gladstone was a member of the House of Commons.

CHAPTER VI.

MEMBER OF PARLIAMENT FOR NEWARK.

We need men in society who stand apart from the little fights, petty controversies, and angry contentions which seem to be part and parcel of daily life, and who shall speak great principles, breathe a heavenly influence, and bring to bear on combatants of all kinds considerations which shall survive all their misunderstandings.
—*Joseph Parker, D. D.*

> No star shines brighter than the kingly man,
> Who nobly earns whatever crown he wears,
> *   *   *   *   *   *
> And the white banner of his manhood bears
> Through all the years uplifted to the skies.
> —*Mrs. J. C. R. Dorr.*

At the close of his University course Mr. Gladstone indulged in what was then the luxury of the few, but which in these days has become the common privilege of the many. In the spring of 1832 he went abroad, and for six months he wandered with growing delight amid the historic fields of sunny Italy. During these eventful months, "England," says Mr. Barnett Smith, "was in a condition of feverish political excitement and expectancy. The people had just fought and won one of the greatest constitutional battles recorded in our parliamentary history. After a prolonged struggle, a defiance of public order, and riots in various parts of the country, the Reform Bill had become a law. The King had clearly perceived the wishes of the people, and, disregarding the advice of those members of the aristocracy who recommended him to brave the national will, had signified his assent to the measure, which could no longer be delayed with safety. The bill became a law on the 7th of June, his Majesty being represented by royal commissioners, although a portion of the press loudly demanded the presence of the King himself at the final stage of a measure which transformed the whole of the electoral arrangements of the United Kingdom. It was alleged that the Sovereign would forfeit the confidence of all true patriots if he did not perform this ceremony in person, and exhibit himself as publicly as possible in testimony of the subjugation to which his crown and the peers had been reduced. But the King, probably considering that he had already made sufficient sacrifices to the popular will, declined to attend the ceremony in the House of Lords."

Walpole says: "King and Queen sat sullenly apart in their palace. Peer and country gentleman moodily awaited the ruin of their country and the destruction of their property. Fanatacism still raved at the wickedness of a people; the people, clamoring for work, still succumbed before the mysterious disease, which was continually claiming more and more victims. But the nation cared not for the sullenness of the court, the forebodings of the landed classes, the ravings of the pulpit, or even the mysterious operations of a new plague. The deep gloom which had overshadowed the land had been relieved by one single ray. The victory had been won. The bill had become law."

Parliament was dissolved, and the first general election after the passage of the Reform Bill was looked forward to with great interest and anxiety. It was to be the opening of a new chapter in English history. What the pages of that chapter would record it was difficult to predict. Trade was bad, the national credit was low, the cholera was raging, filling thousands of graves. Pious people said the vengeance of God was about to fall upon the nation. Some predicted that the end of the world was near, while others declared that they saw the first breaking dawn of a glorious millennium. Early in September of this memorable year, 1832,

Mr. Gladstone having received an overture from the Duke of Newcastle (with whose son, the Earl of Lincoln, he was on terms of intimate friendship) to contest the representation of Newark. hurried back from the Continent for that purpose. Before the close of September, 1832, he was actively engaged in canvassing the borough. He immediately became very popular in the town, and one of the local journals remarked that if candor and ability had any influence upon the electors there would soon be a change in the representation. A week later came accounts of glorious meetings, with the assurance that Gladstone's return might be fully calculated upon.

Mr. Gladstone's first election address was dated "Clinton Arms, Newark, Oct. 9th, 1832," and was inscribed : " To the worthy and independent electors of the Borough of Newark." As this document, in the light of subsequent events, has more than a passing interest, and is distinguished for its ingenious reasoning upon the great question of slavery then agitating the public mind, we present it verbatim :

"Having now completed my canvass, I think it my duty as well to remind you of the principles on which I have solicited your votes, as freely to assure my friends that its result has placed my success beyond a doubt.

"I have not requested your favor on the ground of adherence to the opinions of any man or party, further than such adherence can be fairly understood from the conviction I have not hesitated to avow, that we must watch and resist that uninquiring and undiscriminating desire for change amongst us, which threatens to produce, along with partial good, a melancholy preponderance of mischief ; which, I am persuaded, would aggravate beyond computation the deep-seated evils of our social state, and the heavy burthens of our industrial classes ; which, by disturbing our peace, destroys confidence and strikes at the root of prosperity.

Thus it *has done already;* and thus, we must therefore believe, it *will do.*

"For the mitigation of those evils, we must, I think, look not only to particular measures, but to the restoration of sounder general principles. I mean especially that principle on which alone the incorporation of Religion with the State, in our Constitution, can be defended ; that the duties of governors are strictly and peculiarly religious ; and that legislatures, like individuals, are bound to carry throughout their acts the spirit of the high truths they have acknowledged. Principles are now arrayed against our institutions ; and not by truckling nor by temporizing—not by oppression nor corruption — but by principles they must be met.

"Among the first results should be a sedulous and special attention to the interests of the poor, founded upon the rule that those who are the least able to take care of themselves should be most regarded by others. Particularly it is a duty to endeavor by every means, that *labor may receive adequate remuneration;* which, unhappily, among several classes of our fellow-countrymen, is not now the case. Whatever measures, therefore, whether by correction of the poor laws, allotment of cottage grounds, or otherwise, tend to promote this object, I deem entitled to the warmest support with all such as are calculated to secure sound moral conduct in any class of society.

"I proceed to the momentous question of Slavery, which I have found entertained among you in that candid and temperate spirit which alone befits its nature, or promises to remove its difficulties. If I have not recognized the right of an irresponsible society to interpose between me and the electors, it has not been from any disrespect to its members, nor from unwillingness to answer theirs or any other questions on which the electors may desire to know my views. To the esteemed secretary of the society I submitted my reasons for silence ; and I made a point of stating these views to him, in his character of a voter.

"As regards the abstract lawfulness of Slavery, I acknowledge it simply as importing the right of one man to the labor of another ; and I rest it upon the fact that Scripture, the paramount authority upon such a point, gives directions to persons standing in the relation of master to slave, for their conduct in that relation ; whereas, were the matter absolutely and necessarily *sinful*, it would not regulate the manner. Assuming sin as the cause of degradation, it strives, and strives most effectually, to cure the latter by extirpating the former. We are agreed that both the physical and the moral bondage of the slave are to be abolished. The question is as to the *order*, and the order only ; now Scripture attacks the moral evil *before* the temporal one, and the temporal *through* the moral one, and I am content with the order which Scripture has established.

"To this end, I desire to see immediately set on foot, by impartial and sovereign authority, an universal and efficient system of Christian instruction, not intended to resist designs of individual piety and wisdom for the religious improvement of the negroes, but to do thoroughly what they can only do partially.

"As regards immediate emancipation, whether with or without compensation, there are several minor reasons against it ; but that which weighs with me is, that it would, I much fear, exchange the evils now affecting the negro for others which are weightier—for a relapse into deeper debasement, if not for bloodshed and internal war. Let *fitness* be made a condition for emancipation ; and let us strive to bring him to that fitness by the shortest possible course. Let him enjoy the means of earning his freedom through honest and industrious habits; thus the same instruments which attain his liberty shall likewise render him competent to use it ; and thus, I earnestly trust, without risk of blood, without violation of property, with unimpaired benefit to the negro, and with the utmost speed which prudence will admit, we shall arrive at that exceedingly desirable consummation, the utter extinction of Slavery.

"And now, gentlemen, as regards the enthusiasm with which you have rallied round your ancient flag, and welcomed the humble representative of those principles whose emblem it is, I trust that neither the lapse of time, nor the seductions of prosperity, can ever efface it from my memory. To my opponents, my acknowledgments are due for the good-humor and kindness with which they have received me; and while I would thank my friends for their zealous and unwearied exertions in my favor, I briefly but emphatically assure them, that if promises be an adequate foundation of confidence, or experience a reasonable ground of calculation, our victory *is sure.*

"I have the honor to be, gentlemen,

"Your obliged and obedient servant,

"W. E. GLADSTONE."

The canvass was a very vigorous one, full of hard work and varied experiences. The young student who had so lately come from the stately halls of Oxford was brought into contact with strange characters, for politics like poverty will make a man "acquainted with strange bedfellows." "My Newark recollections," said Mr. Gladstone, writing to an old constituent of Newark, forty years after the memorable election, "do not want much revival. I remember as if it were yesterday my first arrival in the place, at midnight, by the High Flyer Coach in September, 1832, after a journey of forty hours from Torquay, of which we thought nothing in those days. Next morning at eight we sallied forth from the Clinton Arms to begin a canvass, on which I now look back as the most exciting period of my life. I never worked harder or slept so little.   We started our canvass at eight in the morning and worked at it for about nine hours, with a great crowd, band and flags, and innumerable glasses of beer and wine, all jumbled together; then a dinner of thirty or forty, with speeches and songs, until say ten o'clock; then we always

MR. GLADSTONE, M. P. FOR NEWARK.
ÆTAT 23.

played a rubber of whist, and about twelve or one I got to bed, but not to sleep, for never in my life did I undergo any excitement to compare with it.   There was a public house tour of speaking to the Red Clubs—for political parties had their colors in those days, the Tory colors of

Newark being red—with which I often had to top up after the dinner and before the whist." Opportunity will present itself later on to deal more at length with the methods and humors of those old time elections. Mr. Gladstone was really but a boy when he fought his first political battle, but he fought it bravely and well. There was a custom called "heckling," common in the elections of those days, which consisted in asking candidates a series of questions, some of which were wise and serious, and many of which were neither wise nor serious, but were intended to confuse the candidate and make him look rediculous in the eyes of the people. The fact that the Duke of Newcastle had what was called " paramount influence " in those days in the Borough of Newark, and that Mr. Gladstone was in a very real sense his Grace's nominee, gave a radical elector a grand opportunity of "heckling" the young candidate. But as Mrs. Glass says, " First catch your hare then cook it." Mr. Gladstone was too wary to be easily caught. The following amusing dialogue ensued:

Radical Elector. " Are we to understand you, then, as the nominee of the Duke of Newcastle?"

Mr. Gladstone. "I will answer that question if you will tell me what you mean by *nominee.*"

The Elector. "I consider the man as the nominee of the Duke when he is sent by his Grace to be crammed down the throats of the populace whether they like it or not."

Mr. Gladstone. "Then, according to that definition, I am not the nominee of the Duke of Newcastle."

The Elector. "What is your definition of a nominee?"

Mr. Gladstone. "I am not here to give the definition. I asked, what you meant by the word nominee, and according to your own explanation of it I gave the answer."

The crafty "heckler" was silenced, and even the opposing Whigs could scarce forbear applauding the courage and sagacity of the candidate for parliamentary honors.

Mr. Gladstone was opposed by Mr. Handley and Mr. Serjeant Wilde. At the close of the poll the figures stood thus:

Mr. W. E. Gladstone   -   -   -   882
Mr. Handley   -   -   -   -   -   793
Mr. Serjeant Wilde   -   -   -   719

The Tories were delighted beyond measure. The dreaded revolt of the nation was after all only a dream. The *Nottingham Journal* said: "The delusion has now vanished and made room for sound reason and reflection. The shadow satisfies no longer, and the return of Mr. Gladstone has restored the town of Newark to that high rank which it formerly held in the estimation of the friends of order and good government."

Queen Victoria Opening Parliament.

SCENE IN THE HOUSE OF LORDS.

CHAPTER VII.

' Ah God, for a man with heart, head, hand,
Like some of the simple great ones gone
For ever and ever by,
One still strong man in a blatant land,
Whatever they call him, what care I—
Aristocrat, democrat, autocrat—one
Who can rule and dare not lie."

—Tennyson.

The young member from Newark had not begun at the bottom of the ladder in the matter of speech-making and oratory as is generally the case with young members of Parliament. He had already climbed to a most enviable height. His experience and many successes in connection with the Oxford Debating Union had won for him a wide reputation for rare ability and eloquence in debate. Old Oxonians who knew Mr. Gladstone well, prophesied that he would soon take his place in the front rank, and side by side with men who had given the House of Commons the ungrudging fame of being "the greatest deliberative assembly in the world." A vigorous opponent of Mr. Gladstone's, a pronounced Whig, pays this high tribute to his genius, and foretells a brilliant future:

" Yet on one form, whose ear can ne'er refuse
The Muse's tribute, for he loved the Muse
(When the soul the gen'rous virtues raise
A friendly Whig may chant a Tory's praise),
Full many a fond expectant eye is bent
Where Newark's towers are mirror'd in the Trent.
Perchance ere long to shine in senates first,

> If manhood echo what his youth rehears'd,
> Soon Gladstone's brows will bloom with greener bays
> Than twine the chaplet of a minstrel's lays;
> Nor heed, while poring o'er each graver line,
> The far, faint music of a lute like mine,
> His was no head contentedly which press'd
> The downy pillow in obedient rest,
> Where lazy pilots, with their canvas furl'd,
> Set up the Gades of their mental world;
> His was no tongue which meanly stoop'd to wear
> The guise of virtue, while his heart was bare;
> But all he thought through ev'ry action ran;
> God's noblest work—I've known one honest man."

Mr. Gladstone, just before the opening of the Parliament of 1835, made a speech before the Conservative Club of Nottingham, which called from the Conservative journal of that ancient borough the following flattering eulogium:

"Mr. Gladstone is a gentleman of amiable manners and the most extraordinary talent; and we venture to predict, without the slightest exaggeration, that he will one day be classed amongst the most able statesmen of the British Senate."

The prophets were thus early at their tasks, but the boldest of them all was not blessed with vision clear enough to discern the lofty height to which Mr. Gladstone was born to climb. It must not be imagined for one moment that Mr. Gladstone had no enemies. The man who is strong enough to win a wide circle of ardent friends is sure to have a host of bitter foes. The Whig press fell foul on this young Tory, whose youth and brilliance were his chief sins. One of these acrimonious journals, the *Reflector*—let us hope it reflected itself chiefly—said:

"Mr. Gladstone is the son of Gladstone of Liverpool, a person who—we are speaking of the father—has amassed a large fortune by West India dealings. In other words, a great part of his gold has sprung from the blood of black slaves. Respecting the youth himself—a person fresh from college, and whose mind is as much like a sheet of white foolscap as possible—he was utterly unknown. He came recommended by no claim in the world *except the will of the Duke*. The Duke nodded unto Newark, and Newark sent back the man, or rather the boy of his choice. What! Is this to be, now that the Reform Bill has done its work? Are sixteen hundred men still to bow down to a wooden-headed lord, as the people of Egypt used to do to their beasts, to their reptiles and their ropes of onions? There must be something wrong—something imperfect. What is it? What is wanting? Why, the ballot! If there be a doubt of this (and we believe there is a doubt, even amongst intelligent men), the tale of Newark must set the question at rest. Serjeant Wilde was met on his entry into the town by almost the whole population. He was greeted everywhere, cheered everywhere. He was received with delight by his friends, and with good and earnest wishes for his success by his nominal foes. The voters for Gladstone went up to that candidate's booth (the slave-driver, as they called him) with Wilde's colors. People who had before voted for Wilde, on being asked to give their suffrage, said, " We cannot, we dare not. We have lost half our business, and shall lose the rest if we go against the Duke. We would do anything in our power for Serjeant Wilde, for the cause, but we cannot starve! Now what say you, our merry men, touching the ballot?"

The following extract from one of Mr. Gladstone's contributions to the *Eton Miscellany*, read in the light of to-day, awakens a smile at the modest fears of the young aspirant after literary fame :

"In my present undertaking there is one gulf in which I fear to sink, and that gulf is Lethe. There is one stream which I dread my inability to stem, it is the tide of popular opinion. I have ventured, and no doubt rashly ventured—

> Like little wanton boys that swim on bladders,
> To try my fortune in a sea of glory,
> But far beyond my depth.

At present it is hope alone that buoys me up ; for more substantial support I must be indebted to my own exertions, well knowing that in this land of literature merit never wants its reward. That such merit is mine I dare not presume to think ; but still there is something within me that bids me hope that I may be able to glide prosperously down the stream of public estimation ; or, in the words of Virgil—

> ——Celerare viam rumore secundo.

Little could the writer of these words imagine—forecasting the future even by the aid of youth's most ardent desires—that he would live to fill the most exalted office it was in the power of his Sovereign to bestow ; that he was destined to be regarded as an accomplished man of letters, and that, all in good time, he would take rank as one of the greatest orators of his age. It will not be denied by those who are least disposed to idolize Mr. Gladstone that he has won a wider fame in the forum and on the platforms of the nation than Cicero won in the Senate of ancient Rome, or Demosthenes by the sounding, unquiet sea. No man is in a better position to give an authoritative opinion concerning Mr. Gladstone's rare powers of oratory, nor has any man given a more careful and exhaustive analysis of those powers than the brilliant author of "The History of Our Own Times," Justin McCarthy, M. P. We have no apology to offer for quoting at length from the pages of this distinguished Irish leader. He says :

"Mr. Gladstone's first oratorical qualification was his exquisite voice. Such a voice would make commonplace seem interesting and lend something of fascination to dullness itself. It was singularly pure, clear, resonant and sweet. The orator never seemed to use the slightest effort or strain, in filling any hall and reaching the ear of the farthest among the audience. It was not a loud voice or of great volume, but strong, vibrating and silvery. The words were always aided by energetic action and by the deep, gleaming eyes of the orator. Somebody once said that Gladstone was the only man in the House who could talk in italics. The saying was odd, but was nevertheless appropriate and expressive. Gladstone could by the slightest modulation of his voice give all the emphasis of italics, of small print or large print, or any other effect he might desire, to his spoken words. It is not denied that his wonderful gift of words sometimes led him astray. It was often such a fluency as that of a torrent on which the orator was carried away.

"He could seldom resist the temptation to shower too many words on his subject and his hearers. Sometimes he involved his sentence in a parenthesis within parentheses until the ordinary listener began to think extrication an impossibility ; but the orator never failed to unravel all the entanglements and to bring the passage out to a clear and legitimate conclusion. There was never any halt or incoherency, nor did the joints of the sentence fail to fit together in the right way. Harley once described a famous speech as 'a circumgyration of incoherent words.' This description certainly could not be applied even to Mr. Gladstone's most involved passages ; but if some of those were described as a circumgyration of coherent words, the phrase might be considered germane to the matter. His style was commonly too redundant. It seemed as if it belonged to a certain school of exuberant Italian rhetoric. Yet it was hardly to be called florid. Gladstone indulged in few flowers of rhetoric, and his great gift was not imagination. His fault was simply the habitual use of too many words. The defect was indeed a characteristic of the Peelite school of eloquence. Mr. Gladstone retained some of the defects of the school in which he had been trained, even after he had come to surpass its greatest master. Often, however, this superb, exuberant rush of words added indescribable strength to the eloquence of the speaker. In passages of indignant remonstrance or denunciation, when word followed word and stroke came down upon stroke, with a wealth of resource that seemed inexhaustible, the very fluency and variety of the speaker overwhelmed his audience. Interruption only gave him a new stimulus, and appeared to supply him with fresh resources of argument and illustration. His retorts leaped to his lips. His eye caught sometimes even the mere gesture that indicated dissent or question ; and perhaps some unlucky opponent, who was only thinking of what might be said in opposition to the great orator, found himself suddenly dragged into the conflict and overwhelmed with a torrent of remonstrance, argument, and scornful words. Gladstone had not much humor of the playful kind, but he had a certain force of sarcastic and scornful rhetoric. He was always terribly in earnest. Whether the subject were great or small, he threw his whole soul into it. Once, in addressing a schoolboy gathering, he told his young listeners that if a boy ran he ought always to run as fast as he could ; if he jumped, he ought always to jump as far as he could. He illustrated his maxim in his own career. He had no idea apparently of running or jumping in such measure as happened to please the fancy of the moment. He always exercised his splendid powers to their uttermost strain.

" A distinguished critic once pronounced Mr. Gladstone to be the greatest parliamentary orator of our time, on the ground that he had made by far the greatest number of fine speeches, while admitting that two or three speeches had been made by other men of the day which might rank higher than any of his. This is, however, a principle of criticism which posterity never sanctions. The greatest speech, the greatest poem, give the author the highest place, though the effort were but single. Shakespeare would rank beyond Messinger just as he does now had he written only 'The Tempest.' We can not say how many novels, each as good as 'Gil Blas,' would make La Sage the equal of Cervantes. On this point fame is inexorable. We are not, therefore, inclined to call Mr. Gladstone the greatest English orator of our time, when we remember some of the finest speeches of Mr. Bright ; but did we regard parliamentary speaking as a mere instrument of parliamentary business and debate, then unquestionably Mr. Gladstone is not only the greatest, but by far the greatest, English orator of our time ; for he had a richer combination of gifts than any other man we can remember, and he could use them oftenest with effect. He was like a racer, which can not, indeed, always go faster than every rival, but can win more races in the year than any other horse. Mr. Gladstone could get up at any moment, and no matter how many times a night, in the House of Commons, and be argumentative or indignant, pour out a stream of impassioned eloquence or a shower of figures, just as the exigency of debate and the moment required. He was not, of course, always equal ; but he was always eloquent and effective. He seemed as if he could not be anything but eloquent. Perhaps, judged in this way, he never had an equal in the English Parliament. Neither Pitt nor Fox ever made so many speeches combining so many great qualities. Chatham was a great actor rather than a great orator. Burke was the greatest political essayist who ever addressed the House of Commons. Canning did not often rise above the level of burnished rhetorical commonplace. Macaulay, who during his time drew the most crowded houses of any speaker, not even excepting Peel, was not an orator in the true sense. Probably no one, past or present, had in combination so many gifts of voice, manner, fluency and argument, style, reason and passion, as Mr. Gladstone.

"The House of Commons was his ground. There he was himself; there he was always seen to the best advantage. As a rule he was not so successful on the platform. His turn of mind did not fit him well for the work of addressing great public meetings. He loved to look too carefully at every side of a question, and did not always go so quickly to the heart of it as would suit great popular audiences. The principal defect of his mind was probably a lack of simplicity, a tendency to over-refining and super-subtile argument. Not perhaps unnaturally, however, when he did, during some of the later passages of his career, lay himself out for the work of addressing popular audiences, he threw away all discrimination, and gave loose to the full force with which, under the excitement of great pressure, he was wont to rush at a principle. There seemed a certain lack of balance in his mind; a want of the exact poise of all his faculties. Either he must refine too much or he did not refine at all. Thus he became accused, and with some reason, of over-refining and all but quibbling in some of his parliamentary arguments, of looking at all sides of a question so carefully that it was too long in doubt whether he was ever going to form any opinion of his own; and he was sometimes accused with equal justice of pleading one side of a political question before great meetings of his countrymen with all the passionate blindness of a partisan. The accusations might seem self-contradictory, if we did not remember that they will apply, and with great force and justice, to Burke. Burke cut blocks with a razor, and went on refining to an impatient House of Commons, only eager for its dinner; and the same Burke threw himself into antagonism to the French Revolution as if he were the wildest of partisans; as if the question had but one side, and only fools or villains could possibly say it had any other."

It was not possible that the silver-tongued orator of the

Oxford Debating Union could long keep silence. His mind was growing daily richer in that wealth of loving thought that must find utterance. Gray in his matchless "Elegy" talks of "mute, inglorious Miltons," and "Cromwells guiltless of their country's blood." But there are other things besides murder that "will out." With such things to say as Mr. Gladstone had accumulated and was constantly accumulating, the old order was illustrated: "While I mused the fire burned, and at last I spake with my tongue." And from the first speech in Parliament to the last public utterances of his long and illustrious life, he commanded the attention and admiration of his hearers. Millions have listened, spell-bound by his oratory, and when addressing in earnest controversy the ranks of those who were his pronounced opponents in political life, he invariably commanded their respect to such an extent that—

> Even the ranks of Tuscany could scarce forbear to cheer.

The first Parliament summoned after the passing of the Reform Act, and known as "the Reform Parliament," met on the 29th of January, 1833. On the 5th of the following month the King attended and read the speech from the throne. The young member for Newark took his place, little dreaming that in the years to come he would be acknowledged as one of the master spirits of that great deliberative assembly. Sir Robert Peel was the recognized leader of the Tory minority. Under his banner Mr. Gladstone entered on the public service of his country.

This Parliament was celebrated for two great measures of which England has always had occasion to be justly proud. The first was the emancipation of the slaves in the British colonies at a cost of $100,000,000. The second was the breaking up of the monopoly of the East India Company, by which the trade to the East was thrown open to all merchants. It was in connection with the first of these great measures that Mr. Gladstone delivered his maiden speech in the British House of Commons. So much has been said on this matter that we deem it best to present our readers with Mr. Barnett Smith's statement of this interesting episode as being at once impartial, exhaustive and reliable.

"During the debate on the Ministerial proposition for the emancipation of slaves, which was brought forward on the 14th of May, 1833, Lord Howick, ex-Under-Secretary for the Colonies, had referred to an estate in Demerara, owned by Mr. Gladstone's father, for the purpose of showing that a great destruction of human life had taken place in the West Indies, owing to the manner in which the slaves were worked. It was in reply to this accusation that Mr. Gladstone delivered his maiden speech on the 17th of May, the occasion being the presentation of a petition from Portarlington for the abolition of slavery. He challenged the noble lord's statement respecting the decrease of seventy-one slaves upon the estate of Vreeden Hoop, which had been attributed to the increased cultivation of sugar. The real cause of the decrease lay in the very large proportion of Africans upon the estate. When it came into his father's possession, it was so weak, owing to the great number of Africans upon it, that he was obliged to add two hundred people to the gang. It was notorious that Africans were imported into Demerara and Trinidad up to a later period than into any other colony; and he should, when the proper time arrived, be able to prove that the decrease on Vreeden Hoop was among the old Africans, and that there was an increase going on in the Creole population, which would be a sufficient answer to the statement of the noble lord. The quantity of sugar produced was small in proportion to that produced on many other estates. The cultivation of cotton in Demerara had been abandoned, and that of coffee much diminished, and the people employed in these sources of production had been transferred to the cultivation of sugar. Demerara, too, was peculiarly circumstanced, and the labor of the same number of negroes, distributed over the year, would produce in that colony a given quantity of sugar, with less injury to the people, than negroes could produce in other colonies, working only at the stated periods of crop. 'He was ready to admit that this cultivation was of a more severe character than others; and he would ask, were there not certain employments in this and other countries more destructive to life than others? He would only instance those of painting and working in lead mines, both of which were well known to have that tendency. The noble lord attempted to impugn the character of the gentleman acting as manager of his father's estates; and in making this selection he had certainly been most unfortunate; for there was not an individual in the colony more proverbial for humanity, and the kind treatment of his slaves than Mr. Maclean.' Mr. Gladstone, in concluding his warm defense of his relative, said he held in his hand two letters from the agent, in which that gentleman spoke in the kindest terms of the people under his charge; described their state of happiness, content and healthiness—their good conduct and the infrequency of severe punishment—and recommended certain additional comforts, which he said the slaves well deserved.

"On the 3rd of June, on the resumption of the debate on the abolition of slavery, Mr. Gladstone again addressed the House. He now entered more fully into the charges which Lord Howick had brought against the management of his father's estates in Demerara, and showed their groundlessness. When he had discussed the existing aspect of slavery in Trinidad, Jamaica, and other places, he proceeded to deal with the general question. He confessed, with shame and pain, that cases of wanton cruelty had occurred in the

Colonies, but added that they would always exist, particularly under the system of slavery; and this was unquestionably a substantial reason why the British Legislature and public should set themselves in good earnest to provide for its extinction; but he maintained that these instances of cruelty could easily be explained by the West Indians, who represented them as rare and isolated cases, and who maintained that the ordinary relation of master and slave was one of kindliness and not of hostility. He deprecated cruelty, and he deprecated slavery, both of which were abhorrent to the nature of Englishmen; but, conceding these things, he asked, 'Were not Englishmen to retain a right to their own honestly and legally acquired property?' But the cruelty did not exist, and he saw no reason for the attack which had recently been made upon the West India interest. He hoped the house would make a point to adopt the principle of compensation, and to stimulate the slave to genuine and spontaneous industry. If this were done, and moral instruction were not imparted to the slaves, liberty would prove a curse instead of a blessing to them. Touching upon the property question, and the proposed plans for emancipation, Mr. Gladstone said that the house might consume its time and exert its wisdom in devising these plans, but without the concurrence of the Colonial Legislatures success would be hopeless. He thought there was excessive wickedness in any violent interference under the present circumstances. They were still in the midst of unconcluded inquiries, and to pursue the measure then under discussion, at that moment, was to commit an act of great and unnecessary hostility toward the island of Jamaica. 'It was the duty of the House to place as broad a distinction as possible between the idle and the industrious slaves, and nothing could be too strong to secure the freedom of the latter; but, with respect to the idle slaves, no period of emancipation could hasten their improvement. If the labors of the House should be conducted to a satisfactory issue, it would redound to the honor of the nation and to the reputation of his Majesty's Ministers, whilst it would be delightful to the West India planters themselves—for they must feel that to hold in bondage their fellow-men must always involve the greatest responsibility. But let not any man think of carrying this measure by force. England rested her power not upon physical force, but upon her principles, her intellect, and virtue; and if this great measure were not placed on a fair basis, or were conducted by violence, he should lament it as a signal for the ruin of the Colonies, and the downfall of the Empire.' The attitude of Mr. Gladstone, as borne out by the tenor of his speech, was not one of hostility to Emancipation, though he was undoubtedly unfavorable to an immediate and an indiscriminate enfranchisement. He demanded moreover, that the interests of the planters should be duly regarded."

The abolition of Colonial Slavery was decreed. The sum of $100,000,000 was voted to the slave-owners as compensation for their losses. The blot of slavery was wiped from the fair escutcheon of England. William Wilberforce and his brave and untiring comrades saw with boundless joy the success of their labors in the cause of freedom. No slave could now breathe where the flag of England waved.

CHAPTER VIII.

> When he speaks,
> The air, a chartered libertine, is still
> And the mute wonder lurketh in men's ears
> To steal his sweet and honey'd sentences.
> —*William Shakespeare.*

Whatever strengthens our local attachments is favorable both to individual and national character. Our home, our birth-place, our native land—think for a while what the virtues are that arise out of the feelings connected with these words, and if you have any intellectual eyes you will then perceive the connection between topography and patriotism. Show me a man who cares no more for one place than another and I will show you in that same person one who loves nothing but himself.—*Robert Southey.*

It is exceedingly interesting to note that Mr. Gladstone's earliest speeches in Parliament were in the main devoted to the advocacy of principles and institutions that in his riper age he was destined to controvert and overthrow. Take two examples—the Irish church question and the question of the special disadvantages under which all those who were not churchmen or Episcopalians labored in respect to the Universities.

On the 8th of July, 1834, a debate took place on Lord Althorp's Church Temporalities (Ireland) Bill. On the question that this bill should pass, Mr. Gladstone said he would not shelter himself under a silent vote. Silent voting was never a habit with Mr. Gladstone, especially if such voting could be in any way misconstrued. He was prepared to defend the Irish Church, and if it had abuses, which he did not now deny, those abuses were to be ascribed to the ancestors and predecessors of those who then surrounded him. He admitted that the Irish Church had slumbered. He feared that the effect of the bill would be to place the Church on an untenable foundation. He was unwilling to see the number of Irish bishops reduced. He had always regarded it as a well-established principle that as long as a Church was national the State ought to be taxed to support it; and if the Government meant to maintain the Protestant Church in Ireland they ought to enforce this maxim; but it was not the proper way to establish or maintain the Church to proceed by laying further burdens on the body of the clergy, who, God knows, were already not overburthened with money—as was done by that measure. He had little doubt the Government would carry the bill by a large majority, and if they did, he could only hope that it would produce the effects which they had ascribed to it—namely, of securing and propping up the Irish Protestant Church. The bill was carried by 274 votes to 94, Mr. Gladstone's name appearing in the minority.

Thirty years pass by and the question of the Irish Church is once more before the House of Commons. Mr. Dillwyn proposed in March, 1865: "That the present position of the Irish Church is unsatisfactory, and calls for the early attention of Her Majesty's Government." While declining to vote for this motion, on the ground that it was not a matter to which the Government could give its "early" attention, Mr. Gladstone declared that the abstract truth of the former part of the resolution could not be denied. He could come to no other conclusion, he said, than that the Irish Church, as she then stood, was in a false position. This was Mr. Gladstone's first formal utterance in Parliament against the Irish establishment. A few years later he entered upon that memorable conflict which resulted in the disestablishment and disendowment of the Irish Church. In this great conflict the present writer rendered enthusiastic service as a follower in the ranks of the great champion of religious equality and freedom.   Later on attention will be called to some interesting reminiscences of that stirring period.

In this same Parliament of 1834 Mr. Hume presented to the House of Commons the Universities Admission Bill, whose aim was to throw the doors of the Universities open to all applicants, wholly irrespective of their religious opinions or creeds.   The specific purpose of the Bill was to remove the necessity of subscription to the Thirty-nine Articles of the Church of England, as an essential condition of entrance.   Mr. Gladstone's contention was, that although the measure proposed to alter materially the constitution of the Universities, it would be practically inoperative.   Yet the Bill, while not working out its professed objects, would, nevertheless, inevitably lead to great dissension and confusion, and eventually to endless applications and legislation in the House.   It was said of the ancient Romans that they—

Made a solitude and called it peace.

He very much feared that the House, in establishing their present principle of religious liberty, would drive from their functions men who had long done honor and service to their country, and thus inaugurate their reign of religious peace by an act of the grossest tyranny.   Notwithstanding Mr. Gladstone's opposition, the tide in favor of the motion rolled on, and when it came to a vote the Bill was carried by a majority of 89—164 voting for the bill and 75 against.   Rather a handsome and suggestive majority this, showing most surely that the day of a broader liberal spirit was already dawning.   This was the year 1834.   A whole generation passes away ; Mr. Gladstone is at the helm of the state.   "The golden age of Liberalism," as it was proudly called, was in its full-orbed splendor.   Mr. Gladstone, who in those early Newark days—as we have just seen—stood in terror of any radical movement, in respect of University reform, is now the champion of a wide-open University. Under his guidance a Bill receives the Royal assent, the chief feature of which is: "That all lay students, of whatever religious creed, shall in future be admitted to the universities on equal terms."

In the middle of October the King summarily dismissed the Melbourne ministry. Lord Althorp had been transferred to the House of Lords. This gave the King his opportunity. He objected to the reconstruction of the Cabinet. He caused a letter to be sent to the venerable Duke of Wellington, who very warmly recommended Sir Robert as the most suitable man to be at the head of the government. Sir Robert, who was then traveling in Italy, returned to London, and on the 9th of December, 1834, accepted the King's commands to form a Ministry.

On the 24th of December—Christmas Eve of 1834—Mr. Gladstone was tendered the official position of Junior Lord of the Treasury under Sir Robert Peel. He was now twenty-five years of age. This was the first round of the official ladder, to whose sunniest height he was destined to climb, making each step in his upward career increasingly illustrious.

CHAPTER IX.

He who ascends to mountain tops shall find
  The loftiest peaks most wrapped in cloud and snow ;
He who surpasses or subdues mankind,
  Must look down on the hate of those below.

—*Lord Byron.*

Greatness lies not in being strong, but in the right using of strength; and strength is not used rightly when it only serves to carry a man above his fellows for his own solitary glory. He is greatest whose strength carries up the most hearts by the attraction of his own.— *Henry Ward Beecher.*

As we saw in the previous chapter, Mr. Gladstone found himself on his twenty-first birthday, and in his first year of Parliamentary service, started on his official career. The golden honors that some men strive half a lifetime to win, and strive in vain, came to him in the morning of his days, unwooed and uninvited. It was a case of aptitude shaping destiny. Mr. Gladstone was not "born great," nor can it be said that he had "greatness thrust upon him." Greatness came to him in the natural order of things. The judicious use of the one talent made it inevitable that he should be entrusted with increasing power and responsibility. He was not the happy favorite of lucky stars, and yet, as has been most wisely said, "Rarely has a great man at the outset of his career had fewer difficulties to overcome, or been more splendidly helped by favoring circumstances. The son of a rich and influential father, every advantage that wealth, education and position could give was his; and from the first, even from his Eton days, it seems to have been accepted by those who surrounded him that he was one whom destiny had marked out for a great position. He was welcomed into public life, welcomed into office, and while he was still but a youthful Under-Secretary, ecclesiastics were writing to him assuring him that the Premiership awaited him, and advising him to prepare himself with that goal in view." The world-renowned Samuel Wilberforce, Bishop of Oxford, one of the most eloquent divines that ever sat upon an Episcopal throne, wrote to Gladstone in these early days and said : "There is no height to which you may not fairly rise. If it pleases God to spare us violent convulsions and the loss of our liberties, you may at some future day wield the whole government of this lad. Act *now* with a view to *then*."

It was a great Parliament, this first Parliament of the Reform era, the Parliament that welcomed the youthful and brilliant Gladstone to its debates.

The Duke of Wellington, conqueror of Napoleon, not a statesman, but an honest patriot, was there. Lord Brougham, Lord Lyndhurst, Sir Robert Peel, and that greatest Irishman of his age, Daniel O'Connell, were there. Giants of oratory were Peel and O'Connell. It is said nobody in modern times ever swayed the House of Commons by argument and eloquence as did Sir Robert Peel for many years. Both Peel and O'Connell possessed magnificent voices, a characteristic contributing to the forensic power of the man who was to succeed them. Another leader of the new Parliament was Lord John Russell, foremost in enacting the law that had created it. Lord Derby, Macaulay, Grote, the historian, and Bulwer, the novelist, were there. Disraeli had not yet come to astonish the House with his florid fancies and satiric rhetoric, and Palmerston was to be conspicuous later. Earl Grey was Prime Minister. Lord Althorp led the Liberal majority in the House, Peel was the head of the Tory minority.

Before any member of the English House of Commons can exercise the functions of any office to which he has been summoned by the Prime Minister he must first appeal to his constituents for their endorsement. He is the representative of his constituents, and their endorsement or objection is made manifest in the election or non-election of the candidate. On the 24th of December, 1834, Mr. Gladstone issued his address to his constituents at Newark. The warmest adherents of the outgoing Parliament had become incensed by what they regarded as a tendency towards rash, violent, and menacing innovation. Mr. Gladstone said there were even "those among the servants of the King who did not scruple to solicit the suffrages of their constituents, with promises to act on the principles of Radicalism." He further went on to say in his own inimitable style : "The question has then, as it appears to me, become, whether we are to hurry onward at intervals, but not long ones, through the medium of the ballot, short parliaments, and other questions called popular, into republicanism or anarchy ; or whether, independently of all party distinctions, the people will support the Crown in the discharge of its duty to maintain in efficiency, and transmit in safety, those old and valuable institutions under which our country has greatly flourished." In the last paragraph of this address, however, the writer said, "Let me add shortly, but emphatically, concerning the reform of actual abuses, whether in Church or State, that I regard it as a sacred duty—a duty at all times, and certainly not least at a period like this, when the danger of neglecting it is most clear and imminent—a duty not inimical to true and determined Conservative principle, nor a curtailment or modification of such principle, but its legitimate consequences, or rather an actual element of its composition."

If Mr. Gladstone's address met the approval of the thoughtful and patriotic, his speech from the hustings kindled that approval into enthusiasm. The plaudits were long and loud and most persuasive. The waverers became convinced, Mr. Gladstone was triumphantly re-elected for the ancient borough of Newark. In those noisy demonstrative days it was customary to "chair" the successful candidates. A beautiful arm-chair was provided in which the triumphant Member of Parliament was placed, and then chair and occupant were hoisted on the shoulders of sturdy men, a procession was then formed, and the hero of the day was borne along to the great edification and delight of the party on whose banner victory sat enthroned. But Mr. Gladstones "chairing" took on a more elaborate form. The chair, which was one of exceptionally fine workmanship, attracted general admiration; it was placed on a groundwork laid upon the springs of a four-wheel carriage, and drawn by six beautiful grey horses, the riders dressed in silk jackets. As the procession wended its way through the streets the inhabitants were most peaceably inclined. "Never before did the town of Newark present so pleasing and so glorious a sight!" said a local journal of the time. The "red" lion and the "blue" lamb—for the political parties had their colors as well as their names—lay down together (the colors of the quadrupeds may be reversed at pleasure), and all was harmony, and all was peace. Alighting at his committee room, Mr. Gladstone delivered an address of thanks to upwards of 6,000 persons, his speech being greeted with deafening cheers.

Parliament assembled in February, 1835. Mr. Gladstone was promoted to the office of Under Secretary for the Colonies. In a pleasant page of biographical reminiscence Mr. Gladstone details an interview with his Chief, which is exceedingly interesting and reveals the innate modesty of the young minister :

"On an evening in the month of January, 1835, I was sent for by Sir Robert Peel, and received from him the offer, which I accepted, of the Under Secretaryship of the Colonies. From him I went to Lord Aberdeen, who was thus to be, in official home-talk, my master. I may confess that I went in fear and trembling. I knew Lord Aberdeen only by public rumor. Distinction of itself, naturally and properly, rather alarms the young. I had heard of his high character; but I had also heard of him as a man of cold manners, close and even haughty reserve. It was dark when I entered his room—the one on the first floor with the bay window looking to the parlor—so that I could see his figure rather than his countenance. I do not recollect the matter of the conversation, but I well remember that before I had been three minutes with him all my apprehension had melted away like snow in the sun. I came away from that interview conscious—indeed, as who could fail to be conscious?—of his dignity, but of a dignity so tempered by a peculiar purity and gentleness, and so associated with impressions of his kindness, and even friendship, that I believe I felt more about the wonder of his being misunderstood by the outer world than about the duties and responsibilities of my new office."

On the 30th of March, 1835, Lord John Russell introduced a resolution concerning the Irish Church, in the following terms :

"That the House should resolve itself into a committee of the whole to consider of the Temporalities of the Church of Ireland."

The resolution was met with the most determined opposition. In the course of the discussion, Mr. Gladstone said the result of the motion would be first to enfeeble and debase, and then altogether overthrow, the principle on which the church establishment rested. . The noble lord invited them to invade the property of the church in Ireland. The system they were now called upon to agree to was in its essence transitory, and yet it involved the existence of all church establishments. If the separation of church and state was hastening on, the present motion, instead of retarding it, would increase its rapidity. If in the administration of this great country the elements of religion should not enter—if those who were called upon to guide it in its career should be forced to listen to the caprices and to the whims of every body of visionaries, they would lose that station all great men were hitherto proud of. He hoped that he should never live to see the day when any principle leading to such a result would be adopted in this country.

On a division ministers were defeated, the numbers being: For Lord John Russell's motion, 322 ; against, 289. The Irish Church bill was subsequently discussed in committee, when ministers were again defeated on the question of appropriating the surplus funds of the church to the general education of all classes of Christians. Sir Robert Peel, seeing that he and his government had no possibility of conducting the affairs of the country with the substantial support of the House, announced his resignation. Lord Melbourne again became Prime Minister. Mr. Gladstone, of course, stepped down from the office of Under Secretary of the Colonial Department, and retired with his chief into the quiet shades of opposition. The life of the House of Commons was a life of strife and bitter contention. From this Mr. Gladstone kept as much as possible aloof. For great principles he was always ready to fight, but when the conflict was merely between persons and parties he refused to enter the lists, and by the courtesy and urbanity of his manners he won the admiration of the whole House.

An admirer and fellow-member of Parliament with Mr. Gladstone in these early years, thus speaks of him : "He spoke frequently in debates, and the growth of his position in the country is testified to by the fact that in 1837, being in his twenty-eighth year, he was invited to stand as the Tory candidate for Manchester. He declined the proposal, but was nevertheless run, and polled a considerable number of votes. It was at this period of his career that Lord

Macaulay described him in a famous sentence as "a young man of unblemished character, and of distinguished Parliamentary talents, the rising hope of those stern and unbending Tories who follow reluctantly and mutinously a leader whose experience and eloquence are indispensable to them, but whose cautious temper and moderate opinions they abhor."

CHAPTER X.

ACCESSION AND CORONATION OF QUEEN VICTORIA.

This awful responsibility is imposed upon me so suddenly, and at
so early a period of my life, that I should feel myself utterly oppressed
by the burden were I not sustained by the hope that Divine Providence
which has called me to this work will give me strength for the performance of it.   —*Queen Victoria.*

Perhaps our youthful Queen
Remembers what has been—
Her childhood's rest by loving heart,
And sport on grassy sod —
Alas! can others wear
A mother's heart for her?
But calm she lifts her trusting face
And calleth upon God.

Yea! call on God, thou maiden,
Of spirit nobly laden,
And leave such happy days behind.
For happy-making years
A nation looks to thee
For steadfast sympathy.
Make room within thy bright clear eyes,
For all its gathered tears.

And so the grateful isles
Shall give thee back their smiles,
And as thy mother joys in thee,
In them shalt *thou* rejoice;
Rejoice to meekly bow
A somewhat paler brow,
While the King of Kings shall bless thee
By the British people's voice.

      —*Elizabeth Barrett Browning.*

The days of Mr. Gladstone's public service ran parallel
with the days of the reign of Queen Victoria. For sixty
years that illustrious lady has swayed the sceptre of empire,
and for more than sixty years Mr. Gladstone served with

matchless power and rare fidelity his God, his country, and his queen. The historian of the future will find this prolonged reign of so distinct a character that he will in all probability accept the designation already given it; he will describe the reign of Victoria as the "Victorian age." Ardent admirers of Mr. Gladstone have not hesitated to describe him as the greatest moral force in the statesmanship of that eventful era. It seems to us appropriate that at this point a few pages should be devoted to a record of the accession and coronation of the youthful queen. The dawn of that fair June morning in 1837, was the dawn of the most glorious reign England has ever seen or is ever likely to see. In this fair land we have neither monarch nor throne. But if there must be monarchs, well then the land that boasts such a queen as Victoria and such statesmen as Gladstone has everything to hope for, and nothing to fear. Around the accession and coronation of the queen, romance of the most sacred order has woven its delightful traceries.

There is a pretty description which has been often quoted, given by Miss Wynn, of the manner in which the young sovereign received the news of her accession to a throne. The Archbishop of Canterbury, Dr. Howley, and the Lord Chamberlain, the Marquis of Conyngham, left Windsor for Kensington Palace, where the Princess Victoria had been residing, to inform her of the King's death. It was two hours after midnight when they started, and they did not reach Kensington until five o'clock in the morning. "They knocked, they rang, they thumped for a considerable time before they could rouse the porter at the gate; they were again kept waiting in the court yard, then turned into one of the lower rooms, where they seemed forgotten by everybody. They rang the bell, and desired that the attendant of the Princess Victoria might be sent to inform her Royal Highness that they requested an audience on business of importance. After another delay, and another ringing to inquire the cause, the attendant was summoned, who stated that the Princess was in such a sweet sleep that she could not venture to disturb her.   Then they said 'We are come on business of state to the Queen, and even her sleep must give way to that.'   It did; and to prove that she did not keep them waiting, in a few minutes she came into the room in a loose white nightgown and shawl, her nightcap thrown off, and her hair falling upon her shoulders, her feet in slippers, tears in her eyes, but perfectly collected and dignified."   The Prime Minister, Lord Melbourne, was presently sent for, and a meeting of the Privy Council summoned for eleven o'clock, when the Lord Chancellor administered the usual oaths to the Queen, and her Majesty received in return the oaths of allegiance of the Cabinet ministers and other privy councillors present.   Mr. Greville has described the scene:

"The **King** died at twenty minutes after two yesterday morning, and the young Queen met the Council at Kensington Palace at eleven.   Never was anything like the first impression she produced, or the chorus of praise and admiration which is raised about her manner and behavior, and certainly not without justice.   It was very extraordinary, and something far beyond what was looked for.   Her extreme youth and inexperience, and the ignorance of the world concerning her, naturally excited intense curiosity to see how she would act on this trying occasion, and there was a considerable assemblage at the palace, notwithstanding the short notice which was given.   The first thing to be done was to teach her her lesson, which, for this purpose, Melbourne had himself to learn.   .   .   .   .   She bowed to the lords, took her seat, and then read her speech in a clear, distinct, and audible voice, and without any appearance of fear or embarrassment.   She was quite plainly dressed, and in mourning.   After she had read her speech, and taken and signed the oath for the security of the Church of Scotland, the privy councillors were sworn, the two royal dukes first by themselves; and as these two old men, her uncles, knelt before her, swearing allegiance and kissing her hand, I saw her blush up to the eyes, as if she felt the contrast between their civil and their natural relations, and this was the only sign of emotion which she evinced. Her manner to them was very graceful and engaging; she kissed them both, and rose from her chair and moved toward the Duke of Sussex, who was farthest from her, and too infirm to reach her. She seemed rather bewildered at the multitude of men who were sworn, and who came one after another, to kiss her hand, but she did not speak to anybody, nor did she make the slightest difference in her manner, or show any in her countenance, to any individual of any rank, station, or party. I particularly watched her when Melbourne and the ministers, and the Duke of Wellington and Peel approached her. She went through the whole ceremony, occasionally looking at Melbourne for instruction when she had any doubt what to do, which hardly ever occurred, and with perfect calmness and self-possession, but at the same time with a graceful modesty and propriety particularly interesting and ingratiating."

Sir Robert Peel said that he was amazed at " her manner and behavior, at her apparent deep sense of her situation, and at the same time her firmness." The Duke of Wellington said in his blunt way that if she had been his own daughter he could not have desired to see her perform her part better. "At twelve," says Mr. Greville, "she held a Council, at which she presided with as much ease as if she had been doing nothing else all her life; and though Lord Lansdowne and my colleague had contrived between them to make some confusion with the Council papers, she was not put out by it. She looked very well; and though so small in stature, and without much pretension to beauty, the gracefulness of her manner and the good expression of her countenance give her on the whole a very agreeable appearance, and with her youth inspire an excessive interest in all who approach her, and which I can't help feeling myself.   .   .   .   In short, she appears to act with every sort of good taste and good feeling, as well as good sense; and as far as it has gone nothing can be more favorable than the impression she has made, and nothing can promise better than her manner and conduct do; though," Mr. Greville somewhat superfluously adds, "it would be rash to count too confidently upon her judgment and discretion in more weighty matters.

Few remain among the living who were present at that gorgeous ceremony of Coronation. The grand old Abbey had never seen such a pageant, nor had the streets of London ever echoed with more enthusiastic loyalty. The coronation did not take place till the year 1838.

A magnificent new crown had been made for the youthful sovereign. Into its formation all the jewels of the crowns of the Georges and of William had been massed. The jeweler's best skill had been taxed to make this creation one of splendor and of beauty. On this auspicious day it was to rest on the head of her Majesty Queen Victoria.

Escorted by squadrons of the Blues, the Life Guards, the Scots Fusiliers, and other military bodies, and by the great lords and ladies of her kingdom, the girl-sovereign proceeded to Westminster Abbey.

"The great procession," said the London *Times* of that date, "started from Buckingham Palace at 10 o'clock in the morning. The first two state carriages, each drawn by six horses, held the Duchess of Kent and her attendants. The Queen's mother, regally attired, was enthusiastically cheered all along the way. The Queen in the grand state coach drawn by eight magnificent cream-colored horses, with flowing manes and tails, followed.

"Along the line from Buckingham Palace to Westminster Abbey, military bands and battalions were stationed, playing the national airs and presenting arms ; and along the route swarms of people were scattering flowers, waving handkerchiefs, or making other joyous demonstration.

" A scene of the utmost grandeur was displayed in Westminster Abbey on the entrance of the Queen and her train. On each side of the nave, reaching from the western door to the organ screen, were the galleries erected for the spectators. These were all covered with crimson cloth fringed with gold, and below were the lines of footguards. The old stone floor, impressed by footsteps of kings who had been crowned, was covered with purple and crimson, and under the center tower of the Abbey, inside the choir, a few steps from the floor, was a carpet of purple and gold, upon which was a platform covered with cloth of gold, on which was the golden 'Chair of Homage.' The old chair in which all the sovereigns of England since Edward the Confessor had been crowned stood within the chancel, and the 'Stone of Sconce,' on which the ancient Scottish Kings had been crowned, was draped with a cloth of gold. The galleries, in which were seated foreign Princes, Embassadors and members of Parliament, were upholstered in crimson cloth and regal tapestries. In the organ loft the singers were dressed in white and the instrumental performers in scarlet; and far above was a band of trumpeters, whose music, pealing over the heads of the assembly, produced a fine effect.

"The foreign Princes and Embassadors were resplendent in the dazzling costumes of their orders, Prince Esterhazy surpassing all by an exhibition of precious stones sparkling on his person from head to foot.

"In her royal robe of crimson velvet, furred with ermine and trimmed with gold lace, her Majesty entered, wearing the collars of her orders, and on her head a golden circlet, her long train held by eight young ladies of noble birth, looking regal. As she entered the Abbey the choir and orchestra broke out into 'God Save the Queen'; then, as she advanced slowly toward the choir amid deafening cheers, the anthem 'I Was Glad' was sung; and after that the choir boys of Westminster chanted 'Vivat Victoria Regina!' The Queen moved slowly to a chair between the Chair of Homage and the altar, before which she knelt in prayer.

"On the conclusion of the anthem, the Archbishop of Canterbury and the high officers of state moved to the east side of the 'theater,' when the Primate said in a loud voice, 'I here present to you Queen Victoria, the undoubted Queen of the realm, wherefore all of you who are come this day to your homage, are you willing to do the same?'

"The 'recognition,' 'God save Queen Victoria,' was cried by the people and repeated from every side of the 'theater' amid the pealing of trumpets and the beating of drums, the Queen standing through the ceremony and each time turning her head toward the point from which the 'recognition' came.

"This was followed by the receiving and presenting of offerings, the reading of prayers, and by the sermon; then followed the administration of the oath, and the catechism by the Archbishop in regard to the Established Church.

"The Queen was conducted to the altar, where, kneeling with her hand upon the great Bible, she said in a clear, solemn voice: 'The things which I have here before promised I will perform and keep.   So help me God?'

"She then kissed the book; and the hymn 'Come, Holy Ghost, our souls inspire' was sung by the choir, the Queen still kneeling.

"Her Majesty seated herself in St. Edward's chair; a gorgeous cloth of gold was held over her head; and the Archbishop anointed her with holy oil, in the form of a cross. Prayers were offered, the sword and spurs were presented, her Majesty was invested with the imperial robe, the sceptre and the ring, the new crown was consecrated and blessed, and the Queen was crowned.

"The moment the Queen was crowned by the Primate, the Peers and Peeresses lifted to their own heads their coronets and the Queen was conducted to the Chair of Homage.

"The lords spiritual headed by the Primate, performed the first homage to the Queen, kneeling and kissing her hand. Then came the Dukes of Sussex and Cambridge, her Majesty's uncles, who, removing their coronets, and touching them to the crown, solemnly pledged their allegiance and kissed the Queen on the left cheek. Then the other Peers did homage by kneeling, touching coronet to crown, and kissing her Majesty's hands.

"When the sacrament was administered to the Queen she laid aside her crown while partaking, and again assuming it, received the final benediction."

Sixty years have passed since then, and now the venerable Queen, rich in sacred memories and hallowed graves, who has held the chalice of widowhood in her hand for so many years, hears echoing among her Scottish hills the tolling of the Hawarden bells, and sends to that gracious lady who sits silently among the shadows that have fallen a message of tender sympathy and love—a message all the more pathetic because she feels her royal solitude growing more and more intense, as one by one the royal standard-bearers of her reign pass into the silent land.

Sixty years ago! When the Queen was crowned in the grand old Abbey witnesses tell how she wept most gracious tears as she heard the loyal shouts of the mighty multitude. Elizabeth Barrett Browning, the singing, suffering nightingale, who filled the early years of the Victorian Age with deathless song, has crystalized those tears in the following delightful stanzas:

"O Maiden ! heir of kings !
  A king has left his place !
The majesty of death has swept
  All other from his face !
And thou upon thy mother's breast
  No longer lean adown.
But take the glory for the rest,
And rule the land that loves the best !"
    She heard and wept—
  She wept, to wear a crown !

They decked her courtly halls ;
  They reined her hundred steeds ;
They shouted at her palace gate,
  " A noble Queen succeeds !"
Her name has stirred the mountains' sleep
  Her praise has filled the town !
And mourners God had stricken deep
Looked hearkening up, and did not weep.
    Alone she wept,
  Who wept, to wear a crown !

She saw no purple shine,
  For tears had dimmed her eyes ;
She only knew her childhood's flowers
  Were happier pageantries !
And while her heralds played the part,
  For million shouts to drown—
" God save the Queen " from hill to mart—
She heard through all her beating heart,
    And turned and wept—
  She wept, to wear a crown !

God save thee, weeping Queen !
  Thou shalt be well beloved !
The tyrant's sceptre can not move,
  As those pure tears have moved !
The nature in thine eyes we see,
  That tyrants can not own—
The love that guardeth liberties !
Strange blessing on the nation lies,
    Whose Sovereign wept—
  Yea ! wept to wear its crown !

God bless thee, weeping Queen,
  With blessing more divine !
And fill with happier love than earth's
  That tender heart of thine !
That when the thrones of earth shall be
  As low as graves brought down ;
A pierced hand may give to thee
The crown which angels shout to see !
  . Thou wilt not WEEP.
  To wear that heavenly crown !

CHAPTER XI.

The world wants action. The world would move but slowly if all
men were content with good dinners and a quiet life.

—E. P. Roe.

The man most man
Works best for me; and if most man indeed,
He gets his manhood plainest from his soul:
While obviously this stringent soul itself
Obeys our old law of development;
The Spirit ever witnessing in ours,
And Love, the soul of soul, within the soul,
Evolving it sublimely.

—Elizabeth Barrett Browning.

Mr. Gladstone had hardly buckled on the armor of official
service when the whirl-i-gig of time wrought its strange and
unanticipated changes. On the eighth of April, 1835, Sir
Robert Peel resigned with the downfall of the government,
Mr. Gladstone became once more a private member of
Parliament. But though a private member, he led a most
active and interesting life. He occupied rooms at the
Albany, and entered with great zest and enthusiasm into the
thousand and one engagements which were common to
public men in those days. He was regular in attendance in
the House of Commons, and took almost as much interest in
the debates of the House as he would have done had the
responsibility of office rested on his shoulders. He went a
good deal into society, where his presence was regarded as
a great favor. He was very popular in aristocratic circles,
the doors of the noble and the distinguished were wide open
to bid him welcome, but there was little danger that the
young statesman would dwindle down into a mere leader of
fashionable society. Life was always very real, and very

In the Lobby of the House of Lords.

HERBERT GLADSTONE.

earnest with him. An important debate in the House of Commons had power to charm him from the most brilliant assemblage, and from the most delightful entertainment. He rallied to the support of the government when the affairs of Canada were up for discussion.

A debate on the Church Rate question brought forth all his magnificent powers of oratory. This speech delivered in the spring of 1837 occupied no less than thirteen columns in *Hansard*.

The Chancellor of the Exchequer, Mr. Spring Rice, had propounded a plan for the re-arrangement of Church rates, which he hoped would be satisfactory at once to the scruples of Dissenters and the claims of the Establishment. His scheme, in essence, was to take the whole property of the bishops, deans and chapters out of the hands of those dignitaries, and to vest them in the hands of a commission, under whose improved system of management, it was calculated, that after paying to their full present amount all existing incomes, a sum not less than that assigned by Lord Althorp might be saved and applied for the purposes of Church rates. When the House went into committee on Mr. Rice's resolutions, they were opposed by Sir Robert Peel on financial as well as conscientious grounds. Mr. Gladstone followed in the same strain, and the peroration of his speech —in which he drew a comparison between Rome and England, and insisted upon religion being the basis of the greatness of the State—was, perhaps, the most impassioned specimen of oratory with which he had yet favored the House.

"It was not," said Mr. Gladstone, "by the active strength and resistless prowess of her legions, the bold independence of her citizens, or the well-maintained equilibrium of her constitution, or by the judicious adaptation of various measures to the various circumstances of her subject states, that the Roman power was upheld. Its foundation lay in the prevailing feeling of religion. This was the superior power which curbed the license of individual rule, and engendered in the people a lofty disinterestedness and disregard of personal motives and devotion to the glory of the republic. The devotion of the Romans was not enlightened by a knowledge of the precepts of Christianity; here religion was still more deeply rooted and firmly fixed. And would they now consent to compromise the security of its firmest bulwark? No Ministry would dare to propose its unconditional surrender; but with the same earnestness and depth of feeling with which they should deprecate the open avowal of such a determination, they ought to resist the covert and insidious introduction of the principle." When the division came, however, the Ministry obtained a majority of 23, the numbers being — For the resolutions, 273; against, 250.

Close upon the heels of this debate, the Anti-Slavery question came up for consideration. The wildest stories were afloat concerning the horrors to which negro apprentices were subjected, and true or not true, the public mind was aroused, and such men as Lord Brougham and Dr. Lushington led the van in agitation. According to the conditions of the Emancipation Act, slavery had been abolished from the year 1834, but negro apprenticeship was not to terminate until 1840. Lord Brougham introduced the subject in the House of Lords, and moved the immediate abolition of negro apprenticeship. Spite of the harrowing records of cruelty and wrongs perpetrated on helpless youth, spite of the eloquence and logic of the distinguished advocate for freedom, spite of the allegation that attempts were being made to perpetuate slavery in a new form, the noble lords rejected the motion with a marked majority. On the twenty-ninth of March in this same year, Sir George Strickland proposed a similar resolution in the House of Commons. Mr. Gladstone delivered a long address extending over thirty-three columns of the official reports. Mr. Gladstone called attention to the fact that when the Abolition Act of 1833 was brought forward, those who were connected with West Indian slavery joined in the passing of the measure

"We professed a belief," said Mr. Gladstone, that the state of slavery was an evil and a demoralizing state, and desired to be relieved from it; we accepted a price in composition for the loss which was expected to accrue, and if after these professions and that acceptance we have endeavored to prolong its existence and its abuses under another appellation, no language can adequately characterize our baseness, and either everlasting ignominy must be upon us, or you are not justified in carrying this motion." But he utterly and confidently denied the charge, as it affected the mass of the planters, and as it affected the mass of the apprentices. By the facts to be adduced he would stand or fall. "Oh, sir," he continued, "with what depth of desire have I longed for this day! Sore, and wearied, and irritated, perhaps, with the grossly exaggerated misrepresentations, and with the utter calumnies that have been in circulation without the means of reply, how do I rejoice to meet them in free discussion before the face of the British Parliament! And I earnestly wish that I may be enabled to avoid all language and sentiments similar to those I have reprobated in others." He then proceeded to show that the character of the planters was at stake. They were attacked both on moral and pecuniary grounds. The apprenticeship—as Lord Stanley distinctly stated when he introduced the measure—was a part of the compensation. Negro labor had a marketable value, and it would be unjust to those who had the right in it to deprive them of it. Besides, the House had assented to this right as far as the year 1840, and was morally bound to fulfil its compact. The committee presided over by Mr. Buxton had reported against the necessity for this change.

Mr. Gladstone, with great fullness of detail, next examined the relations between the planters and the negroes, and with regard to the cases of alleged cruelty, he showed that they had been constantly and enormously on the decrease since the period of abolition. He strongly deprecated all such appeals as were made to individual instances and exaggerated representations, and endeavored, by elaborate statistics, to prove that the abuses were far from being general. The use of the lash, as a stimulus to labor, had died a natural death in British Guiana. During the preceding five months only eleven corporal punishments had been inflicted in a population of seven thousand persons, yielding an average of seven hundred lashes by the year, and these not for neglect of work, but for theft. Towards the close of his speech, Mr. Gladstone thus effectively turned the tables, in one sense, upon his opponents by a *tu quoque* argument. "Have you," he went on to say, "who are so exasperated with the West Indian apprenticeship that you will not wait two years for its natural expiration,—have you inquired what responsibility lies upon every one of you, at the moment when I speak, with reference to the cultivation of cotton in America? In that country there are near three millions of slaves. You hear not from that land of the abolition—not even of the mitigation—of slavery. It is a domestic institution, and is to pass without limit, we are told, from age to age; and we, much more than they, are responsible for this enormous growth of what purports to be an eternal slavery . . . . You consumed forty-five millions of pounds of cotton in 1837, which proceeded from free labor; and, proceeding from slave labor, three hundred and eighteen millions of pounds! And this while the vast regions of India afford the means of obtaining, at a cheaper rate, and by a slight original outlay to facilitate transport, all that you can require. If, sir, the complaints against the general body of the West Indians had been substantiated, I should have deemed it an unworthy artifice to attempt diverting the attention of the House from the question immediately at issue, by merely proving that other delinquencies existed in other quarters; but feeling as I do that those charges have been overthrown in debate, I think myself entitled and bound to show how capricious are honorable gentlemen in the distribution of their sympathies among those different objects which call for their application." He concluded by asking for justice alone, and demanded that the Legislature should not be deaf to that call. With the influence of this vigorous defense of the planters upon it, the House went to a division. Sir George Strickland's motion was lost, the numbers being—Ayes, 215; Noes, 269—majority, 54. The *Times* newspaper, on the following day, admitted the force of Mr. Gladstone's speech, which, from an oratorical point of view, was completely successful. It also disposed of many allegations that had been made against the planters, although it did not remove the grounds upon which the anti-Slavery agitation was based, and by which evils it was justified. There were complaints of oppression and exaction which could not be denied, and the House of Assembly in Jamaica had by no means shown its readiness to fulfill that portion of the compact of 1833-4 which devolved upon it, and by which there had been secured to the West Indian proprietors a sum of not less than a hundred millions of dollars as an allowance for six years' apprenticeship.

This speech added greatly to Mr. Gladstone's fame as a great debater. Here is an interesting description of the young orator as others saw him in these formative years.

A constant attendant on the House of Commons speaks thus of him:

"Mr. Gladstone's appearance and manners are much in

his favor. He is a fine-looking man. He is about the usual height, and of good figure. His countenance is mild and pleasant, and has a highly intellectual expression. His eyes are clear and quick. His eyebrows are dark and rather prominent. There is not a dandy in the House but envies what Truefit would call his 'fine head of jet-black hair.' It is always carefully parted from the crown downwards to his brow, where it is tastefully shaded. His features are small and regular, and his complexion must be a very unworthy witness if he does not possess an abundant stock of health.

"Mr. Gladstone's gesture is varied, but not violent. When he rises he generally puts both his hands behind his back; and having there suffered them to embrace each other for a short time, he unclasps them, and allows them to drop on either side. They are not permitted to remain long in that locality before you see them again closed together and hanging down before him. Their re-union is not suffered to last for any length of time. Again a separation takes place, and now the right hand is seen moving up and down before him. Having thus exercised it a little, he thrusts it into the pocket of his coat, and then orders the left hand to follow its example. Having granted them a momentary repose there, they are again put into gentle motion; and in a few seconds they are seen reposing *vis-à-vis* on his breast. He moves his face and body from one direction to another, not forgetting to bestow a liberal share of his attention on his own party. He is always listened to with much attention by the House, and appears to be highly respected by men of all parties. He is a man of good business habits: of this he furnished abundant proof when Under-Secretary for the Colonies, during the short-lived administration of Sir Robert Peel."

On the 8th of April, 1840, Mr. Gladstone made another of his impassioned speeches. Sir James Graham brought forward a resolution concerning the war with China arising from the traffic in opium. Mr. Gladstone rallied to the support of Sir James Graham, and in reply to a speech of Mr. Macaulay's on the previous evening, he said:

"The right honorable gentleman opposite spoke last night in eloquent terms of the British flag waving in glory at Canton, and of the animating effects produced on the minds of our sailors by the knowledge that in no country under heaven was it permitted to be insulted. But how comes it to pass that the sight of that flag always raises the spirit of Englishmen? It is because it has always been associated with the cause of justice, with opposition to oppression, with respect for national rights, with honorable commercial enterprise; but now, under the auspices of the noble lord, that flag is hoisted to protect an infamous contraband traffic, and if it were never to be hoisted except as it is now hoisted on the coast of China, we should recoil from its sight with horror, and should never again feel our hearts thrill as they now thrill with emotion, when it floats proudly and magnificently on the breeze." Notwithstanding the eloquence arrayed against them, Ministers obtained a bare majority upon the proposed vote of censure, the numbers being—For Sir J. Graham's motion, 262; against, 271.

CHAPTER XII.

THE CHAMPION OF THE CHURCH.

Religion crowns the statesman and the man,
Sole source of public and of private peace.
—Edward Young.

Christianity rose out of the dying ashes of Paganism, restored conscience to its supremacy, and made real belief in God once more possible.—*L. J. Froude.*

The Church has for long lived upon the divinity of its attitudes and upturned eyes, and the blackness of its cloth. While it was thus postu ing before the altar, the congregation has slipped out into the fresh air to find the life of humanity or the indescribable richness of the fields where there are no vain repetitions.
—David Swing.

Mr. Gladstone's achievements in the fields of literature would entitle him to a very enviable renown. Literature was the recreation rather than the business of his life. The fascinations of logical research wooed him on the one hand, and the romance of classic history and lore charmed him on the other. In the sombre shades of the cloister and the cell, or in the mystic splendors of the Homeric age, he was equally at home. He was bowed with awe amid the thunderings and lightnings of Sinia, or stood enraptured amid the fitful glories of high Olympus. He had unspeakable delight in translating "Rock of Ages" into the Latin tongue, or in reviewing "Ecce Homo," or in writing a treatise on Wedgwood China. He loved the wide fields of literature, and trod them with a free and gracious step, but it is reasonable to conclude that the circumstances of the time had much to do in inspiring his first serious literary task.

In the autumn of 1838, Mr. Gladstone published his first

book : "The State in Its Relations with the Church." In this country, where the dream of " A Free Church in a Free State " is realized to perfection, it is somewhat difficult to explain to an American what such terms as " Dissenter " and " Nonconformist " mean in England even to-day, and much more difficult to explain what such terms involved in the days when the young member for Newark set his glittering lance in rest, and came forth as the champion of the Church as by law established. Nonconformity was becoming a mighty factor in the nation. Nonconformity was young Puritanism full grown, and included all those who from deep religious scruples, sought to worship God according to their conscience. They were the spiritual descendants of the men who in 1618 met King James I. at Hampden Court palace and told him that, while they were loyal to his person and his throne, they could not conform to the teachings of the Church of England nor follow the order of its ritual. The angry, foolish King declared that he would make them conform or he would " harry them out of the land." The former thing he could not do, but the latter he did, and in 1620 they sailed in the Mayflower from Southampton water, and, leaving the homes they loved and the graves that were sacred, they journeyed toward the setting sun that on " the bleak New England shore " they might found a colony for God and King James, where they might enjoy the luxury of religious freedom.

In deathless song Mrs. Hemans has marked and immortalized the landing of this heroic company :

And the heavy night hung dark,
The hills and waters o'er ;
When a band of exiles moored their bark
On the wild New England shore.

Not as the conqueror comes,
They, the true-hearted, came ;
Not with the roll of the stirring drums,
And the trumpet that speaks of fame.

> Not as the flying come—
>   In silence and in fear;
> They shook the depths of the desert gloom
>   With their hymns of lofty cheer.
>
> Amid the storm they sang,
>   And the stars heard, and the sea;
> And the sounding aisles of the dim woods rang
>   To the anthem of the free.
>
> The ocean eagle soared
>   From his nest by the wild waves' foam,
> And the rocking pines of the forest roared—
>   This was their welcome home.
>
> *   *   *   *   *
>
> What sought they thus afar?
>   Bright jewels of the mine?
> The wealth of seas the spoils of war?
>   They sought a faith's pure shrine!
>
> Ay, call it holy ground,
>   The soil where first they trod—
> They have left unstained what there they found—
>   Freedom to worship God

The Nonconformist claimed he was the true Conformist, for he was loyal to his conscience and his God. Nonconformity was growing in numbers, in character, and in influence. It did not care to assume the dignified name of "Church" to its edifices; it was perfectly content to worship in a "Chapel." Its ministers were not regarded by bigoted ecclesiastics as properly "ordained" or duly qualified to discharge the sacred rites of religion, but they preached with power and wrought great work for God. Nonconformity built its sanctuaries and colleges, and opened and conducted schools of education, and voluntarily paid for everything without asking a cent from the national coffer. The leaven of nonconformity was working. In the midland counties of England especially, men who had the confidence of the people, were banding themselves together to agitate for the redress of grievances. Such men as Dr. Legge, the Rev. J. P. Mursell, Carvell Williams and Edward Miall formed

"An Anti-State Church Association," which was merged at last into "The Society for the Liberation of Religion from State Patronage and Control," briefly known as "The Liberation Society," which still exists, as it believes with sufficient cause, and is holding its annual meetings in this month of May, in this year of grace, 1898. That nonconformity was seriously and silently at work Mr. Gladstone knew full well. If he came forth at this interesting and suggestive period to defend and champion the Church of England, it was not because he was afraid. He was not much given to the theory that "There's a divinity that doth hedge a King," but he did believe that the Church of England was God's church, divinely summoned to a divine work. In all of which he was, no doubt, perfectly right. The nonconformist minister held precisely the same view of the church to which God called him to minister in holy things. Mr. Gladstone was not an alarmist. He did not haste to the rescue of a church in danger! He called the serious attention of England to the foundations on which what he regarded the most sacred institution of the country was founded. The book commanded widespread attention at once. Bitter opponents were compelled to recognize the author's remarkable ability. The work was inscribed:

"To the University of Oxford:

"Tried and not found wanting through the vicissitudes of a thousand years; in the belief that she is providentially designed to be a fountain of blessings, spiritual, social and intellectual, to this and other countries, to the present and future times, and in the hope that the temper of these pages may be found not alien to her own."

How this alumnus loved his alma mater!

The brilliant Macaulay in his searching criticism said: "We believe we do him no more than justice when we say that his abilities and demeanor have obtained for him the respect and good will of all parties.   *   *   *   *   That a young politician should, in the intervals afforded by his Parliamentary avocations, have constructed and propounded, with much study and mental toil, an original theory on a great problem in politics, is a circumstance which, abstracted from all considerations of the soundness or unsoundness of his opinions, must be considered as highly creditable to him. We certainly can not wish that Mr. Gladstone's doctrines may become fashionable among public men. But we heartily wish that his laudable desire to penetrate beneath the surface of questions, and to arrive, by long and intent meditation, at the knowledge of great and general laws, were much more fashionable than we at all expect it to become."

This is neither time nor place to enter into any exhaustive criticism of Mr. Gladstone's first contribution to the literature of his age.   Apart altogether from its subject matter, it is well worth careful perusal.   The one word "thoroughness" that marks all his work applies to this carefully written treatise.   One might well imagine that this theme had been the one commanding study of his life.   The book went through four editions, each adition being revised and considerably enlarged.   We quote only one passage, which has become quite famous, by reason of its relation to the Irish Church, which in due time Mr. Gladstone disestablished and disendowed.

"The Protestant legislature of the British Empire maintains in the possession of the Church property of Ireland the ministers of a creed professed, according to the parliamentary enumeration of 1835, by one-ninth of its population, regarded with partial favor by scarcely another ninth, and disowned by the remaining seven.   And not only does this anomaly meet us full in view, but we have also to consider and digest the fact that the maintenance of this Church for near three centuries in Ireland has been contemporaneous with a system of partial and abusive government, varying in degree of culpability, but rarely, until of later years, when we have been forced to look at the subject and to feel it, to be exempted in common fairness from the reproach of gross inattention (to say the very least) to the interests of a noble but neglected people.

"But however formidable at first sight these admissions, which I have no desire to narrow or to qualify, may appear, they in no way shake the foregoing arguments. They do not change the nature of truth and her capability and destiny to benefit mankind. They do not relieve government of its responsibility, if they show that that responsibility was once unfelt and unsatisfied. They place the legislature of this country in the condition, as it were, of one called to do penance for past offenses ; but duty remains unaltered and imperative, and abates nothing of her demand on our services. · It is undoubtedly competent, in a constitutional view, to the government of this country to continue the present disposition of church property in Ireland. It appears not too much to assume that our imperial legislature has been qualified to take, and has taken in point of fact, a sounder view of religious truth than the majority of the people of Ireland, in their destitute and uninstructed state. We believe, accordingly, that that which we place before them is, whether they know it or not, calculated to be beneficial to them, and that if they know it not now they will know it when it is presented to them fairly. Shall we, then, purchase their applause at the expense of their substantial, nay, their spiritual interests ?

"It does, indeed, so happen that there are also powerful motives on the other side, concurring with that which has here been represented as paramount. In the first instance, we are not called upon to establish a creed, but only to maintain an existing legal settlement, where our constitutional right is undoubted. In the second, political considerations tend strongly to recommend that maintenance. A common form of faith binds the Irish Protestants to ourselves, while they, upon the other hand, are fast linked to Ireland ; and thus they supply the most natural bond of connection between the countries. But if England, by overthrowing their Church should weaken their moral position, they would be no longer able, perhaps no longer willing, to counteract the desires of the majority, tending, under the direction of their leaders (however, by a wise policy, revocable from that fatal course), to what is termed national independence. Pride and fear, on the one hand, are, therefore, bearing up against more immediate apprehension and difficulty on the other. And with some men these may be the fundamental consid- erations; but it may be doubted whether such men will not flinch in some stage of the contest, should its aspect at any moment become unfavorable."

Here follow Mr. Gladstone's chief reasons for the main- tenance of the Church Establishment: " Because the gov- ernment stands with us in a paternal relation to the people, and is bound in all things to consider not merely their existing tastes, but the capabilities and ways of their improvement ; because it has both an intrinsic competency and external means to amend and assist their choice ; because to be in accordance with God's mind and will it must have a religion, and because to be in accordance with its con- science that religion must be the truth, as held by it under the most solemn and accumulated responsibilities ; because this is the only sanctifying and preserving principle of soci- ety, as well as to the individual that particular benefit without which all others are worse than valueless ; we must disregard the din of political contention and the pressure of worldly and momentary motives, and in behalf of our regard to man, as well as our allegiance to God, maintain among ourselves, where happily it still exists, the union between Church and State."

Macaulay observed that Mr. Gladstone's whole theory in this work rested upon one great fundamental proposition— viz.: "That the propagation of religious truth is one of the chief ends of government, *as* government," and he proceeded to combat this theory.

The *Quarterly Review* says : "Mr. Gladstone is evidently not an ordinary character ; though it is to be hoped that many others are now forming themselves in the same school with him, to act hereafter upon the same principles. And the highest compliment which we can pay him is to show that we believe him to be what a statesman and philosopher should be—indifferent to his own reputation for talents, and only anxious for truth and right."

Lord Macaulay observed upon the same question of style: "Mr. Gladstone seems to us to be, in many respects, exceedingly well qualified for philosophical investigation. His mind is of large grasp ; nor is he deficient in dialectic skill. But he does not give his intellect fair play. There is no want of light, but a great want of what Bacon would have called dry light. Whatever Mr. Gladstone sees is refracted and distorted by a false medium of passions and prejudices. His style bears a remarkable analogy to his way of thinking, and, indeed, exercises great influence on his mode of thinking. His rhetoric, though often good of its kind, darkens and perplexes the logic which it should illustrate. Half his acuteness and diligence, with a barren imagination and a scanty vocabularly, would have saved him from almost all his mistakes. He has one gift most dangerous to a speculator—a vast command of a kind of language, grave and majestic, but of vague and uncertain import—of a kind of language which affects us much in the same way in which the lofty diction of the Chorus of Clouds affected the simple-hearted Athenian."

CHAPTER XIII.

For contemplation he and valor formed;
For softness she and sweet attractive grace.—*John Milton.*

But happy they! the happiest of their kind,
Whom gentle sta's unite, and in one fate
Their hearts, their fortunes, and their beings blend.
                              —*James Thomson.*

There's bliss beyond all that the minstrel has told,
  When two that are linked in one heavenly tie,
With heart never changing, and brow never cold,
  Love on through all ills, and love on till they die.
One hour of a passion so sacred is worth
  Whole ages of heartless and wandering bliss;
And oh! if there be an Elysium on earth
  It is this — it is this!   —*Thomas Moore.*

"Of making many books there is no end, and much study
is a weariness of the flesh." The labor and research involved
in the production of "The State in its Relation with the
Church," ended in a partial breakdown of Mr. Gladstone's
health. His nervous system had been severely tested, and
his eyesight became seriously impaired. He was ordered
by his doctors to give up reading for a time and go abroad.
To give up reading was almost like giving up breathing,
and wandering about the sleepy cities of Europe was little
to his taste. To this earnest active soul, this kind of thing
was too much like dreaming the useful hours away. But
he was wisely obedient to his doctors and without delay he
packed his portmanteau and started for sunny sleepy Italy.
The winter of 1838-9 was spent in the Eternal City. His
sojourn in Rome was very delightful from the beginning.
He formed and fostered many happy friendships. Among

others, he met with his chief reviewer, the brilliant versatile Macaulay, and his great and admired friend, Edward Manning, afterwards Cardinal Manning, with whom he went frequently to the English College to visit the already renowned Cardinal Wiseman. But these were not all the friends Mr. Gladstone met. The tired student in search of health and better powers of seeing, beheld a vision that brightened and beautified his young life, that afterwards made glad and brave and strong the midway years of a busy public career, and then in mellowing glory filled the sunset of his venerable days with peace and sacred calm. The widow and daughters of Sir Stephen Richard Glynne, of Hawarden Castle, Flintshire, were also spending this same winter in Rome. Mr. Gladstone was not an entire stranger to the family—the eldest son of the Glynne's was a warm personal friend of his. Three years before he had paid a visit to Hawarden Castle, and now the friendship being renewed, Mr. Gladstone became a frequent and always a welcome visitor at the Glynne's. Lady Glynne had two daughters and they were passing fair. Queen Victoria writing to a member of the Glynne family says that when she was a girl, she remembered hearing people about her talking of the "two beautiful Miss Glynne's." Mr. Gladstone was also greatly impressed with the beauty of these young ladies, especially of the elder one, Miss Catharine Glynne, admiration grew into esteem, and esteem developed into love. So the old, old story is repeated; but not the silly story of "love at first sight"—a thoughtless visionary fascinated by the varied splendors of a butterfly's wing—all worship and adoration till the next butterfly comes along— but the story of a love that had time to be born and grow; and taking deep root, blossomed in growing beauty and fragrance with the roses of half a hundred years.

Mr. Gladstone and Miss Catharine Glynne became engaged. What a grand place Rome is for courtship! How this happy pair would wander about the palaces of the Cæsars; they richer, and a thousand times more happy than the Emperors of old renown! What opportunities of quiet strolling these scenes of the dead and buried past afforded! The majestic Coliseum in the glory of noontide or under the paler light of the shimmering moonbeams! He who has not seen the Coliseum by moonlight has not seen it in its most solemn sacred beauty. Doubtless they wandered along the Appian Way, and investigated the Mamertine prison where Paul "the prisoner of the Lord abode," and went down into the Catacombs many and many a time. And what historic stories Mr. Gladstone would tell, until Miss Glynne wondered that so young a gentleman should have learned so much. It was really very wonderful! When next the honeysuckles of July were twining round the cottage homes of the peasants of Hawarden "they two were wed, and merrily rang the bells!" On the 25th of July, 1839, the wedding was celebrated at Hawarden. It was a double wedding. Mr. Gladstone was married to Miss Catharine Glynne ; Miss Mary Glynne was married at the same time to the Fourth Lord Lyttelton. To say that this union of Mr. Gladstone to Miss Glynne was an ideal marriage, is only stating a truth to which fifty eventful years have borne beautiful accumulating testimony.

Mrs. Gladstone was the heiress of Hawarden, her brother —Mr. Gladstone's old time friend—Sir Stephen Glynne, the ninth and last Baronet of the line, being childless. The young couple were welcomed to the Castle of Hawarden as their home, and at the death of Sir Stephen it passed into their sole inheritance.

Their union has been blessed with eight children. Of the four sons the eldest, William Henry, sat in one House of Commons as Member for Whitby, in another representing East Worcestershire. A man of gentle and retiring disposition, he did not take kindly to the turmoil of politics, and when opportunity presented itself, gratefully withdrew. The second son is Rector of Hawarden. In 1875 the torrent of abuse to which Mr. Gladstone was subjected took, in a somewhat obscure London weekly paper, the line of accusation that the ex-Premier had presented his son, ordained in 1870, to one of the richest and easiest livings of the Church. This was a statement that might well have been passed over in silence. It touched Mr. Gladstone to the quick. He wrote: "This easy living entailed the charge of 8,000 people scattered over 17,000 acres, and fast increasing in number. The living is not in the gift of the Crown. I did not present him to the living or recommend him to be presented. He was not ordained in 1870. My relations," he proudly and truthfully added, "have no special cause to thank me for any advice given by me to the Sovereign in the matter of Church patronage."

His third son, Henry, followed the early family traditions by entering upon commercial pursuits, spending some years in India. He married the daughter of Lord Rendel, and still stands apart from politics. The only born politician among the sons is the youngest. Mr. Herbert Gladstone made his first appearance in the political arena by gallantly contesting Middlesex in April, 1880. Defeated there, he was returned for Leeds two months later, and still represents a Leeds Division in the House of Commons. For a while he acted as Private Secretary to his father the Premier, though he received no salary. He became in succession a Lord of the Treasury and Financial Secretary to the War Office, the Secretaryship to the Home Office being the highest post to which his omnipotent father promoted him. Upon Mr. Gladstone's retirement in 1894, colleagues who had long worked with Mr. Herbert Gladstone made haste to do him fuller justice, promoting him to the position of First Commissioner of Works.

A singularly modest record this of the family of an illustrious statesman, four times Chief Minister of a nation whose wealth is illimitable, whose power reaches to the ends of the earth. "We are, happily, so accustomed in England to find our statesmen free from the charge of nepotism, that we take Mr. Gladstone's innocence as a matter of course." But few more suggestive chapters in his history could be written than that which shows the son of a man, who has made many bishops, rector of the family parish in Flintshire ; one of his daughters married to a schoolmaster ; a second a schoolmistress, whilst another of his sons long sat at an office desk.

When not in London engaged in Ministerial or political business Mr. Gladstone has dwelt among his own people in his Flintshire home. Of Hawarden Castle, its history and its belongings, we have the pleasure of presenting a graphic and authoritative account from the pen of the late W. H. Gladstone.

The estate of Hawarden was purchased by Serjeant Glynne from the agents of Sequestration after the execution of James Earl of Derby in 1651. It came first into the Stanley family in 1443, when it was granted by Henry VI. to Sir Thomas Stanley, Comptroller of his Household. This grant was recalled in 1450, but in 1454 it was restored to Sir Thomas, afterwards Lord Stanley. After his death it descended to his second wife, Margaret Countess of Richmond ; on whose decease it returned to Thomas Earl of Derby, and remained in that family till 1651.

On the Restoration, when the Commons rejected the Bill for restoring the estates of those lords which had been alienated in the late usurpation, Charles Earl of Derby compounded with Serjeant Glynne for the property of Hawarden and granted it to him and his heirs.

The old Castle was possessed by the Parliament in 1643, being betrayed to Sir William Brereton, but was besieged soon after by the Royalists, and surrendered to Sir Michael Earnley, December 5th, 1643. The Royalists held it till 1645, when it was taken by General Mytton. It was soon after dismantled, and its further destruction effected by its owner, Sir William Glynne, in 1665.

There is no tradition of the Earls of Derby making the Castle their residence subsequent to the death of the Countess of Richmond; but it is certain that it was not rendered untenable till dismantled by order of the Parliament in 1647.

The Glynne family were first heard of at Glyn Llyvon, in Carnarvonshire, in 1567. A knighthood was conferred on Sir William, father of Serjeant, afterwards Chief Justice, Glynne. Sir William, son of the Chief Justice (who also sat in Parliament for Carnarvonshire in 1660), was created a Baronet in 1661, during his father's lifetime. About this date the family became connected with Oxfordshire, and did not reside at Hawarden till 1727, when Sir Stephen, second Baronet, built a house there. A new one was, however, built shortly after, in 1752, by Sir John Glynne, who, by an alliance with the family of Ravenscroft, acquired the adjoining property of Broadlane. This house, then called Broadlane House, is the kernel of the present residence known as Hawarden Castle. Sir John Glynne (sixth Baronet) applied himself to improving and developing the property on a large scale by inclosing, draining, and planting; and under him the estate grew to its present aspect and dimensions. (The park contains some 200 acres; the plantations cover about 500. The whole estate is upwards of 7,000.) In 1809 the house, built of brick, was much enlarged and cased in stone in the castellated style, and under the name it now bears. Further improvements were made by the late Sir Stephen Glynne in 1831. The new block, however, containing Mr. Gladstone's study, was not added till 1864.

Mr. Gladstone's room has three windows and two fireplaces and is completely lined with bookcases. There are three writing-tables in it. The first Mr. Gladstone uses for political, the second for literary work (Homeric and others) when engaged upon such. The third is occupied by Mrs. Gladstone. The room has busts and other likenesses of Sidney Herbert, Duke of Newcastle, Tennyson, Canning, Cobden, Homer, and others. In a corner may be seen a specimen of an axe from Nottingham, the blade of which is singularly long and narrow, and contrasts strongly with the American pattern, to which Mr. Gladstone is much addicted.

Mr. Gladstone sold his collections of china and pictures in 1874, retaining, however, those of ivories and antique jewels, exhibited at South Kensington and elsewhere.

His library contains over 10,000 volumes, and is very rich in theology. Separate departments are assigned in it to Homer, Shakespeare, and Dante.

Chief portraits in the house are those of Sir Kenelm Digby, by Vandyck, an ancestor of Honora Conway, Sir John Glynne's wife; Lady Lucy Stanley, daughter of Thomas Earl of Northumberland, mother to Sir K. Digby's wife; Jane Warburton, afterwards Duchess of Argyll, great-granddaughter to Chief Justice Glynne; Sir William Glynne, first Baronet, ascribed to Sir Peter Lely; Chief Justice Glynne as a young man, and another in his judicial robes; Lady Sandys, grandmother to Sir William Glynne's wife; Lady Wheler, daughter of Sir Stephen Glynne; Sir John Glynne with Honora Conway his wife, holding a drawing of the new house at Broadlane; Sir Robert Williams, of Penrhyn, who married a daughter of the Chief Justice; Catherine Grenville, afterwards Lady Braybrooke and mother of Lady Glynne; Mrs. Gladstone, by Saye; Lady Lyttelton, by Saye; the late Sir Stephen, by Roden; Mr. Gladstone's own portrait, by W. B. Richmond; Viscountess Vane, *née* Hawes; Charles I., Henrietta Maria his Queen, and Charles II., copies from Vandyck; and several others, one attributed to Gainsborough. There are busts of Pitt, Sir John Glynne, Rev. Henry Glynne, Mrs. Gladstone, Mr. Gladstone by Marochetti, and other statuary.

CHAPTER XIV.

Oh, noble soul! which neither gold, nor love nor scorn can bend.—
Charles Kingsley.

Mr. Gladstone is evidently not an ordinary character. And the
highest compliment which we can pay him is to show that we believe
him to be what a statesman and philosopher should be—indifferent
to his own reputation for talents, and only anxious for truth and
right — *Quarterly Review.*

> Be noble ! and the nobleness that lies
> In other men, sleeping but never dead,
> Will rise in majesty to meet thine own ;
> Then wilt thou see it gleam in many eyes,
> Then will pure light around thy path be shed.
> And thou wilt never more be sad and lone.
> —*James Russell Lowell.*

In the year 1843, Mr. Gladstone, at the age of thirty-three,
became President of the Board of Trade, on the retirement of
Lord Ripon from the Board of Control. The following year
Mr. Gladstone took the remarkable course of resigning his
position, to the great annoyance of his party, on account of
what they had regarded as an eccentric scruple. Sir Robert
Peel proposed to increase the grant which government was
in the habit of making Maynooth College, an establishment
for the education of the Roman Catholic priesthood. In
the course of the debate on the address Mr. Gladstone
explained his reasons for this step, and set a good deal of
speculation at rest by the announcement that his resignation
was due solely to the government intentions with regard to
Maynooth College. The contemplated increase in the Maynooth endowment and the establishment of nonsectarian col-

leges were at variance with the views he had written and uttered upon the relations of the Church and the State. "I am sensible how fallible my judgment is," said Mr. Gladstone, "and how easily I might have erred; but still it has been my conviction that, although I was not to fetter my judgment as a member of Parliament by a reference to abstract theories, yet, on the other hand, it was absolutely due to the public and due to myself that I should, so far as in me lay, place myself in a position to form an opinion upon a matter of so great importance, that should not only be actually free from all bias or leaning with respect to any consideration whatsoever, but an opinion that should be unsuspected. On that account I have taken a course most painful to myself in respect to personal feelings, and have separated myself from men with whom, and under whom, I have long acted in public life, and of whom I am bound to say, although I have now no longer the honor of serving my most gracious Sovereign, that I continue to regard them with unaltered sentiments, both of public regard and private attachment."

Mr. Gladstone added that he was not prepared to war against the religious measures of his friend, Sir Robert Peel. He would not prejudge such questions, but would give them calm and deliberate consideration. A high tribute was paid to the retiring Minister both by Lord John Russell and the Premier. The latter avowed the highest respect and admiration for Mr. Gladstone's character and abilities; admiration only equaled by regard for his private character. He had been most unwilling to lose one whom he regarded as capable of the highest and most eminent services.

This is one of the episodes in Mr. Gladstone's career that justify Mr. Stead in describing him as having a Quixotic conscience.

The fifth decade of the nineteenth century found England beset with anxiety and peril. If the cloud in her fair sky was "no bigger than a man's hand," it was the herald of a wild and pitiless storm.   The young Queen, who had been moved to "gracious tears" as she heard the wild plaudits of her loyal and enthusiastic subjects on the occasion of her coronation, soon became aware of very distinct undertones of discontent on the part of the great masses of the people. The toilers of the land in many thousands "began to be in want."   Wages were dropping lower and lower, and the necessities of life were rising higher and higher in price.

Poverty in its saddest forms stood knocking at hundreds of doors.   Trade was hopelessly bad.   Firms in scores, in all the large cities, counted in the general estimate to be "as safe as the bank," became bankrupt.   The universal confidence gave way.   There had been four or five bad harvests in succession.   Ireland had, of course, her full measure of these sorrows.   Potato-rot, famine and plague threatened all her borders.   Far and near, through all the British isles, there was heard the cry of hard times.   The old wail of the prophet Jeremiah was heard throughout the land: "The children cry for bread and no man breaketh it unto them."

The distress increased on every hand.   In all the large cities of England thousands of people were largely, and very many wholly dependent on the charities the Poor Law administered.   In such towns as Coventry and Nottingham every third or fifth person you met was to some extent a pauper.   Women pawned their wedding rings to keep their children from starving.   The taxes on human food were enormous and iniquitous.   In the interests of the wealthy landlords corn was taxed at such a rate that the poor and their children had to starve.   Of course England was not able to grow corn enough to supply her own great family, but there was corn enough and to spare waiting at the gates of the nation, but it was not allowed to enter until it was so highly taxed that the interests of the landlords were conserved whatever became of the hapless toiling millions. The condition of affairs was threatening and perilous. It was averred that almost the whole cost of government was gained by taxes on raw materials and human food. It was publicly stated, without denial by those who would gladly have made the denial if they could, that the cost of the government reached the vast sum of $120,000,000, and that this sum was obtained in the following manner: $100,000,-000 were gained by taxes on seventeen articles alone, these articles comprising mainly food and raw material; that for the balance of $20,000,000 **not** less than seventeen hundred articles were taxed. The problem before the English nation was an exceedingly difficult one. But it was a problem that must be met. Something had to be done, the people could not be left to starve and die. The question of the taxation of human food became the one absorbing theme of discussion. England has always been celebrated for its various and multitudinous taxes. The conviction was taking deep root that it was a blunder and a crime, an iniquity and a shame to tax human food. In a vigorous speech delivered in Drury Lane theater, John Bright uttered these impressive words:

"What was the state of the population of this country? It was so bad that when he had been abroad he had been ashamed to acknowledge that he was an Englishman. It was said of the celebrated writer, Charles Dickens, that he had described low life so well that he must have lived in a workhouse. The reply was that he had lived in England, which was one great workhouse. The country was filled with paupers, and we were now devouring each other. In Leeds there were 40,000 persons subsisting on charity. A friend of his was then in the room who told him that in Sheffield there were no less than 12,000 paupers, and that there were as many more who were as badly off as paupers."

Concerted action in the direction of the repeal of these iniquitous taxes on the bread of the poor, seemed the only possible way out of the difficulty. We quote a passage from Justin McCarthy's "History of Our Own Times," dealing with this threatening episode in English life in the early forties :

"A movement against the Corn Laws began in London. An Anti-Corn-Law Association on a small scale was formed. Its list of members bore the names of more than twenty members of Parliament, and for a time the society had a look of vigor about it. It came to nothing, however. London has never been found an effective nursery of agitation. It is too large to have any central interest or source of action. It is too dependent socially and economically on the patronage of the higher and wealthier classes. A new centre of operations soon had to be sought, and various causes combined to make Lancashire the proper place. In the year 1838 the town of Bolton-le-Moors, in Lancashire, was the victim of a terrible commercial crisis. Thirty out of the fifty manufacturing establishments which the town contained were closed ; nearly a fourth of all the houses of business were closed and actually deserted ; and more than five thousand workmen were without homes or means of subsistence. All the intelligence and energy of Lancashire was roused. One obvious guarantee against starvation was cheap bread, and cheap bread meant of course the abolition of the Corn Laws, for these laws were constructed on the principle that it was necessary to keep bread dear. A meeting was held in Manchester to consider measures necessary to be adopted for bringing about the complete repeal of these laws. The Manchester Chamber of Commerce adopted a petition to Parliament against the Corn Laws. The Anti-Corn-Law agitation had been fairly launched.

"The real leader of the movement was Mr. Richard Cobden. Mr. Cobden was a man belonging to the yeoman class. He had received but a moderate education. His father dying while the great Free Trader was still young, Richard Cobden was taken in charge by an uncle, who had a wholesale warehouse in the City of London, and who gave him employment there. Cobden afterwards became a partner in a Manchester printed cotton factory; and he traveled occasionally on the commercial interests of this establishment. He had a great liking for travel ; but not by any means as the ordinary tourist travels ; the interest of Cobden was not in scenery, or in art, or in ruins, but in men. He studied the condition of countries with a view to the manner in which it affected the men and women of the present, and through them was likely to affect the future. On everything that he saw he turned a quick and intelligent eye ; he saw for himself and thought for himself. Wherever he went he wanted to learn something. He had in abundance that peculiar faculty which some great men of widely different stamp from him and from each other have possessed ; of which Goethe frankly boasted, and which Mirabeau had more largely than he was always willing to acknowledge ; the faculty which exacts from every one with whom its owner comes into contact some contribution to his stock of information and to his advantage. Cobden could learn something from everybody. It is doubtful whether he ever came even into momentary acquaintance with any one whom he did not compel to yield him something in the way of information. He traveled very widely for a time when traveling was more difficult work than it is at present. He made himself familiar with most of the countries of Europe, with many parts of the East, and what was then a rare accomplishment, with the United States and Canada. He did not make the familiar grand tour and then dismiss the places he had seen from his active memory. He studied them and visited many of them again to compare early with later impressions. This was in itself an education of the highest value for the career he proposed to pursue. When he was about thirty years of age he began to acquire a certain reputation as the author of pamphlets directed against some of the pet doctrines of old-fashioned statesmanship ; the balance of power in Europe; the necessity of maintaining a State Church in Ireland ; the importance of allowing no European quarrel to go on without England's intervention ; and similar dogmas. Mr. Cobden's opinions then were very much as they continued to the day of his death.   He seemed to have come to the maturity of his convictions all at once, and to have passed through no further change either of growth or of decay.   But whatever might be said then or now of the doctrines he maintained, there could be only one opinion as to the skill and force which upheld them with pen as well as tongue.   The tongue, however, was his best weapon.   If oratory were a business and not an art—that is, if its test were its success rather than its form—then it might be contended reasonably enough that Mr. Cobden was one of the greatest orators England has ever known.   Nothing could exceed the persuasiveness of his style.   His manner was simple, sweet, and earnest. It was persuasive, but it had not the sort of persuasiveness which is merely a better kind of plausibility.   It persuaded by convincing.   It was transparently sincere.

Side by side with Richard Cobden stood the eloquent John Bright.   These two were the great apostles of this humane crusade.   It will be interesting to record here the occasions on which these great Tribunes of the people first become associated in this great work.   Mr. Bright says:

"The first time I became acquainted with Mr. Cobden was in connection with the great question of education.   I went over to Manchester to call upon him and invite him to come to Rochdale to speak at a meeting about to be held in the school-room of the Baptist Chapel in West street.   I found him in his counting-house.   I told him what I wanted; his countenance lighted up with pleasure to find that others were working in the same cause.   He without hesitation agreed to come.   He came and he spoke; and though he was then so young a speaker, yet the qualities of his speech were such as remained with him so long as he was able to speak at all—clearness, logic, a conversational eloquence, a persuasiveness which, when combined with the absolute truth there was in his eye and in his countenance, became a power it was almost impossible to resist."

Still more remarkable is the description Mr. Bright has given of Cobden's first appeal to him to join in the agitation for the repeal of the Corn Laws:

"I was in Leamington, and Mr. Cobden called on me. I was then in the depths of grief—I may almost say of despair, for the light and sunshine of my house had been extinguished. All that was left on earth of my young wife, except the memory of a sainted life and a too brief happiness, was lying still and cold in the chamber above us. Mr. Cobden called on me as his friend, and addressed me, as you may suppose, with words of condolence. After a time he looked up and said: 'There are thousands and thousands of homes in England at this moment where wives and mothers and children are dying of hunger. Now when the first paroxysm of your grief is passed, I would advise you to come with me, and we will never rest until the Corn Laws are repealed.'"

Never was more earnest work done in England than by that heroic company of men who vowed that they would give no sleep to eyes and no rest to their eyelids till the taxes were removed from the bread of the poor. Addresses were delivered all over England, Ireland and Scotland. Tons of literature on the subject were distributed far and wide. For five years the work of education went on in the country, and then after three years' struggle in the Houses of Parliament the victory was won. Forced, as it has been often said, by the famine in Ireland, Sir Robert Peel boldly proposed to his cabinet to remove all the restrictions on the importation of human food. His cabinet of course refused to support him in this matter.   In November of 1845, Lord John Russell declared himself a convert to Free Trade. This moved Sir Robert Peel once more to urge his cabinet to accept the inevitable.   They were as stubborn as ever, and Sir Robert Peel resigned.   The Queen sent for Lord John Russell, but he declined the honor of forming a government.   Sir Robert Peel was recalled, and he at once proceeded to construct a cabinet favorable to the repeal of the Corn Laws.   In this cabinet Mr. Gladstone appears. He was given the position of Secretary of State for the Colonies.   In the work of repeal Mr. Gladstone became Sir Robert's right-hand man.

Mr. Gladstone was not in Parliament during these stirring times.   Next to the Premier in the Cabinet, and one of the greatest forces at work bringing about the triumph of the cause of the suffering poor, the House and the Country were deprived of his matchless eloquence in this grand battle for free and untaxed bread.   The Duke of Newcastle who was an implacable Protectionist, was resolved on opposing Mr. Gladstone should he seek re-election for Newark after accepting office in a Free Trade government.   Mr. Gladstone did not contest the borough and remained without a seat in Parliament till the general election of 1847.

Mr. Gladstone had become a thorough Cobdenite in the best sense of the term.   His reverence and regard for the man was deep and intense.   Speaking of him he said: "I do not know that there is in any period a man whose public career and life were nobler or more admirable.   Of course I except Washington.   Washington, to my mind, is the purest figure in history."

On the morning of the 16th of May, 1846, at half past four o'clock in the morning, the Bill for the repeal of the Corn Laws was passed by a majority of ninety-eight.   In the closing scene of this great conflict Mr. Disraeli took part, and poured that memorable tirade of bitterness against

Sir Robert Peel.   He said that Sir Robert Peel throughout his political life had traded on the intelligence of others; that his career was a great appropriation clause; that he was the burglar of other men's intellects; that in our whole history there was no statesman who had committed so much petty larceny on so great a scale *   *   *   *   He had bought his party on the cheapest and had sold it on the dearest terms.

The merciless critic was answered by Lord John Russell in that terse, well remembered phrase in which he pointed out that Mr. Disraeli was much happier in invective than in argument, and that his speech had little relation to the bill before the house.

Sir Robert Peel resigned.   Mr. Cobden said in his own trenchant, homely eloquence, "He has lost office, but he has gained a country."   The closing words of Sir Robert Peel on retiring from office deserve to be held in sacred remembrance.   After a generous testimony to the part Mr. Cobden had played in the battle for untaxed bread, Sir Robert concludes:

"I shall surrender forever, severely censured, I fear, by many honorable gentlemen who from no interested motive, have adhered to the principles of protection as important to the welfare and interest of the country; I shall leave a name execrated by every monopolist who from less honorable motives maintained protection for his own individual benefit, but it may be that I shall leave a name sometimes remembered with expressions of good will in those places which were the abodes of men whose lot it is to labor, and to earn their daily bread by the sweat of their brow—a name remembered with expressions of good will, when they shall recreate their exhausted strength with abundant and untaxed food, the sweeter because it is no longer leavened by a sense of injustice."

LORD HARTINGTON: DUKE OF DEVONSHIRE.
SUCCESSOR OF MR. GLADSTONE AS LEADER OF THE LIBERAL PARTY.

MR. GLADSTONE ADDRESSING HIS CABINET.

CHAPTER XV.

THE BRITISH HOUSE OF COMMONS—A SKETCH.

When any of the four pillars of government are mainly shaken, or weakened—which are religion, justice, counsel and treasure—men had better pray for fair weather —*Lord Bacon.*

Neither Montaigne in writing his essays, nor Descartes in building new worlds, nor Burnet in framing an antediluvian earth, no, nor Newton in discovering and establishing the true laws of nature on experiment and a sublime geometry, felt more intellectual joys than he feels who is a real patriot, who bends all the force of his understanding, and directs all his thoughts and actions, to the good of his country.—*Lord Bolingbroke.*

We assemble parliaments and councils to have the benefit of their collected wisdom; but we necessarily have, at the same time, the inconveniences of their collected passions, prejudices and private interests. By the help of these, artful men overpower their wisdom, and dupe its possessors; and if we may judge by the acts, arrets, and edicts, all the world over, for regulating commerce, an assembly of great men is an assembly of the greatest fools upon earth.—*Benjamin Franklin.*

If you should ask a true-born Englishman where you could find the center of civilization—the very heart of the world—he would instantly unroll a map of England, and without a word point you to the City of London. If further bent on the acquisition of useful knowledge you should ask where you would be likely to find the greatest deliberative assembly in the world, the same complacent gentleman would be sure to answer: "Why in the British House of Commons, of course!" There is so much truth in both these answers that they may be accepted without discussion, and if there be any doubters they will not be found among those who know much of London, or who have been frequent visitors to the House of Commons.

From the far-away days of the old Saxon "Wittenage-mote" down to these later days in which—

> Freedom slowly broadens down
> From precedent to precedent.

the history of the British Parliament, or company of "parlers" or "talkers," is most interesting and instructive. The establishment of the House of Commons in the days of the royal Edwards was practically the recognition of the just right of the people to have a share in their own government. The number of the members of the House of Commons varied in various reigns. In the days of Edward III. they numbered 250. In the reign of Henry VIII. they reached 300. At the dawn of this century the number was fixed at 658, where it now stands.

Some of the most brilliant pages in the history of the British House of Commons were written in the early years of the seventeenth century, in the reigns of James I. and of his son, the hapless Charles. As Carlyle says, the "Iliad" of that age has not yet been written or sung. The conflict of the Commons with the tyranny of the Star Chamber and the High Commission Court is a study for all lovers of freedom for all coming years. It was not so much in the triumphs of Long Marston Moor, of Naseby, of Dunbar, or Worcester, that freedom had occasion to rejoice ; as in the passage of the memorable "Bill of Rights" by the persistence of the outraged Commoners in the third Parliament of Charles I. That bill ranks with such great state documents as Magna Charta, as the Declaration of Independence, and the Proclamation of Emancipation. And even we, in this great free land, owe more than we can ever tell to that Bill of Rights, which won liberty for the world when the seventeenth century was in its early years. That bill was a dream of freedom, which America has interpreted and translated into fact.

The House of Commons in Westminster is one of the most mixed of all public buildings. It seems least of all fitted for the purpose to which it is devoted. Of course there is a great deal of beauty about the House of Parliament. The Victoria Tower, overlooking the Thames, a statelier pile than Giotto's Campanile in Florence, has been called "a dream of architecture." This may all be true. I have no doubt architecture has its dreams. But architecture can have nightmare as well as dreams, or the Houses of Parliament would not be what they are.

The House of Commons is a large building in the form of a parallelogram, with graded benches on either side running the whole length of the hall. At one end is the Speaker's chair, a dark, heavy sort of an affair, that looks a good deal like a bishop's throne that has stolen out of church to play hide and seek and got lost. In front of the chair is a very large table at which sit "three learned clerks," duly wigged and gowned. There are a goodly number of books of reference on the table ; also two large dispatch boxes, one for the leader of the government and one for the leader of the opposition. On the front of the table lies the gorgeous " mace," or " fool's bauble," as Cromwell irreverently called it. The party in power sits at the right hand of the Speaker, the party in opposition on the left. Independent members—"mugwumps," as they may be justly described—sit lower down the House, or " below the gangway." The galleries on the right and left of the Speaker are reserved for noble lords. The lower gallery in front of the Speaker is known as the Speaker's gallery, above which is the smallest gallery of all, where the people of England gather, at least a few of them, whenever they get a chance. Behind the Speaker is another small gallery reserved for ladies. It is screened off from public gaze by a very beautiful gilded lattice work, and has generally been spoken of somewhat rudely as "the ladies' cage."

What a battle field for freedom, for civil and religious liberty this house has been through many generations! And never more so than in the mid-years of this century, when Disraeli and Gladstone and Bright were in all their glory. The sagacious Hebrew, with his Asiatic mysteries, worthy of the devotees of modern Theosophy, has passed away. The silver trumpet of John Bright, the great tribune of the English people, is forever silent. And now Gladstone's fiery eloquence is hushed. He, too, has entered the "silent land." When these three men were in all their prime there was beautiful fighting all along the line. It would be exceedingly difficult to find three more dissimilar men, who yet seemed to be somehow the complement of each other, and so formed a wonderful combination. The spirits of Machiavelli, of Milton, and Cromwell dwelt in these men, and each in his turn did masterly work. The Sphinx of Egypt was not more silent and mystical than Disraeli, when he chose the silent mood. I have often seen him sit with folded arms, and eye-glass in eye, for the space of half an hour, as immovable as though he was stone dead. If silence was ever golden, Disraeli knew its worth. Some said the Prince of the Powers of the air was not more subtle, and in many a campaign speech was applied to him Tennyson's line—

> Only the devil knows what he means.

And yet it cannot be denied that Disraeli did his country grand service. He made the proud—and some thought impertinent—boast that he had "educated his party." But there was truth at the bottom of the boast, and it was good for the party and for the country that this education had taken place.

William Ewart Gladstone was the exact opposite of his great opponent. Where Disraeli was mystical Gladstone was transparent. There was ever the ring of the profoundest sincerity in all he said. He seemed to bring into the contentions and conflicts of political life the mingled atmosphere of the college and the cloister. Life was sacred and earnest, marching to stately music, such as Milton sung. There was no affectation of goodness in Mr. Gladstone. It was all real. Even Disraeli on one occasion paid him the rare compliment of saying: "The right honorable gentleman at the head of Her Majesty's government has not one redeeming *vice*."

The typical Englishman, John Bright, or, as he was called, "The Noblest Roman of Them All," completed a strange trinity of great men. He was the plain, blunt man who talked right on, in simple language, now beautiful, now pathetic, now humorous, and now impassioned. John Bright's organ had a host of stops, and he knew exactly when to pull them out. A member of the Society of Friends, Quaker John, like George Fox, of old, he loved a fight, and his good sword was heard in clanging blows on the shields of his compeers as distinctly as on those of his foes. An anticipated speech from any of these men was enough to crowd the house, and every conceivable subterfuge in any way consistent with truth and honor was resorted to, to beg, buy, borrow or steal a way into the speaker's or the stranger's gallery. Such occasions are burnt in upon the memory. On one occasion when Mr. Gladstone was at the helm of the state, it was deemed necessary to suspend the habeas corpus act in Ireland. A special meeting of Parliament was called for Saturday—a most unusual course.

The house was crowded. Irish members being there in great numbers. Mr. Gladstone announced the purpose of the government, and went into a narrative of sad occurrences just communicated by the Chief Secretary for Ireland, showing the need of immediate action. John Bright was in his seat below the gangway, manifesting by certain signs well known to his friends—such as twitchings at his neck-cloth and movings about on the bench—a more than common interest in the occasion. The Bill was about to pass, more as a matter of form than anything else, giving the executive authority to repress any threatened uprisings—when suddenly cries were heard all over the house :

"Bright! Bright! Bright!"

A moment before there had been the usual indication, "Divide! Divide! Divide!" signifying readiness to vote. But now the cry was for Bright, especially from the Irish members, most of whom sat below the gangway.

Mr. Bright arose and apologizing to the Irish members, said it was not his purpose to oppose the bill before the House, indeed he intended to vote for it, but he had risen to ask if "restraint of liberty" was the best and only cure the government had to offer for Ireland's wrongs. He wanted to know how it was that the Irishman got on well enough and was made much of and found to be useful everywhere except in his own country. Peal after peal of applause broke forth from all quarters of the House, and from Tory and Liberal and Radical came ringing cheers—not all in sympathy with his sentiments, but all in bonds to spell of his masterly oratory—as the grand old champion of righteousness rang out his plea for Ireland.

"What Ireland needs is justice. The only cure for her wounds is the balm of righteousness. If I had my way I would do justice to Ireland, and then I would open the prison doors and let every political prisoner go free and trust to righteousness for the issues!"

Then pointing his finger to Disraeli, he asked if he was not willing to forego all party spirit for the sake of doing a great and lasting good, not to Ireland only, but to the whole empire and the world. Cheer followed cheer, and then turning squarely around to the Treasury bench, he asked his right honorable friends if they had no better things to offer for Ireland, and then, tremulous with passionate fervor, added: "Is this task beyond your power? If so, would it not become you to come down from your high places and learn the business of statesmanship before you assume to discharge its functions?" John Bright sat down, there was silence for a moment, and Mr. Gladstone rose pale and agitated.

He declared he had never heard Mr. Bright exercise his great powers with such consummate skill. He confessed that England had blundered over Ireland generation after generation, and only pleaded that he was as sincere as the honorable member for Birmingham in his desire to heal the sorrows of the Emerald. This was one of Mr. Bright's impromptu speeches. It was a crystal stream suddenly bursting from an exhaustless fountain. Many said it was one of the greatest speeches of his life. I am bold enough to express the opinion that that night was an epoch; that that speech woke up Mr. Gladstone and helped the cause of Ireland to a position where it could successfully challenge the attention of all thoughtful men.

It was a privilege to be in the House of Commons any time during the debate on the disestablishment and disendowment of the Irish church. Disraeli was, as he said, on the side of the angels, and stood firmly for the maintenance of the existing state of things. And he never was over burdened with scruples as to the methods. About this time I remember an amusing scene. Disraeli had been speaking for nearly an hour ; Gladstone was lying with his head well back on the front Treasury bench, one would think, nearly asleep. Disraeli was trying to make the worse appear the better reason, as was his frequent custom. All in a moment Mr. Gladstone sprang to his feet and seized his hat, completely smashing it down out of all shape on the dispatch box in his excitement. The house roared with amazement

> "And even the ranks of Tuscany,
> Could scarce forbear to cheer."

"I rise to a point of order," said Mr. Gladstone, "the right honorable gentleman knows perfectly well that in the statement he has just made he is misleading this House and the country at large, and I call the attention of the House and of the country to a careful consideration of the statement." He then sat down. He had utterly ruined a good silk hat, but then he had gained his point, and punctured William Disraeli's beautiful bubble.

After the tumult had subsided Disraeli readjusted his eye-glasses, and, with a most profound bow, said, smiling sardonically as he spoke: "Mr. Speaker, I congratulate myself that there is a substantial piece of furniture between my right honorable friend and myself."

It was five o'clock on a beautiful morning when the great battle concerning the Irish Church came to an end. Mr. Disreali began to speak about 1:30 o'clock. And his speech, the speech of a forlorn hope, was one of the most wonderful efforts of his brilliant career. It was nearly 4 o'clock when Gladstone rose to close the debate. He was worn, feeble, but he rose to the occasion, and as the growing day broke gently through the stained windows he seized the beautiful omen, "Time is on our side!" he said, "the night has passed, the day is breaking!" And then, with an impassioned peroration he closed that memorable debate which freed Ireland from her religious inequalities.

Disraeli retired to the House of Lords, but he made the name of Disraeli so great that the title "Beaconsfield" will not unlikely fade away. Not long before his death he paid a last visit to the House of Commons. It was quite pathetic to mark the veteran warrior looking down from the peers' gallery on the scene of his former conflicts.

In these memories of the House of Commons it would be unpardonable to forget the bold stand John Bright took as a friend of America, while noble lords and brainless wits were looking on; while America was bleeding at every pore, in their simpering idiocy prophesying that "the American bubble was going to burst," John Bright dared to stand almost alone to plead the cause of the Union. He spoke such words of burning enthusiasm against the departure of the Alabama from Laird's shipyard, that his life was threatened by many who had only threats for arguments. When Roebuck wanted to have the South recognized, John Bright answered him in such words that Roebuck, who had won the unenviable name of "Tearem," was silenced, and silenced forever. A recent visit to the House of Commons revealed the awful ravages of time. What with the changes of time and caprices of constituencies it seemed as if, with but a few exceptions, Charles Lamb's sad line was most appropriate—

"All are gone, the old familiar faces."

CHAPTER XVI.

> Yet I doubt not through the ages,
>   One increasing purpose runs,
> And the thoughts of men are widened
>   With the process of the suns.
> *—Lord Tennyson.*

> We do not serve the dead—the past is past,
> God lives, and lifts his glorious morning up
> Before the eyes of men awake.
> *—Elizabeth Barrett Browning.*

> The less government we have the better—the fewer laws, and the less confided power. The antidote to this abuse of formal government is, the influence of private character, the growth of the individual.*—R. W. Emerson.*

On the 23d of July, 1847, the Queen dissolved Parliament in person. The elections that followed were very considerably influenced by ecclesiastical questions, the Maynooth Grant especially being a considerable factor in the agitation of the time. Many of Mr. Gladstone's friends urged him to stand for the honored seat of the University of Oxford, and truth to tell, he was not without some ambition to represent his beloved *alma mater* in the councils of the nation. In the memorable year 1847 he appeared as a candidate for the University of Oxford.

The seat of Sir R. H. Inglis was regarded as perfectly safe. The real fight was between Mr. Round and Mr. Gladstone. Mr. Round was a member of the ultra Protestant and Tory school. To conserve the existing condition of things, and to stand four-square in bold defense against any innovations, even should they assume the vaunted titles of necessary reforms, was Mr. Round's fixed policy.

Mr. Gladstone was too magnanimous to sail for a moment under false colors. He had struggled for many years for the exclusive support of the national religion by the state, but he had struggled in vain. Voluntaryism was gaining ground on every hand. The champion of the church finally confessed that the time was against him.

In an address to the electors of Oxford, referring to this matter, Mr. Gladstone said :

"I found that scarcely a year passed without the adoption of some fresh measure involving the national recognition and the national support of various forms of religion, and in particular that a recent and fresh provision has been made for the propagation from a public chair of Arian or Socinian doctrines. The question remaining for me was, whether aware of the opposition of the English people, I should set down as equal to nothing, in a matter primarily connected not with our own but with their priesthood, the wishes of the people of Ireland; and whether I should avail myself of the popular feeling in regard to the Roman Catholics for the purpose of enforcing against them a system which we had ceased by common consent to enforce against Arians—a system above all, of which I must say that it never can be conformable to policy, to justice, or even to decency, when it has become avowedly partial and one-sided in its application."

This frank statement antagonized many of the Oxford voters who were somewhat inclined to vote for Mr. Gladstone, and it certainly strengthened the hands of those who were bent on his defeat. The press generally approved of Mr. Gladstone's position and spoke warmly of his talents and industry. They regarded him still as a true and valiant friend of the church, but hailed the advance he had made in ceasing to call upon the Legislature to ignore all forms of religion but those by law established, or which were exactly coincident with his own form of faith. The *Times* said: "His election, unlike that of Mr. Round, while it sends an important member to the House of Commons, will certainly be creditable, and may be valuable to the university; and we heartily hope that no negligence or hesitation among his supporters may impede his success. The candidate for Oxford had been marching along a path of liberal views and broadening sentiments since fifteen years ago he entered the House of Commons, member fo· Newark, and the rising hope of the Tory party."

The election was watched with great interest not only by those deeply concerned about church matters, but far and near it was felt, that Mr. Gladstone was worthy of the honor he asked, and that it would be a very good thing for Oxford that she should have Mr. Gladstone for her representative. The nomination took place on the 29th of July, 1847. The ceremony of nomination having been completed, the voting commenced in the Convocation-house of the University. The place was densely crowded. Mr. Gladstone's friends rallied from far and near. At the close of the poll the members stood:

Inglis,	1,700
Gladstone,	997
Rounds,	824

It was the most enthusiastic election Oxford had ever known, and there were a larger number of votes cast than had ever been cast before.

At this election, to the amazement of many thoughtful people, Baron Rothschild was elected for the City of London. That he should have been elected at all was a surprise, but much more, that he should be elected for so important a seat as the City of London. There was nothing illegal in the election of a Jew, but the difficulty was, that when elected, the statutory declarations required of him virtually precluded him from taking his seat in the House of Commons.

Soon after the meeting of Parliament with a view to overcoming this difficulty, Lord John Russell proposed a resolution, which affirmed the eligibility of Jews to all functions and offices to which Roman Catholics were admissible by law. Sir R. H. Inglis, the senior member of the University of Oxford, bitterly opposed the motion, but it was supported with equal ardor by Mr. Gladstone who asked whether there were any grounds for the disqualification of the Jews which distinguished them from any other class in the community.

"With regard to the stand now made for a Christian Parliament," said Mr. Gladstone, "the present measure did not make a severance between politics and religion; it only amounted to a declaration that there was no necessity for excluding a Jew, as such, from an assembly in which every man felt sure that a vast and overwhelming majority of its members would always be Christian. It is said that by admitting a few Jews they would un-Christianize Parliament; that was true in word, but not in substance. He had no doubt that the majority of the members who composed it would always perform their obligations on the true faith of a Christian. It was too late to say that the measure was un-Christian, and that it would call down the vengeance of heaven. When he opposed the last law for the removal of Jewish disabilities, he forsaw that if we gave the Jew municipal, magisterial, and executive functions, we could not refuse him legislative functions any longer. The Jew was refused entrance into that House because he would then be a maker of the laws; but who made the maker of the law? The constituencies; and into these constituencies we had admitted the Jews. Now, were the constituencies Christian constituencies? If they were, was it probable that the Parliament would cease to be a Christian Parliament?"

The year 1848 was memorable as a year of unrest and agitation, all Europe was perturbed, the French had a revolution in hand, and especially in England the Chartist movement met its Waterloo. This subject cannot be dismissed in a paragraph. Chartism had a much firmer hold on the hearts of the people than was generally understood. Unwise headstrong leaders postponed a great cause as they had done again and again. When they clamored that there should be an entire cessation of work till the Charter was law, they only succeeded in setting back the sunbeams on the dial of time. The late M. M. Trumball gave a most exhaustive essay on the whole question of English Chartism as viewed from an American stand point from which we quote freely. He says:

The People's Charter was a code of principles drawn up in the form of an Act of Parliament, with a long preamble. It is tedious reading, but it may be easily condensed into a demand for the American representative system, although the abolition of monarchy and aristocracy was postponed to a more convenient season. Then the Kings and the Lords were to be quietly supplanted by a President and a Senate. The original draft of the Charter contained a demand for woman suffrage; but as radical sentiment in England was not then quite radical enough for that, it was thought expedient to throw the women overboard, because "they loaded the Charter down." The six points of the Charter were—1. Universal Suffrage. 2. Vote by Ballot. 3. Annual Parliaments. 4. Equal Electoral Districts. 5. No Property Qualification for Members of Parliament. 6. Payment of Members. The name, "The People's Charter," was given to it by O'Connell, who said that the man who was not a Chartist "was either a knave profiting by misrule, or a fool upon whom reason and argument could make no impression." This title also distinguished it from Magna Charta, the charter of the barons and middle classes. In Magna Charta the serfs, the bulk of the English laborers, were not considered as having any rights which other people were bound to respect. The phrase *Nullus liber homo* excluded them from the benefits of the Great Charter.

The People's Charter was a political remedy for social evils, therefore barren. It could not cure hunger, although the Chartists thought it could. The impulse and energy of Chartism came from social injustice, and this could only be removed by social reformation and improvement. The Chartists thought that American abundance came from the Constitution of the United States, and not from the opulent material resources of this imperial domain.

Chartism as an organized menace to the government, was decisively overthrown on April 10, 1848, in a downpour of rain, in a battle of its own seeking, and on a field of its own choice. In February the French revolution was accomplished. This inflamed the imagination of the Chartists and stimulated them to attempt a similar achievement. The French revolution literally forced the hand of the Chartist leaders. They must now crystallize their talk into action or abdicate. Accordingly they appointed the revolution for the 10th of April. To that end a "National Convention," composed of delegates chosen by the various Chartist organizations of Great Britain, was to meet in London as a revolutionary parliament, and direct the campaign. At the meetings where those delegates were elected, the most violent and Jacobinical speeches were made. At Nottingham, where George Julian Harney was chosen delegate, it was resolved that the Chartists "would no longer speak to Parliament in black and white. They would now speak by bayonets." This was the tone and character of all the speeches, and many martial songs were sung to the tune of the Marseillaise.

The "National Convention" met in London and their plan of revolution had as much resemblance to the French method as a Sunday-school picnic has to the battle of Get tysburg. The strategy and tactics were ineffective and weak. A petition containing five million signatures was to be carried to the House of Commons on a wagon drawn by eight stout horses and escorted by half a million men. Another half a million, not in the ranks, were to render outside assistance. The ostensible reason for this vast numerical display was merely an imposing procession of citizens to present a petition to Parliament, but the genuine purpose was to overawe the legislature and the government. The various divisions were to meet in their respective localities and march to Kennington Common. There they were to be formed into one vast army and march to the House of Commons. By this brilliant manœuvre the Chartists put the river Thames between themselves and their objective point, leaving the bridges in possession of the enemy. Had all the rest of the strategy been skilfully carried out, this blunder would have been fatal to the enterprise.

The challenge of the Chartists was at once accepted by the government. The cabinet met and sent for the Duke of Wellington. He was then seventy-nine years old, deaf, rickety and shrunken to about one hundred and ten pounds; but the iron will had not grown rusty, nor was his martial nerve impaired. He was eager to command, and his vanity rejoiced that he had not been passed over for some younger man. He promised to protect the government and defend London against the Chartists. His tactics and strategy were as strong as those of the Chartists were weak. He ordered all the troops to London that could possibly be spared; he fortified the Tower, the Bank of England and all the public buildings; he directed that all shops and places of business be closed on the 10th of April. Three hundred thousand special constables were sworn in, of whom Napoleon III was one. The government, feeling perfectly secure, now assumed the offensive, and on the 9th of April a proclamation was issued prohibiting the procession appointed for the following day.

As soon as the government proclamation appeared, Fergus O'Connor, Member of Parliament for Nottingham, Commander-in-Chief of the Chartists, hoisted the white flag and surrendered. He appeared next morning in the "National Convention" and implored that the whole programme be abandoned. He was overruled by the Convention and compelled to take his seat in the "Triumphial" car. As for the rank and file, most of them weakened when they read the proclamation and saw the preparations made by the government. Some of the divisions, however, assembled at the rendezvous appointed for them, and marched through the city to Kennington. They were not molested by the soldiers or police, but as soon as they had crossed the river, the Duke of Wellington took possession of the bridges and commanded all the approaches to the city with his cannon. An officer was then sent to Kennington to inform the commander of the Chartist army that the procession would not be allowed to cross the bridges, and the information was accompanied by an order for the meeting to disperse. Mr. O'Connor promptly assured the officer that the order would be obeyed. There was a good deal of passionate oratory indulged in by some of the others in the shape of protest against the "arbitrary" order of the government, and Ernest Jones, the most chivalrous of the Chartist leaders, seeing the strategical blunder, exclaimed with bitterness and vexation: "We are on the wrong side of the river; we can do nothing." There were not more than twenty-five thousand men there altogether, and they sullenly melted away. Chartism as a physical force was at an end in England. That evening the monster petition was carted over to the House of Commons like ignominious freight, and Mr. O'Connor presented it amid a tumult of laughter and jeers from every part of the House. It is interesting to note in this connection that many remarkable men were sworn in as special constables, to keep the peace

on this memorable occasion, among whom were Prince Louis
Napoleon, who was then residing in London, the Duke of
Norfolk, Edward Stanley, Earl of Derby, and William
Ewart Gladstone.

Although nobody was killed or wounded at the battle of
Kennington, the victory obtained by the Duke of Wellington, on the 10th of April, was as decisive in its way as the
victory at Waterloo. It put an end to that peculiar social
war which for ten years the Chartists had waged in England. As the victory at Waterloo had eliminated Bona-
partism as a physical power from the politics of Europe, so
the battle of Kennington eliminated Chartism as a physical
force from the politics of England. There was plenty of
sarcasm thrown at the Duke of Wellington, for the tremendous preparations he had made against twenty-five
thousand unarmed working men holding an amiable pic-nic
at Kennington Common; but he answered that he had made
his dispositions to meet what the Chartists intended to do,
not what they actually did. They had proclaimed a revolutionary purpose and he had complimented them by believing what they said.

Many of the social problems now exciting the American
people were first propounded by the Chartists. Even the
"single-tax" and land-confiscation theory, revived by
Mr. Henry George, is of Chartist origin. Indeed, the
ideas, arguments, and some of the phraseology of "Progress
and Poverty" bewilder us in the state papers of the Chartists. A Chartist petition drawn up by Lovett, and presented to Parliament in 1838, calls for such legislation as will
compel the owners of land *"to defray all the expenses of the
state,* and Parliament is informed that "*land was bestowed by
the bountiful Creator upon all his children.*" The petition
denied the right of private ownership of land, and repu-
diated the title of landowners to "*what they call their
property.*" Forty years later, Mr. George reproduces the

argument and doctrine of that petition, and speaks contemptuously of the title of landowners in America to *"what they are pleased to call their land."* William Lovett appears to have had a patent on the "single-tax" contrivance nearly fifty years ahead of Mr. Henry George.

As a matter of fact the best features of the Charter have become part of the law of England, brought about, albeit, by men and methods little dreamed of by the early Chartists.

The condition of affairs excited the sarcasm of Mr. Disraeli, who jeered at the government, which he described as "a man smoking a cigar on a barrel of gunpowder." Ever loyal to his chief, Mr. Gladstone, by a series of incontrovertible statistics, demonstrated the complete success of Sir Robert Peel's policy, and pleaded for the confidence of the country.

"I am sure," said Mr. Gladstone, "that this House of Commons will prove itself to be worthy of the Parliaments which preceded it, worthy of the Sovereign which it has been called to advise, and worthy of the people which it has been chosen to represent, by sustaining this nation, and enabling it to stand firm in the midst of the convulsions that shake European society, by doing all that pertains to us for the purpose of maintaining social order, the stability of trade, and the means of public employment; and by discharging our consciences, on our own part, under the difficult circumstances of the crisis, in the perfect trust that if we set a good example to the nation, for whose interests we are appointed to consult, they too, will stand firm as they have done in other times of almost desperate emergency; and that through their good sense, their moderation, and their attachment to the institutions of the country, we shall see these institutions still exist, a blessing and a benefit to posterity, whatever alarms and whatever misfortunes may unfortunately befall other portions of civilized Europe."

Later on in this session Lord John Russell having moved that the House of Commons resolve itself into a committee on the oaths to be taken by members of the two Houses of Parliament, with a view to further relief upon this subject, Mr. Gladstone rose and said that he should not shrink from stating his opinion thereon. He was deliberately convinced that the civil and political claims of the Jew to the discharge of civil and political duties, ought not, in justice, to be barred, and could not beneficially be barred because of a difference in religion. But there were sufficient grounds for going into committee independent of this main purpose. Oaths, when taken by large masses of men, and under associations not very favorable to solemn religious feelings, had a tendency to degenerate into formalism. Nor could he say that the present oaths had no words in them which could not with advantage be omitted. At the same time he was glad that the noble lord had retained the words "on the true faith of a Christian" in respect to all Christian members of that House. The measure now brought forward should have his support at every stage.

Later on in this session he made important speeches on the navigation laws, and subsequently on a motion for going into committee of supply, introduced the Canadian difficulties by calling attention to certain points of the Indemnity Bill. This address created very considerable influence on the minds of Canadians.

The sky of 1850 was darkened with sorrow that entered into Mr Gladstone's very soul. Early in the year he lost a little daughter. She had lived long enough to become exceedingly precious, and when her young spirit passed away it left a void that was very hard to fill. Mr. Gladstone was a man of ardent affections and impassioned friendships. Those who were bound to him by ties of earthly kindredship were very dear, and hardly less dear were those he called by the endearing name of friend.

In this same year, he lost in another, and to him more poignant sense, two of the most valued friends of his early life. Mr. J. R. Hope-Scott and Archdeacon Henry Manning, afterwards Cardinal, who joined the Church of Rome. They were the godfathers of his eldest son, and in those days a man was in the habit of selecting his dearest and most cherished friends to discharge the functions of this sacred office. The secession of these honored friends from the church of England to the church of Rome left their mutual esteem unimpaired, still it opened an awful gulf between them. They could never be the same to each other again. Mr. Gladstone wrote a letter to Mr. Hope-Scott, a perusal of which will serve to show the intensely sensitive spiritual character of the writer, and the depth and sincerity of his regrets. The realm of Mr. Gladstone's esteem was very near to the kingdom of love. He writes thus:

"Separated we are, but I hope and think not yet estranged. Were I more estranged I should bear the separation better. If estrangement is to come I know not, but it will only be I think, from causes the operation of which is still in its infancy—causes not affecting me. Why should I be estranged from you? I honor you even in what I think you err; why, then, should my feelings to you alter in anything else? It seems to me as though in these fearful times, events were more and more growing too large for our puny grasp, and that we should the more look for and trust the divine purpose in them, when we find they have wholly passed beyond the reach and measure of our own. 'The Lord is in His holy temple; let all the earth keep silence before Him.' The very afflictions of the present are a sign of joy to follow. Thy kingdom come, Thy will be done, is still our prayer in common—the same prayer in the same sense, and a prayer which absorbs every other. That is for the future. For the present we have to endure, trust, and to pray that each day may bring its strength with its burden, and its lamp for its gloom."

How matured that affection was as the swift-rolling years went on we may judge from a single paragraph written long years afterward. In the year 1873, Mrs. Maxwell Scott of Abbotsford asked Mr. Gladstone if he would send her some recollections of her father. He responded in the most generous manner, and closed his account of his friend in these beautiful and impressive words:

"If I have traversed some of the ground in sadness, I now turn to the present thought of his light and peace and progress, and may they be his more and more abundantly, in that world where the shadows that our sins and follies cast, no longer darken the aspect and glory of the truth; and may God ever bless you, the daughter of my friend."

On the 19th of February, 1850, Mr. Disraeli moved for a committee of the whole House to consider such a revision of the Poor Laws of the United Kingdom, as might mitigate the distress of the agricultural classes. Sir James Graham strongly opposed the motion, but Mr. Gladstone heartily supported it. He said that the condition of the farming class and of the agriculturial laborers in a large portion of England, to say nothing of Ireland, was such as to demand the careful attention and consideration of the House.

Twice during this session Mr. Gladstone addressed the House on questions connected with slavery. But the most important debate of the session arose out of the affairs of Greece. Mr. G. Barnett Smith says:

"The Greek government having refused to afford compensation in response to certain demands which the English government had made on account of the claims of specified British subjects, Admiral Sir William Parker was directed to proceed to Athens for the purpose of obtaining satisfaction. Failing in this the Admiral blockaded the Piræus. The news of this somewhat high-handed proceeding produced dissatisfaction in certain quarters in England, the policy being condemned as unworthy of the dignity and discreditable to the reputation of a power like Great Britain. The debates in both Houses initiated upon this Greek question took a wider scope than the facts just enumerated, and eventually included our relations with France. The stability of the Whig administration depended upon the result of the discussions. Lord Palmerston, whose policy as Foreign Minister was thus assailed, before the great debate in the House of Commons came on, tendered an explanation of the circumstances attending the withdrawal of the French minister from London, and related the proceedings which had taken place on the part of the representatives of both governments, alleging also his strong desire to conciliate the French government and to restore an amicable understanding between the two countries. In the House of Lords, upon a resolution moved by Lord Stanley, the government found themselves in a minority of thirty-seven. This gave the impending debate in the Commons additional importance, the fall of the ministry following as a natural consequence, unless the lower house should reverse the condemnation pronounced by the upper. Mr. Roebuck—much to the surprise of many—came to the defense of the government, by proposing the following motion : ‘That the principles which have hitherto regulated the foreign policy of Her Majesty’s government are such as are required to preserve untarnished the honor and dignity of this country, and in times of unexampled difficulty, the best calculated to maintain peace between England and the various nations of the world.’ The debate commenced on the 24th of June and extended over four nights. It was marked on both sides of the House by speeches of unusual oratorical excellence and brilliancy. Sir Robert Peel delivered a powerful speech against the ministers, and one memorable not only for its eloquence but also from the melancholy fact that it was the last speech he was fated to deliver before that assembly, in whose midst he had so long been a conspicuous figure. Lord Palmerston energetically defended his policy in a speech of nearly five hours' duration. At its close he challenged the verdict of the House whether the foreign policy of her Majesty's ministers had been proper and fitting, and whether, as a subject of ancient Rome could hold himself free from indignity by saying *Civis Romanus sum*, a British subject in a foreign country should not be protected by the vigilant eye and strong arm of the government against injustice and wrong.

Mr. Gladstone's speech on the occasion was one of those fine efforts that will never be forgotten by those who heard it. We quote that memorable passage in which the rising statesman entranced his hearers by his reply to Lord Palmerston's allusion to the Roman citizen :

'Sir, great as is the influence and power of Britain, she cannot afford to follow, for any length of time, a self-isolating policy. It would be a contravention of the law of nature and of God, if it were possible for any single nation of Christendom to emancipate itself from the obligations which bind all other nations, and to arrogate. in the face of mankind, a position of peculiar privilege. And now I will grapple with the noble lord on the ground which he selected for himself, in the most tri·mphant portion of his speech, by his reference to those emphatic words, *Civis Romanus sum*. He vaunted, amidst the cheers of his supporters, that under his administration an Englishman should be, throughout the world, what the citizen of Rome had been. What then, sir, was a Roman citizen ? He was the member of a privileged caste ; he belonged to a conquering race, to a nation that held all others bound down by a strong arm of power. For him there was to be an exceptional system of law ; for him principles were to be asserted, and by him rights were to be enjoyed, that were denied to the rest of the world. Is such, then the view of the noble lord as to the relation which is to subsist between England and other countries ? Does he make the claim for us that we are to be uplifted upon a platform high above the standing-ground of all other nations ? It is, indeed, too clear, not only from the expressions but from the whole tone of the speech of the noble viscount, that too much of this notion is lurking in his mind ; that he adopts, in part, that vain conception that we, forsooth, have a mission to be the censors of vice and folly, of abuse and imperfection, among the other countries of the world ;

that we are to be the universal schoolmasters, and that all those who hesitate to recognize our office, can be governed only by prejudice or personal animosity, and should have the blind war of diplomacy forthwith declared against them. And certainly, if the business of a Foreign Secretary were to carry on diplomatic wars, all must admit that the noble lord is a master in the discharge of his functions. What, sir, ought a Foreign Secretary to be? Is he to be like some gallant knight at a tournament of old, pricking forth into the lists, armed at all points, confiding in his sinews and his skill, challenging all comers for the sake of honor, and having no other duty than to lay as many as possible of his adversaries sprawling in the dust? If such is the idea of a good Foreign Secretary, I, for one, would vote to the noble lord his present appointment for his life. But, sir, I do not understand the duty of a Secretary for Foreign Affairs to be of such a character. I understand it to be his duty to conciliate peace with dignity. I think it to be the very first of all his duties studiously to observe, and to exalt in honor among mankind, that great code of principles which is termed the law of nations, which the honorable and learned member for Sheffield has found, indeed, to be very vague in its nature, and greatly dependent on the discretion of each particular country, but in which I find, on the contrary, a great and noble monument of human wisdom, founded on the combined dictates of reason and experience—a precious inheritance bequeathed to us by the generations that have gone before us, and a firm foundation on which we must take care to build whatever it may be our part to add to their acquisitions, if, indeed, we wish to maintain and to consolidate the brotherhood of nations, and to promote the peace and welfare of the world.

'Sir, I say the policy of the noble lord tends to encourage and confirm in us that which is our besetting fault and weakness, both as a nation and as individuals. Let an Englishman travel where he will as a private person, he is found in general to be upright, high-minded, brave, liberal, and true; but with all this, foreigners are too often sensible of something that galls them in his presence, and I apprehend it is because he has too great a tendency to self-esteem—too little disposition to regard the feelings, the habits, and the ideas of others. Sir, I find this characteristic too plainly legible in the policy of the noble lord. I doubt not that use will be made of our present debate to work upon this peculiar weakness of the English mind. The people will be told that those who oppose the motion a e governed by personal motives, have no regard for public principles, and no enlarged ideas of national policy. You will take your case before a favorable jury, and you think to gain your verdict; but, sir, let the House of Commons be warned—let it warn itself—against all illusions. There is in this case also a course of appeal. There is an appeal, such as the honorable and learned member for Sheffield has

made, from the one House of Parliament to the other. There is a
further appeal from this House of Parliament to the peop e of England; but, lastly, there is also an appeal from the people of England
to the general sentiment of the civilized world; and I, for my part,
am of opinion that England will stand shorn of a chief part of her
glory and pride if she shall be found to have separated herself,
through the policy she pursues abroad, from the moral support
which the general and fixed convictions of mankind afford, if the day
shall come when she may continue to excite the wonder and the fear
of other nations, but in which she shall have no part in their affection and regard.

'No, sir, let it not be so; let us recognize, and recognize with
frankness, the equality of the weak with the strong; the principles
of brotherhood among nations, and of their sacred independence.
When we are asking for the maintenance of the rights which belong
to our fellow-subjects resident in Greece, let us do as we would be
done by, and let us pay all the respect to a feeble State, and to the
infancy of free institutions, which we should desire and should exact
from others, towards their maturity and their strength. Let us refrain
from all gratuitous and arbitrary meddling in the internal concerns
of other States, even as we should resent the same interference if it
were attempted to be practiced towards ourselves. If the noble lord
has indeed acted on these principles, let the Government to which he
belongs have your verdict in its favor; but if he has departed from
them, as I contend, and as I humbly think and urge upon you that it
has been too amply proved, then the House of Commons must not
shrink from the performance of its duty, under whatever expectations
of momentary obloquy or reproach, because we shall have done what
is right; we shall enjoy the peace of our own consciences, and
receive, whether a little sooner or a little later, the approval of the
public voice for having entered our solemn protest against a system
of policy which we believe, nay, which we know, whatever may be
its first aspect, must, of necessity, in its final results be unfavorable
even to the security of British subjects resident abroad, which it professes so much to study—unfavorable to the dignity of the country,
which the motion of the honorable and learned member asserts it
preserves—and equally unfavorable to that other great and sacred
object, which also it suggests to our recollections, the maintainance
of peace with the nations of the world.'

This speech is regarded by many as one of Mr. Gladstone's finest efforts. On a division upon Mr. Roebuck's
motion the government succeeded in obtaining a majority of
46. Ayes, 310; Noes, 264."

The day after the famous Don Pacifico debate, June 28, 1850, Sir Robert Peel had left a card at Buckingham Palace, and proceeded thence to enjoy a ride up Constitution Hill, when he was thrown from his horse, and was so severly injured that he died four days later. The tidings of his sad and sudden departure from the ways of men awoke universal regret. On the 3rd of July Mr. Hume alluded to the great loss the nation had sustained, and moved that the House of Commons at once adjourn. In the House of Lords, the Duke of Wellington and Lord Brougham referred in the most impressive terms of respect to the departed statesman.

Lord Brougham, who had frequently been in strong antagonism with Sir Robert Peel, paid this high tribute to his character and worth:

"At the last stage of his public career, chequered as it was—and I told him in private that chequered it would be—when he was differing from those with whom he had been so long connected, and from purely public-spirited feelings was adopting a course which was so galling and unpleasing to them—I told him, I say, that he must turn from the storm without to the sunshine of an approving conscience within. Differing as we may differ on the point whether he was right or wrong, disputing as we may dispute on the results of his policy, we must all agree that to the course which he believed to be advantageous to his country he firmly adhered, and that in pursuing it he made sacrifices compared with which all the sacrifices exacted from public men by a sense of public duty, which I have ever known or read of, sink into nothing."

If Mr Gladstone's tribute to his great chief was brief, it was full of intense feeling. Supporting Mr. Hume's motion, he said:

"I am quite sure that every heart is much too full to allow us, at a period so early, to enter upon a consideration of the amount of that calamity with which the country has been visited in his, I must even now say, premature death; for though he has died full of years and full of honors, yet it is a death which our human eyes will regard as premature, because we had fondly hoped that, in whatever position he was placed, by the weight of his character, by the splendor of his talents, by the purity of his virtues, he would still have been spared to render to his country the most essential services. I will only, sir, quote those most touching and feeling lines which were applied by one of the greatest poets of this country to the memory of a man great indeed, but yet not greater than Sir Robert Peel:

> ' Now is the stately column broke,
> The beacon light is quenched in smoke;
> The trumpet's silver voice is still,
> The warder silent on the hill.'

"Sir, I will add no more. In saying this I have perhaps, said too much. It might have been better had I simply confined myself to seconding the motion. I am sure the tribute of respect which we now offer will be all the more valuable from the silence with which the motion is received, and which I well know has not arisen from the want, but from the excess, of feeling on the part of members of this House."

No tributes to the dead statesman were more impressive and pathetic than those of the poor and needy, who regarded Sir Robert Peel as their savior from poverty and starvation. In the museum of the old town of Leicester there stands a bust purchased by the working people of Leicester in contributions of a penny—two cents each. As they spoke of him they said, with deep and sincere gratitude, "He gave us untaxed bread."

A brief reference will not be out of place here to the first of those great exhibitions of the products and industries of nations which seemed to reach their grand culmination in the marvelous World's Fair of Chicago, in the year 1893.

These exhibitions were healthful signs of the times. The purpose of these gatherings was to bring about a more fraternal feeling between the neighboring nations; to inspire them with zeal for the more perfect development of the resources of their respective countries; and to aid the coming of the good time that alas! seems far distant. Yet when the poet's dream should be realized:

> When the war-drum throbs no longer,
> And the battle-flags are furled;
> In the Parliament of men,
> The Federation of the World.

The first idea of the Exhibition was conceived by Prince Albert; and it was his energy and influence which succeeded in carrying the idea into practical execution. Probably no influence less great than that which his station gave to the Prince would have prevailed to carry to success so difficult an enterprise. There had been industrial exhibitions before on a small scale and of local limit; but if the idea of an exhibition in which all the nations of the world were to compete had occurred to other minds before, as it may well have done, it was merely as a vague thought, a day-dream, without any claim to a practical realization. Prince Albert was President of the Society of Arts, and this position secured him a platform for the effective promulgation of his ideas. On June 30, 1849, he called a meeting of the Royal Society at Buckingham Palace. He proposed that the Society should undertake the initiative in the promotion of an exhibition of the works of all nations. The main idea of Prince Albert was that the exhibition should be divided into four great sections—the first to contain raw materials and products; the second machinery for ordinary industrial and productive purposes and mechanical inventions of the more ingenious kind; the third, manufactured articles; and the fourth, sculpture, models, and the illustration of the plastic arts generally. The idea was at once taken up by the Society of Arts, and by their agency spread abroad. On October 17th in the same year a meeting of merchants and bankers was held in London to promote the success of the undertaking. In the first few days of 1850 a formal commission was appointed "for the promotion of the Exhibition of the Works of All Nations, to be holden in the year 1851." Prince Albert was appointed President of the Commission.

The question of the construction of a building for all the world to meet in, at least by representation, presented a great difficulty. Happily, a sudden inspiration struck Mr. Joseph Paxton, who was then in charge of the Duke of Devonshire's superb grounds at Chatsworth. Why not try glass and iron? he asked himself. Why not build a palace of glass and iron large enough to cover all the intended contents of the Exhibition, and which should be at once light, beautiful and cheap? Mr. Paxton sketched out his plan hastily, and the idea was eagerly accepted by the Royal Commissioners. He made many improvements afterwards in his design ; but the palace of glass and iron arose within the specified time on the green turf of Hyde Park. The idea so happily hit upon was serviceable in more ways than one to the success of the exhibition. It made the building itself as much an object of curiosity and wonder as the collections under its crystal roof. Of the hundreds of thousands who came to the Exhibition, a good proportion was drawn to Hyde Park rather by a wish to see Paxton's palace of glass than all the wonders of industrial and plastic art that it enclosed. Lord Palmerston said : "The building itself is far more worth seeing than anything in it, though many of its contents are worthy of admiration."

The Queen herself has written a very interesting account of the success of the opening day. Her description is interesting as an expression of the feelings of the writer, the sense of profound relief and rapture, as well as for the sake of the picture it gives of the ceremonial itself. The enthusiasm of the wife over the complete success of the project on which her husband had set his heart and staked his name is simple and touching. If the importance of the undertaking, and the amount of fame it was to bring to its author may seem a little overdone, not many readers will complain of the womanly and wifely feeling which could not be denied such fervent expression.

"The great event," wrote the Queen, "has taken place —a complete and beautiful triumph— a glorious and touching sight, one which I shall ever be proud of for my beloved Albert and my country. . . . The Park presented a wonderful spectacle—crowds streaming through it, carriages and troops passing, quite like the Coronation day, and for me the same anxiety—no, much greater anxiety, on account of my beloved Albert. The day was bright, and all bustle and excitement. . . . The Green Park and Hyde Park were one densely crowded mass of human beings in the highest good humor and most enthusiastic. I never saw Hyde Park look as it did—as far as the eye could reach. A little rain fell just as we started, but before we came near the Crystal Palace the sun shone and gleamed upon the gigantic edifice, upon which the flags of all nations were floating. . . . The glimpse of the transept through the iron gates, the waving palms, flowers, statues, myriads of people filling the galleries and seats around, with the flourish of trumpets as we entered, gave us a sensation which I can never forget, and I felt much moved. . . .

The sight as we came to the middle was magical—so vast, so glorious, so touching—one felt, as so many did whom I have since spoken to, filled with devotion—more so than by any service I have ever heard. The tremendous cheers, the joy expressed in every face, the immensity of the building, the mixture of palms, flowers, trees, statues, fountains; the **organ (with two hundred instruments and six hundred voices,** which sounded like nothing), and my beloved husband the author of this peace festival, which united the industry of all nations of the earth. All this was moving indeed, and it was and is a day to live forever ! God bless my dearest Albert ! God bless my dearest country, which has shown itself so great to-day ! One felt so grateful to the great God who seemed to pervade all, and to bless all !"

It is needless to say that in this great movement, Mr. Gladstone took pleasant and helpful interest. Horace Greeley was one of the American Commissioners, and unused though he was to burn incense at any shrine, he was carried away by the grandeur of the scene, and as he stood in this palace of crystal beauty and thought of what it stood for, he confessed that the poet's dream of a golden age might come true after all!

After the exhibition was closed, the main portion of the building was transferred to Sydenham a few miles south of London, where it has been for nearly half a century, and still is, the grandest and most complete place of recreation and entertainment in the world.

Towards the close of this year, 1851, owing to the illness of one of his children, it became necessary for Mr. Gladstone to journey southward. He went to Naples, and while there made such discoveries with regard to the hideous inhumanity which prevailed in high quarters, that very shortly all Europe rang with the voice of his righteous indignation.

Mr. Gladstone remained in Naples for about four months. He had been there but a very short time, when he heard such fearful accounts of thousands of people who were flung into prison, suffering every conceivable indignity for purely imaginary offenses, that he determined upon visiting such of the prisoners as he could, to ascertain for himself what truth there was in the reports he had heard. He found things worse than they had been described to him. Men of all classes were arrested on suspicion, or even without suspicion, and thrown with the ordinary criminals; and many of them loaded with chains, were left there for months, sometimes as long as a couple of years, before they were even put upon their trial, often because it was not possible to work up a case against them. The prisons were terribly overcrowded, dirty and unhealthy—so unhealthy indeed, were many of these dungeons in which the prisoners were herded together, that even the *doctors* dared not visit them!

On his return to England, Mr. Gladstone embodied the result of his investigations in two letters to the Earl of Aberdeen. The letters describe a condition of things that was "an outrage upon religion, upon civilization, upon humanity and upon decency."

"These pages have been written in the hope that by thus making through the press, rather than in another mode, the rejoinder to the Neapolitan reply which was doubtless due from me, I might still, as far as depended on me, keep the question on its true ground, and not of England but of Christendom and of mankind. Again I express that this may be my closing word. I express the hope that it may not become a hard necessity to keep this controversy alive, until it reaches its one only possible issue, which no power of man can possibly intercept. I express the hope that while there is time, while there is quiet, while dignity may yet be saved in showing mercy, and in the blessed work of restoring Justice to her seat, the Government of Naples may set its hand in earnest to the work of real and searching, however quiet, reform; that it may not become unavoidable to reiterate these appeals from the hand of power to the one common heart of mankind; to produce those painful documents, those harrowing descriptions, which might be supplied in rank abundance, of which I have scarcely given the faintest idea or sketch, and which, if they were laid from time to time before the world, would, bear down like a de-

luge every effort at apology or palliation, and would caus-
all that has recently been made known to be forgotten and
eclipsed in deeper horrors yet; lest the strength of offended
and indignant humanity should rise up as a giant refreshed
with wine, and while sweeping away these abominations
from the eye of Heaven, should sweep away along with
them things pure and honest, ancient, venerable, salutary
to mankind, crowned with the glories of the past, and still
capable of bearing future fruit."

But the following may be regarded as the most impressive
passage of his terrible indictment:

" It is such violation of human and written law as this,
carried on for the purpose of violating every other law, un-
written and eternal, human and divine; it is the wholesale
persecution of virtue, when united with intelligence, operat-
ing upon such a scale that entire classes may with truth be
said to be its object, so that the government is in bitter and
cruel, as well as utterly illegal, hostility to whatever in the
nation really lives and moves, and forms the mainspring of
practical progress and improvement. It is the awful pro-
fanation of public religion, by its notorious alliance in the
governing powers, with the violation of every moral rule
under the stimulants of fear and vengeance. It is the perfect
prostitution of the judicial office which has made it, under
veils only too threadbare and transparent, the degraded re-
cipient of the vilest and clumsiest forgeries, got up wilfully
and deliberately by the immediate advisers of the crown for
the purpose of destroying the peace, the freedom, aye, and
even if not by capital sentences, the life of men amongst
the most virtuous, upright, intelligent, distinguished and
refined of the whole community.

The effect of all this is a total inversion of all the moral
and social ideas. Law, instead of being respected, is
odious. Force, and not affection, is the foundation of
government. There is no association, but a violent antagonism, between the idea of freedom and that of order.

The governing power, which teaches of itself that it is the image of God upon earth, is clothed in the view of the overwhelming majority of the thinking public with all the vices for its attributes. I have seen and heard the strong and too true expression used, "This is the negation of God erected into a system of Government."

These letters created the most intense indignation. But was there no issue to be taken? Was there no moral right to interfere? The case had some points that compare with our right to declare war with Spain.

Before the House of Commons was prorogued, attention was drawn to Mr. Gladstone's statements. Sir De Lacy Evans put the following question to the Foreign Secretary:

"From a publication entitled to the highest consideration, it appears that there are at present above 20,000 persons confined in the prisons of Naples for alleged political offenses; that these prisoners have, with extremely few exceptions, been thus immured in violation of the existing laws of the country, and without the slightest legal trial or public inquiry into their respective cases; that they include a late Prime Minister and a majority of the late Neapolitan Parliament, as well as a large proportion of the most respectable and intelligent classes of society; that these prisoners are chained two and two together; that these chains are never undone, day or night, for any purpose whatever, and that they are suffering refinements of cruelty and barbarity, unknown in any other civilized country. It is consequently, asked if the British Minister at the Court of Naples has been instructed to employ his good offices in the cause of humanity, for the diminution of these lamentable severities, and with what result?"

Lord Palmerston replied that her Majesty's Government had received with pain a confirmation of the impressions which had been created by various accounts they had received from other quarters, of the very unfortunate and calamitous condition of the kingdom of Naples. The British Government, however, had not deemed it a part of their duty to make any formal representations to the Government of Naples on a matter that related entirely to the internal affairs of that country.

"At the same time," his lordship continued, "Mr. Gladstone, whom I may freely name, though not in his capacity of a member of Parliament, has done himself, I think, very great honor by the course he pursued at Naples, and by the course he has followed since; for I think that when you see an English gentleman, who goes to pass a winter at Naples, instead of confining himself to those amusements that abound in that city, instead of diving into volcanoes and exploring excavated cities, when we see him going to the courts of justice, visiting prisons, descending into dungeons, and examining great numbers of the cases of unfortunate victims of illegality and injustice, with a view afterwards to enlist public opinion in the endeavor to remedy those abuses, I think that is a course that does honor to the person who pursues it. And concurring in feeling with him that the influence of public opinion in Europe might have some useful effect in setting such matters right, I thought it my duty to send copies of his pamphlet to our Ministers at the various Courts of Europe, directing them to give to each Government copies of the pamphlet, in the hope that by affording them an opportunity of reading it, they might be led to use their influence in promoting what is the object of my honorable and gallant friend— a remedy for the evils to which he has referred." This announcement by the Foreign Secretary was warmly cheered by the House. A few days afterward Lord Palmerston was requested by Prince Castelcicala to forward the reply of the Neapolitan Government to the different European Courts to which Mr. Gladstone's pamphlet had been sent. His lordship, with his wonted courage and independent spirit, replied that he "must decline being accessory to the circulation of a pamphlet which, in my opinion, does no credit to its writer, or the Government which he defends, or to the political party of which he professes to be the champion." He also informed the Prince "that information received from other sources led him to the conclusion that Mr. Gladstone had by no means overstated the various evils which he had described; and he, Lord Palmerston, regretted that the Neapolitan Government had not set to work earnestly and effectually to correct the manifold and grave abuses which clearly existed."

Lord Palmerston, indeed, reflected the national sentiment of England when he declared from his place in the House of Commons, that " Mr. Gladstone had done himself honor by the course he had thus pursued in relation to the Neapolitan prisons. He had lifted his voice with energy and effect on behalf of oppressed humanity, and in condemnation of one of the worst and most despotic Governments that have ever afflicted mankind. This episode remains, and ever will remain, in the estimation both of his fellow-countrymen and the friends of justice and freedom throughout the world, one of the brightest in his career."

The immediate result of this chivalrous advocacy was perhaps not commensurate with the storm of indignation it aroused. But it bore good fruit at last when the heroic Garibaldi and a free people marched into Naples, and King Bomba and his vicious court fled.

On the 14th of September, 1852, the duke of Wellington, who had been for long years the pride and glory of his country, passed into the silent land. One of the grandest public funerals England had ever seen was awarded the hero of Waterloo. On the assembly of Parliament many eloquent tributes were paid to the memory of the man of iron nerve and deathless purpose. The following is part of Mr. Gladstone's eloquence:

"While many of the actions of his life, while many of the qualities he possessed, are unattainable by others, there are lessons which we may all derive from the life and actions of that illustrious man. It may never be given to another subject of the British Crown to perform services so brilliant as he performed; it may never be given to another man to hold the sword which was to gain the independence of Europe, to rally the nations around it, and while England saved herself by her constancy, to save Europe by her example; it may never be given to another man, after having attained such eminence, after such an unexampled series of victories, to show equal moderation in peace as he has shown greatness in war, and to devote the remainder of his life to the cause of internal and external peace for that country which he has so served; it may never be given to another man to have equal authority both with the Sovereign he served, and with the Senate of which he was to the end a venerated member; it may never be given to another man after such a career to preserve even to the last, the full possession of those great faculties with which he was endowed, and to carry on the services of one of the most important departments of the State with unexampled regularity and success, even to the latest day of his life. These are circumstances, these are qualities, which may never occur again in the history of this country. But there are qualities which the Duke of Wellington displayed, of which we may all act in humble imitation—that sincere and unceasing devotion to our country; that honest and upright determination to act for the benefit of the country on every occasion; that devoted loyalty, which, while it made him ever anxious to serve the Crown, never induced him to conceal from the Sovereign that which he believed to be the truth; that devotedness in the constant performance of duty; that temperance of his life, which enabled **him at all times to give his mind and his faculties to the** services which he was called on to perform; that regular, consistent, and unceasing piety by which he was distinguished at all times in his life. These are qualities that are attainable by others, and these are qualities which should not be lost as an example."

Mr. Gladstone himself declared that so late as 1851 he had not left the Tory party. Still, it was as clear as the day that he was marching steadily toward Liberalism. His great and trusted leader was dead. New questions were arising that demanded the most careful consideration. Old questions were assuming still graver importance. The world was marching on. In 1852 the first Derby-Disraeli administration was formed. Mr. Disraeli became Chancellor of the Exchequer, and Lord Derby being in the House of Lords, Mr. Disraeli became also leader in the House of Commons. Mr. Gladstone, being a pronounced Peelite, did not retain office under this administration.

In December of 1852 Mr. Disraeli introduced his budget, which provoked a good deal of severe criticism, to which he replied with scoffs and gibes and sarcasms, Sir James Graham being made the special subject of attack. As Mr. Disraeli sat down Mr. Gladstone sprang to his feet, and the battle that was waged so many years between these two great political gladiators began. In a few minutes the House was wildly cheering the intrepid member for Oxford. Mr. Gladstone began by telling the right honorable gentleman that "he was not entitled to charge with insolence men of as high position and of as high character in the House as himself." Having been prevented by the cheers of the House from completing this sentence, Mr. Gladstone thus concluded :

"I must tell the right honorable gentleman that he is not entitled to say to my right honorable friend, the member for Carlisle, that he regards but does not respect him. And I must tell him that whatever else he has learned, and he has learned much—he has not learned to keep within those limits of discretion, of moderation and of forbearance, that ought to restrain the conduct and language of every member in this House, the disregard of which, while it is an offense in the meanest among us, is an offense of tenfold weight when committed by the leader of the House of Commons."

When Mr. Gladstone concluded, having torn the proposals of the Budget to shreds, a majority followed him into the division lobby, and Mr. Disraeli and his government were beaten by nineteen votes. The first encounter between these great rivals resulted in a pronounced triumph for Mr. Gladstone.

Lord Derby resigned. Politics were plunged into what seemed a condition of hopeless confusion and excitement. At last a coalition government of Whigs, Peelites and even Radicals was formed. In this government Lord Aberdeen was Prime Minister, Lord John Russell was President of the Council, and Mr. Gladstone Chancellor of the Exchequer. If Mr. Gladstone had been making friends in the Camp of Liberalism, he was making bitter enemies in the Tents of Toryism. After having accepted office under Lord Aberdeen, he had of course to seek re-election at the hands of the University of Oxford. His seat was warmly if not bitterly contested.

The nomination took place on the 4th of January. Mr. Gladstone was proposed by Dr. Hawkins, Provost of Oriel, and Mr. Perceval by Archdeacon Denison. In accordance with custom at University elections, neither candidate was present. The opposition to the Chancellor of the Exchequer was based chiefly on his votes on ecclesiastical questions, and on his acceptance of office in a hybrid Ministry.

Two days after the nomination, the Chancellor of the Exchequer wrote the following letter to the Chairman of his Election Committee:

"Unless I had as full and clear conviction that the interests of the Church, whether as relates to the legislative functions of Parliament, or the impartial and wise recommendation of fit persons to her Majesty, for high ecclesiastical offices, were at least as safe in the hands of Lord Aberdeen as in those of Lord Derby (though I would on no account disparage Lord Derby's personal sentiments towards the Church), I should not have accepted office under Lord Aberdeen. As regards the second, if it be thought that during twenty years of public life, or that during the latter part of them, I have failed to give guarantees of attachment to the interests of the Church, to such as so think, I can offer neither apology nor pledge. To those who think otherwise, I tender the assurance that I have not by my recent assumption of office, made any change whatever in that particular, or in any principles relating to it."

The poll lasted for fifteen days, and at its close Mr. Gladstone was found to have been returned. The numbers were—Gladstone, 1,022; Perceval, 898—majority, 124.

On the 18th of April, 1853, he delivered the first of what has proved to be a long series of budget speeches unsurpassed in parliamentary history. There are some members in the present House of Commons who have a vivid recollection of the occasion. Expectation stood on tiptoe. The House was crowded in every part, and it remained crowded and tireless, while for the space of five hours Mr. Gladstone poured forth a flood of oratory which made arithmetic astonishingly easy, and gave an unaccustomed grace to statistics. Merely as an oratorical display, the speech was a rare treat to the crowded assembly that heard it, and to the innumerable company which some hours later read it. But the form was rendered doubly enchanting by the substance. It was clear that Mr. Gladstone could not only adorn the exposition of finance with the glamour of oratory, but could control the developments of finance with a master hand.

His scheme was a bold one. The young and untried Chancellor of the Exchequer found himself with a surplus of something over three-quarters of a million. This was not much; but was enough to make things pleasant in one or two influential quarters, and he might have hoped for a fuller purse next year. To have taken this course, to have dribbled away the surplus; practically to have left matters where they stood, would, moreover, have saved him an infinitude of trouble and relieved him from a tremendous risk. Scorning these considerations, plunging into the troubled sea with the confident daring of genius, he positively increased taxation, chiefly by manipulation of the income tax, and was thereby enabled, in a wholesale manner that seems scarcely less than magical, to reduce or absolutely abolish the duties on nearly three hundred articles of commerce in daily use. The secret of the financier's necromancy lay in that sound principal which he may be said to have inaugurated in British finance, and under the extended application of which trade and commerce have advanced by leaps and bounds. He reckoned upon that property in national finance known as the "elasticity of revenue," now habitually, as a matter of ordinary calculation, counted upon to make good deficiencies immediately accruing upon reduction of taxation.

A contemporary writer states that he never once paused for a word during the whole of the five hours, and awards to him the palm of an unsurpassed fluency and a choice diction. "The impression produced upon the minds of the crowded and brilliant assembly by Mr. Gladstone's evident mastery and grasp of the subject was, that England had at length found a skillful financier, upon whom the mantle of Peel had descended. The cheering when the right hon. gentleman sat down was of the most enthusiastic and prolonged character, and his friends and colleagues hastened to tender him their warm congratulations upon the distinguished success he had achieved in his first budget." When the louder plaudits had subsided, a hum of approbation still went round the House, and extended even to the fair occupants of the ladies' gallery.

The Budget itself was a marvel of ingenious and far-seeing statesmanship. It was a grand effort to equalize taxation. It lifted many burdens that oppressed the poorer classes and very largely obstructed business. It took off no less than $25,000,000 of customs and excise duties; and it balanced these remissions by applying the succession duty to real property, increasing the duty on spirits, and extending the income tax.

In dealing with the income tax, Mr. Gladstone said: "Depend upon it, when you come to close quarters with this subject, when you come to measure and see the respective relations of intelligence and labor and property, and when you come to represent these relations in arithmetical results, you are undertaking an operation which I should say was beyond the power of man to conduct with satisfaction, but which, at any rate, is an operation to which you ought not constantly to recur; for if as my honorable friend once said very properly, this country could not bear a revolution once a year, I will venture to say that it could not bear a reconstruction of the income-tax once a year. Whatever you do in regard to the income-tax, you must be bold, you must be intelligible, you must be decisive. You must not palter with it. If you do, I have striven at least to point out as well as my feeble powers will permit, the almost desecration I would say, certainly the gross breach of duty to your country, of which you will be found guilty, in thus jeopardizing one of the most valuable among all its material resources. I believe it to be of vital importance, whether you keep this tax or whether you part with it, that you should either keep it or leave it in a state in which it would be fit for service in an emergency, and that it will be impossible to do if you break up the basis of your income tax."

In the following magnificent peroration, Mr. Gladstone closed one of the most wonderful financial statements the world has ever heard:

"If the Committee have followed me, they will understand that we stand on the principle that the income-tax ought to be marked as a temporary measure; that the public feeling that relief should be given to intelligence and skill as compared with property ought to be met, and may be met; that the income-tax in its operation ought to be mitigated by every rational means, compatible with its integrity, and, above all, that it should be associated in the last term of its existence, as it was in the first, with those remissions of indirect taxation which have so greatly redounded to the profit of this country, and have set so admirable an example—an example that has already in some quarters proved contagious to other nations of the earth. These are the principles on which we stand, and the figures I have shown you that if you grant us the taxes which we ask, the moderate amount of $12,500,000 in the whole, and much less than that sum for the present year, you. or the Parliament which may be in existence in 1860, will be in the condition, if you so think fit to part with the income-tax. I am almost afraid to look at the clock, shamefully reminding me, as it must, how long I have trespassed on the time of the House. All I can say in apology is, that I have endeavored to keep closely to the topics which I had before me—

> "—immensum spatiis confecimus æquor,
> Et jam tempus equum fumantia solvere colla."

"These are the proposals of the Government. They may be approved, or they may be condemned, but I have this full confidence, that it will be admitted that we have not sought to evade the difficulties of the position; that we have not concealed those difficulties either from ourselves or from others; that we have not attempted to counteract them by narrow or flimsy expedients; that we have prepared plans which, if you will adopt them, will go some way to close up many vexed financial questions, which, if not now settled, may be attended with public inconvenience, and even with public danger, in future years, and under less favorable circumstances; that we have endeavored, in the plans we have now submitted to you, to make the path of our successors in future years not more arduous, but more easy; and I may be permitted to add that, while we have sought to do justice to the great labor community of England, by furthering their relief from indirect taxation, we have not been guided by any desire to put one class against another. We have felt we should best maintain our own honor, that we should best meet the views of Parliament, and best promote the interests of the country, by declining to draw any invidious distinction between class and class, by adapting it to ourselves as a sacred aim to diffuse and distribute the burdens with equal and impartial hand ; and we have the consolation of believing that by proposals such as these, we contribute as far as in us lies, not only to develop the material resources of the country, but to knit the various parts of this great nation yet more closely to than ever, to that Throne and to those institutions under which it is our happiness to live."

During Mr. Gladstone's first tenure of office as Chancellor of the Exchequer, a curious adventure occurred to him in the London offices of the late Mr. W Lindsay, merchant, shipowner, and M. P. There one day entered a brusque and wealthy shipowner of Sunderland, inquiring for Mr. Lindsay. As Mr. Lindsay was out, the visitor was requested to wait in an adjacent room, where he found a person busily engaged in copying some figures. The Sunderland shipowner paced the room several times, and took careful note of the writer's doings, and at length said to him, "Thou writes a bonny hand, thou dost."

"I am glad you think so," was the reply.

"Ah, thou dost. Thou makes thy figures weel. Thou'rt just the chap I want."

"Indeed !" said the Londoner.

"Yes, indeed," said the Sunderland man. "I'm a man of few words. Noo, if thou'lt come over to canny ould Sunderland, thou seest I'll give thee a hundred and twenty pounds a year, and that's a plum thou dost not meet with every day in thy life, I reckon. Noo then."

The Londoner replied that he was much obliged for the offer, and would wait till Mr. Lindsay returned, whom he would consult upon the subject. Accordingly, on the return of the latter, he was informed of the shipowner's tempting offer.

"Very well," said Mr. Lindsay, "I should be sorry to stand in your way. One hundred and fifty pounds is more than I can afford to pay you in the department in which you are at present placed. You will find my friend a good and kind master, and, under the circumstances, the sooner you know each other the better. Allow me, therefore, Mr. ——, to introduce you to the Right Hon. W. E. Gladstone, Chancellor of the Exchequer."

The Sunderland shipowner wished himself back in Sunderland.

It is not necessary to enter at any great length into the story of the Crimean War. The Greek and Latin churches —Russia championing one and France the other—had quarreled of the custody of the Holy Places of Jerusalem, and out of this dispute arose a claim on the part of Russia to a protectorate over all the Greek subjects of the Sultan —a claim which the Sultan of course resisted. Great Britain took the field on the side of Turkey. It has been said again and again that England "drifted" into this war. Be this as it may, it is very certain that Mr. Gladstone took his full share of the responsibility of this very serious step. Long years afterwards, when quite willing to admit that the Crimean War was a great blunder, he nevertheless accepted his full share of blame. Speaking of the war shortly after its conclusion he said: "It was at its commencement, not only a just and necessary war, but it could not have been avoided. It was absolutely necessary to cut the meshes of the net in which Russia had entangled Turkey. It was a war carried on by a united people in the name and on the behalf of Europe, backed by a European combination and by the authority of European law."

The charge made frequently that Mr. Gladstone was "a blind supporter either of Ottoman rule or of the integrity of the Ottoman Empire as such," can hardly be sustained. He expressly stated that the government was not engaged in maintaining the independence and integrity of the Ottoman Empire, as those words might be used with reference to the integrity and independence of England or of France. He further referred to the anomalies of the Eastern Empire, the political solecism of a Mussulman faith exercising a dominion over twelve millions of our fellow-creatures, the weakness inherent in the nature of the Turkish Government, and the eventualities that surrounded the future of that dubious empire, though he added that these were not the things with which any British Government had then to deal. This much will, therefore, be allowed, that Mr. Gladstone admitted and deplored the corruptions of the Turkish Government, and the anomalous relations existing between the Porte and its Christian subjects.

The members of the Peace Society strongly condemned the Aberdeen ministry for the course upon which it now entered. A deputation went to St. Petersburg to interview the Emperor Nicholas, but all in vain. Lord Aberdeen and Mr. Gladstone were both opposed to war in the abstract. On humanitarian as well as on national grounds Mr. Gladstone was bitterly opposed to war. He was almost ready to accept John Bright's comprehensive dictum : "War is always a blunder and always a crime." We have referred to the phrase about England "drifting" into the war, it might rather be said that the war spirit was over all the land and that the government was "driven" to take a part in the conflict. The Emperor Napoleon made a final effort to preserve peace but his appeal was treated with disdain. The Czar was obstinate. A telegraphic dispatch was received in Paris from the French representative at St. Petersburg consisting of this brief but insulting message in answer to Napoleon's note : "I return with refusal." This settled the whole question. War was inevitable and henceforth the French became the warm and **enthusiastic allies of England.**

Mr. Gladstone's attitude is impressively described by Mr. Kinglake, the brilliant historian of the Crimean war, in the following words:

"If he was famous for the splendor of his eloquence, for his unaffected piety, and for his blameless life, he was celebrated far and wide for a more than common liveliness of conscience. He had once imagined it to be his duty to quit a government, and to burst through strong ties of friendship and gratitude, by reason of a thin shade of difference on the subject of white or brown sugar. It was believed that, if he were to commit even a little sin, or to entertain an evil thought, he would instantly arraign himself before the dread tribunal which awaited him within his own bosom; and that, his intellect being subtle and microscopic, and delighting in casuistry and exaggeration, he would be likely to give his soul a very harsh trial, and treat himself as a great criminal for faults too minute to be visible to the naked eyes of laymen. His friends lived in dread of his virtues as tending to make him whimsical and unstable, and the practical politicians, perceiving that he was not to be depended upon for party purposes, and was bent upon none but lofty objects, used to look upon him as dangerous— used to call him behind his back a good man—a good man in the worst sense of the term."

In pleading that those who made war should be prepared to make the sacrifices needful to carry it out, and trusting that the day of honorable peace might not be far away, Mr. Gladstone said:

"We have entered upon a great struggle, but we have entered upon it under favorable circumstances. We have proposed to you to make great efforts, and you have nobly and cheerfully backed our proposals. You have already by your votes added nearly 40,000 men to the establishments of the country; and, taking into account changes that have actually been carried into effect with regard to the return of soldiers from the Colonies, and the arrangements which in the present state of Ireland might be made—but which are not made—with respect to the constabulary force, in order to render the military force disposable to the utmost possible extent. It is not too much to say that we have virtually an addition to the disposable forces of the country, by land and by sea, at the present moment, as compared with our position twelve months ago, to the extent of nearly 50,000 men. This looks like an intention to carry on your war with vigor, and the wish and hope of her Majesty's Government is, that that may be truly said of the people of England, with regard to this war which was, I am afraid, not so truly said of Charles II by a courtly but great poet, Dryden—

> 'He without fear, a dangerous war pursues,
> Which without rashness he began before.'

That, we trust, will be the motto of the people of England; and you have this advantage, that the sentiment of Europe, and we trust the might of Europe, is with you. These circumstances—though we must not be sanguine, though it would be the wildest presumption for any man to say, when the ravages of European war had once begun, where and at what point it would be stayed—these circumstances justify us in cherishing the hope that possibly this may not be a long war."

The history of the war was as sad a chapter as ever was written. After a dreadful winter passed in the Crimea, in which 24,000 British soldiers were sacrificed—largely the result of mismanagement of the War Department in London, the whole country was roused to the deepest sorrow and excitement. Mr. Gladstone described the matter to be one for "weeping all day and praying all night."

On January 26, 1855, Mr. Roebuck moved for a select committee "to inquire into the condition of our army before Sebastopol, and into the conduct of those departments of the government whose duty it has been to minister to the wants of that army."

Mr. Roebuck's motion was carried, with an overwhelming majority.

For Mr. Roebuck's committee, 305.

For ministers, 148

Majority against ministers, 157.

Thus fell the famous coalition cabinet of Lord Aberdeen.

The Queen sent for Lord Derby, but Mr. Gladstone and the Peelites refused to join him, and he failed to form a ministry. Lord Palmerston formed a cabinet, in which Mr. Gladstone served as Chancellor of the Exchequer. Within three weeks Mr. Gladstone and his Peelite colleagues left the government, Lord Palmerston having consented to the appointment of the committee asked for by Mr. Roebuck.

Mr. Gladstone now became a free lance. On a bye question which he had taken—the behavior of British authorities toward the Chinese in the matter of the Lorcha *Arrow*—he succeeded in defeating the government. They were left in a minority of sixteen, and on the 21st of March Parliament was dissolved. The general election which followed gave Lord Palmerston a substantial working majority.

In this Parliament Mr. Gladstone took strong ground in opposition to the divorce bill which the government was supporting.

"Marriage," he declared, was a "mystery" of the Christian religion. "Our Lord had emphatically told us that at and from the beginning marriage was perpetual and was on both sides single." Christian marriage, according to Holy Scripture, was a life-long compact which may sometimes be put in abeyance by the separation of a couple, but which can never be rightfully dissolved so as to set them free during their joint lives to unite with other persons. "I could not," he said, "regard this measure in any other light except one—namely, as the first instalment of change, the first stage in a road of which we know nothing, except that it is different from that of our forefathers, and that it is a point which leads from the point to which Christianity has brought us and carries us back toward the state in which Christianity found the heathenism of man."

The divorce bill was, nevertheless, carried into law.

Mr. Roebuck's Sebastapol Committee presented its report on the 16th of June. The report was voluminous and exhaustive, every detail of the evidence given before the committee was carefully reviewed. The report ended thus :

"Your committee report that the sufferings of the army resulted mainly from the circumstances under which the expedition to the Crimea was undertaken and executed. The administration which ordered that expedition had no adequate information as to the amount of forces in the Crimea. They were not acquainted with the strength of the fortresses to be attacked, or with the resources of the country to be invaded. They hoped and expected the expedition to be immediately successful, and as they did not foresee the probability of a protracted struggle, they made no provision for a winter campaign. The patience and fortitude of the army demand the admiration and gratitude of the nation on whose behalf they have fought, bled and suffered. Their heroic valor and equally heroic patience under sufferings and privations have given them claims on the country which will doubtless be gratefully acknowledged. Your committee will now close their report with a hope that every British army may in future display the valor which this noble army has displayed, and that none may hereafter be exposed to such sufferings as have been recorded in these pages."

When at last the power of Russia was broken, alike on the Baltic and the Black Sea, the Emperor gave up the struggle. Negotiations for peace were entered upon. A treaty of peace was subsequently concluded at Paris in March, 1856.

In the debate on the celebrated Conspiracy Bill, Mr. Gladstone made one of his remarkable speeches, the peroration of which we quote :

"If there is any feeling in this House for the honor of England, don't let us be led away by some vague statement about the necessity of reforming the criminal law. Let us insist upon the necessity of vindicating that law. As far as justice requires, let us have the existing law vindicated, and then let us proceed to amend it if it be found necessary. But do not let us allow it to lie under a cloud of accusations of which we are convinced that it is totally innocent. These times are grave for liberty. We live in the nineteenth century ; we talk of progress ; we believe that we are advancing; but can any man of observation who has watched the events of the last few years in Europe have failed to perceive that there is a movement indeed, but a downward and backward movement ? There are a few spots in which institutions that claim our sympathy still exist and flourish. They are secondary places—nay, they are almost the holes and corners of Europe, so far as mere material greatness is concerned, although their moral greatness will, I trust, insure them long prosperity and happiness. But in these times more than ever, does responsibility center upon the institutions of England ; and if it does center upon England, upon her principles, upon her laws, and upon her governors, then I say, that measure passed by this House of Commons—the chief hope of freedom—which attempts to establish a moral complicity between us and those who seek safety in repressive measures, will be a blow and a discouragement to that sacred cause in every country in the world."

In 1858, the natives of the Ionian Islands—a republic under the protection of Great Britain, were in a very agitated state, being anxious to be annexed by Greece. To this England objected, and Mr. Gladstone was appointed Lord High Commissioner Extraordinary to the Ionian Islands.   He arrived at Corfu with the object of doing his best to reconcile the inhabitants to the British protectorate. He was known to be a Greek student; and we learn that the population of the Islands persisted in regarding him not as the Commissioner of a Conservative English Government, but as "Gladstone the Phil-Hellene!"   He was received wherever he went with the honors due to a liberator.   His path everywhere was made to seem like a triumphal progress.   In vain he repeated his assurances that he came to reconcile the Islands to the protectorate, and not to deliver them from it.   The popular instinct insisted upon regarding him as, at least, the precursor of their union to the kingdom of Greece.

The legislative assembly of the Islands met, and presented a petition to Gladstone, proposing their annexation to Greece.   Finding that this was their firm wish, the Lord High Commissioner dispatched home a copy of the vote, in which the representatives of the Ionian people, declared that "the single and unanimous will of the Ionian people has been and is, for their union with the kingdom of Greece." Mr. Gladstone left the Islands in February, 1859.   The Ionians continued their agitation, and finally, in 1864, were formally given over to the government of Greece.

The year 1860 saw the completion of the Commercial Treaty with France.   Mr. Richard Cobden, Napoleon III and Mr. Gladstone were chiefly responsible for this wise measure which brought France and England into more peaceful relations.   The old hobgoblin of a "French invasion" was laid forever at rest.   As John Bright said: "The Commercial Treaty had made worth while for France and England to keep the peace.   This same year saw the last of the Paper Duty, the abolition of which, in 1861, was a natural sequence to the repeal of the Stamp Duty.

No place would be more suitable than this to refer to the lamented death of the Prince Consort, which took place in December, 1861. In the following April Mr. Gladstone was invited to open a new mechanics' institute in Manchester. From the speech then made and from his "Gleanings of Past Years" we cull the following tribute to Prince Albert:

"Over the tomb of such a man many tears might fall, but not one could be a tear of bitterness. These examples of rare intelligences, yet more rarely cultivated, with their great duties greatly done, are not lights kindled for a moment, in order then to be quenched in the blackness of darkness. While they pass elsewhere to attain their consummation, they live on here in their good deeds, and their venerated memories in their fruitful example. As even a fine figure may be eclipsed by a gorgeous costume, so during life the splendid accompaniments of a Prince Consort's position may for the common eye throw the qualities of his mind and character, his true humanity, into the shade. These hindrances to effectual perception are now removed; and we can see, like the forms of a Greek statue, severely pure in their bath of southern light, all his extraordinary gifts and virtues; his manly force tempered with gentleness, playfulness and love; his intense devotion to duty; his pursuit of the practical, with an unfailing thought of the ideal; his combined allegiance to beauty and to truth; the elevation of his aims, with his painstaking care and thrift of time, and methodizing of life, so as to waste no particle of his appliances and powers. His exact place in the hierarchy of bygone excellence it is not for us to determine; but none can doubt that it is a privilege which, in the revolution of years, but rarely returns, to find such graces and such gifts of mind, heart, character and person, united in one and the same individual, and set so steadily and firmly upon a pedestal of such giddy height, for the instruction and admiration of mankind.

"His comprehensive gaze ranged to and fro between
the base and the summit of society, and examined the
interior forces by which it is kept at once in balance and in
motion. In his well-ordered life there seemed to be room
for all things—for every manly exercise, for the study and
practice of art, for the exacting cares of a splendid court,
for minute attention to every domestic and paternal duty,
for advice and aid toward the discharge of public business
in its innumerable forms, and for meeting the voluntary
calls of an active philanthropy ; one day in considering the
best form for the dwellings of the people ; another day in
bringing his just and gentle influence to bear on the relations
of master and domestic servant; another in suggesting and
supplying the means of culture for the most numerous
classes ; another in some good work of almsgiving or religion. Nor was it a merely external activity which he displayed. His mind, it is evident, was too deeply earnest to
be satisfied in anything, smaller or greater, with resting on
the surface. With a strong grasp on practical life in all its
forms, he united a habit of thought eminently philosophic,
ever referring facts to their causes, and pursuing action to
its consequences. Gone though he be from among us, he,
like other worthies of mankind who have preceded him, is
not altogether gone ; for, in the words of the poet—

> Your heads must come
> To the cold tomb.
> Only the actions of the just
> Smell sweet and blossom in the dust.

"So he has left all men, in all classes, many a useful
lesson, to be learned from the record of his life and character.

"Perhaps no sharper stroke ever cut human lives asunder
than that which parted, so far as this world of sense is concerned, the lives of the Queen of England and of her chosen
Consort. It had been obvious to us all, though necessarily

in different degrees, that they were blessed with the possession of the secret of reconciling the discharge of incessant and wearing public duty with the cultivation of the inner and domestic life. The attachment that binds together wife and husband was known to be, in their case, and to have been from the first, of an unusual force. Through more than twenty years, which flowed past like one long unclouded summer day, that attachment was cherished, exercised and strengthened, by all the forms of family interest, by all the associated pursuits of highly cultivated minds, by all the cares and responsibilities which surround the throne, and which the Prince was called, in his own sphere, both to alleviate and to share. On the one side, such love is rare, even in the annals of the love of woman; on the other, such service can hardly find a parallel, for it is hard to know how a husband could render it to a wife, unless that wife were also Queen."

CHAPTER XVII.

REJECTED BY OXFORD—LIBERAL LEADER.

"Henceforth Mr. Gladstone will belong to the country, and no longer to the University."

—*Times, July 19, 1865.*

"Oxford, I think, will learn to regret her wide severance from one so loyal to the church, and to the faith, and to God."

—*Dr Pusey*

Once the ties had been broken which bound him to his *alma mater*, and Mr. Gladstone felt like a man who breathes the fresh mountain air, after a close confinement in a crowded city.

—*L. Burnett Smith.*

The rejection of Mr. Gladstone by Oxford, after eighteen years of sincere and faithful service, forms an important and almost romantic episode in the career of the great statesman. In the minds of many — the wish being father to the thought—the rejection was a foregone conclusion. For a long time any word or action that could be construed into a point, however feeble and remote, that Mr. Gladstone was fostering Liberal opinions, and that his face was turning toward the Liberal camp, had been eagerly seized upon by members of the Conservative party. In the House of Commons at the close of March 1865, Mr. Dillwyn proposed "That the present position of the Irish church establishment is unsatisfactory, and calls for the early attention of her Majesty's government."

Mr. Gladstone in response arose and said "That although the government were unable to agree to the resolution, they were not prepared to deny the abstract truth of the former part of it." These words were seized upon as practically conceding the whole question involved in Mr. Dillwyn's motion. Some months later Mr. Gladstone explained to Dr. Hannah, warden of Trinity College, Glenalmond, his reasons for not dealing at that time with the Irish Church. The reasons were thus expressed:

"First, because the question is remote and apparently out of all bearing on the practical politics of the day, I think it would be for me worse than superfluous to determine upon any scheme, or basis of a scheme, with respect to it. Secondly, because it is difficult; even if I anticipated any likelihood of being called upon to deal with it, I should think it right to take no decision beforehand on the mode of dealing with the difficulties. But the first reason is that which chiefly weighs. . . I think I have stated strongly my sense of the responsibility attaching to the opening of such a question, except in a state of things which gave promise of satisfactorily closing it. For this reason it is that I have been so silent about the matter, and may probably be so again; but I could not, as a Minister and as member for Oxford University, allow it to be debated an indefinite number of times, and remain silent. One thing, however, I may add, because I think it a clear landmark.—In any measure dealing with the Irish church, I think (though I scarcely expect ever to be called on to share in such a measure) the Act of Union must be recognized, and must have important consequences, especially with reference to the position of the hierarchy."

The sagacious and suspicious Oxford Dons could see in this guarded statement, the straw that indicated the direction of the current.

On the sixth of July, 1865, Parliament was prorogued with a view of immediate dissolution. This parliament died a natural death. The one interesting event towards which all eyes was turning, was the fate of Mr. Gladstone as candidate for the University of Oxford. That his seat was in peril had long been known. When the time for nomination came, Mr. Gathorne Hardy, a pronounced Conservative, was placed in opposition to Mr. Gladstone. On the thirteenth of July, the nomination took place, being conducted as was the custom in Latin. Dr. Liddall proposed Mr. Gladstone; the warden of All Soul's proposed Sir William Heathcote; and the Public Orator proposed Mr. Gathorne Hardy. A period of five days was allowed for keeping open the polls. Mr. Gladstone was in a minority from the beginning. His votes fell six below Mr. Hardy on the first day. On the third day his minority increased to seventy-four and on the fourth to 230. Every effort was made by his friends, but all in vain. The Tory parsons had made up their minds to defeat him. Sir J. T. Coleridge, chairman of Mr. Gladstone's committee sent out the following note:

"The committee do not scruple to advocate his cause on grounds above the common level of politics. They claim for him the gratitude due to one whose public life has for eighteen years reflected a lustre on the University herself. They confidently invite you to consider whether his pure and exalted character, his splendid abilities, and his eminent services to church and state, do not constitute the highest of all qualifications for an academical seat, and entitle him to be judged by his constituents, as he will assuredly be judged by posterity."

Mr. Gladstone's minority was reduced somewhat, but the state of the poll was finally declared as follows :

  Sir William Heathcote,   -   -   3,236
  Mr. Gathorne Hardy,   -   -   - 1,904
  Mr. W. E. Gladstone, -   -   -   1,724

Majority for Mr. Hardy over Mr. Gladstone 180.

Mr. Gladstone's defeat was due to non-residents, yet amongst the distinguished voters who supported him were the following: The Bishops of Durham, Oxford and Chester, Earl Cowper, the Dean of Westminster, the Dean of Christ church, Professors Farrar, Rolleston, and Max

Muller, the Dean of Lichfield, Sir J. T. Coleridge, Sir Henry Thompson, the Rev. Dr. Jelf, the Bodleian Librarian, Sir F. T. Palgrave, the Right Hon. S. Lushington, the Dean of St. Paul's, the Rev. John Keble, the Principal of Brasenose, the Dean of Peterborough, Prof. Conington, the Rev. J. B. Mozley, Mr. E. A. Freeman, Chief Justice Erle, Dr. Pusey, Prof. Jowett, Mr. Cardwell, the Marquis of Kildare, and the Rector of Lincoln.

The whole Liberal party of England had looked forward with ardent hope and desire to the defeat of Mr. Gladstone at Oxford. If Oxford cast out her honored son it would give the Liberal party an irresistible leader. The election in South Lancashire was just pending. At the nomination on the 17th, Mr. Gladstone was proposed as a candidate, in view and hope of the almost certain defeat at Oxford. The die was cast. Mr. Gladstone hastened to Manchester and met the Liberal election committee, and at once issued the following brief address to the electors of South Lancashire:

"To the electors of South Lancashire: Gentlemen—I appear before you as a candidate for the suffrages of your division of my native county. Time forbids me to enlarge on the numerous topics which justly engage the public interest. I will bring them all to a single head. You are conversant—few so much so—with the legislation of the last thirty-five years. You have seen, you have felt its results. You cannot fail to have observed the verdict which the country generally has, within the last eight days, pronounced upon the relative claims and positions of the two great political parties with respect to that legislation in the past, and to the prospective administration of public affairs. I humbly, but confidently, without the least disparagement to many excellent persons, from whom I have the misfortune frequently to differ, ask you to give your powerful voice in confirmation of that verdict, and to pronounce with significance as to the direction in which you desire the wheels of the State to move. Before these words can be read, I hope to be among you in the hives of your teeming enterprise."

At the close of the poll at Oxford, on the 18th of July, 1865, which recorded Mr. Harding's triumph and Mr. Gladstone's defeat, Mr. Gladstone wrote the following impressive valedictory to the members of the convocation :

"After an arduous connection of eighteen years, I bid you respectfully farewell. My earnest purpose to serve you, my many faults and shortcomings, the incidents of the political relation between the University and myself, established in 1847, so often questioned in vain, and now at length, finally dissolved, I leave to the judgment of the future. It is one imperative duty, and one alone, which induces me to trouble you with these few parting words— the duty of expressing my profound and lasting gratitude for indulgences as generous and for support as warm and enthusiastic in itself, and as honorable from the character and distinctions of those who have given it, as has, in my belief, ever been accorded by any constituency to any representative."

On this memorable 18th of July, seven thousand men were wedged into the Free Trade Hall in Manchester, waiting to hear the voice of the defeated of Oxford. The rank and file of the Liberal party regarded this defeat as the "one thing needful" to the national triumph of the party and its principles. "Let Oxford reject him," they said, "and he will come to us 'unmuzzled.'" The word was passed from lip to lip, till it became "familiar as a household word."

When Mr. Gladstone appeared upon the platform he met with an enthusiastic welcome, such as has not often been accorded to the most popular favorite. After silence was restored, he commenced that memorable speech in words which set that vast audience wild with ungovernable delight.

"At last, my friends," he said, "I am come among you, and I am come among you—to use an expression which has become very famous, and is not likely to be forgotten—I am come among you 'unmuzzled.'" At that word "unmuzzled" cheer rose on cheer ; then silence for a breathing space, and then cheers, longer and louder and more intense. At last the cheers ceased from sheer exhaustion, upon which Mr. Gladstone proceeded :

"After an anxious struggle of eighteen years, during which the unbounded devotion and indulgence of my friends maintained me in the arduous position of representative of the University of Oxford, I have been driven from my seat. . . . I have loved the University with a deep and passionate love, and as long as I breathe, that attachment will continue; if my affection is of the smallest advantage to that great, that ancient, that noble institution. That advantage, such as it is, and it is most insignificant, Oxford will possess as long as I live. But don't mistake the issue which has been raised. The University has at length, after eighteen years of self-denial, been drawn by what I might, perhaps, call an overweening exercise of power, into the vortex of mere politics. Well, you will readily understand why, as long as I had a hope that the zeal and kindness of my friends might keep me in my place, it was impossible for me to abandon them. Could they have returned me by a majority of one, painful as it is to a man of my time of life, and feeling the weight of public cares, to be incessantly struggling for his seat, nothing could have induced me to quit that University to which I had so long ago devoted my best care and attachment. But by no act of mine I am free to come among you. And having been thus set free, I need hardly tell you that it is with joy, with thankfulness and enthusiasm, that I now, at this eleventh hour, a candidate without an address, make my appeal to the heart and the mind of South Lancashire, and ask you to pronounce upon that appeal.   As I have said, I am aware of no cause for the votes which have given a majority against me in the University of Oxford, except the fact that the strongest conviction that the human mind can receive, that an overpowering sense of the public interests, that the practical teachings of experience, to which from my youth, Oxford herself taught me to lay open my mind—all these had shown me the folly, and I will say, the madness of refusing to join in the generous sympathies of my countrymen, by adopting what I must call an obstructive policy.

"Without entering into details, without unrolling the long record of all the great measures that have been passed—the emancipation of Roman Catholics, the removal of Tests from Dissenters, the reformation of the Poor Law, the reformation—I had almost said the destruction, but it is the reformation—of the Tariff; the abolition of the Corn laws; the abolition of the Navigation laws; the conclusion of the French treaty; the laws which have relieved Dissenters from stigma and almost ignomy, and which in doing so have not weakened, but have strengthened the church to which I belong—all these great acts accomplished with the same, I had almost said sublime, tranquility of the whole country as that with which your own vast machinery performs its appointed task, as it were in perfect repose—all these things have been done.   You have seen the acts.   You have seen the fruits.

It is natural to inquire who have been the doers.   In a very humble measure and yet according to the degree and capacity of the powers which Providence has bestowed upon me, I have been desirous not to obstruct but to promote and assist, this beneficient and blessed process.   And if I entered Parliament, as I did enter Parliament with a warm and anxious desire to maintain the institutions of my country, I can truly say that there is no period of my life during which my conscience is so clear and renders me so good an answer, as those years in which I have co-operated in the promotion of Liberal measures.   *   *   *   Because they are Liberal measures; they are true measures, and indicate the true policy by which the country is made strong and its institutions preserved."

Mr. Gladstone then proceeded to Liverpool, and in an address to an immense audience in the Royal Amphitheatre in the evening, made the following pathetic reference to his relations to Oxford:—"If I am told that it is only by embracing the narrow interests of a political party that Oxford can discharge her duties to the country, then gentlemen, I at once say, I am with the man for Oxford. We see represented in that ancient institution—represented more nobly, perhaps, and more conspicuously than in any other place, at any rate with more remarkable concentration—the most prominent features that relate to the past of England. I come into South Lancashire, and find here around me an assemblage of different phenomena. I find developments of industry; I find growth of enterprise; I find progress of social philanthropy; I find prevalence of toleration, and I find an ardent desire for freedom.   *   *   *   *   I have honestly, I have earnestly, although I may have feebly, striven to unite, in my insignificant person that which is represented by Oxford and that which is represented by Lancashire. My desire is that they shall know and love one another. If I have clung to the representation of the university with desperate fondness, it was because I would not desert that post in which I seem to have been placed. I have not abandoned it. I have been dismissed from it, not by academical, but by political agencies. I don't complain of those, or those political influences by which I have been displaced. The free constitutional spirit of the country requires that the voice of the majority should prevail. I hope the voice of the majority will prevail in South Lancashire. I do not for a moment complain that it should have prevailed in Oxford.   But, gentlemen, I come now to ask you a question whether, because I have been declared unfit longer to serve the University on account of my political position, there is anything in what I have said and done, in the arduous office which I hold, which is to unfit me for the representation of my native country?

One of the most remarkable comments on this exciting episode, is to be found in a letter addressed by Dr. Pusey, the sainted author of "The Christian Year," to the Editor of the *Churchman*, a pronounced Tory journal.   The letter ran thus: "You are naturally rejoicing over the rejection of Mr. Gladstone, which I mourn.   Some of those who concurred in that election, or who stood aloof, will, I fear, mourn hereafter with a double sorrow, because they were the cause of that rejection.   I, of course, speak only for myself, with whatever degree of anticipation may be the privilege of years.   Yet, on the very ground that I may very probably not live to see the issue of the momentous future now hanging over the Church, let me through you, express to those friends from whom I have been separated, who love the Church in itself, and not the accident of Establishment, my conviction, that we should do it to identify the interests of the Church with any political party; that we have questions before us, compared with which that of the Establishment (important as it is in respect to the possession of our parish churches) is as nothing.   The grounds alleged against Mr. Gladstone, bore at the utmost upon the Establishment.   The Establishment might perish, and the Church but come forth the purer.   If the Church were corrupted, the Establishment would become a curse in proportion to its influence.   As that conflict will thicken, Oxford I think will learn to regret her rude severance from one so loyal to the Church, to the faith and to God."

Mr. G. Barnett Smith reviews the rejection of Mr. Gladstone in the following terse and comprehensive words:

"While the rejection of Mr. Gladstone by the University of Oxford, was regarded in some quarters as a signal triumph of Conservative reaction, in other respects it was felt that the opposition offered to him was a most mistaken stroke of Tory policy. Though he always courageously acted upon his convictions, so long as he retained his seat for Oxford University, he must have remained to some extent fettered. He could not altogether shake off the silent but deep and unmistakable influence which such a connection must necessarily exercise. Once the ties had been broken, which bound him to his *Alma Mater*, Mr. Gladstone felt like a man who breathes the fresh mountain air after a close confinement in the crowded city. There were now many questions whose consideration he could approach without the sense of an invisible but restraining influence. By the whole Liberal party throughout the country, his rejection was immediately regarded with feelings of exaltation—much as (for some reasons) they had desired his return for that distinguished seat of learning which he had represented so long and so well. By a large class of non-resident voters, Mr. Gladstone was viewed as too clever to be a safe man; and it was not anticipated that Mr. Gathorne Hardy would forfeit the confidence of this body, by any eccentricities of genius."

The Times of July 19th, 1865, in dealing with the matter said: "The enemies of the University will make the most of her disgrace. It has hitherto been supposed that a learned constituency was to some extent exempt from the vulgar motives of party spirit, and capable of forming a higher estimate of statesmanship, than common tradesmen or tenant-farmers. It will now stand on record that they have deliberately sacrificed a representative who combined the very highest qualifications, moral and intellectual, for an academical seat, to party-spirit, and party-spirit alone. . . . Henceforth Mr. Gladstone will belong to the country, but no longer to the University. Those Oxford influences and traditions, which have so deeply colored his views, and so greatly interfered with his better judgment, must gradually lose their hold on him."

The *Daily News*, which was then regarded as the organ of the most advanced liberal thought, expressed itself thus :

"Mr. Gladstone's career as a statesman, will certainly not be arrested, nor Mr. Gathorne Hardy's capacity be enlarged by the number of votes which Tory squires or Tory parsons may inflict upon Lord Derby's cheerful and fluent subaltern, or withhold from Lord Palmerston's brilliant colleague. The late Sir Robert Peel was but the chief of a party, until admonished by one ostracism, he became finally emancipated by another. Then, as now, the statesman who was destined to give up to mankind what was never meant for the barren service of a party, could say to the honest bigots who rejected him—

I banish you;
There is a world elsewhere.

" Mediocrity will not be turned into genius, honest and good-natured insignificance into force, fluency into eloquence, if the resident and non-resident Toryism of the University of Oxford, should prefer the safe and sound Mr. Hardy to the illustrious Minister, whom all Europe envies us ; whose name is a household word in every political assembly in the world."

CHAPTER XVIII.

Then, as now, the statesman who was destined to give up to mankind what was never meant for the barren service of a party could say to the honest bigots who rejected him:

"I banish you:
There is a world elsewhere."

—*Daily News, July 19, 1865.*

Who is this man whose words have might
  To lead you from your rest or care,
Who speaks as if the earth were right
  To stop its course and listen there?
He bids you wonder, weep, rejoice,
  Saying "It is yourselves, not I;
I speak but with the people's voice,
  I see but with the people's eye!"

—*Lord Houghton.*

The severing of the political tie with his university after eighteen years' connection with it, may have been in some sense a relief, but it was a very severe blow to so sensitive a man as Mr. Gladstone. How keenly he felt the blow we may gather from the following paragraph of a letter he wrote to Samuel Wilberforce, Lord Bishop of Oxford, his tried and trusted friend:

"There have been two deaths or transmigrations of spirit, in my political existence—one, very slow, the breaking of ties with my original party; the other very short and sharp, the breaking of the tie with Oxford. There will probably be a third and no more."

Mr. Gladstone was returned for South Lancashire, but not at the head of the poll. There were three members returned for this constituency. Of the six candidates who entered the contest Mr. Gladstone came out third on the list. It is worth remarking, however, that he had a considerable majority in all large towns. There was the stronghold of the Liberal party. The general election resulted in a majority for the Liberals, and Lord Palmerston continued in office. But unforeseen changes were at hand.

On the 18th of October, 1865, the venerable Lord Palmerston, at the age of eighty, passed away from toil to rest. Mr. Gladstone offered a eulogy on his late chief, of which the following is the closing paragraph :

"All who knew Lord Palmerston knew his genial temper and the courage with which he entered into the debates of the House ; his incomparable tact and ingenuity—his command of fence—his delight, his old English delight, in a fair stand-up fight. Yet, notwithstanding the possession of these powers, I must say I think there was no man whose inclination and whose habit were more fixed, so far as our discussions were concerned, in avoiding whatever tended to exasperate, and in having recourse to those means by which animosity might be calmed down. He had the power to stir up angry passions, but he chose, like the sea god in the Æneid, rather to pacify. That which, in my opinion, distinguished Lord Palmerston's speaking from the oratory of other men, that which was its most remarkable characteristic, was the degree in which he said precisely that which he meant to express."

Lord John Russell was sent for by the Queen. He reorganized the government. He had been raised to the House of Lords, and now became Prime Minister with Mr. Gladstone as Chancellor of the Exchequer and leader of the House of Commons.

Here were new honors. Here was a higher place, with trying duties and enlarged responsibilities. Would Mr. Gladstone prove equal to the tasks? Many were sanguine and hopeful, but not a few feared. Many years have passed since then, and surely few men have been more thoroughly tested; but the almost universal testimony of those best qualified to judge is that Mr. Gladstone has proved the most able and successful leader of the House of Commons England has ever known. Mr. Gladstone was always an enthusiast, and in this new place and to these new tasks to which he had been so suddenly and so strangely called he devoted himself with most admired devotion. Every detail of the new calling had his most careful attention. "Like Lord Palmerston, he generally remained in the House from the commencement of the sittings to the close of them, however late the adjournment might be. But he did not, like him, slumber during the greater part of the sittings; on the contrary he listened attentively to every speaker, answered fully every question put to him, spoke on every subject, and exhibited a sensitive and conscientious anxiety to discharge his functions as leader of the House, which his friends feared would soon disable him from the performance of the responsible duties which belonged to him, and with his fall precipitate that of the Government of which he was the mainstay."

Mr. Gladstone's first great duty in the new Parliament was to introduce Lord John Russell's reform bill. This bill proposed to create an occupation franchise in counties, including houses at $70 rental, and reaching up to $250 the occupation rental. It was calculated that this would add 171,000 to the electoral list. It was further proposed to introduce into counties the provision which copy-holders and lease-holders within Parliamentary boroughs now possessed for the purpose of county votes. Then came a savings-bank franchise. All male adults who had deposited $250 in a savings-bank for two years would be entitled to be registered for the place in which they resided. This would add 10,000 to 15,000 electors to the constituencies of England and Wales. The rate-paying clauses of the Reform act were to be abolished; this would admit 25,000 voters above the line of $50. There was also to be a lodger franchise, and a $50 annual value of apartments franchise. The bill would add 400,000 new voters to the constituencies Mr. Gladstone's great speech on the introduction of the bill was called for a time "the banner speech of reform." The speech closed thus:

"If issue is taken adversely upon this bill, I hope it will be, above all, a plain and direct issue. I trust it will be taken upon the question, whether there is or is not to be an enfranchisement downwards, if it is to be taken at all. We have felt that to carry enfranchisnment above the present line was essential; essential to character, essential to credit, essential to usefulness ; essential to the character and credit not merely of the Government, not merely of the political party by which it has the honor to be represented, but of this House, and of the successive Parliaments and Governments, who all stand pledged with respect to this question of the representation. We cannot consent to look upon this large addition, considerable although it may be, to the political power of the working classes of this country, as if it was an addition fraught with mischief and with danger. We cannot look, and we hope no man will look, upon it as some Trojan horse approaching the walls of the sacred city, and filled with armed men, bent upon ruin, plunder and conflagration. We cannot join in comparing it with the *monstrum infeiix*—we cannot say—

"——Scandit fatalis machina muros,
Fœta armis : mediæ minans illabitur urbi."

I believe that those persons whom we ask you to enfranchise ought rather to be welcomed, as you would welcome recruits to your army, or children to your family. We ask you to give within what you consider to be the just limits of prudence and circumspection ; but, having once determined those limits, to give with an ungrudging hand. Consider what you can safely and justly afford to do in admitting new subjects and citizens within the pale of the Parliamentary constitution; and having so considered it, do not, I beseech you, perform the act as if you were compounding with danger and misfortune. Do it as if you were conferring a boon that will be felt and reciprocated in grateful attachment. Give to these persons new interests in the Constitution, new interests which, by the beneficent processes of the law of nature and of Providence, shall beget in them new attachment; for the attachment of the people to the Throne, the institutions, and the laws under which they live is, after all, more than gold and silver, or more than fleets and armies, at once the strength, the glory, and the safety of the land.

Mr. Lowe, who had just returned from Austrailia, a brilliant and incisive speaker, attacked the bill. Mr. Laing and Mr. Horsman deserted the Government. The latter observing that Mr. Gladstone's speech was "another promise made to be broken, another political fraud and Parliamentary juggle." This brought John Bright to his feet with one of those caustic retorts, for which the great "Tribune of the People," was celebrated. He ridiculed the idea of Mr. Horsman and Mr. Lowe, forming a third party: Mr. Horsman," he said, "has retired into what may be called his political Cave of Adullam, to which he invited every one who was in distress and every one who was discontented. He has long been anxious to found a party in the House; and there is scarcely a member at this end of the House who is able to address us with effect or to take much part, whom he has not tried to bring over to his party and his cabal. At last he has succeeded in hooking the right hon. gentleman the member for Calne, Mr. Lowe. I know it was the opinion many years ago of a member of the Cabinet that two men could make a party. When a party is formed of two men so amiable and so disinterested as the two right hon. gentlemen, we may hope to see for the first time in

Parliament, a party perfectly harmonious and distinguished by mutual and unbroken trust. But there is one difficulty which it is impossible to remove. This party of two is like the Scotch terrier that was so covered with hair that you could not tell which was the head and which was the tail."

THE THIRD PARTY.

The bill met with fierce opposition. The country was thoroughly aroused. In all the large towns in the north of England, large meetings were held, and hundreds of thousands of those who had no vote, no share in the government of the country whose burdens they bore,—and all because they could not afford to pay $50 rental, began to understand who were their true friends. Mr. Bright wrote a strong letter to his constituents at Rochdale, in which he referred to the opposition as "a dirty conspiracy," and added: "The men who, in every speech they utter, insult the working men, describing them as a multitude given up to ignorance and vice, will be the first to yield when the popular will is loudly and resolutely expressed."

At a great meeting held in Liverpool Mr. Gladstone said: "Having produced this measure, founded in a spirit of moderation, we hope to support it with decision. It is not in our power to secure the passage of the measure; that rests more with you, and more with those whom you represent, and of whom you are a sample, than it does with us. Still, we have a great responsibility, and are conscious of it; and we do not intend to flinch from it. We stake ourselves—we stake our existence as a Government—and we also stake our political character on the adoption of the bill in its main provisions. You have a right to expect from us that we should tell you what we mean, and that the trumpet which it is our business to blow, should give forth no uncertain sound. Its sound has not been, and, I trust, will not be, uncertain. We have passed the Rubicon—we have broken the bridge, and burned the boats behind us. We have advisedly cut off the means of retreat, and having done this, we hope that, as far as time is yet permitted, we have done our duty to the Crown and to the nation.

At the close of this great debate Mr. Gladstone made a reference to Mr. Disraeli's fear lest the Constitution should be reconstructed on American principles:

"At last we have obtained a declaration from an authoritative source that a bill which, in a country with five millions of adult males, proposes to add to a limited constituency 200,000 of the middle class and 200,000 of the working class, is, in the judgment of the leader of the Tory party, a bill to reconstruct the Constitution upon American principles."

But, in the closing speech of that great debate, Mr. Gladstone administered a flagellation to the Right Hon.

Benjamin Disraeli which he probably never forgot. Addressing him, Mr. Gladstone said:

"The right honorable gentleman, secure in the recollection of his own consistency, has taunted me with the errors of my boyhood. When he addressed the honorable member for Westminster, he showed his magnanimity by declaring that he would not take the philosopher to task for what he wrote twenty-five years ago; but when he caught one who, thirty-six years ago, just emerged from boyhood, and still an undergraduate at Oxford, had expressed an opinion adverse to the Reform Bill of 1832, of which he had so long and bitterly repented, then the right honorable gentleman could not resist the temptation. He, a Parliamentary leader of twenty years' standing, is so ignorant of the House of Commons, that he positively thought he got a Parliamentary advantage by exhibiting me as an opponent of the Reform Bill of 1832. As the right honorable gentleman has exhibited me, let me exhibit myself. It is true, I deeply regret it, but I was bred under the shadow of the great name of Canning. Every influence connected with that name governed the politics of my childhood and of my youth. With Canning I rejoiced in the removal of religious disabilities and in the character which he gave to our policy abroad. With Canning I rejoiced in the opening which he made toward the establishment of free commercial interchanges between nations. With Canning, and under the shadow of that great name, and under the shadow of that yet more venerable name of Burke, I grant, my youthful mind and imagination were impressed just the same as the mature mind of the right honorable gentleman is now impressed. I had conceived that fear and alarm of the first Reform Bill in the days of my undergraduate career at Oxford, which the right honorable gentleman now feels; and the only difference between us is this—I thank him for bringing it out—that, having those views, I moved the Oxford Union Debating Society to express them clearly, plainly, forcibly, in downright English, and that the right honorable gentleman is still obliged to skulk under the cover of the amendment of the noble lord. I envy him not one particle of the polemical advantage which he has gained by his discreet reference to the proceedings of the Oxford Union Debating Society, in the year of grace 1831. My position, sir, in regard to the Liberal party, is in all points the opposite of Earl Russell's. . . . . I have none of the claims he possesses. I came among you an outcast from those with whom I associated; driven from them, I admit, by no arbitrary act, but by the slow and resistless forces of conviction. I came among you, to make use of the legal phraseology, *in forma pauperis.* I had nothing to offer you but faithful and honorable service. You received me, as Dido received the shipwrecked Æneas—

'Ejectum littore, egentum accepi.'

and I only trust you may not hereafter at any time have to complete the sentence in regard to me—

' Et regni, demens, in parte locavi.'

You received me with kindness, indulgence, generosity, and, I may even say, with some measure of confidence. And the relation between us has assumed such a form that you can never be my debtors, but that I must forever be in your debt. It is not from me, under such circumstances, that any word will proceed that can savor of the character which the right honorable gentleman imputes to the conduct of the Government with respect to the present bill."

Turning then to the more particular business of the hour, the Chancellor of the Exchequer concluded:

"Sir, we are assailed; this bill is in a state of crisis and of peril, and the Government along with it. We stand or fall with it, as has been declared by my noble friend, Lord Russell. We stand with it now; we may fall with it a short time hence. If we do so fall, we, or others in our places, shall rise with it hereafter. I shall not attempt to measure with precision the forces that are to be arrayed against us in the coming issue. Perhaps the great division of to-night is not the last that must take place in the struggle. At some point of the contest you may possibly succeed. You may drive us from our seats. You may bury the bill that we have introduced, but we will write upon its gravestone for an epitaph this line, with certain confidence in its fulfillment—

' Exoriare aliquis nostris ex ossibus ultor.'

You cannot fight against the future. Time is on our side. The great social forces which move onward in their might and majesty, and which the tumult of our debates does not for a moment impede or disturb—those great social forces are against you; they are marshaled on our side; and the banner which we now carry in this fight, though perhaps at some moment it may droop over our sinking heads, yet it soon again will float in the eye of Heaven, and it will be borne by the firm hands of the united people of the three kingdoms, perhaps not to an easy, but to a certain and to a not far distant victory."

The division took place under circumstances of the greatest excitement. The Speaker having put the question, members withdrew. In due course the result was known—Ayes, 318; noes, 313. Government majority, 5.

It was the privilege of the present writer to be present on this memorable occasion. But, another who was present shall describe the scene:

" Hardly had the words escaped the teller's lips than there arose a wild, raging, mad-brained shout from the floor and gallery such as has never been heard in the present House of Commons. Dozens of half-frantic Tories stood up in their seats, madly waved their hats, and hurrahed at the top of their voices. Strangers in both galleries clapped their hands. The Adullamites on the Ministerial benches, carried away by the delirium of the moment, waved their hats in sympathy with the Opposition, and cheered as loudly as any. The Chancellor of the Exchequer, in his speech, had politely performed the operation of holding a candle to—Lucifer (Mr. Lowe); and he, the prince of the revolt, the leader, instigator, and prime mover of the conspiracy, stood up in the excitement of the moment—flushed, triumphant, and avenged. His hair, brighter than silver, shone and glistened in the brilliant light. His complexion had deepened into something like bishop's purple. His small, regular, and almost woman-like features, always instinct with intelligence 'now mantled with the liveliest pleasure. He took off his hat, waved it in wide and triumphant circles over the heads of the very men who had just gone into the lobby against him. "Who would have thought there were so much in Bob Lowe?" said one member to another; "why, he was one of the cleverest men in Lord Palmerston's Government!" "All this comes of Lord Russell's sending for Goschen," was the reply. "Disraeli did not half so signally avenge himself against Peel," interposed another; "Lowe has very nearly broken up the Liberal party.' These may seem to be exaggerated estimates of the situation; but in that moment of agitation and excitement I dare say a hundred sillier things were said and agreed to. Anyhow, there he stood--that usually cold, undemonstrative, intellectual, white-headed, red faced, venerable-looking arch-conspirator! shouting himself hoarse, like the ringleader of schoolboys at a successful barring-out, and amply repaid at that moment for all Sky-terrier witticisms and any amount of popular obloquy! But see, the Chancellor of the Exchequer lifts up his hand to bespeak silence, as if he had something to say in regard to the result of the division. But the more the great orator lifts his hand beseechingly, the more the cheers are renewed and the hats waved. At length the noise comes to an end by the process of exhaustion, and the Chancellor of the Exchequer rises. Then there is a universal hush, and you might hear a pin drop. He simply says, "Sir, I propose to fix the committee for Monday, and I will then state the order of business." It was twilight, brightening into day, when we got out into the welcome fresh air of New Palace Yard. Early as was the hour, about three hundred persons were assembled to see the members come out, and to cheer the friends of the bill. It was a night to be long remembered. The House of Commons had listened to the grandest oration ever yet delivered by the greatest orator of his age;

and had then to ask itself how it happened that the Liberal party had been disunited, and a Liberal majority of sixty 'muddled away.' "

On the third reading of the Bill, the Government were placed in a minority of 11. The numbers being for the Amendment, 315; against, 304.

The Opposition had at length succeeded in their hostility to Reform and to the Ministry. On the following day, the 19th of June, Earl Russell in the Lords and Mr. Gladstone in the Commons, announced that, in consequence of their late defeat, the Government had felt it their duty to make a communication to her Majesty. On the 26th fuller explanations were furnished in both Houses. In the Lords, Earl Russell stated that Ministers had tendered their resignations, to which they had adhered, notwithstanding an appeal from the Queen to reconsider their determination. In the House of Commons, Mr. Gladstone defended the Government for their resolve to stand or fall by the bill, and explained at length the circumstances which led to that declaration. Such a pledge, he admitted, was one which a Government should rarely give.

" It was the last weapon in the armory of the Government; it should not be lightly taken down from the walls; and if it is taken down, it should not be lightly replaced; nor till it has served the purposes it was meant to fulfill. The pledge had been given, however, under the deepest conviction of public duty, and had the effect of making them use every effort in their power to avoid offence, to conciliate, support, and unite, instead of distracting."

MR. GLADSTONE DELIVERING HIS MAIDEN SPEECH IN PARLIAMENT.

THE SUNDAY ORATOR OF HYDE PARK.

CHAPTER XIX.

HUMORS OF THE OLD ELECTION DAYS.

Dost thou think because thou art virtuous there shall be no more cakes and ale? Yes, by Saint Anne, and ginger shall be hot in the mouth, too —*Shakespeare.*

> The rabble all alive
> From tippling benches, cellars, stalls and sties,
> Swarm in the streets.   —*William Cowper.*

> They praise and they admire, they know not what,
> And know not whom, but as one leads the other ;
> And what delight to be by such extoll'd,
> To live upon their tongues, and be their talk,
> Of whom to be dispraised, were no small praise.
> —*John Milton.*

This is a chapter of personal reminiscences. In the old days of "long ago," when riding in steam cars was somewhat of an experiment; when devout souls thought it was running against providence to ride in coaches driven without horses at the awful rate of twenty miles an hour ; when the telegraph was but a dream, and the weekly newspaper was so expensive, by reason of the absurd and iniquitous stamp duty, that poor folks formed clubs of five or six in order that they might know what was going on " in Lunnon and other parts," it will be easily understood that in these dreary, quiet times, any circumstance out of the common order of things, such as a balloon ascension, or a very small circus, was heartily welcome. The smallest of these things was big enough to break the monotony of life, and stir the sluggish souls of young and old.   The annual election of Mayor, Aldermen and town Councilors was quite a blessing. But a general election of members to serve her gracious Majesty in the Commons House of Parliament was a godsend ! Old political soldiers who had fought in former years, but had never been rich enough to vote, told of the stormy scenes of the old Reform Bill of 1832. They talked of "Billy Pitt" and "Little Lord John" as though they had been next-door neighbors. But in the days of which I speak the older men were mostly given up to memories and reminiscences ; the younger men were full of fight, and they had sufficient cause to be. The Reform Bill of Lord John Russell had given a £10-householder a vote. The man who paid the $50 a year rent, apart altogether from the innumerable taxes—highway tax, poor-law tax, etc., etc.—that formed a perfect chatelaine about the girdle of rent that bound him, was entitled to a vote, but a man might be in all respects the equal, or even the superior of the "Ten Pounder," he might even live in a better house, but if he only paid $49.99 he could not vote. It was the money that did the voting, not the man. The odd cent made all the difference.

Apostles of human rights—such men as Thomas Watson, Henry Hethrington, Thomas Cooper, Henry Vincent among the poor, and such men as John Bright, Joseph Sturge, Earnest Jones and others among the well-to-do classes—found the time ripe for the promulgation of their doctrines, and a general election was just the grandest of all occasions ; a sort of political Pentecost, when men with hearts in earnest and tongues aflame, made the most of their opportunities of unfettered speech. The dissolution of Parliament was the sure and certain sign that there would be real earnest work, beautiful fighting, and merry times all over England for the space of six weeks. Her Majesty issued writs for a new Parliament, her faithful and loving subjects were enjoined to elect their representatives, and they were charged to be in their places in six weeks from the date of the writs, when the gentlemanly usher of the black rod would ring the bell and business would begin.

At the dissolution of Parliament the Queen read a speech, which was always very formal and empty, indicating certain things that everybody knew, expressing royal gratitude to both Houses of Parliament, and then as in duty bound, the Queen committed her lords and commons and the people at large to the care of Almighty God. All this was exceedingly well done. Long before the end of the six weeks' conflict it was painfully manifest that the lords and commons, the electors and the non-electors, and the country at large were all very much in need of divine guidance. The most appropriate prayers for those times would have been "prayers for those that are at sea."

No sooner was the dissolution of Parliament announced, than there was a great desire to get a copy of the Queen's speech. There was not an evening paper in the whole wide world in these days. Enterprising printers printed the speech and soon the ancestors of our newsboys made the streets echo with their cries: "Queen's speech! Parliament 'solved! Queen's speech! Only a penny!"

The Queen's speech had nothing in it to form a text for political oratory, but—as we shall see in a little while—the emptiness of the speech gave the Radical orator themes enough and to spare.

Members of Parliament are not paid a salary, nor are their traveling expenses covered. They would consider it beneath their dignity to accept a cent for their services. The old school English Tory would deplore exceedingly the coming of the time when members of Parliament should be paid for their services, or the hard and fast "property qualifications" should be repealed.

In these old days, now under consideration, there were not a few "pocket boroughs," that is, constituencies in which some noble lord or immense landowner had what was called "paramount influence." He could really send whoever he liked to Parliament. He could send his own butler,

if he chose. And it would have been a good thing if he had
done so sometimes, instead of sending such men as sometimes crept through this subterranean way into the stately
halls of St. Stephen's. Taking him all in all, however, the
English M. P. was fairly representative, and if England
owes nothing else to her worthy Commoners, she owes them
this at least: they have saved her from her Lords many a
time; and it may be that the day is not far distant when the
redemption will be complete, and the House of Lords will
be devoted to some useful purpose.

During the six weeks of a general election the gentleman
who has been M. P. and wants to be M. P. again must put
his dignity in his pocket, for this is the time when the cos-
ter-monger and the cabman, "the brewer, the baker, and
the candlestick maker" will feel called upon to put him
through his facings. He will be asked all sorts of questions, reasonable and unreasonable, especially unreasonable.
Smart men, just for the fun of it, will try to draw from him
the most absurd and foolish pledges. And woe betide the
M. P. who weary of such badgering should remind his tor-
menters of the dignity of his position.

A somewhat short-tempered candidate who had represented the borough before grew tired of this badgering,
and said to the noisy nonelectors:

"My good fellows, do you know who I am? I am the
Representative of the people!"

"Oh, you be blowed!" answered the rude and noisy
enthusiast. "Aint' we the people themselves? Ain't we
a sending of yer? And don't you think we're bloomin'
kind?"

But the day of nomination was the greatest day of all in
an English election till our later civilization came along and
took all the fun out of the fair and made an election as
serious and uneventful as a third-class funeral. In the old,
merry times a temporary covered platform called "The

Hustings" was erected, and on the given day the Mayor, with his stately robes on, and the golden civic chain around his neck, would march in grand procession to the hustings, accompanied by other civic dignitaries, and there, in the presence of an enormous crowd, would show the writ and announce that in loyal obedience to the command of her gracious Majesty that he had called together the electors of this ancient loyal borough to elect two fit and proper persons to represent this borough in the Commons House of Parliament.

Then, with a hearty "God Save the Queen," the business would begin.   According to arrangement the Tories would propose and second their candidate in a brief way ; then the Liberals or Radicals would propose their man.   The Mayor would call for a show of hands on the part of the electors only.   The mayor would usually decide against his own party, by which method he would be sure to win a little glory as "a high-minded, impartial, incorruptible public officer." A "poll" would be demanded by some representative of the supposed minority, all of which the high-minded, incorruptible Mayor would arrange for, and so with another hearty "God Save the Queen" the battle of the election would begin.   Then the walls of the city would be covered with squibs and cartoons.   Each candidate would issue his address, which would form the text for commendation or attack for friends and enemies alike.   Then for five or six weeks life would be well worth living, no matter how poor you were.   The weak points, the foibles, the peculiarities of the candidates would afford topics for boundless amusement. But it is fair to say that the vulgar, brutal vivisection of private life that mars too many of our conflicts, did not enter into these old election fights.   Full to the brim with humor, but free from vicious and bitter slander, they were straightforward, manly fights.   Around the hustings the battle waged hot and fierce.   The rude hustings became a grand arena. Remember these were the days of the $50-voter. The nonelectors were largely in excess of the electors, and they were growing to be a power. They would be heard, and there were many of them well worth hearing. These nonelectors made very lively times for the candidates when they came to deliver addresses. They would give a man a name that would abide with him forever! One candidate I well remember, who was thin enough for exhibition at a dime museum, came before the "electors and nonelectors"; his name was Richardson. He was one of the thinnest men I ever saw. A merry wag in the crowd hailed him as "Fat Dick!" The name was so supremely absurd that it stuck to him. And if ever you go to the town of Never-mind-what, in the north of England, and ask for Mr. Richardson, you will meet with the response: "That means 'Fat Dick' for sure!"

I remember one of his speeches in which he was explaining the reasons that had led him to sever his association with the old Radical party and join the Tories. Just in the midst of his speech, which was really a very able one, a man was hoisted on the shoulders of the crowd, who immediately proceeded to pull off his coat, and turning it inside out, struggled to get it on again. The crowd was uproarious. But "Fat Dick" was equal to the occasion. "Am I to understand," said Candidate Richardson, "that I have turned my coat? Is that your chief objection? Well, what is an honest man to do when he finds he has his coat on wrong side but turn it? And I want to say to my Radical friends, who seem to deplore my loss so much, that if I had continued in their ranks much longer I shouldn't have had a coat to wear or turn." This retort caught the crowd, and "Rah for Fat Dick!" rent the air.

Not infrequently the candidate who was not much of a speaker—though in all other respects just the man to make a most valuable member of Parliament—would content himself with going over the ground of his published address, and then, making a genial bow, would most unwisely undertake to answer any questions that electors or nonelectors might choose to ask.

The man who undertakes to answer any questions that may be asked is not wise.   It is so easy to ask difficult, not to say foolish, questions.

Many and many a time have I seen a political gathering given over to the wildest and most ungovernable merriment by some foolish question, presented with no reason on earth but to create fun and to embarrass the candidate.   Here are a handful of sample questions, some of which were capable of a direct, simple answer, but others could only be answered in a qualified manner, and whenever these qualifications were introduced the trouble began. The questioner always wanted "a simple, straightforward answer."   This is the way the poor candidate was badgered :

"If we send you to Parliament will you vote for the abolition of the House of Lords ?

"Will you move that the civil list be revised or suspended?

"Will you vote for the disestablishment and disendowment of the Established Church?

"Will you vote for universal suffrage?

"Will you vote for the abolition of the property qualification clause ?

"Will you always vote against the declaration of war whatever be the provocation ?

"Will you vote that a man may marry deceased wife's sister ?

" Will you vote that the railroads shall become national property ?

"Will you vote for the Mayworth grant ?

" Will you vote for the repeal of the income tax ?

" Will you vote for the repeal of capital punishment ? "

So the questioning would go on. The only chance for the candidate was to answer "yes" or "no," wherever he had a chance. If he wavered he was lost. There was always some fellow handy with a foolish question. I remember a smart Alec, named Reuben Finn, who could always be relied upon to upset a meeting. He had a question:

"Mr. Candidate," said Reuben, "I have a plain, simple question to ask. A question that is capable of the simplest, shortest answer. And I don't want you to go beating about the bush. I want just a plain, unmistakable 'yes' or 'no.'"

"All right," said the candidate, "go ahead with your question."

"Well, then," said Reuben, "Will you lend me a sovereign?"

The laughter that followed his question was long and loud, but the answer so completely crushed Reuben Finn that it was a long time before he asked any more questions.

"Lend you a sovereign!" said the candidate, "I'll give you a sovereign if you can find a bigger fool than yourself in twenty-four hours, and I'll lend you a lantern to hunt him up."

Sometimes nonconformist clergymen would enter the arena, and they were generally powerful allies. They were earnest and eloquent, and sure of a large following. But sometimes they were terribly roasted by the other side. One case comes to my memory. It was in the good old town of Leicester. The Rev. J. P. Mursell, the successor of Robert Hall, was a man of wonderful ability; a man of grand appearance, with a crown of snowy hair, and a large and prominent nose. He was at a great political meeting in the opera house, and in denouncing the retrograde action of certain wealthy hosiery manufacturers, who had grown conservative as they had grown rich, told an anecdote of Robert Hall, who on being importuned to marry a certain ancient lady, said he would rather "marry Beelzebub's eldest daughter, and go live with the old folks." Mr. Mursell applied the anecdote and turned up his nose very manifestly at the Tory hosiers. Immediately the following jingle was heard sung in the streets of Leicester :

> There is a parson of small renown,
> Lives on the New Walk in Leicester Town ;
> Whose hair has grown gray all over his head
>   Screams aloud for Beelzebub's daughter !
>
> From his peaceful home to the play-house he goes,
> And insults amongst others manufacturers of hose,
> And at them in spite turns up his great nose,
>   And then screams for Beelzebub's daughter.

In a few days the walls of Leicester were placarded with large bills of which the following is a copy :

LECTURE ON NOSES!!!

The Rev. J. P. Mursell,

Having just returned from the Promontory of Noses,

will deliver a series of lectures in

BELVOIR STREET CHAPEL

in the following order :

Lecture 1. The Roman Nose.

Lecture 2. The Pug Nose.

Lecture 3. The Impudent Nose.

ILLUSTRATED BY HIS OWN.

Reserved seats free to Hosiery Manufacturers.

As I have said, the hustings during these six weeks was the arena of a great deal of local oratory. I remember a young Radical who could always gather immense crowds. He was an iconoclast pure and simple and oh how he loved to talk !

" Look here mates," he would say, "there's some things you can reform, and there's others you can only reform by reforming them off the face of the earth ! Now look at me. I'm not such a bad sort of a chap, am I? I tries hard to do fair and square, but I can't vote. 'Cos why? Why it's all a question of money. There's a fellow lives in our street; a drunken, lazy sot, as wallops his wife and lambs his kids, but he can vote. 'Cos why? He's got money; that's why. I pays three and ninepence a week rent, but I can't vote! He pays four shillings a week and he can vote and does vote! But it ain't the man as votes, it's the bloomin' thruppence! Look at the Queen and the Royal family! I should like to know what good they are to the country. They are just a set of royal paupers, that's wot they are. Mind you, I don't say but wot Prince Albert is a likely kind o' cove, and if he had his way things would be different. But, Lord love you, all the big bugs is down on him. 'Cos why? 'Cause he has a good word to say for the workingman, that's why! Look at them lazy fossils in the House o' Lords. Nothing will ever wake 'em up unless somebody yells 'Church in danger,' or 'House afire!' and then they'll march in double quick time! I tell you mates it's time that House was to somebody as has something to do. And then there's the blessed Church, established by law and fed at the public expense! I ain't got nothing particular against the Church, but I think if a man wants either pigs or parsons he should feed them, and not ask the State to do it. But it's no use talking. Half measures won't do! And wot I say is, Down with the Royal family! Down with the House of Lords! Down with the Established Church! Down with everything!"

Since 1832, few of those scenes of violence, and even of bloodshed, which formerly distinguished Parliamentary elections in many English boroughs, have been witnessed. Some of these lawless outbreaks were doubtless due to the unpopularity of the candidates forced upon the electors; but even in the larger towns—where territorial influence had little sway—riots occurred upon which we look back now in almost doubtful amazement. Men holding strong political views have ceased to enforce those views by the aid of brickbats and other dangerous missiles. Yet at the beginning of the present century such arguments were very popular. And to the violence which prevailed was added the most unblushing bribery. Several boroughs long notorious for extensive bribery have since been disfranchised. The practice, however, extended to most towns in the kingdom, though it was not always carried on in the same open manner. By a long-established custom, a voter at Hull received a donation of $10.00 or $20.00 for a plumper. In Liverpool men were openly paid for their votes; and Lord Cochrane stated in the House of Commons that, after his return to Honiton, he sent the town-crier round the borough to tell the voters to go to the chief banker for $50.00 each.

The Drive, Hawarden.

CHAPTER XX.

DISESTABLISHMENT AND DISENDOWMENT OF THE IRISH CHURCH.

It is held
That valor is the chiefest virtue, and
Most dignifies the haver; if it be,
The man I speak of cannot in the world
Be singly counterpoised.   *—Shakespeare.*

If a man stands for the right and the truth, though every man's finger be pointed at him, though every woman's lip be curled at him in scorn, he stands in a majority; for God and good angels are with him, and greater are they that are for him than all that can be against him   *—John B Gough.*

We offer our readers another reminiscent chapter. When Mr. Gladstone rose in the British House of Commons Monday afternoon, Feb. 13, 1886, to present his home rule for Ireland bill many called to mind his first great fight for religious equality for Ireland more than twenty years ago. It may be pleasant to men of this younger generation to be told how that battle for the disestablishment and disendowment of the Irish Church was fought and won.

The condition of affairs may be very briefly told. The population of Ireland in 1867 was about six millions. Of these six millions four and a half millions belonged to the Roman Catholic Church. Half a million only belonged to the Protestant Episcopal Church, another half million owed allegiance to the Presbyterian Church. The census never gave the Irish Church, even from the Episcopal authorities, more than seven hundred thousand. This church of the minority arrogating to itself the title of "The Irish Church," or "The Church of Ireland," had always manifested the warmest sympathy with the oppressors of Ireland, and was spending public money in an unjust and unprofitable manner. This church was absorbing in annual salaries sums amounting to three and a half to four millions of dollars derived from National property amounting to from sixty-five to seventy millions of dollars. Much of this money was wasted in the employment of three or four times as many rectors and curates as the church could possibly have use for. Yet all the while Ireland was in the depths of poverty, famine-threatened, or famine-smitten from year to year.

To change all this, to bring in the reign of religious equality, to place all the churches in Ireland on an equal footing, such as they are in this free land, and to apply these vast funds that were being so shamefully misused to alleviate the sorrows of the maimed and the halt and the blind, and to such as suffered from the sadder lot of mental weakness, these were the grand purposes Mr. Gladstone set his hand and his heart to, in his first great battle on behalf of Ireland.

I am thinking how that great battle was fought and won more than twenty years ago. I am not concerned to discuss at length the merits of this Irish Church measure, nor am I disposed to underestimate the sincerity of those who really thought Mr. Gladstone was endangering the cause of true religion. I am persuaded that Mr. Gladstone was not himself more sincere than many of his opponents. Born and trained a nonconformist of nonconformists all my sympathies, if not my prejudices, ran in favor of disestablishment. Twenty years and more of happy observation of religious equality beneath the Stars and Stripes have only served to deepen my conviction that Count Cavour's dream for Italy of "A Free Church in a free State," is a very good dream for all lands.

I am looking back over the stretch of twenty years. I am calling to mind the grandeur of the battle, of the calm, fixed enthusiasm of Mr. Gladstone, whose personal influence on his followers was largely the secret of the steadfast valor of the conflict and the dignity of its final triumph.

From the very outset this battle for religious equality was elevated to the dignity of a conflict. The battle for Reform had often fallen very near the gutter. On both sides of this religious warfare men were in dead earnest. Mr. Gladstone had scarcely laid his Bill on the table of the House of Commons before the floodgates of abuse were thrown wide open. It was, of course, the easiest thing in the world to charge Mr. Gladstone with treachery to his earliest and deepest convictions, he, the old-time defender of church establishments. He was a "turncoat," a "traitor," a "renegade," and everything else of the kind.

Then uprose the Rt. Hon. Benjamin Disraeli, the champion of the church, and I sometimes think ancient Rome never saw gladiators more thoroughly matched than Gladstone and Disraeli. It was worth while living in those days to see these masters of debate in action. Mr. Disraeli was too wise to make any capital out of the change-of-mind argument. He knew the value of a good cry, and so he started the memorable cry, "Church in Danger!" He saw the sacred fabric of the time-honored Church tottering to its fall. He saw angels in tears over the desecration, and declared himself on the side of the angels. All other points of view were lost sight of in this scare-crow terror of peril to the Church. The ark of God was in danger? And Disraeli came to the rescue!

Punch's picture of the subtle Disraeli soaring heavenward with angel's wings and a wreath of immortal glory about his brows, while there was a smirk of satire and scorn on his lips, will be remembered by every man who had a share in this memorable fight. While Mr. Disraeli was shedding mock tears over the downfall of Zion, his followers were enjoying themselves in belaboring Mr. Gladstone.

The Church and Tory papers supplied Mr. Gladstone with a good deal of information. He was "in league with infidelity," "an atheist at heart," "a sacriligious robber," "a spoliator of the temple of God," he was the "man of sin," the "Anti-Christ" foretold in the "Book of Revelation." He had "the mark of the beast," and "the horns of the evil one" protruding from his wicked brow. So hot and fierce was the conflict that I have seen Mr. Gladstone hung in effigy and burned in more than two or three of the quiet village church-yards in the North of England.

Nothing impresses me more as I look back than Mr. Gladstone's perfect indifference to this whole tirade of abuse. I sometimes wonder if he knew half that was written or said. He did not treat calumny with scorn, he was so absorbed in his mission that he lived above it. I am thinking, too, of his brief visits to our committee-rooms during that grand Lancashire campaign, that campaign in which he delivered speeches which belong to the noblest classics of religious freedom, Mr. Gladstone would crowd his advice into the briefest phrases. "Educate the people! Educate the people! Only enlightened constituencies vote wisely!" And when some fussy committeeman would ask: "What shall we say when asked about the forthcoming Land Bill and the Education Bill?" Mr. Gladstone would answer with manifest impatience: "Tell your friends that it is impossible to redress the wrongs of seven centuries in one session of Parliament."

Mr. Stead has spoken of Mr. Gladstone as having a "Quixotic conscience." I am sure that he impressed that aspect of his character on his followers. And by his followers, I am not speaking of his followers in the House of Commons, but the rank and file of the Liberal party, among the sturdy workmen and middle class of the North of England—followers by thousands, who believed in the perfect integrity, the political sagacity and the incorruptible honor of the man who was then "the People's William," not yet "the Grand Old Man."

Of course there was humor as well as earnestness in this campaign. Soldiers in that war for religious equality will remember Tom Grimshaw's logic. Tom Grimshaw was a Bolton man with a clear head and a witty tongue, rough of speech, but very earnest in purpose. He reduced the whole Irish Church question to a single sentence. There were 5,000 people in Bolton Market place, a large wagon served as a platform. I had labored somewhat painfully with a most indulgent audience for the space of half an hour. I had tried to argue for the voluntary maintenance of the churches of every name. Then came Tom Grimshaw, as burly as Longfellow's blacksmith, and this is what he said:

"Men o' Bowton, there's a sight too much talk. The whole business lies e' a nutshell. Some folks likes pigs, and some folks likes parsons! What I say is, let them as likes pigs *and* parsons feed 'em!" This brief settlement of the Irish Church question was afterward known as "Grimshaw's logic."

No story of this great battle would be complete that lost sight of the hard fighting that took place between Mr. Disraeli and John Bright. Mr. Disraeli recognized in Mr. Bright a foeman worthy of his steel. No man in the House of Commons had more respect for an able and honorable antagonist than the then leader of her Majesty's opposition. As the conflict deepened these doughty warriors measured swords. The question of the appropriation of the vast surplus had especial charms for Mr. Bright, and in answering Mr. Disraeli he had opportunity to deal with this matter, and he dealt with it in words that deserve to be held in long and proud remembrance. Mr. Disraeli had been contend-

ing that this church of the minority, this church that had
assumed to regard itself as "The" Church of Ireland, this
venerable establishment that had always been the protector of
freedom of religion and of toleration ; and that therefore,
being on the side of the angels, he was on the side of the
establishment.   Mr. Bright denied that the establishment
had been the protector of freedom, or religion, or toleration, and in his own quiet, incisive manner remarked that
his right honorable friend seemed to read a different history
from anybody else, or possibly he made his own history,
and, like Voltaire, made it better without facts than with
them.   This, of course, brought down the House.   All
along the ranks of the Liberal party the laughter was long
and loud.

> " And even the ranks of Tuscany
> Could scarce forbear to cheer."

But in all that grand battle for religious equality in
Ireland there was hardly a more brilliant passage than the
closing sentences of John Bright's speech on the uses to be
made of the surplus that would surely follow disendowment.
"Do you think," he said, "it will be a misappropriation of
the surplus funds of this great establishment to apply them
to some objects such as those described in this bill?   Do
you not think that from the charitable dealing with these
matters even a sweeter incense may arise than when these
vast funds were applied to maintain three times the number
of clergy that can be of the slightest use to the church with
which they are connected ?   We can do but little, it is true.
We can not relume the extinguished lamp of reason.   We
can not make the deaf to hear.   We can not make the dumb
to speak.   It is not given to us :

> From the thick film to purge the visual ray,
> And on the sightless eyeballs pour the day.

"But at least we can lessen the load of affliction, and we
can make life more tolerable to vast numbers who are now

suffering. I see this measure giving tranquility to our people, greater strength to the realm, and adding a new lustre and a new dignity to the crown. I dare claim for this bill the support of all good and thoughtful people within the bounds of the British Empire, and I can not doubt that, in its early and great results, it will have the blessing of the Supreme, for I believe it to be founded on those principles of justice and mercy which are the glorious attributes of His eternal reign."

No other man could have spoken with such effect. Other men might have been just as eloquent, but behind this eloquence stood the man, whose character and career gave to his simplest utterances the moral force that made his words almost irresistible.

Mr. Gladstone fired the first shot of this great battle for Ecclesiastical Equality on the 1st of March, 1869. His speech, in introducing his Bill for the Disestablishment and Disendowment of the Irish Church, lasted three hours, and his bitterest opponent, Benjamin Disraeli, said there was not a redundant word in it. Always a master of finance Mr. Gladstone nowhere, except perhaps in some of his famous budgets, revealed his complete mastery of that intricate science more effectively than in his wonderful manipulation of those vast sums involved in the disendowment of the Irish Church. After meeting generously all possible claims, the question of the distribution of the surplus became of grave importance. We rest on the authority of Mr. G. Barnett Smith for the statement of Mr. Gladstone's scheme of distribution.

The tithe rent charge would yield $45,000,000; lands and perpetuity rents, $31,250,000; money, $3,750,000—total, $80,000,000; the present value of the property of the Irish Church. Of this, the bill would dispose of $43,250,000, viz., vested interests of incumbents, $24,500,000; curates, $4,000,000; lay compensation, $4,500,000; private endowments, $2,500,000; building charges, $1,250,000; commutation of the Maynooth Grant and the *Regium Donum*, $5,500,000, and expenses of the commission, $1,000,000.

Consequently, there would remain a surplus of between $35,000,000 and $40,000,000; and the question arose, said the Premier, amid considerable excitement, "What shall we do with it?" He held it to be indispensable, under the circumstances, that the purposes to which the surplus would be applied should be Irish. Further, they should not be religious, although they must be final, and open the door to no new controversy. After discussing various suggestions, some of which he dismissed as impossible, and others as radically wrong, the speaker announced, quoting the preamble of the bill, that the Government had concluded to apply the surplus to the relief of unavoidable calamities and suffering, not provided for by the Poor Law. The sum of $925,000 would be allocated for lunatic asylums; $100,000 a year would be awarded to idiot asylums; $115,000 to training schools for the deaf, dumb and blind; $75,000 for the training of nurses; $50,000 for reformatories, and $225,000 to county infirmaries—in all $1,555,000 a year. Mr. Gladstone claimed that by the provision of all these requirements they would be able to combine very great reforms; and they would also be in a better condition for inviting the Irish landlord to accede to a change in the county-cess, as they were able to offer by this plan a considerable diminution in its burden. The plan for disposing of the residue he believed to be a good and solid plan, full of public advantage. After touching upon possible errors in his statement, and announcing that he should be happy to welcome suggestions from any quarter, Mr. Gladstone referred to the great transition which the Government were asking the clergymen of the Church of Ireland to undergo, and to the privileges which the laity were called upon to debate. He concluded with the following glowing peroration :

"I do not know in what country so great a change, so great a transition has been proposed for the ministers of a religious communion, who have enjoyed for many ages the preferred position of an Established Church. I can well understand that to many in the Irish Establishment such a change appears to be nothing less than ruin and destruction. From the height on which they now stand the future is to them an abyss, and their fears recall the words used in *King Lear*, when Edgar endeavors to persuade Gloster that he has fallen over the cliffs of Dover, and says:

> Ten masts at each, make not the altitude
> Which thou has perpendicularly fallen.
> Thy life's a miracle !

And yet but a little while after the old man is relieved from his delusion, and finds that he has not fallen at all. So I trust that when, instead of the fictitious and adventitious aid on which we have too long taught the Irish Establishment to lean, it should come to place its trust in its own resources, in its own great mission, in all that it can draw from the energy of its ministers and its members, and the high hopes and promises of the gospel that it te ches, it will find that it has entered upon a new era of existence--an era bright with hope and potent for good. At any rate, I think the day has certainly come when an end is finally to be put to that union, not between the Church and religious association, but between the Establishment and the State, which was commenced under circumstances little auspicious, and has endured to be a source of unhappiness to Ireland, and of discredit and scandal to England. There is more to say. This measure is in every sense a great measure--great in its principles, great in the multitude of its dry, technical, but interesting detail, and great as a testing measure; for it will show for one and all of us of what metal we are made. Upon us all it brings a great responsibility—great and foremost upon those who occupy this bench. We are especially chargable, nay, deeply guilty, if we have either dishonestly, as some think, or even prematurely or unwisely challenged so gigantic an issue. I know well the punishments that follow rashness in public affairs, and that ought to fall upon those men, those Phætons of politics, who, with hands unequal to the task, attempt to guide the chariot of the sun. But the responsibility, though heavy, does not exclusively press upon us; it presses upon every man who has to take part in the discussion and decision upon this bill. Every man approaches the discussion under the most solemn obligations to raise the level of his vision and expand its scope in proportion with the greatness of the matter in hand. The working of our constitutional government itself is upon its trial, for I do not believe there ever was a time when the wheels of legislative machinery were set in motion under conditions of peace and order and constitutional regularity to deal with a question greater or more profound. And more especially, sir, is the credit and fame of this great Assembly involved; this Assembly, which has inherited through many ages the accumulated honors of brilliant triumphs, of peaceful but courageous legislation, is now called upon to address itself to a task which would, indeed, have demanded all the best energies of the very best among your fathers and your ancestors. I believe it will prove to be worthy of the task. Should it fail, even the fame of the House of Commons will suffer disparagement; should it succeed, even that fame, I venture to say, will receive no small, no insensible addition. I must not ask gentlemen opposite to concur in this view, emboldened as I am by the kindness they have shown me in listening with patience to a statement which could not have been other than tedious; but I pray them to bear with me for a moment while, for myself and my colleagues, I say we are sanguine of the issue. We believe, and for my part I am deeply convinced, that when the final consummation shall arrive, and when the words are spoken that shall give the force of law to the work embodied in this measure—the work of peace and justice—those words will be echoed upon every shore where the name of Ireland or the name of Great Britain has been heard, and the answer to them will come back in the approving verdict of civilized mankind."

Commenting on this great speech the *Daily Telegraph*, then under the guiding hand of Edwin Arnold, says:

"The night was a night never to be forgotten. We shall not hesitate to say that Mr. Gladstone never before, amidst all the triumphs that mark his long course of honor and success, displayed more vigorous grasp of his subject, more luminous clearness in its development, earnestness more lofty, or eloquence more appropriate and refined, than in the memorable deliverance of last evening. Less than the most complete mastery of the complex scheme, from its mightiest principle to its minutest item, would have brought down that remarkable exhibition of intellect from the high level of an historical oration to a cold and weary evolution of clauses and calculations. But with that consummate skill which in old days made a fine art of finance, and taught us all the romance of the revenue, Mr. Gladstone made his statistics ornamental, and deftly wove the stiffest strings of figures into the web of his exposition. Scarcely even so much as glancing at his notes, he advanced with an oratorical step, which positively never once faltered from exordium to peroration of his amazing task; omitting nothing, slurring nothing, confusing nothing; but pouring from his prodigious faculty of thought, memory, and speech an explanation so lucid that none of all the many points which he made was obscure to any of his listeners when he had finished. And, charged as the speech necessarily was with hard and stern matter of fact and figure, the intense earnestness, the sincere satisfaction of the speaker, at the act of concord and justice he was inaugurating, gave such elasticity and play to his genius, that nowhere was the clause so dry or the calculation so involved, but some gentle phrase of respect, some high invocation of principle, some bright illumination of the theme from actual life, some graceful compliment to his hearers, lightened the passage of these mountains of statistics, and kept the House spell-bound by that rich and energetic voice. This phrase may seem extravagant; but though Mr. Gladstone has done many things of marvellous intellectual and oratorical force, his explosion last evening of the measure from which will assuredly date the pacification and happiness of Ireland, was a Parliamentary achievement unparalleled even by himself.

The long debate that followed on the introduction of the Bill was one of the most illustrious in the annals of the British House of Commons.   It was manifest that the House and the country at large were with the great leader.

On the motion for a second reading of the Bill the votes ran, for the second reading 368, against, 250—majority 118.   Of course there was a long and bitter fight.   In the House of Lords the conflict was waged with intense vigor. The Bishops especially did valiant service on behalf of the Church.   The Bill eventually passed the Lords by 121 to 114.   Thus passed one of the most remarkable measures of Victoria's reign.

A brief but glowing paragraph from Mr. Gladstone on the whole question will fitly close this chapter.

"The Church may have much to regret in respect to temporal splendor, yet the day is to come when it will be said of her, as of the temple of Jerusalem, 'that the glory of the latter house is greater than of the former;' and when the most loyal and faithful of her children will learn not to forget that at length the Parliament of England took courage, and the Irish Church was disestablished and disendowed."

CHAPTER XXI.

Good Knight! No soil of wrong thy spotless shield might stain;
  Thy keen sword served thee long and not in vain.
Oh, high impetuous soul, that mounting to the light,
  Spurned the dull world's control to gain the right!"
—*Lewis Morrison.*

A country is in a good and sound and healthy state when it exhibits the spirit of progress in all its institutions and in all its operations; and when with that spirit of progress it combines the spirit of affectionate retrospect upon the times and the generations that have gone before, and the determination to husband and to turn at every point to the best account, all that these previous generations have accumulated of what is good and worthy for the benefit of us their children. —*W. E. Gladstone.*

Mr. Gladstone's Reform Bill had been defeated, but he was not defeated, nor were the principles for which he so bravely fought to be buried in oblivion. The nation was thoroughly aroused. Reform demonstrations were held all over the country. With singular suicidal folly meetings in Hyde Park were prohibited. Mr. Bright in his trenchant manner asked: "If a public meeting in a public park is denied you, and if millions of intelligent and honest men are denied the franchise, on what foundation do our liberties rest, or is there in this country any liberty but the toleration of the ruling class?" When the police by the order of the government repulsed the procession that had marched in quiet order up to the Marble Arch, a riot ensued, the mob tore down the railings and entered the park. There was a good deal of free fighting, but no very serious damage was done. A body of Life Guards appeared upon the scene, and the riot was quelled. Meantime an enormous meeting was held in Trafalgar Square, where resolutions in favor of Reform and of gratitude to Mr. Gladstone and Mr. Bright, were carried with the wildest enthusiasm. Early in August a meeting was held at Brookfield, near Birmingham, at which it was estimated that not less than 250,000 were present. "Agitate! agitate! agitate!" was John Bright's advice, and with the advice came the assurance "that no Government, however strong, could long withstand the ascertained desire of an intelligent and determined people." It is not necessary to enter at length on any discussion of that remarkable episode of English history in which Mr. Disraeli "educated his party," brought in his Reform Bill, and so, as he gracefully described it, "dished the Whigs."

Passing under the shadow of his monument in Westminster Abbey, one may be forgiven if it should be suggested to the mind, that the three great things that made him famous were, that he made the Queen Empress of India, he "educated his party," and he "dished the Whigs!" On the 25th of February, 1868, it was announced in both Houses of Parliament that Lord Derby, through failing health, had resigned the Premiership, and that the Queen had entrusted Mr. Disraeli with the task of forming a new administration. Thus the "Asian mystery" had reached the highest place, and became Prime Minister of England. Lord Chelmsford in a merry mood said, referring to the two great English horse races the "Derby" and the "Oaks," "The old government was the Derby; this will be the Hoax."

While on the whole the Press spoke kindly and in congratulatory terms of Mr. Disraeli's accession to power, yet he had to bear a good deal of raillery and sarcasm. Of this he could hardly complain, for he had set the example of the merciless and unreasonable satire. One criti. says:

"There was of course but one possible Conservative Premier, Mr. Disraeli—he who had served the Conservative party for more than twenty years, who had led it to victory, and who had long been the ruling spirit of the Cabinet. To have reconstructed the Ministry without Vivian Grey as its chief, would have been to enact in politics a well-known play under proverbial disadvantages."

As Silas Wegg "dropped into poetry," so the *Pall Mall Gazette* dropped into Scripture, in the following caustic manner:

"One of the most grevious and constant puzzles of King David was the prosperity of the wicked and the scornful; and the same tremendous moral enigma has come down to our own days. In this respect, the earth is in its older times what it was in its youth. Even so recently as last week the riddle once more presented itself in its most impressive shape. Like the Psalmist, the Liberal leader may well protest that verily he has cleansed his heart in vain and washed his hands in innocency. All day long he has been plagued by Whig lords, and chastened every morning by Radical manufacturers. As blamelessly as any curate he has written about *Ecce Homo*, and he has never made a speech, even in the smallest country town, without calling out with David, 'How foolish am I, and how ignorant!' For all this, what does he see? The scorner who shot out the lip and shook the head at him across the table of the House of Commons last session, has now more than heart could wish; his eyes, speaking in an Oriental manner, stand out with fatness, he speaketh loftily, and pride compasseth him about as with a chain. . . . That the writer of frivolous stories about *Vivian Grey* and *Coningsby* should grasp the sceptre before the writer of beautiful and serious things about *Ecce Homo*—the man who is epigramatic, flashy, arrogant, before the man who never perpetrated an epigram in his life, is always fervid, and would as soon die as admit that he had a shade more brain than his footman—the Radical corrupted into a Tory before the Tory purified and elevated into a Radical. Is not this enough to make an honest man rend his mantle, and shave his head and sit down among the ashes inconsolable? Let us play the too underrated part of Bildad the Shuhite for a space, while our chiefs thus have unwelcome leisure to scrape themselves with pots herts, and to meditate upon the evil way of the world."

In the election of 1868 the Liberals were successful far beyond their own anticipations. Mr. Gladstone was in southwest Lancashire. The old antagonistic forces were against him. Mr. Cross and Mr. Turner beat him by a majority of three hundred. The possibility of this defeat had been anticipated. The electors of Greenwich, without Mr. Gladstone's solicitation, put him in nomination and elected him, without even an address, along with Mr. Alderman Salomons, a pronounced Liberal. The election proved that the country was with Mr. Gladstone and the Liberal cause. In the large cities the conservatives were completely routed, but in the counties they held their own. Scotland and Ireland both gave very substantial majorities for the Liberals.

Mr. Disraeli did not wait to meet the new Parliament, but resigned, promising, however, to fight the Disestablishment of the Irish Church.

On the 4th of December, 1868, the Queen sent for Mr. Gladstone and gave him instructions to form a ministry. On the 9th of the month he was able to announce the first great Liberal cabinet:

Prime Minister—W. E. Gladstone.
Secretary for Foreign Affairs—Lord Clarendon.
Secretary for the Colonies—Lord Grenville.
Home Secretary—Mr. Bruce.
Secretary of War—Mr. Cardwell.

Secretary for India—Duke of Argyle.
Lord Chancellor—Lord Hetherly.
Lord Privy Seal—Earl Kimberley.
First Lord of the Admiralty—Mr. Childers.
Lord Lieutenant of Ireland—Earl Spencer.
Postmaster-General—Lord Hartington.
Chancellor of the Exchequer—Mr. Robert Lowe.
President of the Board of Trade—Mr. John Bright.

Of the great measure of the Disestablishment and Disendowment of the Irish Church, reference has been made in a previous reminiscent chapter. It is remarkable to what an extent men who had been his sincere admirers up to that point, fell away from him. They could not understand the position he took; he, the old-time champion of the Church, now seeks, as they believed, its destruction. They surely could not have carefully considered these grand works, in which he so lucidly expounded and explained his position:

"There are many who think that to lay hands upon the national Church Establishment of a country is a profane and unhallowed act. I respect that feeling. I sympathize with it. I sympathize with it while I think it my duty to overcome and repress it. But if it be an error, it is an error entitled to respect. There is something in the idea of a national establishment of religion, of a solemn appropriation of a part of the Commonwealth, for conferring upon all who are ready to receive it what we know to be an inestimable benefit; of saving that portion of the inheritance from private selfishness, in order to extract from it, if we can, pure and unmixed advantages of the highest order for the population at large. There is something in this so attractive that it is an image that must always command the homage of the many. It is somewhat like the kingly ghost in *Hamlet*, of which one of the characters of Shakspeare says:—

> We do it wrong, being so majestical,
> To offer it the show of violence;
> For it is, as the air, invulnerable,
> And our vain blows malicious mockery.

But, sir, this is to view a religious establishment upon one side, only upon what I may call the eternal side. It has likewise a side of earth; and here I cannot do better than quote some lines written by the pres-

ent Archbishop of Dublin, at a time when his genius was devoted to
the muses. He said, in speaking of mankind:—

> " We who did our lineage high
>   Draw from beyond the starry sky,
>   And yet upon the other side,
>   To earth and to its dust allied,"

And so the Church Establishment, regarded in its theory and in its
aim, is beautiful and attractive. Yet what is it bnt an appropriation
of public property, an appropriation of the fruits of labor and of skill
to certain purposes, and unless these purposes are fulfilled, that appropriation cannot be justified. Therefore, sir, I cannot but feel that
we must set aside fears which thrust themselves upon the imagination, and act upon the sober dictates of our judgment. I think it has
been shown that the cause for action is strong—not for precipitate
action, not for action beyond our powers, but for such action as the
opportunities of the times and the condition of Parliament, if there
be but a ready will, will amply and easily admit of. If I am asked as
to my expectations of the issue of this struggle, I begin by frankly
avowing that I, for one, would not have entered into it, unless I believed that the final hour was about to sound—

> "Venit summa dies et ineluctabile fatum."

The issue is not in our hands. What we had and have to do is to
consider well and deeply before we take the first step in an engage-
ment such as this; but having enterered into the controversy, there
and then to acquit ourselves like men, and to use every effort to remove what still remains of the scandals and calamities in the relations which exist between England and Ireland, and to make our
best efforts at least to fill up with the cement of human concord the
noble fabric of the British Empire."

On the 15th of February, 1870, Mr. Gladstone brought
forward the Irish Land Bill. The House was crowded with
members and the gallaries were thronged with distinguished
strangers. In the outset, Mr. Gladstone alluded to the pre-
dictions of the opponents of the Irish Church Bill twelve
months before, that it was the land and not the Church
which lay at the root of Irish grievances. He therefore
trusted that the Opposition would approach the question
with a due sense of its importance. The necessity for closing and sealing up the controversy was admitted by all fair-
minded and moderate men on both sides.

The position of the Irish occupier under the existing land system Mr. Gladstone declared to be no better than it had been before the repeal of the Penal Laws. In certain counties of Ulster, there was a traditional custom which secured to the tenant fixity of tenure so long as he paid his rents, and a property or tenant right in his holding in virtue of the improvements which he and his predecessors in title had affected thereon—a tenant-right which he could sell. Throughout the rest of Ireland the tenants were in the main tenants-at-will, their property and themselves at the mercy of landlords and their agents, an evil condition which re-acted upon both tenants and landlords, and produced results of barbarism and cruelty, not matched in any country pretending to be civilized. Mr. Gladstone's Bill legalized the Ulster Customs, and sought to extend its benefits to the rest of Ireland. But Mr. Gladstone shall tell in his own majestic way the moral and social ends he hoped to attain.

"If I am asked," he said "what I hope to effect by this bill, I certainly hope we shall effect a great change in Ireland; but I hope also, and confidently believe, that this change will be accomplished by gentle means. Every line of the measure has been studied with the keenest desire that it shall import as little as possible of shock or violent alteration into any single arrangement now existing between landlord and tenant in Ireland. There is, no doubt, much to be undone; there is, no doubt, much to be improved; but what we desire is that the work of this bill should be like the work of Nature herself, when on face of a desolated land she restores what has been laid waste by the wild and savage hand of man. Its operations, we believe, will be quiet and gradual. We wish to alarm none; we wish to injure no one. What we wish is that where there has been despondency, there shall be hope; where there has been mistrust, there shall be confidence; where there has been alienation and hate, there shall, however gradually, be woven the ties of a strong attachment between man and man. This we know cannot be done in a day. The measure has reference to evils which has long been at work; their roots strike back into bygone centuries; and it is against the ordinance of Providence, as it is against the interest of man, that immediate reparation should in such cases be possible; for one of the main restraints of misdoing would be removed, if the consequences of misdoing could in a moment receive a remedy. For such reparation and such effects it is that we look from this bill; and we reckon on them not less surely and not less confidently because we know they must be gradual and slow; and because we are likewise aware that if it be poisoned by the malignant agency of angry or of bitter passions, it cannot do its proper work. In order that there may be a hope of its entire success, it must be p.ssed--not as a triumph of party over party, or class over class: not as the lifting up of an ensign to record the downfall of that which has once been great and powerful--but as a common work of common love and goodwill to the common good of our common country. With such objects and in such a spirit as that, this House will address itself to the work, and sustain the feeble efforts of the Government. And my hope, at least is high and ardent that we shall live to see our work prosper in our hand, and that in that Ireland, which we desire to unite to England and Scotland by the only enduring ties—th se of free-will and free affection—peace, order, and a settled and cheerful industry will diffuse their blessings from year to year, and from day to day, over a smiling land."

The history of the bill is almost amusing. Not less than *three hundred amendments* were offered to it. But the liberal power was dominant. On the 30th of May, 1870, the bill passed the House of Commons. On the second of June it passed the Lords, and on August 1st, received the royal assent.

In the same Session another important Liberal Measure, Mr. Forster's Education Bill was introduced by the Government providing for Elementary Education in England and Wales. The measure was based on the principle of direct compulsion as regarded the attendance of children, and to effect this, power was to be given to each school board to frame by-laws compelling the attendance at school of all children from five to twelve years of age within their districts.

The Government having shown a decided agreement on some points with the members of the Opposition, Mr. Richards charged the Premier with having thrown the Nonconformists overboard. Mr. Forster became extremely unpopular for a time with the latter body, and he was described by Mr. Richards as "mounting the good steed Conservative, and charging into the ranks of his friends and riding them down roughshod."

On the order for the third reading, Mr. Dixon and Mr. Miall, speaking on behalf of the Nonconformists, denounced the measure, and attacked the Government for having roused the suspicion and distrust of their own supporters, while they had secured the aid of the Opposition.

Mr. Miall said that the Premier had led one section of the Liberal party through the Valley of Humiliation; but "once bit, twice shy," he continued, "and we can't stand this sort of a thing much longer." Mr. Gladstone was roused by this speech, and a sharp passage of arms occurred.

"I hope," said the Premier, replying to Mr. Miall, "that my honorable friend will not continue his support to the Government one moment longer than he deems it consistent with his sense of duty and right. For God's sake, sir, let him withdraw it the moment he thinks it better for the cause he has at heart that he should do so. So long as my honorable friend thinks fit to give us his support we will co-operate with my honorable friend for every purpose we have in common; but when we think his opinions and demands exacting, when we think he looks too much to the section of the community he adorns, and too little to the interests of the people at large, we must then recollect that we are the Government of the Queen, and that those who have assumed the high responsibility of administering the affairs of this Empire, must endeavor to forget the parts in the whole, and must, in the great measures they introduce into the House, propose to themselves no meaner or narrower object—no other object than the welfare of the Empire at large. This second important measure of a memorable session eventually passed both Houses and became a law.

In July, 1870, war broke out between France and Prussia. Mr. Gladstone was pressed hard by Bismarck and by other thoughtless and unprincipled men at home to take sides, but he did himself the honor and his country and age the grand service of maintaining a strict neutrality. This was the Golden Age of Liberalism. Mr. Justin McCarthy speaking of these times and of the wonderful advance of just and liberal legislations says:

"Nothing in modern English history is like the rush of the extraordinary years of reforming energy on which the new Administration had now entered. Mr. Gladstone's Government had to grapple with five or six great questions, any one of which might have seemed enough to engage the whole attention of an ordinary Administration. The new Prime Minister had pledged himself to abolish the State Church in Ireland and to reform the Irish Land Tenure system. He had made up his mind to put an end to the purchase of commissions in the army. Recent events and experiences had convinced him that it was necessary to introduce the system of voting by ballot. He accepted for his Government the responsibility of orignating a complete system of National Education."

The Dissenters' Burials Bill was brought forward by Sir Morton Peto. On the second reading of the Bill, Mr. Gladstone proved his broad and generous sympathy with that spirit of toleration which was rapidly winning its way with all sincere, thoughtful minds, by the following impressive words: "He said he could not refuse his consent to the second reading of the Bill, though he thought some portions of it were open to objection; "but," he added, "I do not see that there is sufficient reason, or indeed, any reason at all, why, having granted, to the entire community the power of professing and practicing what form of religion they please during life, you should say to them as to their relations when dead, 'we will at last lay our hands upon you, and not permit you the privilege of being buried in the church yard, where perhaps the ashes of your ancestors repose, or at any rate in the place of which you are parishioners, unless you appear there as members of the Church of England, and, as members of that Church, have her service read over your remains'—that appears to me an inconsistency and an anomaly in the present state of the law, and is in the nature of a grievance"—Sir Morton Peto's Bill became law.

Another grand reform that marked these years of wonderful years, was the abolition of the University Tests. The tests which existed at the Universities had for their distinct and direct object the limitation of the advantages of these great national seats of learning to the members of the Church of England. Under the arrangement that then existed all Dissenters were excluded. This was naturally felt to be an injustice. A student might pass all examinations with honor, but if he had a conscience and could not swear unfeigned assent and consent to the thirty-nine articles, he was refused his diploma and degree. This was not a gross but a refined injustice in scholarly England. Mr. Gladstone's Bill for the abolition of these tests struggled into law. The result was that all lay students, of whatever religious creed, were in future to be admitted to the universities on equal terms Thus was swept away by this great reformer another shred of religious intolerance. It is singular to note that the first year after the abolition of the Tests, the Senior Wranglership of Cambridge was won by the son of a Baptist minister then resident in Cambridge.

Prior to the passing of the last Reform Bill, there were few safeguards so absolutely necessary for the protection of the ordinary voter as the Ballot. On its first introduction the Bill was particularly offensive to the then Conservative Party, and steps were taken by them to mark their sense of objection, whilst long-continued and virulent opposition was shown. It at length passed the House of Commons, but the House of Peers rejected it with decision, the voting being 97 to 48, or nearly two to one, against the Bill itself. It was re-introduced in the following session by Mr. Forster, and after protracted debates and some important amendments, passed the Lower House, but was again met in the Upper House with amendments, the most important of which was a clause stating that the operation of the Bill should be optional. This was held by the Government to be a direct mode of rendering the Bill utterly useless, and as such was declined. A conference took place, and eventually the Bill passed both houses and became law. It is perhaps, too early to measure the total result of the Ballot Act, although there can be little doubt that its influence is still on the increase. The first effect was a sense of doubt as to how far the voting was really secret, but a conviction is gaining ground that for all practical purposes it answers the end for which it was constructed. It may here be mentioned that the Ballot Act, as it is at present administered, is open to the possibilities of very grave abuse. Further experience will probably demonstrate the necessity for some changes in the actual working of the Act itself.

One of the most daring steps in all Mr. Gladstone's carrer was his abolition by Royal warrant of the system of purchase in the army. By this measure, he made a thousand foes, but he won the heart of the British army by his daring high-handed course. One of the strongest anomalies in connection with a State appointment, was the system which had grown up, and by which an officer purchased his successive steps in rank with the same freedom and certainty as he could purchase a sum in Consols. When stated in its rough outline it seemed too ridiculous to be credible, but it was less ridiculous than it seemed. To say that a man's position as an officer was actualy dependent upon the length of his purse, was to throw contempt on the whole arrangement. It was, however, found in practice that so far as courage and skill were concerned, the men who successively bought their steps in rank, fought with as much courage and ability as though they had earned their position by hard and studious care. The general position, however, remained untouched, that so long as purchase formed a part of the system of the army, each man who had paid for his position had a practical claim for the position he occupied.

This was wisely held to be incompatible with the necessary freedom of action required by the changes which had crept over modern warfare; it was therefore decided that a Bill abolishing the right to purchase should be introduced. Some idea may be formed of the absolute necessity for such a step; when it is stated that the amount required to repay the officers the amount they had disbursed in the purchase of their commissions was between $37 000,000 and $42,000.000.

In the course of the debate Mr. Trevelyan quoted the words of Havelock, who said that he was sick for years waiting for his promotion, which three sots and two fools had purchased over him, and that if he had no family to support he would not serve another hour.

The Bill passed its second reading, but was discussed at inordinate length in Committee. The House of Lords at once came to the rescue, and at a meeting of Conservative Peers, it was resolved to oppose the Bill. After considerable discussion the House of Lords rejected the Bill by 155 to 130. The action was a grave one, and necessitated equal grave action on the part of Mr. Gladstone. This came in due course. On the 20th of July, 1871, Sir George Grey put a question in the House on the subject, and Mr. Gladstone in reply stated:

"That the Government had resolved to advise Her Majesty to cancel the Royal Warrant under which purchase was legal. That advice had been accepted by Her Majesty, and a new warrant had been framed in terms conformable with the law. It was consequently his duty on the part of the Government to state that after the 1st of November ensuing, purchase in the Army would no longer exist."

The House of Lords were very irate at the step which had been taken, and passed a vote of censure on the Government, but at the same time passed the Bill without a division. The use of the Royal Prerogative for the purpose was keenly and bitterly discussed, and the absolute legality of the step was held to be open to discussion. A letter from Sir Roundell Palmer was read on the last day of the Session approving the issue of the Royal Warrant—such a Warrant was within the undoubted powers of the Crown. This settled the legal point, but the question still remained as to how far such a course was justifiable. The answer will probably be found in the recognition that such a course of action probably saved an outburst of public opinion, the results of which might have proved even less agreeable.

This was no doubt a high-handed, not to say autocratic, step. Perhaps the Queen, certainly the House of Lords, never forgave him. It was denounced as Cæsarism and Cromwellism in some quarters. No doubt there were touches both of Cæsar and of Cromwell in Mr. Gladstone, and it may be that more than once he would have been glad to have imitated the courage of the Soldier of St. Ives, and have sent the House of Commons packing. *Punch* of this period had a remarkable picture of Mr. Gladstone as "Ajax Defying the Lightning." Thousands who call in question the wisdom of his course, could not help admiring his pluck, and in the shibboleth of all true Englishmen, "pluck," is a cardinal virtue. Anyway, Purchase in the Army, was a thing of the past.

Prior to the passing of the last Reform Bill, there were few safe-guards so absolutely necessary for the protection of the ordinary voter as the Ballot. On its first introduction the Bill was particularly offensive to the then Conservative Party, and steps were taken by them to mark their sense of objection, whilst long-continued and virulent opposition was shown. It at length passed the House of Commons, but the House of Peers rejected it with decision, the voting being 97 to 48, or nearly two to one, against the Bill itself. It was re-introduced in the following Session by Mr. Foster, and after protracted debates and some important amendments, passed the Lower House, but was again met in the Upper House with amendments, the most important of which was a clause stating that the operation of the Bill should be optional. This was held by the Government to be a direct mode of rendering the Bill utterly useless, and as such was declined. A conference took place, and eventually the Bill passed both Houses and became a law. It is, perhaps, too early to measure the total result of the Ballot Act, although there can be little doubt that its influence is still on the increase. The first effect was a sense of doubt as to how far the voting was really secret, but a conviction is gaining ground that for all practical purposes it answers the end for which it was constructed. It may here be mentioned that the Ballot Act, as it is at present administered, is open to the possibilities of very grave abuse. Further experience will probably demonstrate the necessity for some changes in the actual working of the Act itself.

The years 1869, 1870 and 1871 are banner years of progress in English politics. Those eventful years witnessed the passing of the Irish Church Act, the Endowed Schools Bill, the Bankruptcy Bill, the Habitual Criminals Bill, the Irish Land Act, the Elementary Education Act, the Abolition of Purchase in the Army, the negotiation of the Washington Treaty, the passing of the University Test Bill and of the Trades Union Bill and the repeal of the Ecclesiastical Titles Act.

All through the summer of 1871 it was manifest that Mr. Gladstone's popularity was waning. Something had to be done. The veteran statesman resolved on addressing his Greenwich Constituents. He knew there would be a good deal to face, possibly direct open hostility. But this did not daunt him, and perchance he had some faith in his power over an audience. It was the privilege of the present writer to be one of a goodly company of twenty thousand people who went down to Blackheath on Saturday morning, October 28th, 1871. If a lenghty sketch in detail is given, it is because of the conviction that it was one of the most wonderful political meetings ever held in ancient or modern days, and that the speech was one of the most wonderful ever delivered by this great master of the art of oratory. Early attendance and some degree of persistance secured a place near the temporary hustings. Mrs. Gladstone, as always, was by her husband's side. The *Daily News* tells the story of that turbulent scene:

"The dense mass heaved, and there rose from it an audible gasp as a burst of cheering was heard in the offing. Nearer rolled the cheers, mingled with some yells, but the silence of keen expectancy reigned before the hustings. The door at the back of the booth opened; there was some confusion among its occupants, and then—here was Mr. Gladstone, standing at the right hand of Mr. Angerstein. Then the throng broke the silence of expectancy. Peal after peal of cheering rent the air. There was a waving forest of hats. The cheering was spasmodic—it was too loud to be sustained, and ever as it drooped a little was audible the steady automaton-like hissing. But as yet there was little or no hooting, only the bitter, persistent hissing in the lulls of the cheering. If Mr. Angerstein flatters himself that in the remarks he made introducing Mr. Gladstone, he was audible ten feet to his front, he simply labors under a delusion. The noise that drowned his words was utterly indescribable. When this brief preface was over, Mr. Gladstone stood forward bareheaded. There was something deeply dramatic in the intense silence which fell upon the vast crowd when the renewed burst of cheering, with which he was greeted, had subsided. But the first word he spoke was the signal of a fearful tempest of din. From all around the skirts of the crowd, rose a something between a groan and a howl. So fierce was it that for a little space, it might laugh to scorn the burst of cheering that strove to over-master it. The battle raged between the two sounds, and looking straight upon the excited crowd stood Mr. Gladstone, calm, resolute, patient. It was fine to note the manly British impulse of fair-play that gained him a hearing when the first ebullition had exhausted itself, and the revulsion that followed so quickly and spontaneously. on the realization of the suggestion that it was mean to hoot a man down without giving him a chance to speak for himself. After that Mr. Gladstone may be said to have had it all his own way. Of course at intervals there were repetitions of the interruptions. When he first broached the dock-yard question, there was long, loud, and fervent groaning; when he named Ireland a cry rose of "God save Ireland!" from the serried files of Hibernians that had rendezvoused on the left flank. But long before he had finished, he had so enthralled his audience, that impatient disgust was expressed at the handful who still continued their abortive efforts at interruption. When at length the two hours' oration was over, and the question was put that substantially was, whether Mr. Gladstone had cleared away from the judgment of his constituency the fog of prejudice and ill-feeling that unquestionably encircled him and his Ministry, the affirmative reply was given in bursts of all but unanimous cheering, than which none more earnest ever greeted a political leader. Rarely has an English Premier ventured to throw himself thus completely upon the sympathies of the great mass of the people."

When Mr. Gladstone in the course of his address began to pay his respects to the House of Lords, he was interrupted by a voice, "Leave the constitution of the House of Lords alone!" Whereupon he proceeded to say:—

"I am not prepared to agree with my friend there, because the constitution of the House of Lords has often been a subject of consideration amongst the wisest and most sober-minded men; as, for example, when a proposal—of which my friend disapproves perhaps, —was made a few years ago to make a moderate addition to the House of Lords, of peers holding their peerage for life. I am not going to discuss that particular measure; I will only say, without entering into details that would be highly interesting, but which the vast range of the subject makes impossible on the present occasion—I will only say that I believe there are various particulars in which the constitution of the House of Lords might, under favorable circumstances, be improved. And I am bound to say that, though I believe there are some politicians bearing the name of Liberal who approve the proceedings of the House of Lords with respect to the Ballot Bill at the close of last season, I must own that I deeply lament that proceeding. I have a shrewd suspicion in my mind that a very large proportion of the people of England have a sneaking kindness for the hereditary principle. My observation has not been of a very brief period, and what I have observed is this, that wherever there is anything to be done, or to be given, and there are two candidates for it who are exactly alike—alike in opinions, alike in character, alike in possessions, the one being a commoner and the other a lord—the Englishman is very apt indeed to prefer the lord."

Detailing the great advantages which had accrued from the legislation of the past generation, including Free Trade, the removal of twenty millions of taxation, a cheap press, and an Education bill, Mr. Gladstone enforced the lesson that Englishmen must depend upon themselves for their future well-being and improvement, and thus concluded his wonderful address :

"How, in a country where wealth accumulates with such vast rapidity, are we to check the growth of luxury and selfishness by a sound and healthy opinion ? How are we to secure to labor its due honor; I mean not only to the labor of the hands, but to the labor of the man with any and all the faculties which God has given him ? How are we to make ourselves believe, and how are we to bring the country to believe, that in the sight of God and man labor is honorable and idleness is contemptible? Depend upon it, gentlemen, I do but speak the serious and solemn truth when I say that beneath the political questions which are found on the surface lie, those deeper and more searching questions that enter into the breast and strike home to the conscience and mind of every man; and it is upon the solution of these questions that the well-being of England must depend. Gentlemen, I use the words of a popular poet when I give vent to this sentiment of hope, with which for one I venture to look forward to the future of this country. He says:

> ' The ancient virtue is not dead, and long may it endure
> May wealth in England—'

and I am sure he means by wealth that higher sense of it—prosperity, and sound prosperity—

> ' May wealth in England never fail, nor pity for the poor '

May strength and the means of material prosperity never be wanting to us; but it is far more important that there shall not be wanting the disposition to use those means aright. Gentlemen, I shall go 'rom this meeting, having given you the best account of my position in my feeble power, within the time and under the circumstances of the day. I shall go from this meeting strengthened by the comfort of your kindness and your indulgence, to resume my humble share in public labors. No motive will more operate upon me in stimulating me to the discharge of duty than the gratitude with which I look back upon the, I believe, unexampled circumstances under which you made me your representative. But I shall endeavor—I shall make it my hope—to show that gratitude less by words of idle compliment or hollow flattery, than by a manful endeavor, according to the measure of my gifts, humble as they may be, to render service to a Queen who lives in the hearts of the people, and to a nation, with respect to which I will say that through all posterity, whether it be praised or whether it be blamed, whether it be acquitted or whether it be condemned, it will be acquitted or condemned upon this issue, of having made a good or a bad use of the most splendid opportunities; of having turned to proper account, or failed to turn to account, the powers, the energies, the faculties which rank the people of this little island as among the few great nations that have stamped their name and secured their fame among the greatest nations of the world."

At a great meeting held in Liverpool, Mr. Gladstone said : "Having produced this measure, founded in a spirit of moderation, we hope to support it with decision. It is not in our power to secure the passing of the measure; that rests more with you, and more with those whom you represent, and of whom you are a sample, than it does with us. Still, we have a great responsibilty, and are conscious of it; and we do not intend to flinch from it. We stake ourselves—we stake our existence as a Government—and we also stake our political character on the adoption of the bill in its main provisions. You have a right to expect from us that we should tell you what we mean, and that the trumpet which it is our business to blow should give forth no uncertain sound. Its sound has not been, and, I trust, will not be, uncertain. We have passed the Rubicon—we have broken the bridge, and burned the boats behind us. We have advisedly cut off the means of retreat, and having done this, we hope that, as far as time is yet permitted, we have done our duty to the Crown and to the nation."

Nothing can be more interesting to Americans than the position Mr. Gladstone took on the question of International Arbitration, and especially in relation to the final settlement of the Alabama claims. No man is at all times wise. An impartial and honest judgment will not hesitate to take note of a great man's mistakes. In the matter of our Civil War, Mr. Gladstone was gravely mistaken. But he was honest in his utterances, and we are ready to give them word for word.

In October 1862, Mr. Gladstone visited Newcastle-on-Tyne, and was received with extraordinary demonstrations of popularity. He made what has been called "a royal progress" down the Tyne, which has been fully described by a local journalist. "It was not possible to show to royal visitors more demonstrations of honor than were showered on this illustrious commoner and his wife. . . . At every point, at every bank and hill and factory, in every opening where people could stand or climb, expectant crowds awaited Mr. Gladstone's arrival. Women and children in all costumes and of all conditions lined the shores . . . Mr. and Mrs. Gladstone passed. Cannon boomed from every point; . . . such a succession of cannonading never before greeted triumphant conqueror on the march." A great banquet was given in Gladstone's honor, and in making a speech afterwards, he let fall a few words with regard to the situation of affairs in America, words that were certainly injudicious, a fact which he himself afterwards recognized. He had said, —and the fact of his being a member of the Government of course gave his utterances a ten-fold importance,—"We may have our own opinions about slavery, we may be for or against the South, but there is no doubt, I think, about this— Jefferson Davis and the other leaders of the South have made an army; they are making, it appears, a navy; and they have made, gentlemen, what is even of more importance—they have made a nation. We may anticipate with certainty the success of the Southern States, so far as regards their separation from the North." It is certainly not safe to prophesy, for the prophetic portion of this ill-timed speech was very soon proved entirely wrong. It is curious to remember that Gladstone's great political rival, Disraeli, also foretold the success of the Southern States. He said that the results of the civil war would be "An America of armies, of diplomacy, of rival states, of manœuvering cabinets, of frequent turbulence and probably frequent wars." It is manifest that even shrewd and sagacious statesmen are capable of making egregious blunders, espec-

ially when they venture into the realms of prophesy. All
honor to them however, if having discovered their mistake
they are willing to make a few and generous avowals that
they were mistaken. America has had few sincerer admirers
and no truer friend than William Ewert Gladstone. And
this was abundantly proved in the matter of the Alabama
Claims. Mr. George W. Russell says:

There is no one item of policy in which Mr. Gladstone
has been engaged, that has done so much for the future of
the world, as the final settlement of the Alabama Claims by
arbitration. If it did not inaugurate a new system, it carried the system of arbitration further than it had ever been
before, and under conditions which ensured its future application to causes of great and permanent importance.

This was a gain for humanity.

As is well known, the dispute arose out of the War of
Secession. The South claimed its right, as a partner in the
United States of America, to go its own way, now that a
question of policy had risen in which the views of the North
and South were in entire antagonism. The struggle had
been pending for a considerable period. When the war
broke out a number of vessels escaped from British ports
as cruisers of the Southern States, and inflicted great loss
and damage on the ships and commerce of the North. After
the war closed, the United States put in a claim for compensation. This was not admitted by the English government, and the question remained open, and at times threatening.

At length it was deemed advisable to endeavor to settle
all outstanding differences by arbitration, and Mr. Gladstone's government had the honor of expressing its willing-
ness to abide by the decision of the arbitrators. The Congress met at Geneva, and gave their decision by which
England was called upon to pay $16,154,830 in satisfaction
and final settlement of all claims, including interest. Sir

Alexander Cockburn, who represented Great Britain, differed from the rest of the arbitrators, but admitted the justice of the award so far as the Alabama was concerned. He however counselled the acceptance of the decision of a tribunal by whose award they had freely consented to abide. This advice was followed and has borne good fruit since.

In March 1873, Mr. Gladstone brought forward a Bill for University education in Ireland. It was his third assault on what he called the deadly "Upas tree" of Irish misgovernment which he was determined to cut down. With magnificent enthusiasm he toiled at his task. Bitter opposition proved only to be an inspiration. In closing his address on what he called the solemn nature of the subject he said:—

"We have not spared labor and application in the preparation of this certainly complicated, and, I venture to hope, also, comprehensive plan. We have sought to provide a complete remedy for what we thought, and for what we have long marked and held up to public attention as a palpable grievance—a grievance of conscience. But we have not thought that in removing that grievance, we were discharging either the whole or the main part of our duty. It is one thing to clear obstructions from the ground; it is another to raise the fabric. And the fabric which we seek to raise is a substantive, organized system under which all the sons of Ireland, be their professions, be their opinions what they may, may freely meet in their own ancient, noble, historic university for the advancement of learning in that country. The removal of grievance is the negative portion of the project; the substantive and positive part of it, academic reform. We do not ask the House to embark upon a scheme which can be described as one of mere innovation. We ask you now to give to Ireland that which has long been desired, which has been often attempted, but which has never been attained; and we ask you to give it to Ireland, founding the measure upon the principles on which you have already acted in the universities of England. We commit the plan to the prudence and the patriotism of this House, which we have so often experienced, and in which the country places, as we well know, an entire confidence. I will not lay stress upon the evils which will flow from its failure, from its rejection, in prolonging and embittering the controversies which have for many, for too many years been suffered to exist. I would rather dwell upon a more pleasing prospect—upon my hope, even upon my belief, that this plan in its essential features may meet with the approval of the House and of the country. At any rate I am convinced that if it be your pleasure to adopt it. you will by its means enable Irishmen to raise their country to a height in the sphere of human culture. such as will be worthy of the genius of the people, and such as may perhaps. emulate those oldest, and possibly best, traditions of her history. upon which Ireland still so fondly dwells."

The second reading of the Bill was defeated by a majority of three. Mr. Gladstone resigned. The Queen sent for Mr. Disraeli, but that astute gentleman declined to form a Government, on the ground that the majority of the House was against him. Mr. Gladstone was compelled therefore to continue at his post. But the session dragged on wearily till the dawn of another year, and on the morning of January the 23d, 1874, all London and the world awoke to be startled by what was called for a long time "Gladstone's *coup d'etat.*" Mr. Gladstone issued an address to the Electors of Greenwich, announcing that the existing Parliament would be dissolved and a new one summoned to meet without delay. Such a day had hardly been in London since Cromwell sent the "Rump Parliament" a-packing. Had you walked from the marble arch to the Mansion House, you would have heard on almost every lip the question: "What does Gladstone mean?"

The election took place early in the spring. The Liberals were badly beaten. The Tories rejoiced in a substantial majority of forty-six. Mr. Gladstone resigned without waiting for the meeting of Parliament. Not only did he resign the Premiership, but he resigned also the leadership of the Liberal Party, and resolved on retiring from public life. He met his Cabinet to say farewell on the 13th of March. Mr. Foster, in his diary, records the pathetic incident thus:—

"MARCH 13th, 1874.—Cabinet again at twelve. Decided to resign. * * * * Gladstone made us quite a touching little speech. He began playfully. This was the last of some one hundred and fifty cabinets or so, and he wished to say to his colleagues with what "profound gratitude." And here he completely broke down and could say nothing, except that he could not enter on the details. * * * * * Tears came to my eyes; we were all touched."

Mr. Gladstone was sincerely desirous of enjoying that period of repose which he had fairly earned, though there were not lacking opponents who attributed his comparative retirement from Parliamentary life to personal pique. His letter to Lord Granville, however, dated 11, Carlton House Terrace, March 12, fully explains the reason for that step which took the House and the country somewhat by surprise :—

"My dear Granville,—I have issued a circular to members of Parliament of the Liberal party on the occasion of the opening of Parliamentary business. But I feel it to be necessary that, while discharging this duty, I should explain what a circular could not convey with regard to my individual position at the present time. I need not apologize for addressing these explanations to you. Independently of other reasons for so troubling you, it is enough to observe that you have very long represented the Liberal party, and have also acted on behalf of the late Government, from its commencement to its close, in the House of Lords.

"For a variety of reasons personal to myself, I could not contemplate any unlimited extension of active political service; and I am anxious that it should be clearly understood by those friends with whom I have acted in the direction of affairs, that at my age I must reserve my entire freedom to divest myself of all the responsibilities of leadership at no distant time. The need of rest will prevent me from giving more than occasional attendance in the House of Commons during the present session.

"I should be desirous, shortly before the commencement of the session of 1875, to consider whether there would be advantage in my placing my services for a time at the disposal of the Liberal Party, or whether I should then claim exemption from the duties I have hitherto discharged. If, however, there should be reasonable ground for believing that, instead of the course which I have sketched, it would be preferable, in the view of the party generally, for me to assume at once the place of an independent member, I should willingly adopt the latter alternative. But I shall retain all that desire I have hitherto felt for the welfare of the party, and if the gentlemen composing it should think fit either to choose a leader or make provision *ad interim*, with a view to the convenience of the present year, the person designated would, of course, command from me any assistance which he might find occasion to seek, and which it might be in my power to render."

For a time the Liberal Party enjoyed the partial aid of Mr. Gladstone, but this condition of things was sure to prove unsatisfactory. And so, on the 13th of January, 1875, Mr. Gladstone wrote to Lord Granville:—"Having reviewed the whole question, the result has been that I see no public advantage in my continuing to act as the leader of the Liberal Party; and that, at the age of sixty-five, and after forty-two years of a laborious public life, I think myself entitled to retire on the present opportunity. This retirement is dictated to me by my personal views as to the best method of spending the closing years of my life."

The Liberal party accepted Mr. Gladstone's resignation of the leadership, and elected Lord Hartington, afterwards the Duke of Devonshire in his place. But a little more than a year had elapsed since his "final" retirement when Mr. Gladstone came forth once more.

The Public Worships Bill attracted his attention, and brought forth most impressive advocacy in the direction of religious toleration. But he was most intensely concerned by the Bulgarian atrocities. He threw aside polemics and criticism. He forgot for awhile, Homer and the Pope, as he flung himself with all the impassioned energy of a youth into a new crusade. He, whose keen sense of justice and strong humanitarian sympathies had, a quarter of a century earlier, made Europe ring with the story of the Neapolitan iniquities, was again roused to give eloquent expression to his righteous indignation. Mr. G. W. E. Russell has summed up the reasons for Mr. Gladstone's action in a most eloquent passage:—"The reason of all this passion is not difficult to discover. Mr. Gladstone is a humane man; the Turkish tyranny is founded on cruelty.

He is a worshipper of freedom; the Turk is a slave owner. He is a lover of peace; the Turk is nothing if not a soldier. He is a disciple of progress; the Turkish empire is a synonym for retrogression. But above and beyond and before all else, Mr. Gladstone is a Christian; and in the Turk he saw the great anti-Christian power standing, where it ought not, in the fairest provinces of Christendom, and stained with the record of odious cruelty, practiced through long centuries on its defenceless subjects, who were worshipers of Jesus Christ." Mr. Gladstone—his reappearance among them being loudly cheered by his followers—once more came down to the House, to learn what the Ministers in power meant to do with respect to the Eastern Question.

In the spring of the year, the daily press had been filled with accounts of the terrible cruelties and massacres that were taking place in and around Bulgaria. The Government, however, took no measures to interfere with the barbarous behaviour of our Turkish allies; and in the autumn Mr. Gladstone—the terrible stories of the atrocities, which were continued on during the summer, having been amply verified—published a pamphlet entitled "Bulgarian Horrors and the Question in the East." The daily papers had described many of the atrocities committed in a wholesale manner on men, women, and children indiscriminately. The pamphlet brought home to the English people the idea that for these horrors which were going on, they too, as non-interfering allies of Turkey, were in part responsible.

The Government took no definite action, and were getting rapidly discredited. Following on his pamphlet, Mr. Gladstone, a few days later, addressed a mass meeting of his constituents at Blackheath; and again on the 8th of December, he spoke at a great gathering which was held in St. James' Hall London. Notable men of all ranks were present to give expression to their detestation of the action of Turkey.

It was at this meeting that the late Professor E. A. Freeman used the memorable phrase, "Perish the interests of England, perish our dominion in India, sooner than we should strike one blow or speak one word on behalf of the wrong against the right!"

In the House of Commons Mr. Gladstone concluded one of his grandest speeches in these burning words :

Sir, there were other days when England was the hope of freedom. Wherever in the world a high aspiration was entertained, or a noble blow was struck, it was to England that the eyes of the oppressed were always turned—to this favorite, this darling home of so much privilege and so much happiness, where the people had built up a noble edifice for themselves, would, it was well known, be ready to do what in them lay to secure the benefit of the same inestimable boon for others. You talk to me of the established tradition and policy in regard to Turkey. I appeal to an established tradition, older, wider, nobler far—a tradition not which disregards British interests, but which teaches you to seek the promotion of these interests in obeying the dictates of honor and justice. And, sir, what is to be the end of this? Are we to dress up the fantastic ideas some people entertain about this policy and that policy in the garb of British interests, and then, with a new and base idolatry, fall down and worship them? Or are we to look, not at the sentiment, but at the hard facts of the case, which Lord Derby told us fifteen years ago—viz., that it is the populations of those countries that will ultimately possess them—that will ultimately determine their abiding condition? It is to this fact, this law, that we should look. There is now before the world a glorious prize. A portion of those unhappy people are still as yet, making an effort to retrieve what they have lost so long, but have not ceased to love and to desire. I speak of those in Bosnia and Herzegovina. Another portion—a band of heroes such as the world has rarely seen—stand on the rocks of Montenegro, and are ready now, as they have ever been during the 400 years of their exile from their fertile plains, to sweep down from their fastnesses and meet the Turks at any odds for the re-establishment of justice and of peace in those countries. Another portion still, the 5,000,000 of Bulgarians, cowed and beaten down to the ground, hardly venturing to look upward, even to their Father in heaven, have extended their hands to you; they have sent you their petition, they have prayed for your help and protection. They have told you that they do not seek alliance with Russia, or with any foreign power, but that they seek to be delivered from an intolerable burden of woe and shame. That burden of woe and shame—the greatest that exists on God's earth—is one that we thought united Europe was about to remove ; but to the removing which, for the present, you seem to have no efficacious means of offering even the smallest practical contribution. But, sir, the removal of that load of woe and shame is a grand and noble prize. It is a prize well worth competing for. It is not yet too late to try to win it. I believe there are men in the Cabinet who would try to win it if they were free to act on their own beliefs and aspirations. It is not yet too late, I say to become competitors for that prize ; but be assured that even whether you mean to claim for yourselves even a single leaf in that immortal chaplet of renown, which will be the reward of true labor in that cause, or whether you turn your backs upon that cause and upon your own duty, I believe, for one, that the knell of Turkish tyranny in these provinces has sounded. So far as human eye can judge, it is about to be destroyed. The destruction may not come in the way or by the means that we should choose ; but come this boon from what hands it may, it will be a noble boon, and as a noble boon will gladly be accepted by Christendom and the world.

Meetings were addressed by Mr. Gladstone all over the country; a new lease of youth seemed to have been allotted to him, his fervor and his energy alike seeming inexhaustible.

During 1877–78 the Russo-Turkish war took place; and in July of the latter year the celebrated Berlin Conference met. Returning from the Conference, Benjamin Disraeli then Earl of Beaconsfield and Lord Salisbury, were hailed in London with every demonstration of enthusiasm. The "jingo" policy, as it was called, had asserted itself, and had undoubtedly taken the public fancy. So much so that for a time, despite his energetic action on behalf of suffering and oppressed peoples, despite his long years of noble service in the cause of reform, Mr. Gladstone was discredited and unpopular. His time of triumph, however, was not far off.

The Afghan and Zulu wars broke out, and Parliament was called upon to vote $32,000,000 to defray the cost.

The budgets of 1878 and 1879 both showed large deficits, notwithstanding the fact that when Mr. Gladstone's Ministry left office, there had been a surplus of over fifteen millions. The people who had applauded the "imperial policy," the "jingoism" of the preceding two or three years, did not appreciate it so well when they found it was so costly a one. Business, too, was in a very depressed condition. The fate of unpopularity which had grown upon the Liberal Government, and had culminated in its defeat in 1873, was now growing upon their opponents; as in 1879 the term of their office tenure, was drawing to its close.

Gladstone was once more, in every sense of the word, the Liberal leader, and was taking as active a part as ever in Parliamentary business. He decided to contest the election for Midlothian. Never in the history of modern times has such a reception been accorded to any man as that which he met on visiting the North. When he reached Edinburgh, "his progress was as the progress of a nation's guest or a king returning to his own again." For three weeks he delivered speeches all over the constituency, being received everywhere with most extraordinary demonstrations of good-will and admiration from thousands of persons. "Being a man of Scotch blood, I am very much attached to Scotland, and like even the Scottish accent," Mr. Gladstone once said; and Scotland showed herself equally proud of her son. Although Midlothian had been one of the Conservative strongholds, Mr. Gladstone won it by a majority of 211 against the son of the Duke of Buccleugh. The result of the general election was a return of the Liberals to power with a considerable majority.

Lord Beaconsfield followed the precedent he had himself set in 1868, and resigned before meeting Parliament. As Lord Hartington was at the time titular leader of the Liberal party, Mr. Gladstone being still technically in retirement, the Queen sent for Lord Hartington, but it was manifest that Mr. Gladstone was the only available, indeed the only possible Prime Minister. The country demanded him. The old popularity came back with increased volume. The " People's William" was now beginning to be regarded as the "Grand Old Man." Both Lord Granville and Lord Hartington assured Her Majesty that there was no other course but to recall Mr. Gladstone to power. The royal summons came, Mr. Gladstone went down to Windsor, received the royal mandate, kissed the royal hand, and came back to take a second time the helm of state, and lead the nation that now almost idolized him, in an upward and an onward course.

CHAPTER XXII.

" A soul as full of worth, as void of pride,
  Which nothing seeks to show, or needs to hide,
  Which nor to guilt nor fear its caution owes,
  And boasts a warmth that from no passion flows.
  A face untaught to feign; a judging eye
  That darts severe upon a rising lie,
  And strikes a blush through frontless flattery.
  All this thou wert."

—Alexander Pope.

Surely the love of our country is a lesson of reason, not an institution of nature. Education and habit, obligation and interest, attach us to it, not instinct. It is, however, necessary to be cultivated, and the prosperity of all societies, as well as the grandeur of some, depends upon it so much, that orators by their eloquence, and poets by their enthusiasm, have endeavored to work up this precept of morality into a principle of passion. But the examples which we find in history, improved by the lively descriptions and the just applauses or censures of historians, will have a much better and more permanent effect than declamation, or song, or the dry ethics of mere philosophy.

—Lord Bolingbroke.

The Parliament of 1880–1885 opened full of promise.

When the Ministry was completed, the list presented an appearance of strength and stability that promised a long, honorable and useful career. Lord Granville and Lord Hartington, cordially accepting the situation, resumed their allegiance to their former chief, the one serving the new Ministry as Foreign Secretary, the other as Secretary of State for India. Mr. Gladstone coupled with the office of First Lord of the Treasury the duties of Chancellor of the Exchequer. Sir William Harcourt, preferring not to pursue the pathway opened for him when he was made a Law

Officer of the Crown, became Home Secretary. Mr. Childers was Secretary for War. Lord Kimberley cared for the Colonies. Lord Northbrook was First Lord of the Admiralty. Mr. Forster was Chief Secretary for Ireland. The Earl of Selborne presided in the House of Lords as Lord Chancellor. Earl Spencer was Lord President of the Council. The Duke of Argyll and Mr. Bright divided between them the posts of Lord Privy Seal and Chancellor of the Duchy of Lancaster, whose importance arose almost exclusively from the fact that they carried with them seats in the Cabinet.

In this Parliament at the opening of the session of 1881, a Home Rule Party appeared, composed of sixty-one members, with Charles Stuart Parnell at its head. He had been in Parliament since 1875, and had acquired a thorough political education. Such a leader, with more than three-score determined men at his back, formed a very serious contingent. They were men of one idea mainly, and while they were generally in harmony with the Liberal party and its principles, they set before themselves the attainment of Home Rule for Ireland, as the only cure for her manifold wrongs and sorrows. Under the inspiration of Mr. Parnell the Irish Land League became established, which assumed the form of a powerful trade union of the tenant farmers, which Mr. Michael Davitt had been very diligent in promoting. For a time government took no notice of the Irish party, but Mr Parnell with his colleague, Mr. Biggar, sought to force attention to the great Irish question by a policy of obstruction. At the opening of Parliament in January, 1881, it was found that the Irish Party could no longer be ignored. The condition of Ireland was growing more and more distressing. Suffering, want and oppression bred, as they always do, hatred, resentment and rebellion.

The winter was a black one in Ireland. The class of landlords who had swelled the list of evictions, finding them-

selves sustained by the action of the Lords, ran them up
with freer hand. By the end of the year, there was record
of 2,110 families turned out on the roadside. The Land
League, growing in numbers and in power, held meetings
all over the country, advising tenants whose rents were fixed
above Griffith's valuation, to pay no rent and passively resist eviction. Attention was concentrated on the case of
Captain Boycott, agent of Lord Erne, farming a considerable acreage at Lough Mask. He having served notices
upon some of Lord Erne's tenants, the countryside, with
one consent, agreed it would hold no communication with
him. None would work for him. None would sell him
feed or fetch him water. The Ulster Orangemen responded
to his cry for help by despatching a body of armed men to
gather in his imperilled harvest. The unhappy Chief Secretary apprehending disturbance when the emergency men
came within pistol shot of the peasants of Connemara,
hastily despatched a small army to keep the peace. A blow
was struck in another direction, the officials of the Land
League being indicted for seditious conspiracy. Amongst
those who stood in the dock on this charge were Mr. Parnell, Mr. Dillon, Mr. T D. Sullivan, Mr. Sexton, and Mr.
Biggar, all members of the House of Commons. The jury,
as might have been expected, did not agree on a verdict,
and amidst the huzzas of the Dublin populace, the prisoners
were set free.

A winter of such discontent was not a harbinger of peace
in the spring. Parliament was summoned to meet on the
6th of January, an unusually early date. Of two measures
in a long list, upon which attention was chiefly centered, both
related to Ireland. One was a new Coercion bill, the other
a Land bill, a nicely balancing arrangement which the fatal-
ity that seemed to dog the steps of the government, succeeded in enraging both sections of the Opposition. Mr.
Gladstone announced that priority should be given to the

Coercion measures, which were divided into two bills, one "For the Better Protection of Persons and Property in Ireland," the other Amending the Law relating to the Carrying and Possession of Arms. On Monday, the 24th January, Mr. Forster introduced the Coercion measure, which he studiously called the Protection Bill. On the next day Mr. Gladstone moved a resolution giving priority to the bill till it should have passed all its stages. The resolution was carried by 251 votes against 33, a conclusion arrived at only at the close of a sitting that had lasted uninterruptedly for twenty-two hours, in the course of which Mr. Biggar succeeded in getting himself suspended under the new rules of procedure

It was the purpose of this Coercion Bill to put down with a strong hand all those who were disturbing the peace of Ireland. It was a formidable measure, it practically suspended the liberties of Ireland. The Irish Party resisted the passing of the Bill by every conceivable method of obstruction. This ended in the famous suspension of the Thirty-Seven Members, a page in Parliamentary history that is to be most seriously regretted.

On the 25th of February, 1881, the Coercion Bill was passed, and on the 7th of April, Mr. Gladstone introduced his Land Bill which was offered as a measure of conciliation. The bill contained the novel and far-reaching feature of the State stepping in between landlord and tenant and fixing the rents. It was, notwithstanding some defects, the greatest measure of land reform ever passed by the Imperial Parliament. The act was to be administered by Land Commissioners appointed by the Government. The Irish members had no confidenc in the Commissioners. They said they would belong almost entirely to the landlord class and would defeat the purposes of the act.

Speaking at Leeds on the 7th October, 1881, Mr. Gladstone uttered an ominous warning. "I have," he said, "not lost confidence in the people of Ireland. The progress they have made in many points is to me a proof that we ought to rely upon them. But they have dangers and temptations and seductions offered to them such as never were before presented to a people, and the trial of their virtue is severe. Nevertheless, they will have to go through that trial ; we have endeavored to pay them the debt of justice, and of liberal justice. We have no reason to believe they do not acknowledge it. We wish they may have the courage to acknowledge it manfully and openly, and to repudiate, as they ought to repudiate, the evil counsels with which it is sought to seduce them from the path of duty and of right, as well as of public law and of public order. We are convinced that the Irish nation desires to take full and free advantage of the Land Act. But Mr. Parnell says: 'No, you must wait until I have submitted cases ; until I tell you whether the court that Parliament has established can be trusted. ' Trusted for what? Trusted to reduce what he says is seventeen millions a year of property, to three millions which he graciously allows. And when he finds it is not to be trusted for that—and I hope in God it is not to be trusted for any such purpose— then he will endeavor to work his will by attempting to procure for the Irish people the repeal of the Act. But in the meantime what says he? That until he has submitted his test cases any farmer who pays his rent is a fool—a dangerous denunciation in Ireland, a dangerous thing to be denounced as a fool by a man who has made himself the head of the most violent party in Ireland, and who has offered the greatest temptations to the Irish people. That is no small matter. He desires to arrest the operation of the Act, to stand as Aaron stood, between the living and the dead ; but to stand there, not as Aaron stood, to arrest, but to spread the plague.

"These opinions are called forth by the grave state of the facts. I do not give them to you as anything more, but they are opinions sustained by reference to words and to actions. They all have regard to this great impending crisis in which we depend upon the good sense of the people, and in which we are determined that no force, and no fear of force, and no fear of ruin through force, shall, so far as we are concerned, and as it is in our power to decide the question, prevent the Irish people from having the full and free benefit of the Land Act. But if, when we have that short further experience to which I have referred, it shall then appear that there is still to be fought a final conflict in Ireland, between law on one side and sheer lawlessness on the other. If the law, purged from defect and from any taint of injustice, is still to be repelled and refused, and the first conditions of political society are to be set at nought, then I say with out hesitation that the resources of civilization against its enemies are not yet exhausted. I shall recognize in full, when the facts are ripe—and there ripeness is approaching—the duty and responsibility of the Government. I call upon all orders and degrees of men, not in these two kingdoms, but in these three, to support the Government in the discharge of its duty and in acquitting itself of that responsibility. I, for one, in that state of facts, relying upon my fellow-countrymen in these three nations associated together, have not a doubt of the results."

Mr. Parnell replied at Wexford in a defiant speech, in which he characterized Mr. Gladstone's remarks as "unscrupulous and dishonest." The Irish people, he declared, would not rest or relax their efforts till they had regained their lost legislative independence.

Swift on these two speeches fell a heavy blow. On the 13th of October, Mr. Parnell was arrested in Dublin, and carried off to Kilmainham. Mr. John Dillon, Mr. Sexton and Mr. O'Kelly, members of Parliament, were also lodged in Kilmainham with the chief officials of the League.

Mr. Egan, the Treasurer of the League, fled to Paris. Mr. Biggar and other Irish members escaped the fate of their colleagues by keeping out of Ireland.

When the House of Commons met for the Session of 1882, the Irish Leader and some of his principal lieutenants were still in Kilmainham. Coercion was in full swing. In April it was stated in the House of Commons that Mr. Forster had under lock and key not less than six hundred persons, imprisoned under the Coercion Acts, Ireland, its rights and its wrongs, blazed up fiercely night after night.

Mr. Forster resigned the post of Chief Secretary for Ireland. Mr. Gladstone appointed Lord Frederick Cavendish to succeed him. Mr. Lucy tells in his own graphic way the story of the sad tragedy that followed:

On Saturday morning, the 6th of May, Lord Frederick arrived in Dublin to assume his new duties. Late that evening the Marquis of Hartington, present at a party given at the Admiralty to meet the Duke and Duchess of Edinburgh, was taken aside by a colleague in the Cabinet and told that his brother had been murdered. Walking to the Viceregal Lodge in company with Mr. Burke, after taking part in the State entry of the new Viceroy, Earl Spencer, Lord Frederick was fallen upon by a gang of men and stabbed in the chest. It was a fair summer evening, so light that Lord Spencer, standing at the window of the Viceregal Lodge, saw what he afterwards knew to have been the death-struggle. Some boys on bicycles, passing down the broad highway, saw the two gentlemen walking and talking together. Returning after a spin, they found them lying side by side on the pathway, Mr. Burke stabbed to the heart, Lord Frederick with a knife through his right lung.

This outrage upon the person of an inoffensive man, who had gone over to Ireland carrying the olive-leaf of peace, created a profound sensation. Mr. Parnell took the earliest opportunity of expressing in the House of Commons, on the part of his friends and himself, and, he believed, on the part of every Irishman throughout the world, his detestation of the horrible crime committed. Some years later Mr. Gladstone incidentally mentioned that the Irish leader had privately written to him, offering, if he thought it would be useful, to retire from public life. In the temper of the House and the country there was no difficulty in hurrying through Parliament a fresh and more stringent Coercion Bill.

On the 13th of May, 1885, the government announced their intention to renew the Spencer-Trevelyan coercion act. On the 8th of June the opportunity of the Parnellites arrived. In alliance with the Tories they defeated the government on one of the resolutions of the budget.

Mr. Gladstone resigned and was succeeded by Lord Salisbury. But the government of Lord Salisbury expired after an existence of only eight months. Mr. Gladstone was sent for by the Queen, and for the third time he became Prime Minister of England.

On the 8th of April the Grand Old Man, now in his seventy-seventh year, introduced, in a speech of three hours' duration, his Home Rule Bill. At the close of his masterly speech friends and foes alike expressed their profound admiration of the masterly way in which he set forth the provisions of the bill. Many of Mr. Gladstone's old-time followers deserted him because of the concessions he made to the Irish party.

On his defeat, the Premier advised the Queen to dissolve Parliament, and though her Majesty demurred to the trouble of another general election so soon after the last, Mr. Gladstone had his way, and Parliament was dissolved on June 26th.

The result of the " appeal to the country " was the return of a decided majority against Home Rule ; and thus, after a short term of five months in power, Mr. Gladstone found his third Premiership at an end and himself, once more the leader of the opposition. Conscious of the fact that no great reform had been inaugurated on a first attempt, he thenceforward dedicated all his energies to the furthering of the Home Rule cause. The same autumn, before leaving England for a holiday rest on the Continent, he issued a pamphlet on the Home Rule question, dividing it into two sections, called respectively "History of an Idea" and "Lessons of the Elections." In May he had issued in the form of an address to the electors of Midlothian a manifesto, declaring the reasons which had induced him to espouse the cause of Home Rule for Ireland.

In November, 1890, a great disaster occurred to the Irish party. Its leader, Mr. Parnell, by a set of circumstances of which we do not desire to enter into detail, lost his hold upon his followers. Before the clean moral sense of Mr. Gladstone, it seemed that the only course before Mr. Parnell was to retire. He wrote a letter to Mr. Morley, which was intended to be private, but which, fortunately or unfortunately, as the case may be, became public. So much has been said about this letter that we deem it desirable to insert it in this place :

"1, CARLTON GARDENS, Nov. 24, 1890.

"MY DEAR MORLEY,—Having arrived at a certain conclusion with regard to the continuance at the present moment of Mr. Parnell's leadership of the Irish party, I have seen Mr. McCarthy on my arrival in town, and have inquired from him whether I was likely to receive from Mr. Parnell himself any communication on the subject. Mr. McCarthy replied that he was unable to give me any communication on the subject. I mentioned to him that in 1882, after the terrible murder in Phœnix Park, Mr. Parnell, although totally removed from any idea of responsibility, had spontaneously written to me and offered to take the Chiltern Hundreds, an offer much to his honor, but one which I thought it my duty to decline.

"While clinging to the hope of a communication from Mr Parnell to whomsoever addressed, I thought it necessary, viewing the arrangements for the commencement of the Session to-morrow, to acquaint Mr. McCarthy of the conclusion at which, after using all the means of observation and reflection in my power, I had myself arrived. It was that, notwithstanding the splendid services rendered by Mr. Parnell to his country, his continuance at the present moment in the leadership would be productive of consequences disastrous in the highest degree to the cause of Ireland. I think I may be warranted in asking you so far to explain the conclusion I have given above as to add that the continuance which I speak of would not only place many hearty and effective friends of the Irish cause in a position of great embarrassment, but would render my retention of the leadership of the Liberal party, based as it has been mainly upon the prosecution of the Irish cause, almost a nullity.

"This explanation of my own view I begged Mr. McCarthy to regard as confidential, and not intended for his colleagues generally, if he found that Mr. Parnell contemplated spontaneous action. But I also begged that he would make known to the Irish party at their meeting to-morrow afternoon, that such was my conclusion if he should find that Mr. Parnell had not in contemplation any step of the nature indicated.

"I now write to you in case Mr. McCarthy should be unable to communicate with Mr. Parnell, as I understand you may possibly have an opening to-morrow through another channel. Should you have such an opening I would beg you to make known, to Mr. Parnell the conclusion itself, which I have stated in the earlier part of this letter. I have thought it best to put it in terms simple and direct, much as I should have desired had it been within my power to alleviate the painful nature of the situation. As respects the manner of conveying what my public duty has made it an obligation to say, I rely entirely on your good feeling, tact, and judgment."

On the 28th of June, 1892, Parliament was once more dissolved, and Mr. Gladstone, octogenarian though he was, entered on that marvelous Midlothian campaign—a record of which will be found in the next chapter—which ranks among the most remarkable campaigns of his long, illustrious life. It was a grand, winning fight all along the Liberal lines. The election went against the Conservatives, who were able to return only 269 members. The Liberal-Unionists were now reduced to 46 representatives. The Liberals elected 274 members, and the Home Rulers 81, making a total in this combination of 355, or a majority against the existing moribund government.

On the 5th of August a new Parliament was opened. The Conservative ministers had not resigned. On the reply to the address from the throne a vote of no confidence was moved from the Liberal benches. The motion was debated three days, and finally carried by a majority of forty. Thus ended the Salisbury ministry. Parliament was prorogued till the 1st of February, 1893. On the 13th of February Mr. Gladstone—for the fourth time Prime Minister of England—brought in his second Home Rule Bill, a complete copy of which will be found later on.

The streets leading to the House of Commons were crowded with hundreds of persons anxious to get a glimpse of the Prime Minister on his way to the scene of so many former oratorical triumphs. As his carriage drove to the House, he was greeted with great enthusiasm and lusty cheers, which were echoed, as he walked up the floor of the House, by the close throng of members.

At a quarter to four Mr. Gladstone rose, and after reminding the House that for seven years the voices which used to plead the cause of Irish government in Irish affairs, had been mute within the walls of the House, he proceeded to outline the main points of the scheme embodied in the Bill which he was asking leave to introduce. The much-debated subject as to whether Ireland, if granted a parliament of its own, was to continue to send representatives to Westminster, is to be solved by its sending eighty members with power to vote only on matters of Imperial interest or matters affecting Ireland. The "five propositions" of the Bill were summed up by Mr. Gladstone thus:

"First, then, Imperial unity was to be observed. Secondly, the equality of all the kingdoms was to be borne in mind. Thirdly, there was to be an equitable repartition of Imperial charges. Fourthly, any and every practicable provision for the protection of minorities was to be adopted. And, fifthly, the plan that was to be proposed was to be such as, at least in the judgment of its promoters, presented the necessary characteristics—I will not say finality, because it is a discredited word—but of a real and continuing settlement. That is the basis on which we continue to stand."

Then for two and a quarter hours did the Premier unfold in detail such parts of the scheme as time allowed, and as could be explained in a speech. Never before had the House of Commons had a Prime Minister over eighty-three years of age, to deliver a two hours' speech advocating a new legislation. And yet the orator, who sixty years earlier, had first exercised his gifts in the House, delivered his latest speech with all his old fire and *verve*, making it hard for his hearers to realize his great age. This unique oration ended with these appealing words:

"It would be a misery to me if I had forgotten or omitted in these my closing years, any measure possible for me to take towards upholding and promoting the cause, which I believe to be the cause, not of one party or another, of one nation or another, but of all parties and of all nations inhabiting these islands; and to these nations, viewing them as I do, with all their vast opportunities under a living union for power and for happiness, I do entreat you—if it were with my latest breath I would entreat you—to let the dead bury the dead, and to cast behind you every recollection of bygone evils, and to cherish and love and sustain one another through all the vicissitudes of human affairs in the times that are to come."

The time for laying down the great burden was at hand. His eyesight began to fail, and on the 3rd of March he and Mrs. Gladstone went down to Osborne, where he delivered up for the last time, his seals of office to the Queen. Her Majesty offered, as she had done in 1874, to raise him to the peerage as an Earl, but he respectfully declined the honor.

So ended the public life of William Ewart Gladstone, England's greatest commoner.

Lord Roseberry was sent for to undertake the duty of reconstructing the Government.

In 1886, with Gladstone's return to power, Lord Rosebery attained the Foreign Office. Although he had but a short time to prove his fitness for the post, he won general approval and throughout all the civilized world became known as a statesman of the first rank.

"But he has more stuff in him than will ever find expression in Blue Books," was said of him after his life of Pitt appeared. He is also a scholar of first rank. In a cabinet rich in literary men—Morley, Sir George Trevelyan, and Gladstone himself—Lord Rosebery held his own. His style is keen and incisive, but careful and full of evidences of discriminative research, while now and then he betrays a close study of Macauley in his own interminable sentences." His learning has won for him the honorary degree of LL. D. from Cambridge University; the distinction of being president of the Social Science Congress, Lord Rector of Aberdeen University and Lord Rector of Edinburgh University.

He is proudest of the acts that identify him with the people—the equipment of the People's Palace, the improvement and the importation of farm horses, and the removal of religious disabilities from university tests that barred to high honors all but Church of England students. He advocated the abolition of the catechism from Scotch and Irish schools, but the spiritual peers were too much for him there. He pulled down squalid huts and tenements and put comfortable homes in their places by the Artisans' Dwelling Act; and while thousands of her Majesty's subjects were on the verge of starvation, he protested against Lord Beaconsfield's bill for conferring the title of Empress of India on the Queen as being repugnant to popular feeling at that time, by heaping up honors on royalty against the heaped-up misery of the people.

CHAPTER XXIII.

THE MIDLOTHIAN MANIFESTO.

Hark to that shrill, sudden shout,
The cry of an applauding multitude,
Swayed by some loud-voiced orator who wields
The living mass as if he were its soul !
—William Cullen Bryant.

Thus an admonition when it comes at the proper moment, from the lips of a man who enjoys the respect of the world, is often able not only to deter men from the commission of crime, but leads them into the right path. For when the life of a speaker is known to be in unison with his words it is impossible that his advice should not have the greatest weight.—*Polybius.*

In this chapter we present the entire platform, as we should call it in this country, of the memorable Midlothian campaign of 1892. Mr. Gladstone delivered his first address at the Music Hall, Edinborough. It is the most wonderful instance of "The Old Man Eloquent" on record. This chapter forms an exhaustive text-book of Mr. Gladstone's political philosophy. Mr. Gladstone said:

"The question has been much discussed what the Home Rule Bill is to be. Some people have conceived that it was a dark and deep secret hatched in our breasts ready to be let loose upon the world, all prepared with its clauses and its sections, every important principle of it and every unimportant principle of it ready to spring as a surprise upon the country. That has been a favorite doctrine of the Tories. Well, with regard to the Home Rule Bill, undoubtedly, in my opinion, the first duty and the greatest duty of a Liberal government, if it should be formed, would be the preparation and the introduction of such a bill. It would be a violation of every principle we profess, of every pledge we have given for the last six years, if we were to propose to adopt any other view than that. With regard to the principles of such a bill, pray let me remind you that even our opponents do not say that it would be wise or practicable to set out all those particulars; but they sometimes complain that they know nothing about the principles upon which it is to be founded. Now I state that they know a great deal about the principles upon which it is to be founded, and for that purpose I go back to the declarations of 1886. Those declarations it was my duty to make on the part of the government of that year, and they have never been retracted, never disowned, not a word has ever been spoken in the way of recession of any one of them. What we stated then was this— that the object of such a bill was to give to Ireland full and effective control of her own properly local affairs. And then it was my duty to state the conditions under which, as far as we were concerned, alone, that control could be given, and the conditions named by me were five. The first of them was the full and effective maintenance of the supremacy of Parliament. Now shall I say one word to you upon that important phrase 'the supremacy of Parliament'? Lord Salisbury says it is or will be in the case of Ireland a sham. Well, is it a thing unknown to us now beyond the limits of our own country? Have we not scattered over the world a number of states, colonial in their origin, which have in more than one case swollen to national dimensions? Is it not true that every one of those is subject to the supremacy of Parliament? And I want to know whether you consider that that supremacy is or is not a shadow or a fiction. In my opinion it is a real, overshadowing, controlling power. The second condition was a fair adjustment of pecuniary burdens. That seems to have been not made in principle the subject of objection. The third condition was the special care of minorities. We declared our intention to go all possible lengths in considering—ay, in adopting—every reasonable method of guarantee to defend the minority as against the possibility of injustice, by wise provision in the local constitution. We made those declarations without the smallest objection from the Nationalists.

We even went the immense length of saying that possibly the counties of Down and Antrim, the only two counties in which the Orange feeling appears to be so dominant, that the language held and the temper indulged about the Nationalists of Ireland—that is, about the body of the nation—seem to present the greatest difficulty in the way of permanent reconciliation — we even went the length of saying that if a proposal were made by Ireland— by these counties of Ireland in particular—for the purpose of severing them from the rest of their countrymen and keeping them under the British Parliament, even that proposal ought to be entitled to respectful and tender consideration. That was the third of these conditions. But I am bound to say, and I say it in honor of the inhabitants of these counties, that, as far as they made any declaration, their declaration was "No ; we refuse to be severed from the rest of Ireland."

The fourth condition was—and here we had Scotland especially in view—that no principle should be laid down for Ireland with respect to which we were not to admit that Scotland, if she thought fit, was entitled to claim the benefit. I say nothing further upon that subject. The same course applied to England. What we meant and what we contended was that the principle of political equality between the three countries in every substantial respect, and subject to Imperial laws and considerations, was to remain absolute and inviolate. The last condition was that we should not propose a mere piecemeal or halfway measure, but something which should really constitute a substantial settlement of a long and inveterate controversy and should give reasonable hope of peace and satisfaction to

the country and freedom from the frightful strife and from
the intolerable burden which that controversy has imposed
upon us for the last fifty years. He who knows those five
conditions of a Home Rule Bill, knows already a great deal
about the Home Rule Bill. One other condition has been
suggested to us by the voice of public opinion, and in
respect and deference to that voice has been adopted by us.
You will readily perceive that I mean the retention of an
Irish representation at Westminster. That was not our
opinion, but it was an opinion with respect to which we felt
these two things—first, that the country was entitled to
impose it upon us if it thought fit; and, secondly, that the
motive upon which it was founded was a motive in which
we ourselves entirely and absolutely shared—namely, the
desire that everything should be done to testify to the unity
of the Empire and the supremacy of Parliament. We have
never concealed—I do not conceal now—that while the
retention of Irish members has a most valuable meaning as
a living assertion of the unity of the Empire, it will and
must be, attended, as far as we can see, by certain inconveniences. Now I will just point out to you some of the
questions that arise in regard to this retention of Irish
members. As to the mode in which they are to be retained,
one question that arises is, are you to retain a portion of
them, or are you to retain the whole of them? I am not
going to discuss this subject now; it would be too long and
must be ineffectual. I am only going to state them as lying
on the surface of the case, being palpable to every man who
gives it a moment's serious or practical consideration. The
first is, shall you retain the whole of the Irish members or
shall you retain a part? The next is, shall those who are
retained vote on all questions coming before Parliament, or
shall you endeavor, if you can, to make a division of questions, and to limit them to one portion, excluding them
from another portion? The third is, will you have for Ire-

land one set of members or two? As you call it, I think, in the arrangement of a mine, will you have one shift of laborers or two? And another is, will you proceed upon the basis of the present Parliamentary system in Ireland, the present division of the country into districts, and the present number of its members, or will you endeavor to reconstruct that system and readjust it with reference to its relations with England and Scotland or with reference to any other consideration? Now you will at once see that all these are practical matters which must be approached in a practical spirit. They do not raise difficulties of a character to be compared for one instant with the dreadful difficulties of the present Irish controversy.

We scout wholly the preposterous representations of those who—mark my words—when we get into this discussion, will take up these difficulties and exaggerate them and endeavor to raise them as objections to the principle of the scheme which we all have at heart. They are not of that character at all. They are secondary difficulties. They may involve, as almost all practical adjustments do involve, certain inconveniences. And how are those to be dealt with? Why, gentlemen, they are to be dealt with by the responsible Ministers of the Crown, and if the result of your action and the result of the action of other constituencies should be that a Liberal Government is to be established, then it will be the obvious duty of that Government to consider this important subject of the retention of the Irish members in conjunction with every other part of the case, to make to Parliament the propositions which in detail they consider upon the whole the best, and to use every effort in their power to carry it into law. Now I hope you will be able, both in your own minds and in discourse with others, to see how this question stands—a purely practical question, a question that ought not to be prematurely decided, a question in respect to which, so far as we know, the country

holds to the principle, but has not given any marked pref-
erence to any particular form of detail. A Liberal
Government would have to accept that responsibility, and
would meet that responsibility, as I hope we have in other
times met like men the responsibilities that have fallen upon
us. Mr. Gladstone next contrasted the reception of the
Home Rule proposals by the "educated classes" who were
said to compose the Unionist party with the spirit with
which the people of Ireland accepted them, and he concluded
by speaking upon the subject of the Irish Local Government
Bill. There never was, he said, a more gross breach of
faith than the offering of the Local Government Bill to that
still distracted country.

Mr. Gladstone visited Glasgow on Saturday for the purpose of delivering an address to the representatives of the
Liberal associations of Glasgow and the West of Scotland.
The Theatre Royal was crowded, and so were the streets
along the route. In the course of his speech Mr. Gladstone
referred thus to the Ulster agitation:—The alarmists of
northeastern Ireland—who constitute the bulk of the population, or the large majority of the population, nowhere
except in the little narrow strip of country along the northeastern coast —call themselves by the name of Ulster. But
yet Ulster does not consist of two counties; it consists of
nine counties. Of these nine counties, four are represented
exclusively by Home Rulers (cheers); one, the county of
Tyrone, is equally divided; four have a majority opposed
to Home Rule, and that majority is concentrated in a great
degree in the two counties of Down and Antrim. Is it not
a most astonishing circumstance that apprehension and alarm
should be so active where the Protestants are in the vast
majority, and that, on the contrary, where the Protestants
are scattered in the great bulk of Ireland, almost man by
man, with immense thousands of Roman Catholics around
them, these Protestants are perfectly calm, perfectly com-

posed, and make none of those appeals to which our tory friends desire to give such extravagant weight?

Dealing with the danger to civil liberty from ecclesiastical power, Mr. Gladstone said :—I am not a man to disparage or undervalue such a danger. It exists in many conditions of society. It has existed in many religious communities, and not the least unnaturally in the Roman Catholic communion, where the clergy are the best organized, and where they are the great distinctive character, as they depend upon a foreign centre. This danger of ecclesiastical power is supposed to arise from the Roman Catholic priesthood, the local clergy in Ireland. That is one source, undoubtedly, from which it may arise. I cannot say that it impresses me with any very great alarms, because I very greatly doubt if the power the Roman Catholic priesthood in Ireland have over their flocks is as great as it was fifty or sixty years ago. (Hear, hear.) We have, thank God, in spite of the great bulk of those who are now teaching to us this doctrine of danger—we have, thank God, during the interval redressed with strong hands many of the particular grievances of Ireland; and I believe that the more liberty you give to the mass of the Irish people the less risk there will or can possibly be of their surrendering that liberty into the hands of ecclesiastical power. I do not wish to speak with dishonor of the Irish priesthood. I will not speak in their disparagement—I have often differed from them before and I may differ from them again, but this I know, that there never was a clergy that entered more profoundly into the deepest wrongs that ever were inflicted by one nation upon another (cheers), there never was a clergy which secured for itself a more intimate and more truly consecrated place in the hearts of the people. There never was a clergy that practically built its power more upon the recollection of inestimable services. And if I want to diminish the power that that clergy may have for raising

its influence to an abusive height, my secret and nostrum
for doing that is this—to put the people upon a footing of
justice in which they will no longer have a motive for seeking out to themselves extraneous force, but will rest protected and happy under the guidance of a beneficent government and of equal laws.

Mr. Gladstone next spoke of the Maltese marriage question, and read this clause from the draft ordinance:—"A
marriage (meaning always civil marriages, remember), "a
marriage between persons who, with a view to elude the
law of the Catholic Church concerning marriage, have abandoned the Catholic religion is invalid." I call that an
astounding provision.   Surely we understand at this time
of day that a change under the impulse of conscience from
one religion to another is a matter of private and personal
concern (cheers), and that the law cannot interfere between
the private conscience and the God who ought to rule. Yes,
but what says this ordinance? Two persons have abandoned
the Roman Catholic Church; they fall in love with one
another and contract a marriage, and that marriage may at
any time under this draft ordinance be questioned, and
questioned not as it affects spiritual efficacy—let us leave
that to the Roman Catholic Church—but as to its civil effect
and as to the legitimacy of the children, that may be
brought into question and decided in a way we know not
what in a Maltese court of justice, on the plea that these
p ople left the Catholic Church in order to elude the Catholic Church law.   Can you conceive a state of things more
monstrous?   But this is practically the result of the mission
of Sir Lintern Simmons, which sprang from Lord Salisbury's Government, and Lord Salisbury's government is
receiving the allegiance of the Presbyterians, or a large
part of the Presbyterians of Ireland, who are now soliciting
you in Scotland to give your confidence as being the per-

sons best qualified to watch the designs and to restrain the excesses of ecclesiastical power.

On Monday afternoon Mr. Gladstone spoke briefly at Stow. A resolution of confidence was passed, with about fifteen dissentients, an amendment having been proposed to the effect that the meeting sorrowfully disapproved of Mr. Gladstone's action with regard to the disestablishment of the Church of Scotland, and also his policy of Home Rule for Ireland.

THE LABOR QUESTION.

At five o'clock Mr. Gladstone addressed a crowded assemblage in the public hall, Gorebridge. The streets all the way between the railway station and the hall were decorated with flags. The centre flag of a line of bannerets stretched across the street bore the inscription "Welcome Gladstone, man of God." Mr. Gladstone, on his arrival at the railway station, was loudly cheered. Preceded by a local band which played "Rule Britannia" and "See the conquering hero comes," he drove to the Free Church manse, where he received a deputation of miners. He afterwards drove to the public hall, where he was received with great enthusiasm, and devoted a lengthy address to labor questions. After advocating in the interests of the working classes registration reform, payment of public election expenses, payment of members, and an increased number of Labor representatives in the House of Commons, he went on to ask: What, then, is it reasonable that the laboring interest should do with the Liberal party? I will endeavor respectfully to point out one thing which they should not do. I do not think they ought to fasten themselves to the Liberal party so as to qualify their independence. I have always told the Irish Nationalists that it was their duty to maintain, however closely we may be agreed in regard to Irish measures—and I am happy to believe that we are thoroughly and heartily agreed—yet I have always told them that it was their duty to maintain their position of independence as Irishmen, and I have told them again and again that if the Tories will, in their judgment, do better for Ireland than we can, let them go to the Tories. The Tories once gave them promises to that effect before an election. They believed them, and voted for the Tories at that election. The next scene in the drama was the proposal by the Tories of a Coercion Bill. (Laughter and cheers.) But, gentlemen, let the labor party and the labor interest maintain their independence; but I should be very sorry to say that laboring men are not to vote for Liberals when they think that Liberals are the fairest and best representatives of their interests. Referring to his interview with the miners, Mr. Gladstone said: I would not wish to have mining interests and feelings represented either here or elsewhere by persons either more temperate or apparently more competent and qualified in every respect to do them full justice. I thank you for having given me the immediate opportunity of communication which, although it was succinct, was most interesting and most valuable.

As for strikes, Mr. Gladstone went on to say, they are a rough, costly, and wasteful proceeding. But that which is evil in itself is often a relative good under the conditions of human life when it prevents a greater evil, and, though in my own mind I may be wrong and have no other faculty of judgment than may obtain in a greater degree with other people, upon the whole I believe that that rough-and-ready and costly instrument has done much in the long run in securing the rights and raising the condition of working men. Do not let me be misunderstood. I hope we may get to something better, something cheaper, something more effective; but I am not one of those who are prepared to say that the laboring classes of this country have been either uniformly or generally unwise in resorting to that method when they thought they had a just and a substantial cause and when they had no other instrument open to them.

(Cheers.) There is another instrument of great importance to the laboring classes that I cannot help valuing very highly indeed, and that is the method of co-operation both for distributive and for productive purposes. The hours of labor question Mr. Gladstone dealt with thus: However, we all look back with unbounded satisfaction upon the great progress that has been made by voluntary arrangement in that vitally important process which is now specially before you —namely, the shortening of the hours of labor. (Hear, hear.) You must allow me, if you please, to say one word upon the proposals for a general shortening of the hours of labor. I had the advantage of a long and tolerably tough discussion a few weeks ago in London with the representatives of a movement, and an important movement, for securing the adoption of a general compulsory Eight Hours' Bill. In my opinion that deputation clearly had not measured accurately the difficulties—I would almost say, at the present moment, the impossibility—of so vast a measure. I do not think that they had fully considered the enormous variations that prevail between different kinds and classes of labor. I do not think that they had accurately estimated the amount of legal and Parliamentary interference which a law such as they were disposed to recommend would require in what is now perfectly free—namely, the nature and character of trade organization. But what I ventured to tell those gentlemen I repeat to you.

THE EIGHT HOURS' QUESTION.

If the consent or refusal of the majority of a given trade was to determine the lengths of legal labor, and to entail the infliction of a legal penalty by a sentence of a court of justice, in order to come at that state of things which they did not appear to me to have at all considered, you would be obliged to fix the conditions of a trade organization which was to say that ay or no as rigidly by law as you now fix the conditions of a constituency of a county. I lay that before you as a practical consideration very far from being a matter connected with any question of political excitement or of party interest. But now I will tell you my interpretation of that movement in London, which I think is very, very far indeed as yet from being a general movement of the laboring classes in favor of a universal eight hour day. My idea of it is this—that it is not at all a thing to be complained of, not at all to be regretted, though I was obliged to point out difficulties rather than to hold out any premature encouragement, for in my opinion that man is a bad friend of the working class who holds out encouragements which are or may be premature. He tempts them to walk upon slippery paths where they may have very awkward falls, or where they may feel impediments in their way on which they had not reckoned. (Hear, hear.) That is the spirit in which I should always rather wish to speak, to make my conversations or my speeches to laboring men somewhat less favorable than my own views really are, rather than to put an appearance favorable to them which I might not afterwards be able entirely to sustain. The way in which I interpret that universal eight hours' movement is this. It was supported in a general way by a large mass meeting of laboring men in Hyde Park. I do not treat it as an insignificent phenomenon at all. I think there is a good deal of substance and meaning in it, and the substance and meaning I think are, then, these—the indeterminate, if I may so say, the inarticulate expression of a sentiment which is strong, substantial, and just.

The feeling of the laboring man on the eight hours' movement, if I might consider the whole of those who support it as concentrated into one individual, is this—he knows, the laboring man knows, that in time past distribution between labor and capital, the distribution of the profits of production, in his opinion, has not been equitably made. Capital

has had too much and labor has had too little. I have not a
doubt that in the vast majority of cases, if we look widely
and comprehensively over the past, that in that partnership
—for it always has been a partnership—between capital and
labor capital has had too much, and a great deal too much,
and labor has had too little, and in many cases a great deal
too little, a lamentable deal too little. We ought not to be
content with showing that it is premature and perhaps impossible to propose—at any rate most certainly premature
to propose—an Eight Hours' Bill for all descriptions and
kinds of labor throughout the community. We ought not
to be content with that. We ought to do more. We ought
to get at that which is substantial and reasonable in the
workman's mind, and see if we cannot aid him in making
some progress in the road which he desires to go. The subject of a miners' eight hours is undoubtedly in various particulars, and from many points of view, a very different
subject, a far more accessible subject, and a far more hopeful subject than the subject of a universal Eight Hour Bill.
All men are heartily united in the doctrine that eight hours
below ground out of twenty-four on six days—if on five
days so much the better—is enough for a human being.
(Cheers.) First of all, are the mining classes practically
unanimous? Well, I received in this very place and in the
House of Commons from one whom you much respect a most
interesting assurance on that subject, so far as this district
is concerned. I was assured that in every colliery except
one in this immediate district the eight hours' system is established by the consent both of employers and of laborers,
and that it works admirably well (cheers), having for its results even this—about which some might have been scepti-
cal—an increase of output, and not a decrease. (Hear, hear.)
Now supposing, as it is here, there is a unanimity—except
in the case of a particular employer—of the men in this district; supposing, on the other hand, that the miners of

Northumberland and Durham adhere to their doctrine and offer a united front in objection to the universal Eight Hours' Miners' Bill. Then I am led to ask myself this question—Would it be possible to introduce into the mining business, for the purpose of imposing locally an eight hours' limit, that which is called in the case of the liquor laws local option? (Cheers.) I do not presume to give you a positive opinion. All I can say is that until universal unanimity has prevailed, and in cases where local unanimity exists, I should be very glad indeed to see that principle of local option made available to avoid the difficulty of violent interference with the individual freedom of bodies of men that are unwilling to give it up, and on the other hand, to give full scope to the honorable and legitimate aspirations of the miners of a district like this, who value the eight hours for high social and moral purposes and who are unanimous in their desire to attain it.

On Tuesday Mr. Gladstone went to Dalkeith, and spoke chiefly on Scottish Home Rule and disestablishment. The case of Scotland, he said, was different from that of Ireland. Mr. Gladstone continued: Scotland enjoys, happily, a system of justice and administration which is in itself as truly national as the system of justice and administration in England is truly English. Scotland differs, happily, in that respect. Scotland has the most harmonious and the most complex relations with England. I do not know what shape, I do not venture to predict or forecast what shape, the mediation of Scotland will finally take upon this subject of satisfaction for Scotch nationality; but this I undoubtedly will say, that the practical working of the present system is by no means what it ought to be, and beyond all doubt it is our business to maintain the perfect national right of Scotland to ask from the Imperial Parliament, and to obtain from the Imperial Parliament, whatever in her ultimate and thoroughly reasoned conviction she finds to be necessary for her welfare. I hope I have spoken plainly upon that subject, but I have told you that the present system does not work satisfactorily, and I am going to illustrate that in a way that I think you will understand tolerably well. I will tell you what my great complaint with the present system is. My great complaint is that when there is an anti-Liberal majority—and I use the word anti-Liberal because it saves me the trouble of using two names, which express the same thing (cheers), one of which would be Tory and the other Dissentient Liberal; I call them both anti-Liberal—well, whenever there is an anti-Liberal majority the vote of Scotland is put down by that anti-Liberal majority. Now, that, in my opinion, is a serious national grievance.

"I have spoken plainly on the subject of Scottish nationality, and now I come to another subject—namely, disestablishment (cheers)—and on that subject no man can accuse me of any want of frankness. I will tell you upon that, as upon other matters, exactly what I think, what I have done, and why I have done it. The first question is, what did I promise to do? This question was alive even when I first came into Mid Lothian. I saw it stated, because I believe a casual inadvertence of a friend of my own, who undertook the very difficult task of editing four volumes of my speeches made in Scotland, gave some color to the doctrine which has been stated, that I said the question of disestablishment or establishment in Scotland can never be considered with propriety, excepting when the general election had been based upon that issue as its principal issue. Why, I should have been mad if I had said anything of the kind. I never did say anything of the kind. What I said was this—that the question of Scottish disestablishment ought not to be carried by storm ; that there ought to be ample opportunity for bringing it home to the mind of every Scotsman, that it should have full, sufficient, effectual consideration. That is what I said, and what I say now (cheers); and I promised that I at any rate would take no part in promoting Scottish disestablishment, until in my opinion that condition had been realized. Well, that was the first thing. What have I done? This is what I have done. I came here in 1879, and in 1886 Mr. Finlay proposed a bill intended to prop up the Established Church of Scotland. The votes against that bill were not conclusive, but they showed that Scottish opinion were not in his favor. I took no part—I had regarded this as an entirely Scottish question—and I determined to take no part until I knew what Scottish electors desired and required. In 1888 a regular division was taken, and three-fifths—more than three-fifths, I think—of the Scottish members voted in favor of disestablishment. (Cheers.) When in 1890 the great question came forward I was aware that disestablishment would be supported by a still larger majority. I had kept my eyes open, and I had observed its effect. First of all, the majority had increased, and it was known it was going to increase, on the approximate question, from three-sixths to two to one—that is, two-thirds. Secondly, proof of the deep interest of Scotland in the matter, and a proof how thoroughly Scotsmen had attended to it was given in this way? Scotland having, I think, seventy-two members for her share, no less than sixty-seven Scottish members took part in the division, and those sixty-seven Scottish members voted in the proportion of forty-three to twenty-four, or nearly two to one. And I observed another fact, and it was this—that Scotland, of course, had her share of vacancies, and her share of bye-elections happily resulted in the return of Liberals, and that invariably those Liberals were advocates of disestablishment. If I was to give fair weight to Scottish opinion could I overlook these facts? In 1890 I fell into the ranks behind Dr. Cameron, and in those ranks I continue."

CHAPTER XXIV.

IRELAND:—MR. GLADSTONE'S HOME RULE BILL.

> Tyranny
> Is far the worst of treasons.   Dost thou deem
> None rebels except subjects? The prince who
> Neglects or violates his trust, is more
> A brigand than the robber-chief.
>
> —*Lord Byron.*

Mr. Gladstone's sympathies were with humanity. His aspirations were toward the everlasting right. In measurably realizing this right in practical and political affairs he had to be expedient. But between right and expediency there is no necessary conflict. A truly great man is he who can be so expedient that the right shall u'timately prevail.

> —*Bishop Fallows.*

When Edmund Burke died in 1797, Canning wrote: "There is but one event, but it is an event of the world; Burke is dead." And now that Gladstone hath passed from the strife of politics to where beyond these voices there is rest and peace, England and America have but one heart; that heart is very sore. For this man, who reverenced his conscience as his king, was also one whose "glory was redressing human wrong." At once the child of genius, wealth and power, this young patrician took as his clients not the rich and great, but the poor and weak.

> —*Dr. Hillis.*

We have no apology to offer for presenting Mr. Gladstone's Home Rule Bill verbatim. It ranks among the few great national documents of world-wide and permanent interest. It belongs to that group that includes Magna Charta, the Bill of Rights, the Declaration of Independence, and the Proclamation of Emancipation. It will be studied for generations by all lovers of freedom. We count it among the grandest efforts of that colossal brain and that great heart large as humanity which has just been taken from us.

The following is the full text of Mr. Gladstone's Home Rule Bill as presented to Parliament, and issued to the members thereof in printed form :

WHEREAS, It is expedient that without impairing or restricting the supreme authority of Parliament, an Irish Legislature be created for such purposes in Ireland as are in this Act mentioned; be it therefore enacted by the Queen's most excellent Majesty, by and with the advice and consent of the lords spiritual and temporal and commons, in this present Parliament assembled, and by the authority of the same as follows:

1. On and after the appointed day there shall be estab'ished in Ire and a Legislature consisting of her Majesty the Queen and two houses, a legis ative council and a legis'ative assembly

2. With the exceptions and subject to the restrictions in this Act mentioned, there shall be granted to the Irish Legislature power to make laws for the peace, order and good government of Ireland in respect to matters excl sively relating to Ireland or some part thereof.

3 The Irish Legislature shall not have the power to make laws in respect to the following matters or any of them: The status of d gnity of the crown or regency; the Lord Lieutenant as representative of the crown; the making of peace or war; matters arising from a state of war; the naval or military forces, or the defense of the rea m; treaties and other relations with foreign S ates, or the relations between the different parts of her Majesty's dominions, or offenses connected with such treaties; dignities or titles of honor; treason or treason-fe'ony; alienage or naturaiization; trade with any place out of Ireland; quarantine or navigation; except in respect to inland waters; local health or harbor regulations; beacons, lighthouses or seamarks. except so far as they can consistently with any general Act of Parliament be constructed or maintained by loca' harbor authority; coinage; legal tender; standard weights and measures; trade marks: merchandise marks; copyr'ght of patent rights. Any law made in contravention to t' is section shall be void.

POWERS OF THE IRISH PARLIAMENT.

4. The powers of the Irish Legislature shall not extend to the making of any law respecting the establishment or endowment of religion or prohibiting the free exercise thereof, imposing any disability or conferring any privi'ege on account of religious belief or abrogating or prejudicially affecting the right to establish or maintain any place of denominational education or any denominational institution or charity, or prejudicially affecting the right of any child

to attend a school receiving public money without attending the religious instruction at the school, or whereby any person may be deprived of life, liberty, or property without due process of law.

5.   The executive power of Ireland shall continue to be vested in the Queen.   The Lord Lieutenant, on behalf of her Majesty, shall e ercise any prerogatives other than the executive power of the Queen, which may be delegated to him by her Majesty, and shall, in her Majesty's name, summon, prorogue, and disso ve the Irish Legislature.

6.   The Irish Legislative Council shall consist of forty-eight councilors.   Each of the constituencies mentioned in the first schedule of this Act shall return the number of councilors named opposite thereto in the schedule.   Every man shall be entitled to be registered as an elector, and when registered to vote at the election of the councilor for a constituency, who owns or occupies land or a tenement in the constituency of the ratable value of more than twenty pounds. subject to like conditions as the man who is entitled at the passage of the Act to be registered and to vote as a parliamentary elector with respect to ownership qualification; or provided that a man shall not be entitled to be registered, nor if registered to vote at the election of a councilor in more than one constituency in the same year.   The term of office of every councilor shall be eight years.   They shall not be affected by dissolution.   Half the counci ors shall retire every fourth year, and their seats shall be filled by a new election.

LIFE OF THE LEGISLATURE.

7.   The Irish legislative assembly shall consist of members returned by the existing parliamentary constituencies of Ireland or the existing divisions thereof and elected by the parliamentary electors in those constituencies.   The Irish legislative assembly when summoned may, unless sooner dissolved, have continuance for five years from the day on which the summons directs it to meet, and no longer.

8.   After six years from the passing of the Act, the Irish legislature may alter the qua ifications of e ectors and constituencies, provided that in such distribution due regard be had for the population of the constituencies.   If a bill or any provision of a bill adopted by the legislative assembly be lost by the disagreement of the legislative council, and after dissolution, or a period of two years from such disagreement, such bill or a bill for enacting said provisions be again adopted by the legislative assembly, and fails within three months afterward to be adopted by the legislative coun il, the same shall forthwith be submitted to the members of the two houses deliberating and voting together thereon, and shall be adopted or rejected, according to the decision of a majority of those members on the question.

9. Unless and until Parliament otherwise determines, the follow iug provisions shall have effect: Each of the constituencies named in the second schedule shall return to serve in Parliament the number of members named opposite thereto in that schedule and no more. Dublin University shall cease to return a member. The existing divisions of the constituencies shall, save as provided in that schedule, be abolished. An Irish representative peer in the House of Lords and a member in the House of Commons for an Irish constituency shall not be entitled to deliberate or vote on any bill or motion in relation thereto, the operation of which bill or motion is confined to Great Britain or some part thereof; and any motion or resolution relating solely to a tax not raised or to be raised in Ireland, or any vote on an appropriation of money made exclusively for some services not men t oned in the third schedule; any motion or resolution referring exclusively to Great Britain or some part thereof, or some local authority, or some person or thing therein. Any motion incidental to such motion or resolution, either as last mentioned or that relates solely to s me tax not raised in Ireland, or incidental to any such vote or appropriation of money aforesaid in c mpliance with the provisions of this section shall not be questioned otherwise than in each House, in the manner provided by the House.

QUALIFICATIONS OF ELECTORS.

The election laws and laws relating to the qualification of Parliamentary electors shall not, so far as they relate to Parliamentary electors, be altered by the Irish leg slature, but this enactment shall not prevent the Irish legislature from dealing with any officers concerned with the issue of writs of election. If any officers are so dealt with it shall be lawful for her Majesty in council to arrange for the issue of such writs. Writs issued in pursuance of such orders shall be of the same effect as if issued in the manner heretofore accustomed.

IRISH FINANCES.

10. There shall be an Irish exchequer and consolidated fund separate from the United Kingdom. The duties of customs and excise and the duties of postage shall be imposed by act of Parliament, but subject to the provisions of this act The Irish Legislature may in order to provide for the public service in Ireland impose other taxes, save as in this act mentioned. All matters relating to taxes in Ireland and the collection and management therof shall be regulated by Irish act. The same shall be collected and managed by the Irish government and shall form part of the public revenues of Ireland, provided that duties and customs shall be regulated, collected, managed and paid into the exchequer of the United Kingdom as heretofore, and all prohibitions in connection with duties and excise, and so far as regards articles sent out of Ireland, and all matters relating

to those duties shall be regulated by act of Parliament   Excise duties on articles consumed in Great Britain shall be paid in Great Britain, or to an officer of the government of the United Kingdom, save as in the act mentioned.   All public revenues in Ireland shall be paid into the Irish exchequer and for a consolidated fund appropriated to the public service of Ireland by Irish act.   If the duties of excise are increased above the rates in force on the first day of March, the net proceeds in Ireland of the duties in excess of said rates shall be paid from the Irish exchequer to the exchequer of the United Kingdom.   If the duties of excise are reduced below the rates in force on said day, and the net proceeds of such duties in Ireland are in consequence less than the net proceeds of the duties before reduction, a sum equal to the deficiency shall, unless otherwise agreed between the treasury and the Irish government, be paid from the exchequer of the United Kingdom into the Irish exchequer.

PROTECTING ROYAL PREROGATIVES.

11.   The hereditary revenues of the crown in Ireland, which are managed by the Commissioners of her Majesty's woods, forests, and land revenues, shall continue during the life of her present Majesty and shall be managed and collected by those Commissioners.   The net amount payable by them to the exchequer on account of those revenues, after deducting all expenses, but including an allowance for interest on such proceeds of the sale of those revenues as have not been reinvested by Ireland, shall be paid into the treasury account (Ireland) hereinafter mentioned, for the benefit of the Irish exchequer.

RELATING TO TAXATION.

A person shall not be required to pay an income tax in Great Britain in respect to property situate or business carried on in Ireland, and a person shall not be required to pay an income tax in Ireland in respect to property situate or business carried on in Great Britain.   For the purpose of giving Ireland the benefit of the difference between the income tax collected by Great Britain from the British Colonial and foreign securities held by residents of Ireland and the income tax collected by Ireland from Irish securities held by residents of Great Britain, there shall be made to Ireland out of the income tax collected in Great Britain an allowance of such an amount as may from time to time be determined by the treasury, in accordance with a minute of the treasury laid before Parliament.   Before the appointed day such allowance shall be paid into the treasury account (Ireland) for the benefit of the Irish exchequer, provided that the provisions of this section with respect to the income tax shall not apply to any excess in the income tax of Great Britain above the rate of Ireland or to the rate of the income tax of Ireland above the rate of Great Britain.

12. The duties and customs contributed by Ireland and (save as provided in this act) that portion of the public revenues of the United Kingdom to which Ireland may claim to be entitled, whether specified in the third schedule or not, shall be carried to the consolidated fund of the United Kingdom as the contribution of Ireland to imperial liabilities and expenditures, as defined in the schedule. The civil charges of the government of Ireland shall be subject, as in this act mentioned, to be borne after the appointed day by Ireland. After fifteen years from the passage of this act the arrangements made by the act for the contribution of Ireland to imperial liabilities and expenditure, and otherwise for the financial relations of Ireland, may be revived in pursuance of an address to Her Majesty from the House of Commons or from the Irish assembly.

HOW THE BOOKS SHALL BE KEPT.

13. There shall be established under the direction of the treasury an account, in this act referred to as " treasury account" (Ireland). There shall be paid into such account all sums payable from the Irish exchequer to the exchequer of the United Kingdom, or from the latter to the former exchequer. All sums directed to be paid into such account for the benefit of either of said exchequers, and all sums which are payable from either of said exchequers to the other of them, or, being payable out of one of said exchequers, are payable by the other exchequer, shall in the first instance be payable out of said account. So far as the money standing on account is sufficient for the purpose of meeting such sums, the treasury, out of the customs revenues collected in Ireland, and the Irish government, out of any public revenues of Ireland, may direct money to be paid into the treasury account (Ireland) instead of into the exchequer. Any surplus standing on account of the credit of either exchequer, and not required for meeting payments, shall at convenient times be paid into that exchequer. Any sum so payable into the exchequer of the United Kingdom is required by law to be forthwith paid to the National Debt Commissioners, that sum paid may be to those Commissioners without being paid into the exchequer All sums payable by virtue of this act out of the consolidated fund of the United Kingdom or of Ireland, shall be payable from the exchequer of the United Kingdom or of Ireland, as the case may be, within the meaning of this act. All sums by this act made payable from the exchequer of the United Kingdom, shall, if not otherwise paid, be charged on or paid out of the consolidated fund of the United Kingdom.

CHARGES AGAINST THE IRISH EXCHEQUER.

14. There shall be charged on the Irish consolidated fund in favor of the exchequer of the United Kingdom, as a first charge on

that fund, all sums which are payable to that exchequer from the Irish exchequer, or are required to repay to the exchequer of the United Kingdom sums issued to meet dividends or sinking fund on guaranteed land stock under the purchase of land in Ireland act of 1891, or otherwise have been or are required to be paid out of the exchequer of the United Kingdom in consequence of the non-payment thereof out of the exchequer of Ireland or otherwise by the Irish government. If at any time the Comptroller or Auditor-General of the United Kingdom is satisfied that any such charge is due, he shall certify the amount, and the treasury shall send such certificate to the Lord Lieutenant, who shall thereupon by order, without countersignature, direct the payment of the amount from the Irish exchequer to the exchequer of the United Kingdom, and such order shall be duly obeyed by all persons. Until the amount is wholly paid no other payment shall be made out of the Irish exchequer for any purpose whatever. There shall be charged on the Irish consolidated fund next after the foregoing charge all funds for dividends or sinking fund on guaranteed land stock, under the purchase of land in Ireland act of 1891, which the land purchase account and guarantee fund were insufficient to pay; all sums due with respect to any debt incurred by the government of Ireland, whether for interest, management, or for sinking fund; an annual sum of £5,000 for the expenses of the household and establishment of the Lord Lieutenant, all existing charges on the consolidated fund of the United Kingdom in respect to Irish services, other than the salary of the Lord Lieutenant, the salaries and pensions of all judges of the Supreme Court, or other superior courts of Ireland or any county, or other like court who may be appointed after the passing of the act, and are not exchequer judges hereafter mentioned. Until all charges created by the act upon the Irish consolidated fund and f r the time being due are paid, no money shall be issued by the Irish exchequer for any other purpose whatever.

CHARGES ON CHURCH PROPERTY.

15. All existing charges on Church property in Ireland, that is, all property accruing under the Irish Church Act of 1869 and transferred to the Irish Land Commission by the Irish Church Amendment Act of 1881, shall, so far as not paid out of said property, be charged on the Irish consolidated fund. Any of these charges guaranteed by the treasury, if and so far as not paid, shall be paid out of the exchequer of the United Kingdom. Subject to existing charges thereon, said church property shall belong to the Irish government and shall be managed, administered, and disposed of as directed by Irish Act.

16. All sums paid or applicable in or toward the discharge of the interest or principal of any local loan advanced before the appointed day, on the security of Ireland or otherwise, in respect to such loan,

which but for the Act would be paid to the National Debt Commissioners and carried to the Local Loans Fund, shall, after the appointed day, be paid, until otherwise provided by Irish Act, into the Irish exchequer for payment to the Local Loans Fund of the principal and interest of such loans The Irish Government shall after the appointed day pay, by half-yearly payments, an annuity for forty-nine years, at the rate of 14 per cent. on the principal of said loans, exclusive of any sums written off before the appointed day for the account of the assets of the Local Loans Fund. Such annuity shall be paid from the Irish exchequer to the exchequer of the United Kingdom, and when so paid shall forthwith be paid to the National Debt Commissioners for the credit of the Local Loans Fund. After the appointed day the money for the loans to Ireland shall cease to be advanced either by the Public Works Loan Commissioners or out of the Local Loans Fund.

RELATING TO THE SETTLEMENT OF ESTATES.

17. So much of any act as directs the payment to the local taxation (Ireland) account of any share of probate, excise of customs duties payable to the exchequer of the United Kingdom shall, together with any enactment amending the same be repealed as from the appointed day, without prejudice to the adjustment of balances after that day, but l ke amounts shall continue to be paid on the local taxation accounts in England and Scotland as would have been paid if this act had not passed. Any residue of said shares shall be paid into the exchequer of the United Kingdom. Stamp duties, chargeable in respect to the personality of a deceased person, shall not in case the administration was granted by Great Britain be chargeable in respect to any personality situate in Ireland, nor in case administration be granted in Ireland be chargeable with respect to personality situate in Great Britain. Any administration granted in Great Britain shall not, if resealed in Ireland, be exempt from stamp duty on administration granted in Ireland. Any administration granted in Ireland shall not, if resealed in Great Britain, be exempt from stamp duty on administration granted in Great Britain.

18. Bills appropriating any part of the public revenue or for imposing a tax, shall originate in the legislative assembly. It shall not be lawful for the legislative assembly to adopt or pass a vote, resolution, address, or bill for an appropriation for any purpose or any tax except in pursuance of the recommendation of the Lord Lieutenant in the session wherein such vote, resolution, address, or bill is proposed.

THE JUDICIARY.

19. Two Judges of the Supreme Court of Ireland shall be exchequer judges. They shall be appointed under the great seal of the United Kingdom. Their salaries and pensions shall be charged to and paid

out of the consolidated fund of the United Kingdom.   The exchequer judges shall be removable only by her Majesty on an address from the two houses of Parliament.   Each such Judge shall, save as otherwise provided by Parliament, receive the same salary and be entitled to the same pension as at the time of his appointment, fixed for puisne judges of the Supreme Court, and during his continuance in office, his salary shall not be diminished or his right to a pension altered without his consent.   Alterations of any rules relating to such legal proceedings as mentioned in this section, shall not be made except with the approval of her Majesty in council.   The sittings of the exchequer judges shall be regulated by like approval.   All legal proceedings in Ireland which are instituted at the instance of or against the treasury or the commissioners of customs or their officers, or which relate to the election of members of Parliament, or touch a matter not within the powers of the Irish legislature, or touch a matter affected by a law which the Irish legisla ure has not power to repeal or alter, shall, if so required by any party to such proceedings, be heard and determined before exchequer judges or, except where the case requires to be determined by two judges before one of them.   In such legal proceedings an appeal shall, if any party so requires, lie from any court of first instance in Ireland to the exchequer j dges. The decision of the exchequer judges shall be subject to appeal to the Queen in council and not to any other tribunal.   If it is made to appear to an exchequer judge that any decree or judgment in such proceeding as aforesaid is not duly enforced by the sheriff, or other officer whose duty it is to enforce the same, such judge shall appoint an officer whose duty it shall be to enforce that judgment.   For that purpose that officer and all persons employed by him shall be entitled to the same privileges, immunities, and powers as are by law conferred upon the sheriff and his officers.   Exchequer judges when not engaged in hearing and determining such legal proceedings above mentioned shall perform such duties ordinarily performed by other judges of the Supreme Court of Ireland as may be assigned by the Queen in council.   All sums recovered by the treasury or the commissioners of customs or their office s, or recovered under any act relating to customs, shall, notwithstanding anything in any other act, be paid to such public ac ount as the treasury or the commissioner of customs shall dir ct.

MEANS OF COMMUNICATION.

20.   From the appointed day the postal and telegraph service of Ireland shall be transferred to the Irish Government, and may be regulated by Irish act, except as in this act mentioned and except as regards matters relating to such conditions of transmission and delivery of postal packets and telegrams as are incide tal to duties on postage, or foreign mails, or submarine telegraphs, or through lines

in connection therewith, or any other postal or telegraphic business in connection with places out of the United Kingdom. The administration incidental to said excepted matters shall, save as may otherwise be arranged with the Irish postoffice, rema'n with the Postmaster General. As regards revenue and expenses of the postal telegraph service, the Postmaster General shall retain the revenues collected and defray the expenses incurred in Great Britain, and the Irish postoffice shall retain the revenue collected and defray the expenses incurred in Ireland, subject to the fourth schedule of this act, which schedule shall be in full effect, but may be varied or added to by agreement between the Postmaster General and the Irish postoffice. Sums payable by the Postmaster General or the Irish postoffice to the other of them in the pursuance of this act shall, if not paid out of the postoffice money, be paid from the exchequer of the United Kingdom or of Ireland, as the case require, to the other exchequer. Sections 48 to 52 of the telegraphic act of 1863 and any enactment amending the same shall apply to all telegraphic lines of the Irish Government in a like manner as telegraphs of the company within the meaning of the act.

REGULATING POSTAL SAVINGS BANKS.

21. As from the appointed day there shall be transferred to the Irish Government the postoffice savings banks of Ireland and all such powers and duties of any department or officer of Great Britain as are connected with the postoffice savings banks, trusts of savings banks, or friendly societies in Ireland, and the same may be regulated by Irish act, the treasury shall publish, not less than six months previous, a notice of transfer of the savings banks. If before due transfer any depositor of the postoffice savings bank requests his deposit it shall, according to his request, be paid to him or transferred to the postoffice savings bank of Great Britain. After said date the depositors of the postoffice savings banks of Ireland shall cease to have any claim against the Postmaster General or the consolidated fund of the United Kingdom, but shall have a like claim against the government of the consolidated fund of Ireland. If before the date of transfer the trustees of any trustee savings bank request, then according to their request either all sums due them shall be repaid and the savings bank closed, or those sums shall be paid to the Irish government, and after said date the trustees shall cease from having any claim against the national debt commissioners or the consolidated fund of the United Kingdom, but shall have a like claim against the government or the consolidated fund of Ireland. Notwithstanding the foregoing provisions, a sum due on account of any annuity or policy of insurance which has before the above-mentioned notice been granted through the postoffice or a trustee savings bank is not paid by the Irish Government, that sum shall be paid out of the exchequer of the United Kingdom.

GOVERNING APPEALS FROM COURT DECISIONS.

22.   Appeal from the courts of Ireland to the House of Lords shall cease   Where any persons would but for this act have the right to appeal from any court in Ireland to the House of Lords, such person shall have the right to appeal to the Queen in council.   The right to so appeal shall not be affected by any Irish act.   All enactments relating to appeal to the Queen in council and the judicial committee of the privy council shall apply accordingly.   When the judicial committee sit in hearing upon appeals from a court in Ireland there shall be present not less than four lords of appeal and at least one member who is or has been a judge of the Supreme Court of Ireland.   The rota of privy councilors to sit for the hearing of appeals from courts of Ireland shall be made annually by her Majesty in council.   The privy councilors or some of them on that rota shall sit to hear appeals. A casual vacancy in such rota may be filled by order of council. Nothing in this act shall affect the jurisdiction of the House of Lords to determine claims to Irish peerages.

TO AVOID CONFLICT OF AUTHORITY.

23.   If it appears to the Lord Lieutenant or the Secretary of the State expedient for the public interest that steps be taken for the speedy determination of the question whether any Irish act or any provision thereof is beyond the powers of the Irish Legislature, he may represent the same to her Majesty in council, and thereupon said question shall forthwith be referred to and heard and determined by judicial committee of the privy Council constituted as if hearing and appeal from a court of Ireland.   Upon the hearing of the question such persons as seem to the judicial committee to be interested may be allowed to appear and be heard as parties to this case.   The decision of the judicial committee shall be given in like manner, as if it were a decision on appeal, the nature of the report or recommendation to her Majesty being stated in open court.   Nothing in this act shall prejudice any other power of her Majesty in council to refer any question to the judicial committee, or the right of any person to petition her Majesty for such reference.

RELIGION NO BARRIER.

24.   Notwithstanding anything to the contrary in any act, every subject of the Queen shall be qualified to hold the office of the Lord Lieutenant of Ireland without reference to his religious belief.   The office of the Lord Lieutenant shall be for the term of six years, without prejudice to the power of the Queen at any time to revoke the appointment.

25.   The Queen in Council may place under the control of the Irish Government for the purposes of that government such lands and buildings in Ireland as are vested in or held in trust for Her

Majesty, subject to such conditions or restrictions as may seem expedient.

WHEN JUDGES MAY BE REMOVED.

26. A judge of the Supreme Court, or other superior courts of
Ireland, or county court, or other court with like jurisdiction appointed after the passage of this act, shall not be removed from office
except in pursuance of an address from the two houses of the legislature, nor during his continuance in office shall the salary be diminished or the right of pension altered without his consent.

27. All existing judges of the Supreme Court, County Court
judges land commissioners in Ireland, and all existing officers serving in Ireland in the permanent civil service of the crown, and receiving salaries charged to the consolidated fund of the United Kingdom, shall, if they are removable at present. on address to the houses
of Parliament, continue removable only upon such address; if removable in any other manner, they shall cont nue removable only in the
same manner as heretofore. They shall continue to receive the same
salaries, gratuities, and pensions, and shall be liable to perform the
same duties as heretofore, or such duties as her Majesty may declare
analogous. Their salaries and pensions if, and as far as, not p id out
of the Irish consolidated fund, shall be paid out of the exchequer of
the United Kingdom provided this section shall be subject to the
provisions of the act with respect to exchequer judges. If any of the
said judges, commissioners, or officers retire from office with the
Queens approbation before the comp etion of the period of service
entitling them to a pension, her Maje ty may, if she thinks it fit,
grant a pen ion not exceeding the pension to which they would, on
the completion of their period of service, have been entitled.

THE REMAINING CIVIL LIST.

28. All the existing officers of the permanent civil service of the
crown who are not above provided for, and at the appoin ed day serving Ireland shall, after that day, continue to hold their offices by the
same tenure, receive the same salaries, gratuities, and pensions, and
be liable to perform the same duties as heretofore, or such duties as
the treasury may declare analogous to their gratuities and pensions,
and until three years after the passing of the act the sa aries due to
any officers, if remaining in the existing office, shall be paid to the
payee by the treasury out of the exchequer of the United Kingdom.
Any such officer may after three years from the passing of this act
retire from office, and shall at any time during those three years if
required by the Irish government retire from office, and on such
retirement may be awarded by the treasury a gratuity or pension,
provided that a six months' written notice shall, unless otherwise
agreed, be given either by said officer or the Irish government; and
such a number of officers only shall retire at one time and at such in-

tervals of time as the treasury, in communication with the Irish government, shall sanction. If any such officer does not so retire the treasury may award him after the said three years a pension. The gratuities and pensions awarded in accordance with the act shall be paid by the treasury to the payees out of the exchequer of the United Kingdom. All sums paid out of the exchequer of the United Kingdom in pursuance of this section, shall be repaid to that exchequer from the Irish exchequer. This section does not apply to officers retained by the United Kingdom.

PENSIONS TO JUDGES.

29. Any existing pension granted on account of service in Ireland as Judge of the Supreme Court or any court consolidated into that court, or as a County Court Judge or any other judicial position, or as an officer in the permanent civil service of the Crown other than an office-holder who is after the appointed day retained in the service of the United Kingdom, shall be charged on the Irish consolidated fund, and if, and as far as, it is not paid out of that fund, it shall be paid out of the exchequer of the United Kingdom.

TO ABOLISH THE CONSTABULARY.

30. The forces of the Royal Irish constabulary and Dublin metropolitan police shall, when and as local police forces are from time to time established in Ireland in accordance with the sixth schedule of this act, be gradually reduced and ultimately cease to exist as mentioned in the schedule. After the passing of this act no officer or man shall be appointed to either of these forces; provided, that until the expiration of six years from the appointed day nothing in the act shall require the Lord Lieutenant to cause either of said forces to cease to exist; if, as representing the Queen, he considers it expedient that the said two forces shall for awhile continue and be subject to the control of the Lord Lieutenant, representing her Majesty, and the members thereof shall continue to receive the same salaries, gratuities, and pensions, and shall hold appointments of the same tenure as heretofore; and those salaries, gratuities, pensions, and all expenditure incidental to either of the forces shall be paid out of the exchequer of the United Kingdom. When any existing member of either force retires under the provision of the sixth schedule the treasury may award a gratuity or pension, in accordance with the schedule, and those gratuities or pensions and all existing pensions payable with respect to the service of either force shall be paid by the treasury to the payees out of the exchequer of the United Kingdom, and two-thirds of the net amount payable in pursuance of this section out of the exchequer of the United Kingdom shall be repaid to that exchequer from the Irish exchequer.

WILL CHECK THE ACCOUNTS.

31.   Save as may be otherwise provided by Irish act the existing law relating to the exchequer and the consolidated fund of the United Kingdom shall apply with necessary modifications to the exchequer and consolidated fund of Ireland.   An official shall be appointed by the Lord Lieutenant to be the Irish comptroller and auditor general.

32.   Subject as in this act, particularly to the seventh schedule of this act, all existing election laws relating to the House of Commons and the members thereof shall, as far as applicable, extend to each of the houses of the Irish Legislature and the members thereof, but such election laws may be altered in accordance with the Irish act, and the privileges, rights, and immunities held and enjoyed by each house and the members thereof shall be such as may be defined by the Irish act, but so that the same shall never exceed those for the time being held and enjoyed by the House of Commons and the members thereof.

MAY REPEAL PROVISIONS OF THIS ACT.

33.   The Irish Legislature may repeal or alter any provision of this act, which is by this act expressly made alterable by that Legislature; also, any enactments in force in Ireland, except such as either relate to matters beyond the powers of the Irish Legislature, or, being enacted by Parliament after the passing of this act, may be expressly extended to Ireland.   An Irish act, notwithsianding it is in any respect repugnant to any enactment excepted as aforesaid, shall, though read subject to that enactment, be valid except to the extent of that repugnancy.   An order, rule, or regulation made in pursuance of or having the force of an act of Parliament shall be deemed to be an enactment within in the meaning of this section. Nothing in this act shall affect bills relating to the divorce or marriage of individuals.   Any such bill shall be introduced and proceed in parliament in a like manner as if this act was not passed.

WHEN LOANS MAY BE CONTRACTED.

34.   The local authority of any county or borough or any other area shall not borrow money without either the special authority of the Irish Legislature or the sanction of the proper department of the Irish Government.   Such authority shall not, without such special authority, borrow, in the case of a municipal borough or town or area less than a county any loan, which, together with the then outstanding debt of the local authority, will exceed twice the annual ratable value of the property of municipal borough, town or area, or. in the case of a county or larger area, any loan which, together with the then outstanding debt of the local authority, will exceed one-tenth of the annual ratable value of the property of the county or area, or in any case, a loan exceeding one-half the above limits with-

out local inquiry held in the county, borough or area, by a person appointed for the purpose by said department.

NO LAND LEGISLATION FOR THREE YEARS.

35.   During three years from the passing of the act, and if Parliament is then sitting until the end of that session of Parliament, the Irish Legislature shall not pass an act respecting the relations of landlord and tenant or the sale, purchase, or letting of land generally; provided that nothing in this section shall prevent the passing of any Irish act with a view to the purchase of land for railways, harbors, water works, town improvements, or other local undertakings.   During six years from the passing of the act, the appointment of Judges of the Supreme Court or other Superior Court in Ireland, other than one of the Exchequer judges, shall be made in pursuance of a warrant from Her Majesty.

36.   Subject to the provisions of this act the Queen in council may make or direct such arrangements as may seem necessary for setting in motion the Irish Legislature and government, and for otherwise bringing the act into operation.   The Irish Legislature shall be summoned to meet the first Tuesday in September, 1894.   The first election for members of the houses of the Irish Legislature shall be held such a time before that day as may be fixed by her Majesty in council.   Upon the first meeting of the Legi lature the members of the House of Commons, then sitting for Irish constituencies, including the members for Dublin University, shall vacate their seats.   Writs shall, as soon as they conveniently may be, be issued by the Lord Chancellor in Ireland for the purpose of holding elections for members to serve in Parliament for the constituencies named in the second schedule of this act.   The existing Chief Baron of the Exchequer and the senior existing puisne Judges of the Exchequer division of the Supreme Court, or if they or either of them be dead or unable or unwilling to act, such other Judges of the Supreme Court as Her Majesty may appoint, shall be the first Exchequer Judges.   Where it appears to the Queen in council before the expiration of one year after the appointed day that any existing enactment respecting matters within the powers of the Irish Legislature requires adaptation to Ireland, whether, first, by substitution of the Lord Lieutenant in council or any department or office of the executive government of Ireland for her Majesty in council, the Secretary of State, Secretary of the Treasury, Postmaster General, board of inland revenue or any other public department or officer of Great Britain; or, second, by the substitution of the Irish consolidated fund or moneys provided by the Irish legislature for the consolidated fund of the United Kingdom, or moneys provided by Parliament; or, third, by the substitution of confirmation by, or other act to be done by or to the Irish legislature for confirmation by or other act to be done by or to Parlia-

ment; or, fourth, by any other adaptation, her Majesty by order of council may make that adaptation. The Queen in council may provide for the transfer of such property rights and liabilities and the doing of such other things as appear to her Majesty necessary and proper for carrying into effect this act, or any order in council under this act. An order in council under this section may make adaptation or provide for transfer, either unconditionally or subject to such exceptions, conditions or restrictions as may seem expedient. A draft of every order in council under this section shall be laid before both Houses of Parliament for not less than two months before it is made. Such order when made shall be subject as respects Ireland to the provisions of the Irish Act, have full effect, but shall not interfere with the continued application to any place, authority, person or thing not in Ireland, of the enactment to which the order relates.

37. Except as otherwise provided by this Act, all existing laws, institutions, authorities and officers of Ireland, whether judicial, administrative or ministerial and all existing taxes for Ireland, shall continue as if this Act had not been passed, but with modifications necessary for adapting the same to this Act and subject to be repealed, abolished, altered of adapted in the manner and not the extent authorized by this Act.

38. Subject as in this Act mentioned, the appointed day for the purposes of this Act shall be the day of the first meeting of the Irish Legislature, or such other—not more than seven months earlier or later, as may be fixed by order of her Majesty in council either generally or with reference to any particular provision of this Act. Different days may be appointed for different purposes and different provisions of this Act.

First Schedule—Legislative Council constituencies shall consist as follows:

Antrim.............3	Galway.............2	Meath 1
Armagh............1	Kerry. 1	Monaghan..........1
Carlow.............1	Kildare. 1	Queens............. 1
Cavan..............1	Kilkenny...........1	Roscommon 1
Clare...............1	Kings...............1	Tipperary......... 2
Cork, East Riding..3	Leitrim and Sligo..1	Tyrone 1
Cork, West Riding..1	Limerick 2	Waterford..........1
Donegal 1	Londonderry.......1	West Meath 1
Down..............3	Longford...........1	Wexford...........1
Dublin............3	Louth...... 1	Wicklow...........1
Fermanagh.........1	Mayo..............1	

Boroughs:

Dublin.............2	Belfast.............2	Cork...............1

Second Schedule—Irish members in House of Commons shall be apportioned as follows:

Antrim 3	Kerry..............3	Monaghan..........2
Armagh......... 2	Kildare 1	Queens.............1
Carlow...........1	Kilkenny...........1	Roscommon........2
Cavan.............2	Kings..............1	Sligo 2
Clare 2	Leitrim 2	Tipperary..........3
Cork.............5	Limerick...........2	Tyrone........... 3
Donegal...........3	Londonderry.......2	Waterford.........1
Down......... 3	Longford.... 1	West Meath.......1
Dublin.............2	Louth.............1	Wexford 2
Fermanagh 1	Mayo 3	Wicklow 1
Galway 3	Meath 2	

Boroughs :

Belfast............4	Galway 1	Derry.. 1
Cork.... 2	Kilkenny...........1	Newry.............1
Dublin.. 4	Limerick 1	Waterford...... ...1

FINANCIAL LIABILITIES.

Third Schedule—The imperial liabilities shall consist of the funded and unfunded debt of the United Kingdom, inclusive of terminable annuities paid out of the permanent annual charge for the national debt, inclusive of the cost of management of said funded and unfunded debt, but exclusive of local loans, stock, and guaranteed land stock and the cost of management thereof, and all other charges on the consolidated funds of the United Kingdom for the repayment of borrowed money or the fulfillment of guaranteed expenditures. For the purpose of this act the imper al expenditure shall consist of the naval and military expenditure; civil expenditure, that is to say, the civil list and royal family salaries, pensions, allowances, incidental expenses of the Lord Lieutenant of Ireland, exchequer judges in Ireland, buildings, works, salaries, pensions, printing, stationery allowances, and incidental expenses of parliament; the national debt commissioners; foreign office; diplomatic and consular service, including secret service, special service and telegraph subsidies; the Colonial office, including special services and telegraph subsidies; the Privy Council; Board of Trade; the mint; the meterologic service; the slave trade; the service of foreign mails and telegraphic communication with places outside the United Kingdom. The public revenue, to a portion of which Ireland may claim to be entitled, consists of revenue from these sources : Suez Canal shares; loans and advances to foreign countries; annual payments by the British possessions; fees, stamps, and extra receipts received by departments, the expenses of which are a part of the imperial expenditure; and the small branches of the hereditary revenues from the crown foreshores.

Fourth Schedule—The Postmaster General shall pay the Irish postoffice with respect to foreign mails sent through Ireland, and the Irish postoffices shall pay the Postmaster General with respect to foreign mails sent through Great Britain such sums as may be agreed upon for the carriage of those mails. The Irish postoffice shall pay the Postmaster General one-half the expense of the packet service, the submarine and telegraph lines between Great Britain and Ireland after deducting from that expense the sum fixed by the Postmaster General as incurred on account of the foriegn mails or telegraphic communication with places out of the United Kingdom, and five per cent of the expense of conveyance outside the United Kingdom of the foreign mails and the transmission of telegrams to places outside the United Kingdom. The Postmaster General or the Irish postoffices shall pay one to the other of them on account foreign money orders as compensation with respect to postal packets such sums as may be agreed upon.

Fifth Schedule—(Blank).

Sixth Schedule—Such local police forces shall be established, under such local authorities and for such counties, municipal boroughs or other larger areas as shall be provided by Irish act. Whenever the executive committee of the Privy Council of Ireland shall certify to the Lord Lieutenant that a police force adequate for local purposes has been established in any area, then he shall within six months thereafter direct the Royal Irish Constabulary to be withdrawn from the performance of regular police duties in such area. Upon any such withdrawal the Lord Lieutenant shall order measures to be taken for a proportionate reduction of the members of the Royal Irish Constabulary. Upon the executive committee of the Privy Council certifying to the Lord Lieutenant that adequate local police forces have been established in every part of Ireland, then the Lord Lieutenant shall, within six months after such certificate, order measures to be taken for causing the whole Royal Irish Constabulary force to cease to exist as a police force. Wherever the area in which a local police force is established is part of the Dublin metropolitan police district, the foregoing regulations shall apply to the Dublin metropolitan police.

Seventh Schedule—Regulations as to the House of the Legislature, the members thereof, and the legislative council. There shall be a separate register of the electors and councilors of the legislative council, which shall be made until otherwise provided by Irish act, in like manner with the parliamentary register of electors. Writs shall be issued for the election of councilors at such time, not less than one nor more than three months before the day for the periodical retirement of councillors, as the Lord Lieutenant in council shall fix.

LEGISLATIVE ASSEMBLY.

The Parliamentary register for electors for the time being, and until otherwise provided by Irish act, shall be the register of electors of the legislative assembly.

BOTH HOUSES.

Annual sessions of the Legislature shall be held. Any peer, whether of the United Kingdom or Great Britain, England, Scotland or Ireland, shall be qualified to be a member of either house, but the same person shall not be a member of both houses. Until otherwise provided by Irish act, if the same person is elected to a seat in each house, he sha'l, before the eighth day after the next sitting of either house, elect in which house he will serve. Upon his making such election the seat in the other house will be declared vacant. If he does not so elect the seats in both houses will be vacant.

The Lord Lieutenant in council may make regulations for summoning the two houses of the Legislature of Ireland, and he may issue writs, and may do any other thing appearing necessary for the election of members of the two houses for the election of a chairman, whether called "Speaker," "President," or any other name in each house for a quorum of each house, for communications between the two houses, and the adaptation to the two houses and the members thereof of any laws or customs relating to the House of Commons and the deliberation and voting together of the two houses, in cases provided by this act.

CHAPTER XXV.

THE CHAMPION OF THE GREEKS.

The Isles of Greece, the Isle of Greece,
  Where burning Sappho loved and sung;
Where grew the arts of war and peace,
  Where Delos rose and Phœbus sprung.
Eternal summer gilds them yet,
But all except their sin is set.   *—Lord Byron.*

The crisis in the history of modern Greece stirred the heart of Mr. Gladstone to intense excitement and interest. In championing the cause of those descendants of the old heroic race, Mr. Gladstone has not opened himself in plain language concerning the European powers. The message is in the form of a letter written to the Duke of Westminster. The following is the full text:

"My Dear Duke of Westminster:—Had we at the present date been in our ordinary relation of near neighborhood you would have run no risk of being addressed by me in print without your previous knowledge or permission. But the present position of the eastern question is peculiar. Transactions—such only for the moment I am content to call them—have been occurring in the east at short intervals during the last two years of such a nature as to stir our common humanity from its innermost recesses and to lodge a trustworthy appeal from the official to the personal conscience. Until the most recent dates these transactions had seemed to awaken no echo save in England, but now a light has flashed at least upon western Europe and an uneasy consciousness that nations as well as cabinets are concerned in what has been and is going on has taken strong hold upon the public mind, and the time seems to have come when men should speak or be forever silent."

300

My ambition is for rest, and rest alone. But every grain of sand is part of the seashore, and, connected as I have been for nearly half a century, with the eastern question, often when in positions of responsibility, I feel that inclination does not suffice to justify silence. In yielding to this belief I keep another conviction steadily in view—namely, that to infuse into this discussion the spirit of language of party would be to give a cover and an apology to every sluggish and unmanly mind for refusing to offer its tribute to a common cause, and I have felt that, taking into view the attitude you have consistently held in our domestic politics during the last decade of years, I can offer to my countrymen of all opinions no more appropriate guarantee of my careful fidelity to this conviction than, if only by the exercise of an unusual freedom, to place the expression of my views under shelter of your name.

It is more easy thus to forego the liberty and license of partisanship because it is my firm inward belief that the deplorable position which the concerted action or non-action of the powers of Europe has brought about and maintained, has been mainly due, not to a common accord but to a want of it; that the unwise and mistaken views of some of the powers have brought dishonor upon the whole, and that when the time comes for the distribution with full knowledge of praise and blame, it will not be on the British government or on those in sympathy with it that the heaviest sentence of condemnation will descend. Let us succinctly review the situation.

The Armenian massacres, judiciously interspersed with intervals of breathing time, have surpassed in their scale and in the intensity and diversity of their wickedness all modern, if not all historical experience. All this was done under the eyes of six powers, who were represented by their ambassadors, and who thought their feeble verbiage a sufficient counterpoise to the instruments of death, shame, and torture, provided if in framing it they all chimed in with one another. Growing in confidence with each successive triumph of deeds over words, and having exhausted in Armenia every expedient of deliberate and wholesale wickedness, the sultan, whom I have not scrupled to call the great assassin, recollected that he had not yet reached his climax. It yet remained to show to the powers and their ambassadors, under their own eyes and within the hearing of their own ears, in Constantinople itself, what their organs were too dull to see and hear.

From amid the fastnesses of the Armenian hills to this height of daring he boldly ascended, and his triumph was not less complete than before. They did, indeed, make bold to interfere with his prerogatives by protecting or exporting some Armenians who would otherwise have swelled the festering heaps of those murdered in the streets of Constantinople, but as to punishment, reparation, or even prevention, the world has yet to learn that any one of them was effectually cared for. Every extreme of wickedness is sacrosanct when it passes in Turkish garb. All comers may, as in a tournament of old, be challenged to point to any two years of diplomatic history which have been marked by more glaring inequality of forces; by more uniform and complete success of weakness combined with wrong, over strength associated with right, of which it had, unhappily, neither consciousness nor confidence; by so vast an aggregation of blood-red records of massacre, or by so profound a disgrace inflicted upon and still clinging as a shirt of Nessus to collective Europe.

All these terrible occurrences the six powers appear to treat as past and gone, as dead and buried. They forget that every one of them will revive in history, to say nothing of a higher record still, and in proceeding calmly to handle those further developments of the great drama which is now in progress they appear blissfully unconscious that at every step they take they are treading on the burning cinders of the Armenian massacres.

To inform and sway the public mind amid the disastrous confusions of the last two years there have been set up as supreme and guiding ideas those expressed firstly in the phrase "The Concert of Europe" and secondly "The Integrity of the Turkish Empire." Of these phrases the first denotes an instrument indescribably valuable where it can be made available for purposes of good, but it is an instrument only, and as such it must be tried by the question of adaptation to its ends. When it can be made subservient to the purposes of honor, duty, liberty and humanity, it has the immense and otherwise unattainable advantage of leaving the selfish aims of each power to neutralize and destroy one another, and of acting with resistless force for such objects as will bear the light.

In the years 1876-80 it was the influence of England in European diplomacy which principally distracted the concert of the powers. In determining the particulars of the treaty of Berlin, she made herself conspicuous by taking the side least favorable to liberty in the last. In that state of things I for one used my best exertions to set up a European concert. In public estimation it would at least have qualified our activity in the support of Turkey, which had then sufficiently displayed her iniquitous character and policy in Bulgaria, though she has since surpassed herself.

When the ministry of 1880 came into power we made it one of our first objects to organize a European concert for the purpose of procuring the fulfillment of two important provisions of the treaty of 1878, referring to Montenegro and to Greece, respectively. Fair and smiling were the first results of our endeavors. The forces of suasion had been visibly exhausted and the emblems of force were accordingly displayed, a squadron consisting of ships of war carrying the flags of each of the powers, being speedily gathered on the Montenegrin or Albanian coast. But we soon discovered that for several of the powers "concert of Europe" bore a signification totally at variance with that which we attached to it, and that it included toy demonstrations which might be made under a condition that they should not pass into reality.

We did not waste our time in vain endeavors to galvanize a corpse, but framed a plan for the seizure of an important port of the sultan's dominions. To this we confidently believed that some of the powers would accede, and in concert with these we prepared to go forward. It hardly needs be said that we found our principal support in wise and brave Alexander II., who then reigned over Russia. Still less need it be specified that there was no war in Europe, though, doubtless, this bugbear would have been used for intimidation, had our proceedings passed beyond the stage of privacy; but the effect was perfect—the effect produced, be it observed, on Abdul Hamid, on him who has since proved himself to be the great assassin. Our plan became known to the sultan, and without our encountering a single serious difficulty, Montenegro obtained the considerable extension which she now enjoys, and Thessaly was added to Greece.

But as nothing can be better, nay, nothing so good, as the "concert of Europe," where it can be made to work; so, as the best when in its corruption always changes to the worst, nothing can be more mischievous than the pretense to be working with this tool when it is not really in working order. The concert of Europe then comes to mean the concealment of dissents, the lapse into generalities, and the settling down upon negotiations at junctures when duty loudly calls for positive action. Lord Granville was the mildest of men, but mildness may keep company with resolution, and we have seen how he dealt with the " concert of Europe," Very brief intercommunications enable a man of common sense to see in cases where the principles involved are clear,

whether there is a true concert.   But the mischief of setting
up a false one is immense.

*   *   *

After a most exhaustive discussion of the whole matter,
Mr. Gladstone concludes with the following impressive
paragraph:

*   *

Let it be borne in mind that in this unhappy business all
along, under the cover of the "concert of Europe," power
and speech have been the monopoly of the goverments and
their organs, while the people have been shut out.   Give us
at length both light and air.   The nations of Europe are in
very various stages of their training, but I do not believe
there is a European people whose judgment, could it be had,
would ordain or tolerate the infliction of punishment upon
Greece for the good deed she has recently performed.   Certainly it would not be the French, who so largely contributed to the foundation of the kingdom, nor the Italians, still
so mindful of what they and their fathers have undergone;
and, least of all, I will say, the English, to whom the air of
freedom is the very breath of their nostrils, who have already shown in every way open to them how they are minded, and who, were the road now laid open to them by a
dissolution of parliament, would show it by returning a parliament which upon that question would speak with
unanimity.

Waiving any further trespass on your time by a repetition
of apologies, I remain, my dear duke, sincerely yours,

W. E. GLADSTONE.

Chateau Thorenc, Cannes, March 13.

CHAPTER XXVI.

> The first sure symptoms of a mind in health,
> Is rest of heart and pleasure felt at home.
>
> —*Edward Young.*

Go into the house. If the proprietor is constrained and deferring, 'tis of no importance how large his house, how beautiful his grounds, you quickly come to the end of all. But if the man is self-possessed, happy, and at home, his house is deep founded, indefinitely large and interesting, the roof and dome, buoyant as the sky.—*R. W. Emerson.*

The home at Hawarden Castle was eminently calculated to mould the thoughts and direct the course of an intelligent and receptive nature. There was the father's masterful will and keen perception, the sweetness and piety of the mother, wealth, with all its substantial advantages and few of its mischiefs, a strong sense of the value of money, a rigid avoidance of extravagance and excess, everywhere a strenuous purpose in life, constant employment, and concentrated ambition. The spirit that ruled was the spirit of simplicity itself; not ascetic, not indifference to the good things of the world, but alien alike to pomp, ceremony and epicureanism. Time was held as a trust to be accounted for minute by minute. A wilful, purposeless idler would have found himself aloof and estranged, as in few other places. Not the head of the house alone, but mother, sons and daughters, following his example, found employment to fill the day from an early rising to an early bedtime.

The daily routine of Mr. Gladstone's life at Hawarden

MR. GLADSTONE READING PRAYERS IN HAWARDEN CHURCH.

is well known. The early walk to church before breakfast; the morning devoted chiefly to literary work and the
severer kinds of business and study; half an hour or an
hour for reading and writing after luncheon; the afternoon walk or visit, or tree cutting; correspondence and
reading after a cup of tea until dinner-time. As a rule,
Mr. Gladstone read after dinner until about 11:15. He
occasionally enjoyed a game at backgammon. Of chess
as a game, he had the very highest opinion, but he found
it too long and exciting. Music he delighted in, and all
the members of his family were musical, and two or
three were performers above the average. His wishes
in this direction, led the evening to be spent in a sacred
home concert in which Mr. Gladstone took an earnest
and interested part. "Rock of Ages," "Lead, Kindly
Light," and "Depths of Mercy," were among his favorite hymns.

During the later years Mr. Gladstone's family dis-
couraged him from cutting down trees. Few forms of
exercise are more violent and trying to the heart, and at
Mr. Gladstone's age the risk was considerable. Tree-
cutting had its dangers, but in his thirty years' experience of it, Mr. Gladstone had been fortunate in escaping
them. The only serious inconvenience he ever suffered
was from a chip which caused a slight abrasion of the
eyeball. Once an accident almost occurred. Mr. Henry
Gladstone had climbed a large lime tree which Gladstone
had begun to cut, when without any warning, and owing
to unexpected rot in its center, the tree fell. At the
moment Mr. Henry was high up, and on the underneath
side. To the onlooker's relief, he managed to get around
the trunk as the tree was falling, and escaped with a shak-
ing. The bough on which he stood was smashed. Mr.
Gladstone never cut down a tree for the sake of exercise.
A doubtful tree was tried judicially.

When Mr. and Mrs. Gladstone entertained visitors, politics were seldom discussed; party politics never, unless introduced by their guests. This is partly because men of opposite sides were not infrequently present, but mainly because Mrs. Gladstone considered it desirable that her distinguished husband should be relieved of the cares and worries of public life, and should breathe in the shelter of home a more quiet and serene atmosphere. "I have never," says Theodore Stanton, "in any private company, large or small, known Mr. Gladstone himself to start a political controversy. If such is begun by others he manages, as soon as possible, to change the subject.

"Alike as a talker and an orator he is full of resources, he draws upon a long and rich experience, having associated with some of the greatest statesmen and litterateurs of the last sixty years. His conversation is enriched by anecdotes and incidents connected with the notable men that he has met. He is a great lover of books, and they form one of his favorite topics. How varied and world-wide are his tastes! From Homer and Dante to the latest work of fiction and romance. Nothing comes amiss to him. I remember visiting his official residence in Downing street when he was Prime Minister. On the drawing-room table lay 'Silas Lapham,' and 'Treasure Island,' side by side with other books of a more solid, but, perhaps, of a less entertaining character. Among novelists, Scott is his favorite. He considers it a sign of the degeneracy of public taste that the 'Wizard of the North' should be so largely superseded by writers of inferior power. In conversation with him on one occasion he instituted a comparison between Scott and George Eliot rather to the disadvantage of the latter. As a warm admirer of George Eliot, I ventured to put in a plea for her. I spoke of her deep philosophy, her humor, her knowledge of human nature, her graphic descriptions of country scenery, life and character."

Mrs. Gladstone's entire life has been passed in the pretty village of Hawarden, as she did not consider her residence in London to be really living, but merely a concession to duties of state. She was born in Hawarden castle, which belonged to her father, Sir Stephen Glynne, a baronet of a fine old family. She was one of those royal-hearted women of whom George Eliot says :

"They the royal-hearted women are, who nobly love the noblest, yet have grace for needy suffering lives in lowliest places, carrying a choicer sunlight in their smile, the heavenliest ray that pitieth the vile."

Of the eight children who came to Mr. and Mrs. Gladstone, five are now living. Of the sons, two are in England, one as rector of the village church in which his father and mother were married; the other represented West Leeds in Parliament. The third is engaged in commercial pursuits in India. One of the daughters is married; while Helen Gladstone, named for her father's only sister, who died in early womanhood, holds the honorable position of principal of Newham College at Cambridge. She is one of the most profoundly educated women in England; and the college of which she is the head, is one of two founded for the higher education of women. Both Mr. and Mrs. Gladstone have always been on the most tender and affectionate terms with their children. Mrs. Gladstone nursed them all herself. She watched their infancy and growing years as religiously as for the past thirty-five years she has protected the waking and sleeping hours of her husband. She looked after them all along, as if she had been the mistress of a humble cottage, instead of a lady of a proud castle against which the storms of centuries have hurled themselves. When out of office, Mr. Gladstone taught his children Italian. The girls were educated at home by governesses in English, French and German. The boys wore the jackets of Eton, and afterward had lodgings in the grounds at Oxford.

MRS. GLADSTONE.

Mrs. Gladstone's social, education and charitable plans always met with the hearty approval of her husband. Their children were wont to say that he was more proud of her than of anything else in the world, not excepting his own honor and splendid achievements.

MR. GLADSTONE AND DOROTHY DREW.

Mr. Gladstone is a great lover of his grand-children They are all his favorites—especially Dorothy Drew. She has a nursery at the top of the castle, and a beautiful pigeon-house in the park below. On the gracious golden wedding day Mr. Gladstone wrote the following charming poem to Dorothy Drew:

AD DOROTHEAM.

I know where there is honey in a jar,
    Meet for a certain little friend of mine;
And, Dorothy, I know where daisies are
    That only wait small hands to entwine
    A wreath for such a golden head as thine

The thought that thou art coming makes all glad;
    The house is bright with blossoms high and low.
And many a little lass and little lad
    Expectantly are running to and fro;
    The fire within our hearts is all aglow.

We want thee, child, to share in our delight
    On this high day, the holiest and best,
Because 'twas then, ere youth had taken flight.
    Thy grandmamma, of women loveliest,
    Made me of men most honored and most blest.

That naughty boy who led you to suppose
    He was thy sweetheart has, I grieve to tell,
Been seen to pick the garden's choicest rose
    And toddle with it to another belle.
    Who does not treat him altogether well.

But mind not that, or let it teach thee this—
    To waste no love on any youthful rover
(All youths are rovers, I assure thee, Miss):
    No, if thou wouldst true constancy discover
    Thy grandpapa is perfect as a lover.

So come, thou playmate of my closing day,
    The latest treasure life can offer me,
And with thy baby laughing make us gay.
    Thy fresh young voice shall sing, my Dorothy,
    Songs that shall bid the feet of sorrow flee.

GRANDPA GLADSTONE AND DOROTHY DREW.

On the 25th of July, 1889, Mr. and Mrs. Gladstone celebrated their Golden Wedding in the quietude of their mountain- home.   On that day Hawarden Castle was invaded with kindliest greetings.   From every continent of earth and from ships that were far out at sea came loving congratulations.   Kings and princes and peers, the sons and daughters of toil, " old men and maidens, young men and children,"—all the world was one that July day in its benediction and its prayers.   The venerable peasants of Hawarden, with their wives, men and women from the cottages and the fields, and little children in the rosy dawn of life, came in goodly companies to pay their reverential respect to Mr. Gladstone and his gracious wife, who through fifty beautiful years had taught by their devoted lives the grand lesson, that—

> 'Tis only noble to be good ;
> Kind hearts are more than coronets
> And simple faith that Norman blood.

England was proud of Mr. Gladstone for his greatness, and honored Mrs. Gladstone for her grace; but these simple country-folk loved them for their goodness—so deep, so gentle and so true.   All day long the bells of Hawarden rang out the merry chimes, and the hearts of the Hawarden people kept time to the music of the bells.

> While the stars burn.
> And the moons increase,
> And the great ages onward roll.
>
> > --H. W. Longfellow.

> My love, when life was young, I knew
> But little what you were to be,
> A light more bounteous to me
> While lengthening shadows grew.
> Have I been silent, love ? or cold ?
> It may be you have little guessed
> All the strong love, half-unexpressed—
> Stronger, as I grew old.

CHAPTER XXVII.

"SUNSET AND EVENING STAR."

Sunset and evening star,
    And one clear call for me !
And may there be no moaning of the bar,
When I put out to sea.

But such a tide as, moving, seems asleep,
    Too full for sound and foam,
When that which drew from the boundless deep
    Turns again home.

Twilight and evening bell,
    And after that the dark !
And may there be no sadness of farewell
    When I embark.

For tho' from out our bourne of Time and Place
    The flood may bear me far,
I hope to see my Pilot face to face
    When I have crossed the bar.

                        —*Lord Tennyson.*

Of all the thoughts of God that are
Borne inward unto souls afar,
  Along the psalmist's music deep,
Now tell me if there any is,
For gift or grace surpassing this—
  " He giveth His beloved sleep"?
    *   *   *   *   *
And friends, dear friends—when it shall be
That this low breath is gone from me,
  And round my bier ye come to weep,
Let one most loving of you all,
Say,—" Not a tear must o'er him fall—
  He giveth His beloved sleep."

                   —*Elizabeth Barrett Browning.*

Long expected events come suddenly at last. The English nation, and the world at large, watched for many months, with pathetic interest the records of Mr. Gladstone's declining health. It was manifest that in spite of his magnificent constitution and of the fidelity with which he had obeyed the laws of health, the end of the long, illustrious journey was not far away. The sun, and the light, and the moon, and the stars, grew dark; the keepers of the house began to tremble, and those that looked out of the windows were darkened; he rose up at the voice of the bird, and the daughters of music were brought sweet and low; the almond tree flourished; the silver cord was loosened; the majestic golden bowl was growing frail; and the pitcher went slowly to the fountain. The blossoms of the May time had made the pastures of Harwarden beautiful. Mr. Gladstone knew the day of his departure was near, and so one by one he bade his more intimate friends farewell. His chief delight and solace was in joining in the singing of sacred hymns. "Lead, Kindly Light," "Abide with Me," "Son of My Soul," and especially "Rock of Ages." The last vesper service came. His son Stephen read part of the litany. The last conscious effort of his life was in feeble responses to its prayers. His utterances grew less and less distinct. The litany drew near its close:

That it may please Thee to defend and provide for the fatherless children and widows, and all who are desolate and oppressed.

We beseech Thee to hear us, good Lord.

That it may please Thee to have mercy upon all men.

We beseech Thee to hear us, good Lord.

That it may please Thee to forgive our enemies, persecutors and slanderers, and to turn their hearts.

We beseech Thee to hear us, good Lord.

That it may please Thee to give to our use the kindly fruits of the earth, so that in due time we may enjoy them.

We beseech Thee to hear us, good Lord.

That it may please Thee to give us true repentance; to forgive us all our sins, negligence, and ignorance; and to endow us with the grace of Thy Holy Spirit, to amend our lives according to Thy Holy Word.

We beseech Thee to hear us, good Lord.

Son of God, we beseech Thee to hear us.

Son of God, we beseech Thee to hear us.

O Lamb of God, who taketh away the sins of the world.

Grant us Thy peace.

O Lamb of God, who taketh away the sins of the world.

Have mercy upon us.

And then with life's last breath the dying Christian said, "Amen!" That was the last utterance of the venerable saint. The light began to break through the castle windows; and in the dawn of a beautiful May morning, the spirit of William Ewart Gladstone passed to where "beyond these voices there is peace."

On the 25th of May the great statesman was laid to rest in Westminster Abbey. In the procession the members of the last Liberal Government walked together, followed by the representatives of the various members of the Royal Family, and these by representatives of the Tsar, the Kings of Italy, Denmark, Norway and Sweden, the King of the Belgians and the Queen of the Netherlands. Prince Christian and the Dukes of Cambridge and Connaught were present in person, and the Queen was represented by the Earl of Pembroke.

Over and around the grave a dais was erected, on which the chief mourners took their places. At the foot of the grave a chair was placed for Mrs. Gladstone, but the venerable lady, with her daughters and the children, continued during the remainder of the service kneeling or standing.

Dean Bradley repeated the customary sentences, while the coffin was lowered to its last resting-place, and the aged clerk of the works dropped upon it earth from the Garden of Gethsemane, the gift of an anonymous friend.

The Bishop of London, standing at the head of the coffin, in ringing tones offered the prayer:

"Almighty God, with Whom live the spirits of just men made perfect, we give Thee hearty thanks for the life and example of Thy servant, William Ewart Gladstone, whom Thou hast been pleased to call from the trials and troubles of this world to the realm of eternal rest; and we beseech Thee to grant us Thy grace that, as we commit his body to the ground, our hearts and minds may be so moved by the remembrance of his life and manifold labors for the service of mankind, his country, and his Queen, begun, continued, and ended in Thy faith and fear, that we fail not to learn the lessons that Thou teachest Thy faithful people, by the lives of those who live and serve Thee, through Jesus Christ, our only Lord and Savior.

A loud heartfelt "Amen" was said by the whole company.

THE QUEEN'S MESSAGE TO MRS. GLADSTONE.

My thoughts are much with you to-day when your dear husband is laid to rest. To-day's ceremony will be most trying and painful for you, but it will be, at the same time, gratifying to you to see the respect and regret evinced by the nation for the memory of one whose character and intellectual abilities marked him as one of the most distinguished statesmen of my reign. I shall ever gratefully remember his devotion and zeal in all that concerned my personal welfare and that of my family.

VICTORIA R. I.

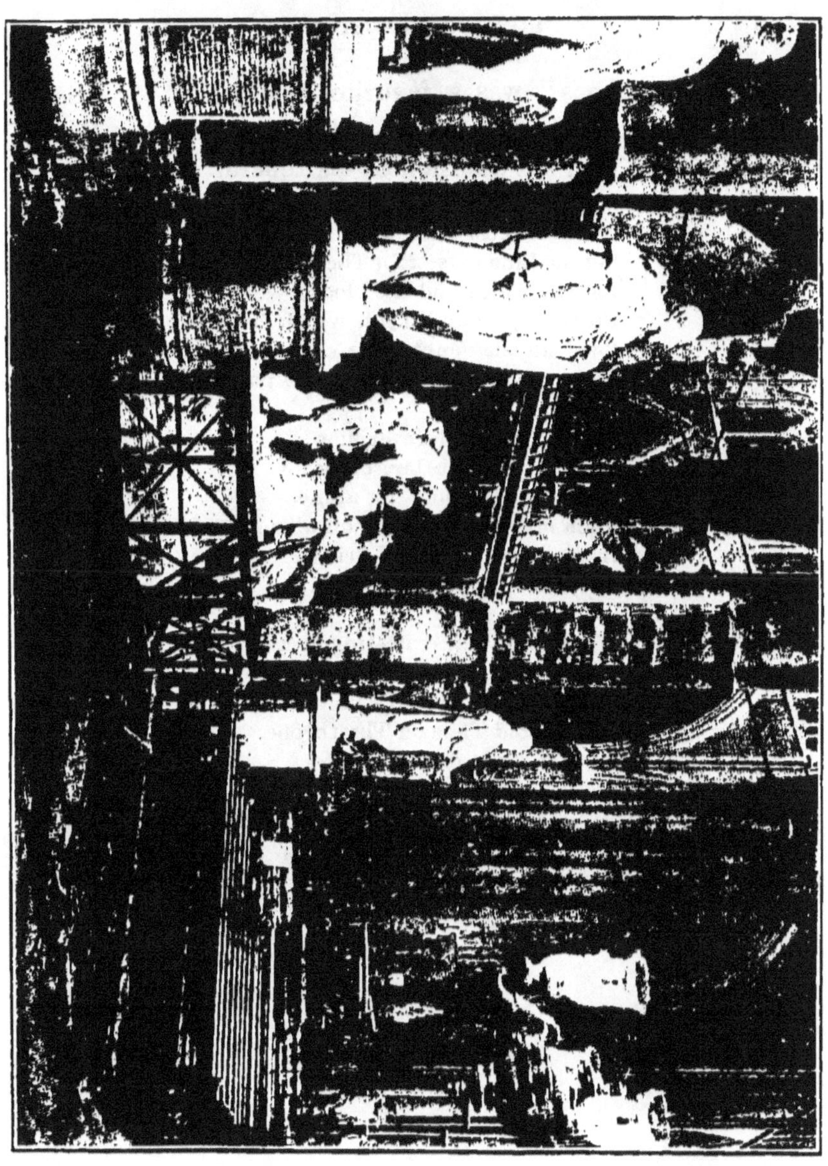

"Rock of Ages" was a favorite hymn with Mr. Gladstone. It was the last hymn he sang. It was sung in Westminster Abbey on the occasion of his funeral:

> Rock of Ages! cleft for me,
> Let me hide myself in Thee;
> Let the water and the blood,
> From Thy wounded side which flowed,
> Be of sin the double cure,
> Save from wrath and make me pure.
>
> Could my tears forever flow,
> Could my zeal no languor know,
> These for sin could not atone.
> Thou must save, and Thou alone.
> In my hand no price I bring;
> Simply to Thy cross I cling.
>
> When I draw this fleeting breath,
> When my eyes shall close in death,
> When I rise to world's unknown,
> And behold Thee on Thy throne,
> Rock of Ages, cleft for me,
> Let me hide myself in Thee.